Stum

...captivating look at the challenges faced by an immigrant family as they navigate life in multicultural Canada...sprinkled with fun and delicious reminiscing...dares to expose underlying issues of short-sighted immigration policies... Canada's immigrants stumble as they try to find a way to practise their professions that are so needed, yet wasted... human spirit prevails...family triumphs, Canada advances... thought-provoking read for all.

Esmie Gayo McLaren, Director, Vancouver Asia Heritage Month Society

...depicts the real problems encountered by immigrants in Canada...parallels some of our survey findings about the difficulties of immigrants...their strength and resilience... a worthy addition to the genre of "ethnic literature"...the first such novel focused on Filipino immigrants in a positive and balanced manner...will interest many readers not only in Canada but in other countries...

Aprodicio and Eleanor Laquian, authors of Seeking a Better Life Abroad: A study of Filipinos in Canada and The Silent Debate: Asian Immigration and Racism in Canada

...puts into words ...emotions many immigrants feel as they live their new life...storytelling felt so real that I found myself in tears...makes you feel the pain, struggles and triumphs of characters skillfully depicted...Very good book to read!

Irene Querubin, TV and Radio Host

To Anita —
Thank you for your poetry.
Hope you enjoy this! *Eleanor*

Eleanor Guerrero-Campbell

Stumbling Through Paradise

A Feast of Mercy
for Manuel del Mundo

by Eleanor Guerrero-Campbell

 FriesenPress

Suite 300 - 990 Fort St
Victoria, BC, Canada, V8V 3K2
www.friesenpress.com

Copyright © 2016 by Eleanor Guerrero-Campbell
First Edition — 2016

This is a work of fiction. Names, characters, businesses, places, events and incidents are either the products of the author's imagination or used in a fictitious manner. Any resemblance to actual persons, living or dead, or actual events is purely coincidental.

All rights reserved. No part of this publication may be reproduced in any form, or by any means, electronic or mechanical, including photocopying, recording, or any information browsing, storage, or retrieval system, without permission in writing from FriesenPress.

ISBN
978-1-4602-8362-2 (Hardcover)
978-1-4602-8363-9 (Paperback)
978-1-4602-8364-6 (eBook)

1. Fiction, Cultural Heritage

Distributed to the trade by The Ingram Book Company

This book is dedicated to all immigrants.

Which is to say, all of us.

For, excepting indigenous peoples, we, our ancestors, all came from somewhere else.

Some of us simply came earlier.

We are pilgrims all, searching for our sacred home.

If only we remember this always.

There will be no discrimination, only compassion.

This is a work of fiction inspired by real experiences.

Similarities to people alive or dead, events past and present, are entirely coincidental.

Eleanor Guerrero-Campbell

CONTENTS

1
PROLOGUE

3
PART 1
JOSIE AND MANUEL'S JOURNEY:
The Comfort of Green Papaya Soup and Pandesal

155
PART 2
SONIA AND BOBBY'S SEARCH:
The Scent of Black Cigarettes and Money

333
PART 3
THE MAKING OF MANOLITA and JUN JUN:
Soup or Salad for the Canadian Soul?

491
EPILOGUE

492
ACKNOWLEDGEMENTS

495
ABOUT THE AUTHOR

PROLOGUE

Since 1869, Canada has been inviting people throughout the world to live and work in Canada. Mostly, the reason was to fill labour needs, and later, to fill skilled labour shortages with foreign skilled workers. In the 1970s–2000s, hundreds of thousands of people from different countries — armed with talent, experience, degrees and dreams — applied to Canada's various skilled-worker programs. When they arrived in Canada, many of them found that they could not practice their skills and professions. To keep bodies and souls together for their families, foreign-trained engineers, doctors, nurses and teachers accepted work driving taxis, working as late-night 7-Eleven cashiers, and cleaning floors. It is estimated that only one in four skilled immigrants work in their field.

"Although recent immigrants are more educated than their Canadian-born counterparts — three times as many have undergraduate degrees according to Stats Canada — only 24% work in their fields, less than half the rate for those native in Canada." Huffington Post, Dec 19, 2012.

Why and how did this waste of talent happen? How did it affect the lives of many immigrants who came to Canada dreaming of paradise?

Over a million Filipinos leave the Philippines every year to work abroad. In 2008, the Philippines became the leading source country of immigrants for Canada, where an estimated 500,000 people of Filipino origin live. This story tells of one fictional Filipino family — the del Mundos — who came to Canada. In the del Mundo family, we see the struggle of all immigrants stumbling through the paradise they uprooted their lives for — some rising, some falling, and still others, through the second and third generations, rising gloriously after the fall.

PART 1
JOSIE AND MANUEL'S JOURNEY:

The Comfort of Green Papaya Soup and Pandesal

CHAPTER 1

Canada
Josie, 1991

I promised Manuel this: that he would come home one day, when he was ready, and I would let him. But I never thought it would be this way. That he would come home to die.

Why bother to fathom things? Why do some things I ask for happen, and others not? But then most of what I ask for happens, whatever I ask, really. Quit complaining.

* * *

"Hija, child. What are you praying for?" said a nun, as I walked out of the San Marcelino Church in Ermita, Manila where I went to mass every day.

I was surprised to be asked about my prayers. I had just finished my novena and was leaving the church when the nun stepped beside me. "I see you every day walking on your knees from the back of the church to the altar," she assured me. Then I remembered a nun with a long white habit and a tall square black veil arranging the flowers on the altar of the church. Close up, her face looked tiny underneath her headdress. Small pinprick eyes peered at me through thick eyeglasses. Her face glowed with a leathery sheen, and she smelled of mothballs.

"Yes, sister. I'm praying for a job. A teaching job in Manila," I confessed.

"Why don't you see my friend Sister Nieves? She's the principal at the school across the street. She may have something for you. They always need good teachers. Tell her I spoke to you," she smiled, showing her yellow teeth.

I was so surprised. I wanted to hug her. I felt so happy, but as I started to walk towards the street, I remembered that I didn't even know her name. I looked back, and she said right away, as though she already knew my question, "Sister Redempta. Tell her Sister Redempta referred you."

"Thank you, Sister. Thank you so much! You answered my prayers!"

"No, I didn't. I'm only His instrument, hija. Go."

* * *

"Josie, people are starting to come in. You want to sit? You've been standing here by the casket for so long," Lily squeezes my hand. Her hands are so warm. So competent. Everybody relies on Lily. I take a look at my husband, his grey face against the white pleated satin sheet of the casket. He's the only man I've ever loved. My husband, who's been lying in the bed of another woman for nine years now, would no longer be able to come to his senses and choose to come back to me, to us, the children.

I feel Lily's arms firmly guiding me towards the chair in the front row. I sit. She sits beside me, holding my hand. I stare at the brass base of the casket, the gleaming black mahogany, and on top of the coffin, a framed picture of Manuel during his engineer days in Manila. Perhaps if he looked at this picture often enough, it would have reminded him of his best self, and made him persist on being an engineer, to go back to school. But instead, he slid away from respectability, and from us.

* * *

"Plumber? Carpenter? Electrician? I did not come here to be a labourer. Just because you have decided to become labourers does not mean I have to do it too," Manuel replied to his friends.

"You are too proud," I interrupted. "We can't eat pride," I added.

"Just give me more time, Josie. I'm not the same as you. Teaching is not much to give up for cooking," said Manuel.

"You think I'm only a teacher so I can give it up for anything? Who do you think you are, engineer that can't get a job, refusing to take lowly jobs. Insulting other people who at least pay for their drinks. At least my cooking pays for our bills!" I cried, and stormed out of the room.

* * *

God, why? Why did you not answer that prayer? Even a small engineering job would have lifted his spirits. What possible good came out of that? My business success? Was that the payoff, Lord? It seemed so simple in the beginning, so harmless.

* * *

It was the ninth day of my novena at Our Lady of Perpetual Help, a bus ride away from the kids' school. A big event was happening in the church vestry. The commotion distracted me from my prayers. When I finished, I stuck my head in the next-door room to find out what was going on. People were putting up streamers, pulling out tables from cabinets hidden in the walls of the room, rolling out carts of folded chairs stacked on top of each other. Someone ran in from a door and spoke to the woman who seemed to be in charge.

"What? That's not possible. We need the food tonight!" said the person in charge. She was short and stocky. She held her feet apart like a commander.

"They can't do it, the place is burned to a crisp. You can't even speak to the owner. She's dumbstruck and useless. Everybody's crying," said the messenger from St. Joseph.

From somewhere deep in my heart, where my prayers lodged — already answered before they materialized into reality — I boldly addressed the woman in charge.

"How much food do you need?" I asked.

"We're expecting 150. It's a fundraiser. They've already paid $25 per ticket. They're expecting good food."

"Are they mostly Filipino?"

"How did you know?"

"Catholic Churches here have mostly Filipino parishioners. I can make the food if you don't mind Filipino food mostly."

"Are you kidding? They would love it," said the commander.

"How much did you plan to pay for the food?"

"$10 per head.

"I can manage that. I'll make five dishes: a salad, a noodle dish, a chicken dish, a vegetable dish and a dessert. Good enough?"

"Perfect."

"I don't have time to get cutlery and drinks," I said, remembering that caterers usually bring those things as well.

"No worries, we'll look after that, if you can live with $8 per head," said the commander.

As though St Joseph was putting words in my mouth, I said "$9 per head."

"Done," said the commander.

* * *

Dear Lily, my champion. Thank you God for Lily. But I didn't ask for so much business success Lord, a little would have been enough. Why did I need to be the CEO of Plates of Paradise catering, food and manufacturing and export company? I'm just a simple Pililla girl; I don't need very much. How did I get so caught up in the business? If I were just a little successful, maybe Manuel would not have been so threatened, and I would not have been so busy and proud, impatient with him. He would not have lost his temper too much, would not have spent a lot of time away with his friends, and would not have met that woman.

"Josie, the dining table is all ready for you now." Someone sits on the other side of me, holds my other hand. I raise my head from my reveries. It's Ching: my sister-in-law, married to Manuel's brother, who sponsored us to Canada. Something's different. She looks so much older. It's the hat.

"You remember that big round hat you used to wear in Manila when you and Mario met? Where's that? You should wear hats again," I say. "Manuel thought all Canadian women wore hats. I was so excited to wear a hat, but Manuel said 'over my dead body.' He was always so conservative."

I suddenly feel tearful, remembering those early times. Ching folds me in her arms. I let her. The old feelings creep up, the girly crush I had over the handsome dark engineer with the piercing eyes, the storm that swept over my life.

* * *

"You're under arrest, Miss," said the student dressed up as a policewoman.

"Why?" I asked gamely. I felt wild in that Ann-Margret hairdo that my boarding mate had fixed for me so that I wouldn't look so siyana at the school fair, *"with all those rich people,"* she said. Siyana, or simple village girl, was not the woman staring back at me in the mirror that fateful morning.

"Because you're too pretty," teased a smiling man who stood behind the policewoman. She snapped plastic handcuffs over my wrist and his.

"For you lovebirds, jail for 15 minutes," pronounced the policewoman, locking us up in a large cage set on a platform in the middle of the school playground.

That 15 minutes turned into 30 minutes, then 45 minutes, until we were ejected by force because of other couples lined up paying to be jailed.

He never let me go the rest of the day at that school fair. I walked around in a daze, held under the spell of the devastatingly handsome charming engineer. No one's ever paid that kind of attention to me. We were together all day, until his little sister, a grade 3 Theresian, had to be taken home. After that it was daily visits, in school, at my boarding house, taking me to movies, strolling Luneta Park, driving around in his fancy red Malibu. Until I couldn't help but say yes to his question — *"will you marry me"*?

* * *

Love. I never asked you for that Lord, still, you gave it to me. But betrayal — I never expected that. They were small betrayals at first, easily forgivable. Having an affair with the maid while I was pregnant with my first child. Okay. He was hungry and I could not provide. So. He said that he would not do it again. I believed him. But later, it was too much.

"Josie, the table?" Ching reminds me.

"Yes, of course," I comply. We walk quickly towards the dining area. I look at the long table, not really seeing.

"Josie," Ching nudges me. "Is it okay?"

I scan the long banquet table. It is bicultural, as planned. *Pancit, empanadas, puto* and *cuchinta, cassava* pastries, all good on this side, the Filipino side. Cascading towers of white triangular sandwiches, and a long tray of charcuteries on the Canadian side. Between the Filipino and Canadian sides there is a giant basket of fruit. Yes, it brims over like I wanted, to look like a cornucopia, with mangoes on top, even if from Mexico, and bananas, even if not the sweet orange *lakatan* kind of Pililla. Oh well. Difficult to get an equal mix of Philippine and Canadian fruits, have to sacrifice one for the other. The tray of charcuteries has small *lumpia* spring rolls scattered amongst the cheeses and salamis and parsley. Rosie did well.

Is there enough food on each side? Manolita's friends for sure would be Canadians, and Bobby's. Sonia would bring a mix of Canadians and Filipinos, but mostly Canadians. Manuel's would mostly be Filipinos, and what about mine. No, more is needed on the Filipino side. Something missing. The breads. The *pandesal* of course, how could I forget?

"No, it's not fine. Where's the *pandesal*?"

"Oh yeah, it must still be in the kitchen," said Ching.

"In the middle, okay? Right there, where the gladiolas are."

"Where do we put the gladiolas? There's no more room at the table." Ching's voice trails off.

Manuel's *pandesals*. In the early morning was when he wanted to bake them. The smell woke us up — a warm, sweet, salty and slightly fermented smell.

* * *

"Smells like kili-kili," giggled little Manolita.

"Armpit smell ha, probably your armpit!" says Manuel running after Manolita to reach her arm.

Manolita ran behind big brother Bobby, who pretended to protect her, but ended up raising Manolita's arm. Manolita squealed and ran to big sis Sonia.

"Enough, kids! The pandesal *is getting cold,"* warned Sonia.

Manuel loved tearing the pandesal *open, releasing the bread's steaming heat, then slathering it with butter. Sonia loved it with cheese whiz, Bobby stuffed it with langgonisa, and Manolita ate it plain. I liked it any way, but specially dipping it into anything — coffee, hot chocolate, green papaya soup.*

* * *

Baking *pandesals* was the one thing Manuel could do well, well enough in fact to make a business of it. But he was too proud to sell anything.

"Give them away and you make friends. Isn't it better to have a lot of friends than a lot of money?" Manuel used to say.

"*Ate*, Father Carlos has arrived," someone calls from the door.

"Go, I'll look after this," Ching says. I give her a hug, whisper thanks. Father Carlos has entered the dining room.

"Ah Father, thank you for coming. You are the only one who would."

"It's not for us to judge, but for the Lord," said Father Carlos, embracing me. "I brought the prayers, who will lead?"

"I don't know yet, Father. I would like Manolita to do it, but she will be late coming from a singing engagement. I suppose Sonia could do it, but she might just change the words, you never know with her. Forget about Bobby. I'm no good with this sort of thing. Can you just do it Father, if Manolita doesn't?"

"Don't worry *hija*. And the eulogy?"

"Manuel has a lot of friends who will say something. Maybe that's enough? Manolita said she will sing Manuel's favourite song and that would be the eulogy." I am worried.

"Father, what if she comes? I'll not be responsible for my actions if she comes," I stiffen.

"We'll play it by ear. Go meet your friends," Father Carlos gives me another hug and walks away.

"There you are." Sonia stands in front of me, a worried look on her face. My good girl. The best. So responsible.

"You look so worried," I straighten her collar, which doesn't need it.

"Carla. She's out there," whispers Sonia.

"I don't want to be there," I say.

"I know. Bobby's looking after it," Sonia assures me.

There's a scuffle. Loud sounds from the foyer. I don't want to see, but my legs have their own mind, and I find myself in the corridor watching a scene that looks like it belongs to a movie.

Bobby and another man are holding that woman by her arms, dragging her towards the door at the end of the hallway away from the chapel. She pulls her body back, feet trying to gain traction on the carpet, arms flailing trying to get away from the hold.

"Let me go! I just want to see him! He's already dead, what's the harm?" she cries.

"What's the harm? You have harmed us all our life, *puta*, and now you want to ruin even this?" Bobby's handsome face flushes red with the anger he is trying to control.

"Sonia, do something please with that *scandalosa*," urges Tita Lily who has somehow appeared beside Sonia and me.

Sonia pushes her way through the people standing around watching, transfixed.

I hear Sonia's level voice. "Carla, for heaven's sake. Show some respect. Where's your shame?" Sonia bends her head near Carla's ear and whispers something that quiets her down. Sonia holds Carla's elbow, and helps her up. "Let her go Bobby, she'll walk out on her own."

Bobby reluctantly lets go of Carla's arm. She stands up. She looks so tiny in that mid-calf black dress. Her long wavy hair reaches down to her waist, uncontained by a black lacy veil. He always liked old-fashioned long hair, liked them free and loose, sexy he said. I touch the small bun at the base of my neck. So I like it neat this way. Carla picks up her purse and does not look up as she shuffles towards the door that Bobby holds open. She is gone. Bobby whispers something to the other man.

The music starts. People begin making their way to the chapel. Sonia takes Bobby's arm, and walks with him to the front pew. Tita Lily guides me to the front. Before sitting, Bobby turns to Sonia. "What did you promise her?" he asks bitterly. Sonia does not reply.

They made it up like a stage. The casket at the centre, a big white screen at the back, various musical instruments on the far side and a podium off-centre. Two standing wreaths of calla lilies frame the stage.

"We are gathered today to say farewell to our dear friend, Manuel del Mundo. He died as he lived, in quiet simplicity, in the arms of his beloved family. Let us pray that he rest in peace with the Lord," Father Carlos intones. How amazing that priests could lie so well. Beloved family? Yes, indeed.

I look sideways at Bobby, so handsome in his leather jacket, eyes framed by long curly lashes. He has so many girls chasing after him but he is only interested in looking after our family; he's the self-appointed father since the separation. He is looking down, hunched, elbows on his muscular thighs, shoulders stooped, carrying the unnaturally heavy burden of hate. Lord, please help him forgive Manuel. And himself. Look at me, when I can't even do that myself. God, give me the strength. I rub Bobby's back slowly, and gently massage his shoulders.

I feel arms around my waist, bushy wild hair against my back. Sonia. I let Bobby go and turn to Sonia. I wrap my arms around her. Dear dependable, loving, caring Sonia who advocates for everybody. She's usually so strong; how vulnerable she is now. Sonia raises her head. I hear a sigh of exhaustion. Sonia takes the deep brown complexion of her father, but her wild stringy Afro hairdo is a step up from Manuel's wavy locks. My social activist. Her black-rimmed eyeglasses are fogged up. I take her eyeglasses to clean them, but she stops my hand. She lifts her glasses and wipes the tears underneath. She looks at me, as though searching for something. I feel the fight going out from me. She pulls me to her in an embrace, and I let her. I smell the frying cooking oil on my suit underneath her lavender fragrance and my Chanel. I feel so tired.

Bobby turns towards us. I feel his helplessness. I know he is battling the anger towards his father while feeling responsible for his father's death. All these people mourning, who have no idea of what can come between a father and a son. Bobby confessed his prayer to me: please God, give me one good memory of my father.

The choir stands up from the front-row seats on the right side of the chapel, and begins to sing "Amazing Grace." Their voices soar like a great wind taking my thoughts with them. 'Was lost, and now was found.' Manuel found? Lost yes, but found? I see Bobby's fist pushing his tears away. The voices are so soothing they are melting Bobby's hardness. Could they be loosening the resentments, the hate, making him able to cry? 'Amazing grace, how sweet the sound that saved a wreck like me.' There's something wrong with Bobby. His face is twisting in pain. I reach out for him. Bobby shoots up from his seat, flies down the aisle. Here's Manolita finally, as usual late and unperturbed, gliding up the aisle. Bobby stumbles into her.

"Bobby!" cries Manolita. Bobby brushes her away and runs. I see Lily following after Bobby. She signals for me to stay.

"Manolita. About time you arrived," says Sonia.

Manolita. So lovely that no one can stay angry with her. How tall she has become, almost as tall as Bobby now, and so pretty in her plaid school uniform. Even now, eyes turn admiringly towards her. But she is as thin as a needle, so thin she could disappear with a rush of wind. She is not eating again. Her face is so arresting. The way her hair is cut at a slant like a dagger on one side of her face; she is so sophisticated, with an earring glistening on the visible ear. Her sweet smile begs your pardon for the sophistication. Already grade 12, but she would always be Manuel's little girl. He would do anything for her. She plops down beside me carelessly, embraces me first, and then reaches out to embrace Sonia next.

"Sorry, sorry. The Mayor was late. We had to wait for him before I could sing," she whispers.

Sonia eyes Manolita with reservation. I can hear what she is thinking. The apple of everyone's eye. The brilliant one. The beautiful one. Top grades. Skipped several grades. Jock. Debater. Singer. Model looks. Not a word of Tagalog. Don't need it. You all have enough Tagalog for me. So spoiled. The only one their father loved, the only one he saw on the side through it all. Wants to be the first woman Prime Minister of Canada. The rising star of the Filipino Canadian community. Too full of herself. I can't say I disagree with Sonia. Everyone and everything waits for Manolita. Including burying their father.

"I call on Manolita del Mundo to give the eulogy," says Father Carlos.

Dear Lord. You gave me wonderful children. I'm not ungrateful. And you did bring Manuel back, but so late. And how it happened, Lord, how could you. I feel a cold wind rush around my heart. I look at the seat Bobby vacated. Lord, you've already taken Manuel away from me; that means you owe me. That will be Bobby. Let him be the good that will come out of this that I must keep faith with. The blessing in return. Promise me.

* * *

CHAPTER 2

Philippines
Josie, 1946–1968

I was born on April 11, 1946, of Marcelino and Francisca de Jesus, in the small village of Pililla, Rizal, two-and-a-half hours east of Manila. I was named Maria Josefina Godebertha in honour of my mother's mother, who was also Josefina, and in honour of St. Godebertha, on whose feast day I was born. My father was pleased about me being born on April 11, as "she will have a fierce patron saint to guard her in her life." St. Godebertha was a 7th-century saint from France who entered the convent rather than marrying, and became an abbess. She was proclaimed a saint when her death stopped a plague and a raging fire that protected the village of Amiens. My mother, whom I called *Inay*, thought it might be a little greedy, giving me a name that had both Jesus and God in it, to which *Itay*, my father, said you can't get too close to God. I was a good student, but even with my good spelling and penmanship, I left out the Godebertha when I wrote my name. The only times anyone called me by that name was when I had done something wrong.

As eldest in the family, I helped *Inay* around the house with all the chores while *Itay* taught at the local elementary school. Siblings came fast — two, three, four of them in a row, all boys — until I begged *Itay* to stop as *Inay* and I couldn't keep up with the babies. "Gifts of God should not be stopped," *Itay* said. I understood. *Inay* is very beautiful, but really. In the end, they slept on the floor with the children in between them, and that took care of it.

Our family was well respected in the village, and *Itay* was known as a fair and kind man. When people fought, they came to him for a resolution. He was such a popular godfather to many baptisms and weddings that *Inay* complained of the expense. Our house was often filled with people on the veranda at the end of the day, just talking about the latest gossip in the village. *Inay* always served *kakanins* and coffee, which made people come even more often. In this way, I grew up learning to make *bibingkas* and *suman,* sewing fabrics into tablecloths and pillowcases, drying flowers, picking out interesting shells to make into unique flower arrangements and vases, as presents of my father to his godchildren.

I graduated from high school as valedictorian. It was assumed that I would go away to Manila to study teaching. *Inay* prepared herself as best she could, but it was still difficult to accept my leaving. I made life easier for her. *Itay* was inconsolable. He and I were so close. I kept saying "It's only two hours away. You can always visit, and I can too." But everyone knew it was not the same. "I hope Manila will not change our angel," I heard *Itay* say to *Inay* one night. I wasn't so sure how I would get along in Manila without my family. I already missed everyone just thinking of it.

On the bus bound for Manila the day I left, I prayed hard that each day in Manila would pass by fast so I could come home for the two months of summer. I knew there was no frequent going back and forth for my parents or me once I was in Manila, because of the expense. As the bus rolled away, I looked back at *Inay, Itay* and my brothers waving at the bus, and felt suddenly afraid. Of how it would be without them, of being alone in the big city and living with Uncle Asiong's family, whom I did not know at all. As the bus drove on, our home became smaller and smaller, my family looking like long thin leaves of cogon grass waving in the wind. I stuck my head out of the bus to wave at them some more, and then they were gone.

The bus passed by Pililla Elementary School, and I thought of graduation day, how proud I felt when the principal said: "Do not forget us when you have succeeded in Manila." What would it be like studying at the Centro Escolar University? I felt nervous but thrilled thinking about university. I promised myself to do well in school, so my parents would be proud of me. How can I possibly forget them when I succeed? What an odd thing for the principal to say. The only future I could imagine was coming back to my old school to teach there.

I felt better at the thought of returning. As the bus sped along, I planted in my mind everything I saw so I would never forget: the old Church where *Inay* and I went to mass everyday, the basketball court where my brothers played in tournaments, where I cheered for them, and especially for the star shooter of my class, Sendong. I blushed thinking of him. There was the plaza in front of the city hall where bands and majorettes compete during fiestas. How I'd miss the fiestas. There was the shallow river and the boulevard where we hang out on moonlit nights.

"You'll forget us. I know I'm not good enough for you," was the last thing Sendong said to me when I did not accept his offer to be my date for the prom. But it was not because he was the black sheep of the class, or that he was fast with all the girls, or that he was an orphan raised by the *manangs* in the church — I just didn't know how to have a date. He confused me too much. Besides, I was too busy organizing the prom, how could I have a date myself?

There was the graveyard where we played ghost games on All Saints' Day, the girls collecting candle wax drippings from the candles lighting the old graves, the boys sneaking into backyards, stealing underwear from the clotheslines and hanging them between the posts on the plaza in front of the municipal hall next day.

I watched and planted them all in my heart: the trees and trees of coconuts, mangos, bananas heavy with fruit, the unending fields of rice, carabaos pulling carts, carabaos lazing on mud puddles, their tails swatting flies away, little birds perched on their hard leather backs.

* * *

In Cubao, I thought I would die. It seemed that the whole Philippines came to Cubao that day. The place teemed with people. Jeepneys honked, and wooden carts pulled sacks, bags and luggage. The air was hot with asphalt and sweat. Everyone seemed so busy, walking determinedly to somewhere, worry on their faces. Everyone seemed like they wanted something from me, like to ride in their jeepney, buy a *sampaguita* garland or give them money. New smells assaulted me: the scent of gas fumes from the exhausted buses, the stink of rotted fish lying on oily puddles snaking their way from the market, the smell of charred meat grilling over charcoals. Strange sights frightened me. An old man with no legs sat on a wooden platform on wheels, pushing himself on the sidewalk by one hand,

and on the other, carrying a carton of cigarettes and gum for sale. Children lay on the pavement asleep on flattened cardboard boxes.

A shirtless boy tugged at my skirt, his unseeing eyes blank and his palm open. As I was about to open my purse, someone tried to pull it away. I held on to my purse, and was dragged away until I fell on the ground.

People began forming around me, and I heard a voice from the crowd. "Josie! It's me, Uncle Asiong." A short fat man wearing a white polo shirt and dark eyeglasses picked me up from the ground.

"When did you arrive? Who's with you?" asked Uncle Asiong.

When I gestured that I was alone, Uncle Asiong blurted, "*Ay lintik!* I told them to have someone accompany you. You could have been killed here!" As Uncle Asiong helped me up, the circle began dispersing. With bags firmly in hand, Uncle Asiong led me to the street corner where he flagged a jeepney and we piled in.

Uncle Asiong and his wife Auntie Marita, an older woman with a limp, lived on the second floor of a two-level house. We couldn't see the house from the street. We had to walk between two houses, along a wooden plank over an *estero*. The house sat at the end of the plank, where the fetid canal ended. We walked up a flight of stairs from a door at the front of the house. The ground level was rented out to two other families, the units separated by the stairs. The upstairs had two units as well, connected by a corridor with the toilet. Uncle Asiong's unit was an open space with three sides. The side with the window had a counter against the wall, which contained a sink and a two-burner stove. In front of the stove and in the middle of the space was a dining table with a sewing machine on it.

The two other sides of the space were 'bedrooms,' separated from the open space by curtains. One bedroom had a wardrobe and a bed for Uncle Asiong and Auntie Marita. The other bedroom, separated by another curtain, contained a double-deck bed and a clothesline groaning with clothes.

"*Pasensiya na*. We have a small house. You will share the room with our other boarder. You'll meet her soon. She's in school," said Auntie Marita, who drew open the curtain of the bedroom while Uncle Asiong shoved my bags under the bed.

"Why don't you rest a little and your Auntie Marita will have supper ready soon. The toilet is outside. We share it with our neighbour," Uncle Asiong said. He took off his eyeglasses, revealing one empty eye socket. "Accident," he pointed to his eye, and drew the curtain close.

I sat down on the lower bunk and inspected my new room. I'd never slept in a double-decker bed ever. Not even on a one-decker bed. We always slept on floors. What a treat. I passed my hand over the colourful *banig* covering the bed, the pillow and blanket folded on top of it. What would it be like sleeping on the upper bunk? It should feel more private there, noting the rail guarding the side of the upstairs bunk. I envied the other boarder who slept there, imagining how pretty she must be, based on the fancy clothes on the clothesline.

The curtain hung by a wire about a foot from the ceiling, and I could hear everything going on in the house: pots banging, the kitchen water turning on and off, the sizzle and smell of fish frying. There was another smell that I couldn't figure out, a stink like urine and rotting garbage. It must come from the canal. Outside, I heard Uncle Asiong and Auntie Marita whispering, and from the window beyond, the sounds of children playing. An image of my brothers playing flashed before my eyes, of *Inay* and *Itay*, and I felt a wave of homesickness. I tried to look on the positive side. I'll have a kind of sister here, imagining the other boarder. Uncle Asiong and Auntie Marita seem nice. I decided to join them outside to stop feeling sorry for myself.

The curtain swung open and in came the most beautiful girl I ever saw. She had a triangular-shaped face framed by straight bangs that ended just below her eyebrows. She had long black hair down to her shoulders. She wore a white uniform. She stood still, moving her eyes all over me, as though inspecting me. She walked over to the clothesline, and started undressing.

"You must be the other boarder?" I said. I felt embarrassed seeing a total stranger undressing. The girl did not speak. "My name is Josie, what's yours?" I said, extending my hand. The girl did not seem to hear, nor see me. She didn't say anything, but made a forced smile on her pretty face. She turned away with an unmistakeable *irap*. I knew a snub when I saw one. I watched her climb up to the upper bunk, feeling humiliated and self-conscious. I may have come from a small town, but I was educated, and a valedictorian. I looked at the plain blouse I was wearing, then at my roommate's clothes, and determined to get some new ones like hers.

That night, I didn't feel well. I ate little of the *kangkong adobo,* fried *galunggong* and rice. Only quiet Auntie Marita and I had supper. Uncle Asiong promised to take me to school the next day, and then had gone out. My roommate, whose name turned out to be Cristy, did not join us at the table and instead made herself a plate and ate inside the room. There was nothing else to do after supper but go to sleep. I lay on my lower bunk bed, and tucked a rosary under my pillow. I lay the thin cotton blanket over myself, and tried not to think of the person above the bunk.

I recited my nightly prayer, naming things I was grateful for that day: a bed of my own, a new *Inay* and *Itay* in Manila who seemed nice enough, my purse which did not get lost even after someone tried to steal it, being found in the Cubao jungle just when I needed someone, a house to sleep in instead of the street pavement, two legs and two eyes all intact, a father and mother and brothers in Pililla whom I loved so much and who loved me, a new school next day where I would meet nice classmates, and make excellent grades, become a teacher, and soon be back home. It was the sort of day when I had to work hard to find things to be grateful for. On my first night in Manila, I cried myself to sleep, as I would for the next whole year.

* * *

The years passed swiftly. I put my whole heart into my studies. I lived to study. It showed in my grades. My teachers liked me. I made a few friends, girls who also came from the provinces, specially the ones near Pililla. With no spending money for transportation or anything else, I walked to and from Centro Escolar University every day, an hour walk each way, and going to morning mass along the way. I began making a few things to sell. Auntie Marita let me use her sewing machine when she was not using it for sewing potholders, place mats and dishcloths, and let me use the scraps for my projects. I sewed purses from the leftover fabrics, and embroidered them with sequins. I wore the purses to school, attracting the attention of classmates, and when they praised the purse, I offered to make them a similar purse, for a price.

I noticed that there were no desserts in the school canteen. I missed *bibingkas* from home. I made *bibingkas* once and let my classmates sample them. Seeing how they enjoyed the *bibingkas,* I offered the native pastries to the school canteen, which agreed to sell the *bibingkas* on trial. With the sales from the purses, I bought ingredients and made *bibingkas*. The *bibingkas* were a wild success.

Thereafter, I hurried up my studies so I could sew and cook. Auntie Marita started helping me with the projects, and I gave her some money for her help. I was even able to send some money home for birthday presents. Auntie Marita and I became close friends over the years, spending much time together.

Uncle Asiong was always away, and I wondered what he did for a living. 'Buy and sell,' he said. Until one day I discovered what he did.

In Cubao, I was about to board a bus to Pililla, when I saw Uncle Asiong herding a group of scrawny kids towards an alley. I followed them. Uncle Asiong opened a paper bag, and the kids threw coins in it. "This is very little. You've been sleeping on the job. I told you to bring your baby sister with you! That makes people give more. If you don't make better tomorrow, don't come back. I can't afford to keep you. That's my best corner. *'T'angina!*" He shooed the kids away, who scattered like birds. I hid myself, feeling as terrified as the children.

"You mean you only knew now?" said Cristy the night I told her about what I saw. "You are really something," shaking her head. "And I guess you think I'm the Virgin Mary," she added laughing. That was the night I learned Cristy was a prostitute, "but a high class one," Cristy boasted. "I do it only in hotels with rich important men. And when I graduate nursing, I'm done with this. I'm going to Canada."

That was the first time I heard about a place called Canada.

"I'll be a nurse there. Nurses get paid really well there. I'll make lots of dollars, marry a nice handsome Canadian and have a big house with a swimming pool. I'll buy a cream-coloured mustang convertible and drive it with the top down wearing a white scarf over my hair, blowing in the wind, like Marilyn Monroe, you know?" Cristy gushed.

The way Cristy talked about it, Canada sounded like paradise.

* * *

The years flew by and I graduated teaching with honours. *Inay* and *Itay* were eager to have me back in Pililla where a class was waiting for me to teach. But I was not as eager; in fact, I began to dread it, as I had grown to like life in the big city.

I continued to go to mass every day, and began a special campaign with God so that I could teach and continue to live in Manila. I began to walk to the altar on my knees every day for a whole month as my offering. The San Marcelino Church was one of my favourite churches, as it was airy and modern. It was out of my way to school, a greater sacrifice, and therefore more pleasing to God. That's where I met Sister Redempta, who referred me to the school across the street, which was how I ended up teaching at St Theresa's College, where Marites del Mundo studied, whose brother Manuel del Mundo regularly dropped her off and picked her up — which is how I met Manuel.

* * *

CHAPTER 3

Philippines
Manuel, 1967

It's a hot summer evening in a nightclub on Roxas Boulevard in Manila. I tagged along with my brother, Mario, as I had nothing else to do. He knew the band that played there and they let him sing with them every now and then. Mario greets everyone with a slap on the back, or they slap him on the back, and everyone says *pare*. Buddy. He is everyone's buddy and I don't have to do anything to be accepted. When you're with my brother, you'll be fine. A party of revellers sat at a table beside the band, where we usually sit. We take a table next to it.

"Is it really like Paradise?" asks one.

"Yes, everything you need is there, except...no eligible handsome Filipinos!" says the woman wearing a hat, who is the centre of attention. Giggles, laughter.

"Why, what's wrong with Canadians?" asks another.

"Not big enough for you?" More laughter.

"No, they're too...well...serious...dry..." says the woman with the hat, giggling.

"YOU'RE the one who's dry, miss old maid Ching!" More laughter.

"So why hasn't anyone introduced me to a nice sexy Filipino bachelor?" the hat woman teases. I guess her name is Ching.

"Did anyone call me?" inserts Mario, rising from our table to join the laughter.

Ching stops and looks at my brother, who is not laughing but looking intensely at her. She blushes deep red.

"Uuuuy!" cries the crowd in unison.

Mario bows to Ching and gestures a playful salute with his hand on his brow. He smiles directly at her. He moves toward the band while still keeping his eyes on her. What a flirt. I could never be as bold as that. Mario holds the microphone and announces, "This song is dedicated to our lovely Canadian guest, from all the sexy Filipino bachelors in this room." Hoots and howls from the audience. Mario smiles teasingly, pleased with himself, looking towards Ching's table. The band plays the first low notes of "Lighter Shade of Pale" and the audience cheers in recognition. Mario sings with an exceptionally strong voice, buoyed by the game. Ching's eyes are glued to Mario as he sings. Everyone on Ching's table watches Ching and Mario closely, and I sense a feeling of secret titillation in the air. It is hard to see Ching's face with the hat in the way and the dim lights in the room, but I feel the electricity between those two.

That night, Mario and Ching had eyes for no one but each other. That they would marry came as no surprise to anyone, except for the swiftness of it all.

"You must be kidding, right?" I asked Mario, who was driving effortlessly through the early morning traffic of Manila on the return home from the party. "You just met her tonight, *'tangina naman!'* I protested.

"She likes me, anyone can see that. She's not bad. Why shouldn't I like her? She's the one in a hurry. She said it takes only a few months to sponsor me to Canada after we marry. She leaves for Vancouver next week, so we'll do it this weekend. We'll just go to the judge, and do it." Mario said, blowing smoke through the open window.

The night was humid, the stars were out, and a tinge of light peeked behind the midnight blue sky, the dawn patiently waiting to break out. It was four am; Manila was only starting to wake up. By the time we reached our home in Bel Air, Makati, it would be light enough that if we got caught, we could pretend we were actually on our way out.

Mario parked the Malibu on the street, rather than in the garage, so as not to disturb the household with the opening of the garage doors. We sneaked into the house by the back door. The maid was already making breakfast but no one else was up. Mario slid his finger along his lips gesturing to the maid not to say anything. We silently crept up the stairs to our room.

"You are crazy," I half-screamed in a whisper when we reached our room and the door was shut.

"And when I get there, I will sponsor you. You'll see," Mario said.

"Dad will kill you."

"He won't have a chance. No one knows until the day I leave, understood?"

I felt frightened and excited for Mario. Ching looked older than Mario. All Mario's girlfriends were prettier than Ching. She could pass as Mario's aunt. How long would this crazy marriage last? And how would Mario fare in Canada? What work could he do there? He's not even finished college.

"What will you do for money?" I asked.

"Whatever. Sing. Do business. Work in an architectural office drafting. I'm almost finished anyway, just a few courses left to do. She's a nurse. Nurses make lots of money. She can keep working until I find something. I have enough savings for the trip anyway. We'll be okay. I don't need Dad's money."

"I can lend you some if you need it," I offered.

"Keep it," he said.

I felt somehow triumphant for Mario. Our dad seemed to be losing out to Destiny. Destiny was on our side. Canada. What an escape! A paradise. Would Mario really sponsor me?

I couldn't sleep anymore. The light began to seep into our bedroom. Mario looked like he was sleeping soundly. He is so capable of going with the flow. So careless with his life but things always work for him. The Mario charm. Wish I had a little of it. He's got Dad's blood, while I've got Mom's, everybody says. I miss her. It was all his fault, and that woman's. I feel the anger rising in me again.

"Do you think Mom would agree if she were alive?" I threw the question up in the air above our beds. No answer.

"She's gone. And anywhere is better than here. So get some sleep," said Mario.

I tried to see her face again, but it is fading with the years. I feel her softness and it warms me. I miss her so much. I try to think of Canada, and the image that comes up is of snow and mountains and forests, gleaming skyscrapers, mansions, shopping malls, offices, hospitals. I look for Mario in the picture, but all the people were snow men and snow women.

* * *

Ching went back to Canada. After a few months, the sponsorship of Mario was approved. He began preparations to leave for Vancouver. He no longer kept the relationship a secret. It did not take long for the del Mundo clan, the Bel Air neighbourhood, the village of Makati and the City of Manila to learn about the elopement.

I hate breakfast. That's when both of them will be there for sure. Dad sits at the head of the table buried in the paper. I see the top of his balding head above the page. He puts the paper down to take a sip of coffee. Dad is in his sixties but doesn't look it, even with the balding head. He is elegant in a *barong tagalog* suit, framed by the spray of bird of paradise in the middle of the table. The table is set for breakfast for four, the birds of paradise pattern repeated in embossed colors on the place mats. Mom didn't like formal breakfasts, formal anything in fact.

Beside Dad sits Lolita, his beautiful second wife, after mom died. In fact, she was his mistress all along. Lolita's silky black hair is parted at the middle and flows down bare alabaster shoulders, like the ghostly mother of the Addams family. She is scanning a newspaper, then reads out loud:

"'Whose son of a socialite actress and a development baron secretly married a maid from a foreign country?' Goodness, and this one. 'Nurse, maid or nursemaid to wed Manila bachelor?' That's the caption under a picture of a woman, whose face is hidden by a big hat. God, there's not even a face, they must have just got any old picture here," says Lolita, giggling. She continues to read.

"'Rumours have it that a 40-year-old nanny from a country which shall not be named has bagged one of Manila's up-and-coming top bachelors, and all she had to do was waive a citizenship card...'"

"It won't last. I'll get it annulled," interrupts Dad.

"You wish. How? They are both of legal age. Doesn't matter. I've got several offers come up because of my renewed infamy. I should thank Mario and his sugar nanny," says Lolita, turning the newspaper page. "Let it go, Ben. Isn't that what you wanted? For Mario to get on with his life and grow up?"

"You give them everything, and they throw everything back at you," Dad says, staring at the bottom of his cup.

"Your problem is you keep picking up the pieces they break. Let them live with their broken pieces, then you see, they'll come back to you," says the witch, topping up Dad's coffee.

"I promised their mother they would practise in professions," says Dad.

"She's dead, Ben. What's wrong with marrying a maid, anyway? She's a Canadian maid, earning Canadian dollars, and she's really a nurse anyway. Didn't they say the same of you? Marrying an actress! No, no... not for the del Mundos." She rolls her eyes.

"But you're a star, the most beautiful of them all. You win awards. You're different," Dad says, adding, "While she is nobody," he continues while tossing back the coffee.

"That's what they said of me too, remember? And what did you do?" Lolita reaches out across the table to touch Dad's hand. Dad brings her hand to his lips and kisses it. I want to puke.

"You fought for me. And now, Mario is fighting for her. He's your son alright," Lolita smiles.

"I was already successful when I married you. I can do whatever I want. He's only a kid, not even finished with his architecture. What kind of job can he have in Canada?" Dad stands up, agitated. "He is determined to make me a fool, that's what," he continues, stabbing the table with his finger. "He wants to prove a del Mundo can be bum. He wants to show me up. Destroy me. By destroying his life, he destroys me." Dad shakes his head and starts pacing.

He stops and looks Lolita in the eye. "He can expect nothing from me now. When he takes off on that plane, he can forget he has a family."

He turns around and leaves the room, ignoring Marites, who just walks in the door.

Marites plops onto the chair and looks around at the dishes on the table. "Where's my French toast?" she asks, then pauses. She says again, louder this time, to somebody outside the room, "My French toast?!"

The new maid — a pretty girl in a white uniform and black apron — runs into the room bearing a plate. "Sorry *po* mam. I tot you still dressing."

"Maybe YOU should dress up. I saw you take off your blouse as Dad stood by your open door. You think we're blind, you …*alembong*…!" Tease. Another of Dad's victims. Marites pushes the plate into the maid's face. The maid drops the plate and runs away.

Marites stares at the floral place mat in front of her.

I look at Lolita with something like a victorious sneer.

"It's not him. It's her! It's always…these…girls!" Lolita cries out defensively. I shrug. She looks towards the empty doorway, stands up and walks out.

In the silence, you could smell the burnt butter of the French toast on the floor, mixed with the fragrance left behind by Lolita's swishing hair. You could hear the chirping of birds in the garden outside.

"*Kuya* Mario didn't even say goodbye. I wish I could go with him," says Marites.

"I'm taking them to the airport this afternoon. Come," I say.

Marites bursts out in tears.

* * *

The Manila International Airport is not an airport. It is a place of joyful homecoming, of tearful farewells, a place of gathering for families, friends, neighbours, whole communities saying welcome and goodbye. It is where the Filipino character is truly revealed, how Filipinos show love for each other — seeing a loved person off till the very last minute before takeoff, and being there to welcome the loved person, as they step out of the Customs Checkpoint. They come in cars, jeepneys and buses all the way from the provinces, to say goodbye, and to welcome back. There is not an international airport that can ever hold this kind of meet and greet, as Filipino designers have tried to do. There is nothing airport authorities can do to discourage the mass welcomes and send-offs to free up traffic. Somehow, people find a way to come and send off loved ones in large droves.

That afternoon at the airport, Ching's family and friends from Lingayen, Pangasinan came in full force. They filled two jeepneys and a small bus. They came with full food provisions for lunch in the parking lot. After lunch, they joined Mario and Ching, Marites and me at the lobby, still talking about the lunch of *adobo* and green mangoes with *bagoong,* and 'newly-married jokes.' Our section of the lobby started to fill up with more guests whom I didn't know — Ching's family, most likely. Ching looked radiant in a bright green suit and her regulation wide-brim hat, *sampaguita* garlands hanging around her neck. Mario looked serious, nervous and movie-star-handsome in a dark suit. Ching's mother kept crying, while everyone else was chatting, laughing. Someone was taking pictures, making people pose. Some sat on the luggage, waiting till four pm when the newlyweds had to go inside the departure gates.

Marites huddled close to Mario. "Promise you'll visit soon?" she said.

"Yes, or you visit us. In one year," Mario said.

"Christmas! Promise?" He shouldn't promise Marites if he couldn't do it.

"Yes, I promise you your first white Christmas," Mario said.

"How about me, *utol*?" I reminded him.

"I'll begin sponsorship papers as soon as I can," Mario assured me.

"It's 4:30 pm folks. Time to go through departure gates," someone announced.

Everyone started hugging Ching and Mario. There was more crying from Ching's mother, sisters and girlfriends. Marites began crying, and pretty soon, I felt myself crying too as I wrapped my arms tight around my big brother, who began crying as well. Ching took Mario's arm and led him away as everyone waved them goodbye. We followed them along the glass corridor until they disappeared in the secured room beyond.

* * *

CHAPTER 4

Philippines
Josie, 1968–1981

It was St. Theresa's day, the annual fair when Theresians come to school not wearing uniforms, bringing family and friends to the fair. It's a day when teachers mingle socially with students, their families, other teachers and nuns. I had been teaching grade one for a few months, and couldn't believe my luck. Teaching the bright, clean and well-behaved grade one children of rich families was easy. The teachers were mostly friendly, and the nuns were kind. The parents were another matter though. I was warned. I was anxious and excited to meet some of them at the fair.

"Enjoy yourself, *hija*, it's a fair, not a homeroom meeting," advised Sr. Redempta, who had become a close friend, and who it turns out was the kindergarten teacher at St Theresa's.

The school quadrangle was decked out in festive banners. Classrooms around the quadrangle were turned into displays of science, crafts and arts of different classes. Food stands competed with game stands for the attention of students.

A large cage stood in the middle of the quadrangle where you could have someone 'arrested' and handcuffed with another person, so that the 'lovebirds' would be 'jailed.' It was a popular game for girls and boys to get introduced to their crushes, or spend a little time in the spotlight with them, in a way that was socially acceptable and fun. Boys and girls, dressed in bright fancy clothes, hovered around the cage. The high school students specially were difficult to distinguish from their normal selves — some wore makeup and high heels, and looked older than us, their teachers.

I had borrowed one of Christy's outfits for the day, at her insistence. "So you won't look so *siyana* with those socialites," Christy had said. She fixed up my hair so it was teased and sat on my head high and round as a ball, and then gently curled up in a small tight wave at the shoulders. Standing me in front of the mirror, Christy pronounced: "Now you look like Ann-Margret." I knew that name from the Hollywood movies. I felt confident that I should be good enough for the Theresian parents.

"You look lovely," said Sr. Redempta.

"Is that you, Josie?" remarked Sr. Nieves, the principal, with a rare smile on her face that seemed mixed with disapproval.

I caught a few young men looking at me in a strange way, making me feel secretly excited. I smiled at a couple of high school girls I knew, but they shot back a hostile look, unmistakably one of competition. I felt thrilled at not being recognized, feeling like a new person.

That's when I got 'arrested.'

I'd never been arrested before, and I didn't know how this game worked. The man who came behind the 'police officer' was not much taller than me. What I remember about him was the piercing look he had on me, part serious, part teasing, and I felt confused. He seemed to enjoy my being flustered, which made me even more flustered. I don't exactly know how we got handcuffed, and next thing I knew, I was alone with him in a huge cage raised on a stage in the middle of the quadrangle. I felt very self-conscious, wondering what Sister Nieves thought of me.

His name was Manuel. Manuel del Mundo. But really, it was Manolo del Mundo, he said. He chucked Manolo as it was too serious and made him feel like an old man. I told him my full name, with the Godebertha. "Seriously?" he asked, and almost choked laughing.

The policewoman rattled the cage. "One more minute, lovebirds!" she said.

"This woman carries a vicious name, and is too funny. She is a danger to society. She should stay in prison," he said, pulling out a string of orange tickets.

"If you say so," said the policewoman, tearing off two tickets.

I don't remember anything else about our conversation in that cage except I kept laughing. He made harmless little jokes and winked at the policewoman every time I laughed. He made me feel so unburdened, took down my defenses, made me feel free as a child. I felt I was the only person in his world that moment. No one ever made me feel like that.

I'll never forget the rest of that day. He occupied me completely, fascinated me. I was captivated by the way he smiled with his eyes, his long lashes, those full lips, his gentlemanly way. He treated me like a princess. We went from display to display not seeing any of it. I felt deliciously happy. This was the first time a handsome and interesting man paid such attention to me. Manuel spoke of his family, which intimidated me. I told him about mine, which fascinated him. We walked around the quadrangle wrapped in each other.

The next day, we were the talk of the faculty. He dropped by the school, and everyday thereafter. He always had some special activity planned — a walk in Intramuros park, a movie, an out-of-the-way restaurant, watching the sun set over Manila Bay. I had never been to such places. It confounded me, all the attention.

"I'm an ordinary person. I come from a poor family and I'm a simple grade one teacher. You're from an affluent family, a gentleman, good-looking, an engineer. You can have any woman you want. Why me?" I asked finally.

"That's why. See? How innocent you are of your own beauty and strength. You are solid as a rock, the way you are so responsible and caring of your family. I love the way you listen and don't make demands. The way you make everything feel all right. I feel so supported with you, safe. You are the sort of woman any man would like to have for a partner in life. Don't ever change."

What seemed like a proposition was soon followed by a real one.

The next month, we were married — by a justice of the peace. That way, not one of our families could interfere.

After our marriage, we visited Pililla. I never needed to worry. My family welcomed us with open arms. *Inay* and *Itay* had a pig killed and roasted, and with the *lechon*, a small impromptu fiesta happened with most of the townsfolk attending, bearing native cakes and various dishes. "We are so proud that one of our own students is marrying a rich handsome engineer from a great family of Manila. A toast to the Rose of Pililla," said the principal of Pililla Elementary School. I felt like disappearing from the embarrassment. Manuel seemed to enjoy it all. Unlike everybody else, *Inay* worried about how the aristocratic del Mundos would treat me. She was right.

The del Mundos were not pleased. Manuel brought me one day to his home for dinner. To a stunned Benjamin and Lolita del Mundo, Manuel introduced me as his wife. Don Benjamin stood up and left. Manuel followed him to his room where their raised voices could be heard in the dining room. Dona Lolita, Marites and I sat quietly in our chairs. I felt afraid of so much wealth, as it usually came with so much power. What could they do to us? Manuel came back to the dining room, his face flushed, and pulled me up to go.

That was all the contact we had with Manuel's family until much later, when our first baby came.

* * *

Manuel and I moved to a small apartment near St Theresa's College on San Marcelino Street, in Ermita. We lived on my small salary, as Manuel quit working for the family business. He did not want to be in his father's employ, or anywhere around him, so long as he could remember the ugly words his father said about me, and my family. He could not find work. Construction companies would not hire him for one reason or another, until he figured out that his influential father must have put out the word. He sought companies based outside Manila where his father's influence might not reach, and landed a job in a small contracting company doing a renovation for the University of the Philippines in Los Banos, about two-hours away from Manila. It was a difficult but sweet time for us, when our hardships only brought us closer.

Soon, I was pregnant with our first baby. I continued to work, but later, I increasingly found it difficult to do both teaching and housework. We decided to hire a maid, Nena, a young girl from Pililla recommended by a cousin of mine. With Nena, I was able to manage teaching better, but at home became lethargic and unkempt, lying in bed mostly, reading or sleeping. By the time Manuel came home, I was already asleep, and Manuel was left dining by himself served by Nena.

That was the excuse anyway that Manuel gave me, when I found out one day that Manuel was having an affair with Nena. I was so upset that I bled, and was rushed to the hospital. I confided in Sr. Redempta and my parents. *Itay* was livid and promised to come to Manila to kill Manuel. Instead, *Inay* gave strict instruction to my brothers to keep their father under strict surveillance, packed a bag, and took a bus to Manila. Arriving in our house, *Inay* packed Nena off in a bus back home to Pililla, and stayed to look after me until Bobby was born.

Our life improved with the birth of Bobby. I hired a new maid to help look after Bobby. When I searched for a maid, I insisted on "an older ugly woman." One was readily found in Pililla. Maring was the spinster aunt of a third-degree cousin. I was so lucky with Maring. Small and hard as a raisin, her beady eyes and thin mouth were all a front for a soul at the margins of life, longing to love someone wholeheartedly, and which she did Bobby.

Manuel's parents softened, opened their hearts to their first grandchild and became the doting grandparents. I soon went back to work where my natural flair for teaching was recognized. I rose in prominence. Manuel's career also improved, getting better contracts with referrals from his father's friends. Soon we had a second child — Sonia. After our third child, Manolita, was born, so taken with her were Manuel's parents that they insisted on our whole family moving in with them in the big Bel Air house. We resisted, naturally, but they did not let off the pressure until we consented to accepting a house gift: a three-bedroom bungalow on the same street in Bel Air. And that was how our growing family of Manuel and myself, Bobby, Sonia and Manolita came to live in posh Makati on the small salaries of teacher and engineer.

The seventies were a great time to be an architect, an engineer, a contractor, a road builder, a developer — anything to do with construction in the Philippines. The First Lady Imelda Marcos was a great builder and visionary. She wanted to create innovative institutions: a health centre, an arts centre, a cultural centre. It was an honour to build any of the Madame's buildings, as the project would spare no expense. It would be grand and make a name for the designers associated with it. Anyone she liked would surely get more referrals, assured of a name, a future.

Also, she always needed the project done yesterday. When the First Lady returned from Cannes International Film Festival, she was reported to have been inspired to create a world-class Film Centre in Manila to host world-class films. The favoured contractors were already busy on other Imelda projects and could not take on a new project to finish in less than 12 months. Papa Ben got the building contract and gave Manuel the engineering sub-contract.

Manuel was delighted. I was not. For with every new commission, we got more comfortable financially, but Manuel had become a different person. He no longer spent time with the children, except perhaps Manolita. Bobby was not doing well in school. Sonia was having bouts of Tourette syndrome. Manuel seemed angry with me somehow, for what, I didn't know. He spent more time with his colleagues, businessmen who drove fancy cars and drank whisky. They spent hours meeting in nightclubs, and Manuel came home drunk many nights. Once, I found a gun tucked away among his underwear. Manuel said that the gun was a gift.

"What kind of friend would give a gun for a gift?" I implored.

"One who understands the need for safety. You are being too moralistic. There's nothing wrong with a gun — it's only something to protect us with. It's how you use it that makes the difference. Of course, I will use it only for our protection. What else will I use it for?" argued Manuel.

"It's so tempting when it's around. You have an argument with someone, and you reach out for it. Or what if it just blasts off accidentally. These things happen all the time. I read about them in the papers," I continued.

"You worry too much. This is very expensive. I'll never use it except for protecting us — okay? That's a promise."

"Leave it at home then," I negotiated, something I would regret forever.

"Okay," he said reluctantly.

"Somewhere the kids would never see or reach," I said, thinking how insignificant my demand was: just to hide the gun from the kids. Perhaps I should have followed my instinct then and threw the gun away. Then perhaps Manuel would still be alive today.

The night Manuel announced he had received the commission for the Film Centre, I told him that Bobby's homeroom teacher had called and inquired about Bobby. The teacher asked whether Bobby was ill, as he had not been to school two days in a row. We were in our bedroom. It was our first out-and-out fight.

"You need to deal with this. I don't care how busy you are, "I told Manuel.

"He's only what, 13 years old? You're a teacher — can't discipline your own boy?" said Manuel.

"Don't you even care what Bobby was doing, where he was when he was not in school?" I cried.

Silence. Manuel went to the sideboard and poured himself a Johnny Walker. "So where was he?" he asked.

"Watching movies. Drinking with his buddy Butch Fuentes. Smoking. Gallivanting about. Then coming home as though nothing happened."

"*Puneta*! Where's that boy?" Manuel made a dash for the door. Manuel had become hotheaded. It was something new that alarmed me. There was a side of him that was temperamental and so easily triggered to anger. Too much stress at work I said. He needed to slow down with his contracts. I've never heard him swear at his own son. I barred his way.

"Sit down and let's talk this out," I tried to calm him. I pulled him to the bed.

"I managed to get it from Bobby that he spent the days with Butch. I went to Butch's house to talk with his parents, but no adults were home, except a maid. Turns out, the parents are in France vacationing. The maid had the parents' phone number in Paris, and I talked to the mother. They are so shocked. They are cutting their vacation short, and are on their way home. Butch is grounded until they get home. Bobby said this is the first time he and Butch have done this. He has promised they won't do it again," I explained.

"And you believed him?" cried Manuel, still angry.

"I don't know. It's his first time. His homeroom teacher says his grades are falling, and he may need a good threat like expulsion if he does it again, and that might scare him enough. His teacher is willing to take a 'united front with us' on how to act on this matter," I said.

"What united front? He's grounded — no allowance, no TV, no parties. School and home, nothing else. One month." Manuel finished his drink.

"But you have to be here for him, Manuel. Be here for dinners with us. Talk to him. He is sleeping now. I said he is not going to school tomorrow. Neither am I. Tomorrow, all of us will be more relaxed. You can talk to him after breakfast, then I can join you." I took Manuel's hand. I continued. "And I think you need to stop drinking. He is copying you, being a 'man' like you."

The door opened, and Sonia walked in, her eyes red from crying.

"Bobby is crying," she said, and put her head on my lap. "He won't talk to me. What's wrong with Bobby?" Sonia cried, blinking her eyes, then sniffling and then shrugging her shoulders.

I hugged my sweet Sonia. Ten years old and already so caring like a mother. Sonia's tics seem to be getting worse. Sonia did it again: blinked her eyes, sniffled several times and shrugged her shoulders. Poor Sonia. This anxiety is only making it worse.

Manuel looked at me, with what seemed like accusing eyes. It was my fault again. He walked to the bathroom, leaving me alone with Sonia.

I set Sonia down in the middle of the bed and lay beside her. I rubbed Sonia's back gently, caressed her hair slowly, until the tics subsided.

When Manuel came out of the shower. Sonia was asleep. I felt too tired to continue the fight. Manuel sat on the other side of Sonia, and stroked her shoulder that continued shrugging faintly.

"We should really take this Tourrete syndrome more seriously," I said quietly. "The doctor suggested it could get worse."

"Yup. You do that," he said. "Is that Bobby crying?" he asked, almost to himself.

I didn't answer.

"You know, I can't remember a time when I cried and anyone came to me? Not Mom, not Dad," he said. I sat up.

"I have to be a better father, but I don't know what that means," he continued. I walked over to Manuel's side and held his head against my breast.

"We'll figure it out together," I said, kissing his newly showered head. "Go. He needs you as much as you need him."

* * *

CHAPTER 5

Philippines
Manuel, 1981

The Film Centre was to house the first-ever Manila International Film Festival, scheduled for January 1982. The site was a reclaimed area off of Manila Bay, within the cultural complex of Manila, which included magnificent edifices such as the Cultural Centre of the Philippines.

It was October 1981, and the foundations were only beginning to be set up. I was worried. I told the architect that the building could not possibly finish by January. The building program had already been simplified to include only two basic components: an auditorium and the film archives. The deadline of the structure was tight. It required 4,000 workers, working in three shifts across 24 hours. One thousand workers constructed the lobby in 72 hours, a job which would normally entail six weeks of labour.

At 3:00 am on November 17, 1981, tragedy struck. The scaffolding supporting hundreds of workers collapsed and fell into freshly formed wet cement. At least 169 workers fell and were buried in quick-drying wet cement. A security blanket was immediately imposed by the government. Neither rescuers nor ambulances were permitted on the site until an official statement had been prepared. The rescuers were only permitted access to the accident site nine hours after the collapse.

I was not on site when the collapse happened. I was not even called to the site. I learned about it only at noon, when Dad phoned me. By then, the construction site was in chaos. Only six bodies had been recovered from the cement. To my horror, the order to continue construction work had been given, and workers were pouring more cement on top of the cement where bodies of dead workers lay. Dad said orders were orders and his hands were tied. I screamed at him and resigned on the spot. He barked back: "No you can't resign, because you no longer work here. You're fired. Get out."

In the jumble of events, it was never clear what exactly caused the accident. One version was that some workers were drunk, had a fight, and caused one part of the platform to sway, causing a cascade of scaffolding to fall. Another version was that the construction work had been sped up so much that the scaffolding was put together carelessly, and further, that more men were on the platform than it could carry, therefore causing the collapse. Still one other version referred to the structural design of the building, and that an 'unnamed junior engineer, who was immediately fired, made a mistake.' This version said the mistake was in calculating the load on a pillar that supported the scaffolding, thus causing the pillar to sway, which caused the scaffolding to fall.

My blood boiled. I wanted to fight the allegations. But Dad said to leave it alone and that things would blow over.

* * *

I always look forward to Saturdays, my tennis day. Playing tennis, and then coming home to a relaxed lunch with Josie and the kids. I like driving myself, no chauffeur. Arriving home this Saturday, I was surprised to see the whole house littered with big boxes, newspaper wrapping and different types of tapes. Seems like Josie had begun packing for the move. I didn't think we decided yet.

Josie stood by the bar in a smashing red outfit holding out a cold San Miguel beer, and a plate of my favourite chicken barbecue on a stick. The other thing can wait. I took a quick sip of the beer and bit a piece of chicken from the stick as I put my racket and bags down. With the tip of the stick, I speared some of the pickled *achara* and stuffed that in my mouth.

"Cooked with love!" I said.

"Always," Josie teased. "Did you win?" She kissed my lips.

"Of course, Mommy. Singles and doubles, two out of three both. You're looking at the singles champ of the Nagtahan Tennis Club!" I smacked her bum lightly with my tennis racket. "What's all this?" I asked, pointing to the boxes.

"Packing for Canada, what else?"

"We don't have to. They are right now digging out whatever bodies can be dug out. They said the Government is giving out 5000 pesos to each of the families," I said.

"And that's okay?" Josie raised her voice. "They dig out six out of the 169 construction workers, and we're supposed to be satisfied? That buy-out is pathetic." Josie straightened out the box nearest her, and continued.

"Have you read the latest version in the papers as to what caused the collapsed? Blaming an 'unnamed junior engineer' for faulty design of a pillar that swayed and caused all the scaffolding to fall!"

"Dad said don't pay attention to all that gossip. It's just some competitor taking advantage of the mess to destroy us. Dad said some workers were drunk, fought and caused a scaffolding to collapse. It's not our fault. Dad said the First Lady just wants it done, and things will blow over," I said.

Josie had that look she gets when there's no more arguing. "Well, we're going. Even if you're not. The kids. I'll take them. Who will hire you after this? I don't like this…this project is cursed. Rushing right from the beginning. I can believe the rumour that they rushed the building of the scaffolding, put it together carelessly, and put too many workers on it that it fell. And all for what? A stupid film festival for foreign celebrities. Meantime the poor continue to be poorer, and construction workers die for this…this…stupid thing, and rushing again, no time to bury them properly. It's evil, I tell you."

Josie walked to one of the boxes by the dining table and started filling it with crumpled newspapers. She kept up with the tough talk. "The sponsorship papers have been approved, and we have another month before it runs out. Your brother says if we let the deadline pass, we'll have to start over. That's how many years again? How lucky we are that he is sponsoring us. He has worked so hard to get us to this point. What will he say?" It was all true.

"It's our life, our decision," I said.

"Well my decision is to go. You can stay. You can follow later, when you finally see I was right," Josie said.

"What will I do without you? How will you support yourselves in a strange land?" I asked.

Our eyes met. She continued. "Let's leave now. There are more projects in Canada, and more money. Bloodless money. I can work, do whatever. You don't have to work all day and night, at somebody's beck and call. We will have more time together, a quiet, peaceful life. More time with the kids. Especially Bobby. That's all he needs: time with you. We don't have to slave for a decent life, like we have to do here. Have you forgotten all of our dreams?"

"No, I haven't," I leaned back on the chair, raised my hands over his head, then lay them over my closed eyes, and stayed still. I felt soft hands on my shoulders, massaging them. I smelled Josie's sweet lavender scent and felt my tense muscles softening. No, I can't live without this.

"Daddy, daddy! What did you bring me?" Manolita. Pigtails bouncing as she rushes to occupy her favourite seat: my lap. Lucy followed behind.

"Ah, my baby. Where've you been? Daddy's been looking all over for you. You love your *yaya* more than me," I said with a mock pout.

"Yes I do. Yaya Lucy loves me more, right, Yaya? She is always here and you're always away. And you didn't bring me chocolates," Manolita said, feeling my pockets.

"What if I did?" I said, tickling her.

"Did you? Where?" Manolita giggled.

"First, sing for Daddy," I said.

"What do you like?" she asked.

"How about my favourite?" I asked.

"Somewhere Over the Rainbow!" exclaimed Manolita.

Manolita sang the verses easily, with a pure soaring voice:
Somewhere over the rainbow, bluebirds fly.
Somewhere over the rainbow, why and oh why can't I?

When the song was finished, I hugged Manolita in a tight embrace. She squirmed out of my arms and demanded, "So where?"

"See that red bag? Open it and you'll find a surprise!" I said.

Manolita jumped from my lap and ran to the bag, extracting a white plastic shopping bag. She poured the contents on the floor, and out rolled M&M's, Nestle and Cadbury bars, Hershey's Kisses, a box of Black Magic, a long stick of Toblerone. "Wow! All my favourites!" She ran and climbed up to my lap and planted a kiss. "I love you, Daddy. You're the best daddy in the world!"

* * *

Dear Dad and Mommy dearest,

Swear you will change your mind, and when we come home from Pililla, we are staying in Manila for good. I hate cold Canada. I will look after Lola Iska forever if you leave me behind. She needs so much looking after. She is already blind, did they tell you? I will be her eyes, her arms, her legs. She needs me. And Canada doesn't. Please, please, promise? Bobby is a brag. He thinks he's already Canadian, and I can't stand him! I'm already homesick just being around him! Kiss my little bratty sister for me.

Your loving daughter,
Sonia

PS. Bekang's baby sister got a tummy ache because they didn't ask permission from the dwarf who owned the tree of the kayamito she ate. Tell Manolita she better ask permission from the dwarf of the santol tree in our backyard she likes so much, or she'll be in real trouble. And also tell Lucy, because it's no excuse if you don't know or are too little to know. Someone has to ask permission. Don't forget!!!

* * *

Dear Mom (and Dad),

Sonia and I are having a great time here. We heard. When I think that this will be our last vacation in Pililla, I feel sad. But I'm also excited! Sonia is adamant. We may need to chain her with one of the luggages so she will come. Heh heh. If Dad doesn't want to come, don't worry; I'll look after us. They say McDonalds hires kids and pays good money. I told Lola Iska she doesn't have to wait for Dad's promise. I'll save up to get her eyes fixed. Her cataracts are getting worse. Maybe I don't have to go to school there, if I can just work, maybe even two jobs! The boys are so envious. Me in Canada! I'll get a Harley and send them pictures of me and my Harley surrounded by my Canadian girlfriends! Ha ha! Don't worry. I'll convince Sonia to come without causing trouble. When we come home, she'll be begging to go to Canada! My miserable cousins are calling. Got to go. Wish you were here!

Your pogi son,
Bobby

PS. Don't worry about packing for me. I'm not bringing anything! Hah hah. Everything's much nicer in Canada anyway. I'll buy my own clothes there. And yours too!

* * *

I smiled, reading Sonia's letter.

"What's that?" asked Josie.

"Oh nothing. Just a note from the kids," I gave her Sonia's letter.

She smiled reading the letter. "My sweet girl. Let's see the other one." I gave her the second letter, saying, "The blowhard. Who does he think he is? That boy is too big for his breeches. So he thinks he can look after everyone. Maybe he plans to deal in his precious drugs. Ya, maybe that's how he means to support you."

"What does he say?" Josie read quickly.

"Bobby's just trying to be helpful, Daddy. You always misinterpret him, that's the problem. Sure he makes mistakes. But when he's good, can't you give him that? Isn't it sweet how he cares for his Lola, and Sonia, and me? And to think he's only 13. He's not a bad kid," she said.

"Sure, and I'm a terrible father, right?" I said.

"Yes, sometimes. But mostly.... so-so," she teased.

"So-so like this?" I whispered, and took her in my arms.

* * *

That night, Josie shook me awake from a nightmare.

"Manuel, wake up! Wake up, you're screaming!"

I groaned. She made me sit up. The light was too bright. I closed my eyes trying to remember the dream. Through eyes closed, I recalled my nightmare. "A dead construction worker pulled my leg. I fell into the quick sand of wet cement. I screamed for help but no sounds came out from my mouth. My mouth was filling fast with cold lumps of gravel. I couldn't breathe. Good thing you woke me."

Josie hugged me tight.

"It's over for us here. You're right. When is the soonest we can go?" I said.

* * *

On December 1, 1981, our little family of Josie, Bobby, Sonia, Manolita and myself boarded a Cathay Pacific jumbo jet from the Manila International Airport en route to Vancouver, British Columbia, Canada.

Huddled close together in the plane, Josie and I watched the clouds, lost in our respective thoughts. I squeezed her hand.

"We'll be fine," I said.

"Of course, we'll be fine. Watch out, Canada, here come the del Mundos!" she joked.

"They must have great schools there, I'm excited to teach Canadians!" My hardworking Josie. Already thinking of the work in Canada.

"Maybe you shouldn't work for a while, get the kids settled. I'll work. Engineers get real good pay in Canada, I hear. Get a vacation, you've worked so hard." I kissed her hand. I felt so close to her. When was the last time I kissed her hand?

"Hey, let's not work right away. Let's tour around the city first. I'm sure when you start working, you'll overwork again," she brightened.

"You seem to have a lot of money, *dona*?" I teased.

"Not as much as I want, but enough to enjoy a little," she said.

"A little? We brought a lot! You always worry. I don't want you to ever worry again," I said.

Later, I said, "You know, Mommy, our life in Canada will be different. Didn't they say it's Paradise? Canada will be our paradise."

"Promise?" Josie asked.

"Promise," I repeated.

We huddled closer together.

* * *

CHAPTER 6

Canada
Josie, December 1981

Sonia has been crying for the last seven nights before our flight to Canada, already missing her friends, school, Pililla. But when she looked out the window of the airplane as it approached Vancouver, she couldn't help getting excited. She was seated with Bobby across the aisle from Manuel, Manolita and me.

"Look, Bobby, the subdivisions look like keys," said Sonia.

"Oh yeah?" Bobby peers over Sonia's shoulder. 'You're right. I can't believe it. You're actually making sense!" teased Bobby.

"Where's the key?" asked Manolita, crossing the aisle from her seat to Bobby's lap.

"See that long thing, and then the round thing at the end, and the houses around it? In one of those houses, Tito Mario lives," said Bobby.

"Oh shut up, Mr. Know-it-all. You don't even know that! Hey, is that snow?" cried Sonia.

"Where?" Even I got excited. I crossed over the aisle and strained to see down below.

"See that layer of white on the ground — is that snow?" repeated Sonia.

"Could be," said Manuel who was looking out his window too. "There's a freak snowfall in Vancouver, they said."

"What's freak?" asked Manolita.

"Means unusual. Strange. It never snows in Vancouver. Sometimes it snows in November, but only for a short while. That's why it's a freak snow," said Manuel.

"Just like you. Freak kid," said Bobby, tickling Manolita.

"Sssh….we're landing," said Sonia.

The stewardess walked down the aisle checking seatbelts. I took Manolita and settled her between Manuel and me, and gave her the teddy bear. She took my hand and Manuel's hand. "Don't be afraid, hold my hand," she said. My brave carefree little girl. Nothing will faze her.

"I told you there will be snow. Snowball fight?" challenged Bobby.

Sonia didn't answer. My cautious one. I can't imagine her throwing snowballs or skating on ice.

"Sure," I heard Sonia answer weakly. "You're on!" said Bobby. My big gallant boy.

When we got off the plane, I noticed how clean and cool everything was in the airport, how few people there were. It was not at all chaotic and busy and hot like in the Manila airport. You could see people's faces instead of crowds. You could breathe. Canadian airport people smiled a lot, as though everything was fine in their lives, and that was why they smiled and said kind things like "how was your trip?" and sounding like they meant it. The immigration officer gave Manuel a whole bunch of brochures and papers, stamped something on the papers, then smiled, stood up and shook hands with him and me, saying "Welcome to Canada." Thus, were we ushered into Canada.

We piled up our baggage onto a tall rack on wheels, pushed by a man in uniform.

The man pushed it across another uniformed man who looked at the tickets Manuel gave him, made a mark, and smiled. "Have a good day," he pronounced, and waved our group on.

Our little del Mundo group marched through the open glass door, to an audience of people standing along the glass railing, sitting on galley seats, the welcoming parties. I scanned through the faces, looking for Mario and Ching.

"Manuel, Manuel!" cried someone from the crowd. Mario appeared at the bottom of the ramp to greet us. Mario seemed smaller somehow, drowned by a thick black coat, and his smile was wide and warm. Manuel fell into his arms and the brothers hugged long and hard. I noticed that Mario's eyes were moist when he hugged Manuel, then each of the kids in turn, then me.

"Where's Ching?" I asked.

"At home, making us dinner. Come, I'll get the car, you wait by the lobby, and I'll pick you up in a few minutes. Stay indoors; it's cold. Freak snow is continuing another day, they say," Mario added.

"Can I come with you to the parking lot? I want to see the snow," said Bobby.

"It will be cold, your jacket won't be good enough," said Mario.

"I can do it, *Tito*. It shouldn't be too long a walk anyway," said Bobby.

"There you go again, the big hero. Do you want to catch a cold so fast in Canada?" snarled Manuel.

"You can have my coat," I offered. "It's not that far, right Mario?"

"I guess, with the added coat, it should be okay. Let's go, snow buddy," said Mario.

"You really shouldn't do that," Manuel said to me when Mario and Bobby left. "Crossing me in front of everybody, including my brother. What must he think? That's why that blowhard kid thinks he can get away with anything."

"It's only a walk in the snow. It's his first snow, come on, Manuel," I said.

Manuel was looking around, "Where's Manolita?"

"She was just here a while ago," said Sonia. We all began looking around.

It was easy to see in the uncrowded lobby of the airport that there were no little girls holding a teddy bear. The three of us dispersed to look for Manolita. I talked to other passengers, asking if they saw Manolita. I couldn't see a little girl anywhere. I began to feel frantic. Manuel approached a security guard. I joined him. The guard listened intently, then talked on his phone. Sonia was somewhere out there. I noticed how fair most people were, and tall. A lot of Asians — Indian, Chinese, some Filipinos. Two more security guards arrived, they fanned out, and one of them walked out of the lobby towards the street.

The doors opened automatically and I felt the cold wind blow in. Could Manolita have slipped out? I rushed out and turned left, then right, and then saw a small figure by a steel post. I ran towards it, and there was Manolita, her tongue stuck on the pole, and wailing.

"*Santisima!*" I cried.

Manolita's face was red and her eyes showed panic. "Good God, what have you done?" I asked no one, pulling the little tongue away from the post, but it would not budge. Manolita cried more.

A security guard appeared beside me. "No, don't pull. It will tear," he said. He called someone on the phone again. I didn't know what to do. "Hush, baby, hush, baby… it'll be ok," I kept saying. Her little hands were cold. I blew on them.

Manuel and Sonia appeared suddenly. "Manolita! What now?" cried Sonia. She tried to pry the tongue loose like I did earlier. "No, no… it's tearing… help is coming," I said. "Just keep her warm."

"Crazy, crazy girl," said Sonia.

"What's happening now? She's freezing!" Manuel screamed at the security guard. Manuel took off his coat and laid it around Manolita's little shoulders.

"Take it easy sir. Someone's coming with help. Don't worry, it'll be ok," said the security guard. "Keep her still if you can, and don't move the tongue. Help will be here shortly," he continued.

Soon enough, another security guard came running, carrying a pail of water. "Can you hold her please," he asked. Manuel held Manolita by her shoulders. "This won't hurt, it's only warm water," the guard continued. Sonia crouched on the ground, holding Manolita's hand and the teddy bear. The guard poured the water slowly over where the tongue was stuck to the pole. Manolita cried out even more. In about thirty seconds, the tongue detached from the pole.

"Open your mouth," he told Manolita. "Please massage the tongue for about a minute," he asked. I reached out and did as I was told. Such a small slippery thing. Manolita's crying subsided, till she was finally quiet.

"That should be okay now," said the security guard. I released the tongue and Manuel hugged his little girl. He carried Manolita in his arms and walked towards the door and into the airport lobby. He kept kissing Manolita.

In the warm lobby, Manuel scolded all of us. "How did we let her out of our sight? What are you there for if not to watch your little sister?" he said to Sonia, but Sonia was laughing through her tears.

"Here. Wear my jacket. Dad's is too big," said Sonia. Manuel put down Manolita and they all exchanged jackets. Then Manuel carried Manolita again.

"Just like you! Always getting into trouble! Can you just please keep your tongue in your mouth?" he said.

The security guards encircled us. A feeling of relief. One of the guards said, "Well, welcome to Canada." We felt safe enough to laugh.

From the street, a car honked. A burgundy Cutlass sedan pulled up by the sidewalk. Bobby happily waved to us from the front seat. The porter began loading the baggage while Manuel stuffed Manolita in the car first. "You won't believe what happened," he said.

* * *

Mario and Ching lived in a place called Surrey, a suburb of Vancouver. The house had two levels. They lived in the upper floor, and another family lived in the lower floor. When we arrived, a party was waiting for us. It didn't feel cold at all inside the house, even after the snowy cold outside. The driveway was lined with cars and the house packed with Filipinos. Our luggage was put away in one of the rooms.

"This is your room," said Mario. I noted the double bed, and wondered where the kids might sleep. Oh well, time for that later. We joined the party in full bloom.

"What's the occasion," I asked.

"Your arrival, of course!" said Mario.

"Where's Ching?" I asked.

"In the kitchen cooking," said Mario.

I felt happy meeting so many people welcoming us. Mario and Ching have so many friends, they must be so successful! I made my way through the living room full of people. Manuel sat in the middle of a group regaling them with stories about Manolita's escapade. I could not find any of the kids among the many other kids playing on the floor and running about. I noticed the dining table already had a platter of *pancit*, a tray of *puto* and *cuchinta*, a big bowl of *dinuguan*, the blackness of the soup accentuated by a bright green chilli pepper sticking out. My mouth began to water.

I smelled frying from the kitchen. Ching, without a hat, looked different, un-Canadian. She looked tiny and ordinary, like a maid almost, ladling a large *bangus* fish from the sizzling hot oil.

"O, how was your trip?" asked Ching not even looking up at me. "Heard about the ice escapade," she said laughing. "This is a lucky omen, it never snows in Vancouver!" she continued, sliding in another piece of fish into the oil. The oil hissed and splattered and Ching and I automatically moved away from the stove. Ching opened the cabinet underneath the sink, took out the plastic pail full of garbage. She adroitly lifted the ends of the plastic bag, tied the ends in a knot, lifted the bag, opened the door leading to the backyard, and set it down there.

Ching touched her cheeks to mine and said, "This is how we are here, we do everything, the cooking, throwing out the garbage," she said. Then she opened up a drawer, lifted a white plastic bag, lined the garbage pail with it, and set it back in the cabinet. She looked at my beautiful lime green suit and said '"You'll get used to it."

Another woman came in bearing a tray of big fat fried pork hocks.

"Wow! Crispy *pata*! Thank you, thank you!" cried Ching.

"Of course! For my friend's in-laws. We don't want them to be homesick so soon, right?' said the new arrival.

"This is my sister-in-law Josie. And this is the best crispy *pata* cook in the whole of Canada, my dear friend Rosie. If you're nice to her, she'll tell you her secret," Ching beamed as she touched her cheeks to Rosie's.

"Uuumm, that smells yummy," Rosie said, lifting the lid of the pot on the stove. "*Sinigang*! With salmon heads! The best!" she cried.

"Yeah, for free too," said Ching.

"Really?" asked Josie.

"They just throw it away anyway, so just ask in the fish section for the heads, and they'll give it to you for nothing," answered Ching.

"What did you use for *asim*?" asked Rosie, tasting a bit of broth from a spoon.

"Just lemon," said Ching.

"That's what I thought. You know, I saw *sampalok* in a small store in Chinatown. I'll get you some when I'm there next time. Store's just beside my employer's *suki* for fresh fish," she continued.

"I know, nothing beats *sampalok*. There's just nothing out here in Surrey," said Ching.

"*Oy mga kumare!*" said another woman waltzing into the kitchen, carrying a foil-covered tray.

"Here's your *turon*," she said, touching her cheeks to Josie's, then Rosie. "You must be the in-law from Manila?" the new arrival smiled briefly, set the tray down and lifted the foil, exposing golden banana rolls caramelized with sugar.

"Smells great, Carmen!" said Rosie welcoming the new arrival.

"Of course, the filling is real *saging na saba* and *langka*," said Carmen proudly. She continued, "None of this dole banana stuff that tastes like cardboard."

"Thanks, Carmen. *Turon* is Mario's favourite!" Ching beamed.

"Hey, did you hear about what happened to Carla?" asked someone carrying a pitcher of *gulaman* juice into the kitchen.

"Didn't she just get back from the Philippines?" asked Ching.

"Yes, and true enough her husband is living with another woman. She got the truth out of a neighbour," said the one with the pitcher.

"How do you know that, Anita?' asked Ching, taking the pitcher from her.

"Her cousin told me," said Anita. "Apparently it's been going on for some time. The whole neighbourhood knows except Carla. She found out where the girl lived, and threw acid on her face, but it caught only her arm. Her husband stopped her," continued Anita.

"*Susmaryosep*," cried Rosie.

"She better drop his sponsorship papers," said Ching.

"No, speed it up! She should keep him here where she can guard him," said Rosie.

Stumbling Through Paradise

"Carla said she will stop the sponsorship, but we'll see. You know how she is. The last time, she said she'd separate from him, and then she took him back when he romanced her all over again. He's just using her. He's always had the same girlfriend apparently. And to think she saves up everything she earns to send to that guy. She just gave him money for a tricycle for extra income," explained Carmen.

"Who looks after the daughter?" asked Ching.

"The girlfriend. They're like a family," said Carmen.

"The ingrates. *Ay punemas!* She should just forget about them, live it up here," said Rosie.

"And to think the sponsorship papers are just about ready for approval. Six years in this place slaving, cleaning somebody else's toilets, all so that you can lose your entire family to somebody else? It's not right," said Carmen.

"Carla's stupid. If I were as young and pretty as her, I'd get myself a Canadian boyfriend," said Rosie.

"Or dump your philandering husband, go back and get a rich handsome Filipino one...like someone here...Uuuuy...!" teased Carmen.

Everybody laughed. I felt embarrassed for Ching, and confused. Did they say Ching dumped a husband? Ching married before? I didn't know that.

Ching said, "So ladies, get your Canadian citizenship cards quick, your passport to Paradise. And let's go and start dinner, before you poison the mind of my sweet sister-in-law here." She shooed us all towards the living room.

The table groaned with food and everybody had a great laughing time. I felt so welcomed. After eating, everybody helped put the dishes away, including me. I remembered Ching's warning: "No maids, okay?" How easily everyone did the chores. In the end, everyone left with almost as much food as they brought. Ching insisted on everyone taking home the leftovers, which they happily did. So, just about everything is the same as back home. Homesickness will not be a problem!

* * *

CHAPTER 7

Canada
Manuel, 1982

The first months of our stay in Canada were an eye opener. It turned out that Ching had a husband, he fooled around on her, and then she dumped him. But then how did she and my brother Mario get married?

Ching never declared in her papers to Canada that she was married, the better to get approval faster. When she met and married Mario, she could sponsor her 'real' husband to Canada. What about the legality of Mario's marriage certificate? "Nothing that a few dollars couldn't pay for. There are many hungry justices of the peace and clerks at city hall," Ching explained. Did Mario know? Apparently, he did all along. He wanted to go to Canada badly. Mario and Ching kept it a secret from everyone in the Philippines. No wonder, it was so rushed.

It also turned out that Mario was unemployed. Well, not really. He sang at parties and got paid sometimes. He sold soap products, called Amway, but not really. He recruited people to sell the soap products, and he got a cut out of anything they sold. With all the caregiver friends of Ching, he made a good commission from their purchases on behalf of their employers.

Mario recruited Josie and me to sell Amway. I couldn't believe Mario was doing it. "I didn't come to Canada to sell soap. I'm an engineer," I said. Josie signed up, but couldn't go through with it. All the people we met were already signed on with Mario. Josie felt shy to approach strangers.

It was a strange time. On the one hand, so many friends of Mario and Ching welcomed us, but I felt alone. They all seemed to be happy and set in their own lives, lives that seems to be one step below their lives in the Philippines. Nurses are working as cleaners, domestic workers and caregivers. Accountants, teachers and lawyers are working as 7-Eleven night workers, clerks in department stores and security guards. They all had nice houses anyway, and a car, and partied with each other every week. They all seemed fine with having no maids. Working all day then coming home and working some more on house chores. What a life. Well, they seemed to be earning well, saving up to bring the family over, buy a house, college for the kids.

It had been several months now, and I had not met too many Canadians at all. Where were the Canadians? Even in the Holy Rosary Catholic Church, most people were Filipinos. Mario and Ching lived in what looked like a small Philippine island, surrounded by Canada.

I asked around for schools, and it looked like most everyone had their kids in public school. A few took their kids to Catholic private schools where the kids wore uniforms, and were taught religion, but they had to pay so many dollars per month, whereas the public schools were completely free. Josie and I calculated what that meant in pesos. We couldn't afford it. I thought that if the public schools here were as bad as those in the Philippines, then we must find a way of sending the kids to private school.

"I did not go to Canada to send my kids to public school," I told Josie.

"We don't have a job yet, couldn't they go to public school first and then they can transfer when we have a job? Our peso savings won't last too long," my ever-frugal wife said.

"You worry too much. I'll find an engineering job. I read an engineering job advertised in the *Vancouver Sun*. You know how much they pay? $40,000 a year. That's 30,000 pesos a month — that's 10 times more than both our incomes in the Philippines combined. Hah! You don't even have to work. Just be patient Josie," I said.

* * *

Several months passed, and I was growing frustrated with the lack of replies to my job applications.

"What's the matter with Canadians? It's like they never even received my application. Are they too good for Filipinos?"

"That's how they are. They don't recognize Philippine engineering degrees. I applied to so many companies, and heard from no one, until finally I asked a personnel officer why they did not call me for an interview. She said they do not recognize engineering degrees from the Philippines," said Paquito. Paquito was a friend of Mario's, and an engineering graduate of the University of the East in Manila. He worked as a night cashier for a 7-Eleven store in Vancouver.

"So what are we supposed to do?" I asked.

"Study all over again here in Canada," said Paquito.

"You must be joking. A building in the Philippines is the same as a building in Vancouver, last time I looked, or have they never been to the Philippines?" I said.

"They think we still live in tree houses," said Paquito.

The story was the same everywhere I applied. Josie and I were becoming anxious. Mario and Ching were getting tired of referring jobs to me, and I began to tire of saying 'I did not come to Canada to...'. The cramped living arrangements were getting to everybody. Sonia slept on the living room couch, Bobby on the floor in the living room, Manolita slept on the bed with Josie and me. The people living downstairs, another Filipino family, had regular arguments with Ching over walking noises at night. After the first month, Mario accepted grocery money contribution from me. Ching and Josie argued over the kinds of meals being prepared.

"You think you're still the rich *senorita* in Manila? One dish is good enough, why have three dishes, and so much to prepare? Your kids, little *senoritas* and *senorito* — let them clean up their mess, wash dishes. You do it all, you spoil them," said Ching. Mario always took Ching's side.

"My poor brother is *'under di saya'*," I acknowledged. I had to agree that Mario seemed to be under Ching's skirt.

"It's bad enough that the kids are having troubles in school, they have to wash dishes at home?" Josie said. "She should mind her own business. Don't I clean up everything before she arrives?"

*   *   *

And so it was that after three months, on a rainy February day, my little family moved our few belongings to a basement suite in a house across the Holy Rosary Catholic School. We had to part with four hundred precious dollars a month for the rent. Plus we had to buy a used dining table and chairs. We had to have something to eat on. Someone gave us an old sofa, and others gave blankets and cushions, which Josie happily accepted, over my objections. We used the donated blankets as mattresses to sleep on, and promised the kids that the container of goods from the Philippines should arrive any day now with good towels and dinnerware and such.

I still had no work.

I heard about a security guard job. I applied, had a short interview, and was offered the job. I accepted readily, and on the way out, the man said "It's graveyard, ok with you?" I wasn't sure about working in a graveyard but, thinking of my family, I nodded just the same. At least no one would see me there. On the bus, the ridiculousness of the idea dawned on me. Did I come to Canada to do this? I resolved not to come back to work there. Paquito slapped me on the back laughing. "*Gago*! You fool! That means working 11 pm to 7 am, not in a graveyard!"

That was the last time I tried to apply for security guard jobs.

Through Paquito, I met a few Filipino engineering graduates from the same school in the Philippines, one of whom worked on a construction site as a day labourer. Gary was 10 years younger than me. "The place is called Labour Inc. I come early in the morning, and if I'm lucky, I get called for a job that day. One day, I might construct kitchen cabinets; another day, I might do drywall, or clean up construction debris. Just whatever. Pays better than 7-Eleven. Why not give it a try?" said Gary.

I gave it a try. But I couldn't qualify for anything.

Have you laid tile before? No.

Put up drywall? No.

Paint? No.

Sorry, that's all we have today.

I came home empty handed. That night Gary asked me where I went, as he did not see me on site.

"No, no! Just say yes when they ask you for experience. Then stick with me, and I can show you what to do. And never, never say you're an engineer. They won't get you because you would be overqualified," said Gary.

That was the last time I tried to do construction labour work.

Someone said, why not McDonald's?

I went to McDonalds in the local town centre. There was a job opening for a bus boy and for a janitor. I did not want the bus boy job because people would see me. The janitorial job was better, because it was hidden from view.

I accepted the job.

The manager must not have been older than Bobby. The boy manager showed me a cart full of cleaning tools, and pointed me to the toilet.

I took one look at the mess in the first cubicle, thought of how I came to Canada to do this, and retched on the floor. After cleaning myself up, I walked out of the restaurant.

That was the last time I applied for a janitorial job.

Josie began to look for work herself. It was the same story. They do not recognize education degrees from the Philippines. She had to start over. Not even teaching assistant they said. She needed a special certificate to be teaching assistant.

"Well, there's good old cooking and baking and sewing. It made me enough money in college, didn't it?" With that, my wife, who never ceases to amaze me with her ingenuity, began making plans for a small business.

* * *

CHAPTER 8

Canada
Josie, 1982

Dear Inay and Itay,

We are happy here. Mario and Ching are so kind to us and we have so many friends already. Canada is not all that cold, except for that first day of snow, when Manolita got her tongue stuck trying to lick snow off a pole. Must have thought it was a giant popsicle. Don't worry — she got more scared than hurt. The nice security guards poured warm water and it got unstuck right away.

Snow on the ground is like white snow cone, like packed ice. Snow when it falls is something else. There's what's called wet snow, you see it coming from above — tiny soft white things so small they look like dandruff and when they fall to the ground, they have become rain. Then there are snowflakes that look just like that, white flakes, dancing on their way down, dropping silently on the ground where they lie like a thick white blanket. On Grouse Mountain, we saw people ski down snow-covered hills in the bright sunshine. No amount of sunshine melts snow when it has become as thick as blankets. The kids lie down on it, wave their hands up and down, then when they get up, they have made an angel on the snow. I did it when no one was looking. I felt so giggly when the snowflakes fell on my face; they felt tingly, like soft rain except cold and dry. They say that in real snow country like Alberta, the province next door to British Columbia, snow can be real dangerous, what's called a blizzard. It falls down like white sheets, so fast it can be blinding. They say snow can build up to one storey high, locking people indoors for months. Lucky we live in Vancouver where it snows only gently.

The real joke is the rain. Canadians are wimps about rain. Everyone complains about it, but it's hardly rain, only showers and short-lived rains. They do not know rain like in the Philippines, thunder and lightning, typhoons and floods. But the rain here is cold. The cold comes from inside the body, and hard to warm with jackets. I have to wear several sweaters to feel warm, but the kids have no problem at all! They are having great fun, and Manuel is too.

Canada is not at all what I imagined. I don't know now what I imagined then. White streets I guess and snow-covered pine trees. But it's only a big clean place with lots of shopping centres and highways, no traffic, big clean buses that are on time. Green parks everywhere. The city of Vancouver is like a dream. Mario took us there one day. There's a real beach in the middle of the city. It's called English Bay, and it's so clean, surrounded by mountains. High-rise after high-rise on streets lined with leafy trees. Little restaurants and shops everywhere, but nice and not at all crowded. A real forest in the city, called Stanley Park. The trees are so old and big, and when you walk under them, it feels so quiet like a church. When we have jobs, we will move to Vancouver.

We love it here, but I miss you very much. One day, God willing, we will all be together here, if you like. I promise.

Missing you all,
Josie

I reread my letter and decided to change "When we have jobs" to "One day," so it didn't call too much attention to the fact that we had no jobs still. Rereading it, even I felt happy. None of the sad stuff. I sealed the letter, put a stamp on it and laid it by the door to take with me on my walk to the bus stop where the mailbox was located. Nowadays, I wrote home every two weeks, whereas before, I wrote every day. It was harder making up happiness lately.

Bobby was uncommunicative. He said things are fine in school, but I don't think so. He didn't mention friends, teachers. And when I pressed him, he got mad. He had become demanding. One day he blurted out: "We're so poor we don't even have a TV. Why did we even come here?"

Manuel slapped him on the mouth. I got frightened. Manuel never laid a hand on the kids before. I went out to get a used TV from Value Village.

Sonia's Tourette syndrome had come back. She blinked her eyes rapidly, and then raised her shoulders up and down like a shrug. She must be suffering for it in school. Sonia seemed quiet lately, mostly reading her books. I knew Sonia was worried about something when she said once, "When will I have my own room?" Sonia was always accommodating, not one to complain. She was always chatty and giggling, and nowadays she did not smile much.

Manolita was the lucky one, spending a lot of time with her father. She is his one joy.

Manuel seemed to have given up on working as an engineer. He hung out with Paquito in the afternoons, drinking beer, before Paquito went to work at 7-Eleven. Paquito's wife Ludy was a teller in a bank, and they hardly saw each other because their working hours crossed. When it was time to work for Paquito, it was time to sleep for Ludy. Just when

Ludy was getting up to go to work, Paquito was coming in from work to get some sleep. What a life.

"Why don't you apply for a teller job?" Ludy offered one day. I watched out for teller job postings and applied. Again, like Manuel, no one replied to my applications.

I intensified my prayers. I began scouting about for a good time when I might be able to walk on my knees to the altar in church when not too many people were present. Unlike in the Philippines, Canadian churches were open only at certain times and days. I felt assured, remembering how God supplied an answer for my Manila job search through Sr. Redempta.

Like clockwork, you answered my prayers again, Lord. On the ninth day of the novena exactly, at Our Lady of Perpetual Help Church, you created an emergency that required a lot of food quickly. You put me where I could learn about it. You gave me the courage and boldness to offer to provide the food. You gave me Lily, my best friend who gave me the contract. My God. What a ride!

I remember my whole body tingling with excitement. What came upon me, to offer to cook for 150 people in less than 12 hours, just like that? If St. Joseph put it in my head, it must be because it's something I can do. On the bus, I planned the attack. Call Carmen to make the *pancit*, it's her specialty, and she just lost her job. Maybe she can make the *chop suey* vegetables too — that's easy enough, but needs a lot of cutting. We'll see, maybe she's got someone who can help her. If not, Manuel and the kids can help. Call Rosie to make *puto* and *cuchinta* — easy to do, it's her day off today. I decided to make the chicken *adobo*, my specialty. Sonia can help with the green salad. Need groceries. Call Mario to drive around for groceries and errands.

Whenever I recall this life-changing episode, I cannot believe how it happened.

It was a whirlwind of a day. What if Carmen already got a job and couldn't do the *pancit*? What if Rosie went out shopping as she normally does on her days off? Who would have done the *puto* and *cuchinta*? What if Mario had an Amway conference and I had no car to buy the groceries and the large foil trays to serve the food in, to pick up the food from the other girls, and deliver all the food to the event that night? As it turned out, I had lots of time as soon as the calls were made and the groceries bought. It's amazing how three dishes for 150 people could be made in a basement apartment with just common everyday pots and pans and utensils. I borrowed some implements and pots from a neighbour. The *adobo* cooked in one go in four pots. While the *adobo* cooked, the veggies for *chop suey* were prepared. When the *adobo* finished cooking, veggies were ready to be sautéed. It took three batches of sautéing. While the veggies sautéed, the greens were washed up and torn. Then the rice was cooked in the pots where the *adobo* was cooked. Manuel was a great help, and Manolita sat at the table as his little assistant. When Sonia and Bobby arrived, they too helped cutting up veggies.

The food was a success at the banquet. The additional tomato peach salsa that I dreamed up and added as a bonus was a hit. It should have been mango, but since there were no mangoes in season, I used peaches instead. There was not much extra, and people kept coming back. Father Carlos, the parish priest, was so pleased he made a special announcement on stage thanking me for the food. He even asked me to stand up and be recognized. I felt so proud. Lily was very happy and booked me for the next fundraisers.

I met many people that night, Filipinos and non-Filipinos, as I helped serve the food to the guests at the buffet. When they said they liked the food, I asked which in particular, and remembered it. Several women expressed interest in my catering, and I wrote their names and phone numbers down. At the end of the evening, Father Carlos approached me and thanked me for the food, and especially for the quick turnaround. He sounded sincere and down to earth, and I warmed to him.

Rosie and Carmen were happy with the extra money. Mario refused to take anything. "Happy to be of service, sis," he said. After the groceries were netted out, I still had $600 profit. For a day's labour? Not bad.

I will always remember it as the first time, not just in Canada, but in the whole of our lives, that our small family did a project together where everybody just helped, no questions asked, and enjoyed it. Much later, when we became financially comfortable, I always marked this time in our life as the beginning of our real journey in Canada, when we met face to face with opportunity and took it and ran with it and it rewarded us. In a way, how simple everything was — I sincerely asked for something, then let it go, then acted according to what was presented to me. I felt fresh and excited. I felt so close to God for answering more than my job request but the bigger more worrisome one, my family. I no longer felt alone.

The next day, Manuel helped me clean up the mess. We prepared a special supper for the family that no one had to cook: pizza!

* * *

My family enjoyed a 'honeymoon period' following the birth of my catering business. It seemed we communicated with each other better, including the kids writing home to their grandparents. Our letter envelopes bulged with drawings from Manolita, and fat letters from Bobby and Sonia. I enjoyed reading them before I mailed them out. I even copied these two letters for posterity.

Dear Lolo Lino and Lola Iska,

Hello from Canada! Your pogi grandson is now in grade 6 at the Holy Rosary Catholic School, where everybody is a giant and I feel like a dwarf. It's like hell here. But me, I'm ok. You gotta hear this!

The first day of school, I passed a group of boys, and heard someone say, "chink." Another time, I heard "flip." I asked my seatmate Jane, she's Chinese, what these words meant and she explained — chink for Chinese, and flip for Filipino. They are supposed to be bad names.

One day, Jane and I were walking down the corridor when I heard someone say, "Flip" as we passed. I went back to the group and said: "Who called me Flip?"

"I did. So what, Flip," said a tall skinny boy, whose lips were about the only visible feature of his face because of the streaks of blonde straight hair hanging down his sunglasses.

"Don't ever call me that again," I said.

"Flip," taunted the boy.

I swung my arm to hit the boy's face with my fist. Someone blocked my arm, and another one held my other arm behind my back. I pulled my arms away and kicked wildly. I managed to tear one of my arms away and swung it at his sunglasses. He dodged, held out his long hand and grasped my head, while one of the boys held back my arm again.

"You get your face out of here, or I'll send you back where you belong, Flip. And take that Chink with you," said the boy. That got me angrier and I prepared to hit him again, but someone cried

"Teacher! Teacher!" and everyone ran away leaving Jane and me alone.

Jane said that guy was Ian, alias Ivan the Terrible, head of the Scorpion gang, the biggest gang in school. She warned me that he's a bully and to get out of his way.

Then a Filipino guy with a pockmarked face approached me from the side, I guess he was watching all along. Ding brought me to meet his group, the Diablos. They've got a house behind the school where they learn karate in the basement. They were practicing with an instructor when we arrived. Most of them were Filipinos and looked older than Ding or me. The instructor was a short muscular Filipino, with a red bandana around his head, and his belt was black. The rest only wore white belts, except one who wore a brown belt. When the practice ended, the brown belt approached Ding. He was taller than either Ding or me, lean but well built. He had a quiet face, confident, no nonsense. Turns out he's Dante, leader of the Diablos. He wore a tattoo of a red and black trident on his right arm, the Diablo symbol.

Ding told Dante about my fight with Ivan the Terrible, which impressed Dante no end. So now, I'm a member of the Diablos. I get to learn karate with them every afternoon after school, to toughen me up. Diablos look after their members. No one touches you when you're with Diablos. They took me with them to dinner and said I'm now a member of the family.

So now, I'm okay. Don't worry about me. Now I can even take care of Sonia in school. When anyone bullies her, she tells them her brother is a Diablo and they stay away. Now I can go about in school without fear. I'm even doing a part time job with Dante's business and saving some money, for Lola's eye operation.

Jane? No, she's just a friend. I'm saving me for someone really special. I don't know who yet. Too many chicks to choose from, heh heh.

Stumbling Through Paradise

Luv u,

Bobby, your best-looking grandson in Canada

PS. My grades are ok, don't you worry. I'm curling up my English, so they don't laugh at me anymore.

* * *

Dear Lola Iska and Lolo Lino,

It's me! Your devoted granddaughter from Canada who hasn't written you in a long time! That doesn't mean that I don't miss you! I do! I haven't written you in a while because there's nothing much to write about — school is soooo boring! It's too easy!

The only class I really like is the one of Miss Sahota. She is so perfect, and kind. She looks like a model. She is so thin! Her hair is silky black and tied up in what they call a French knot. So glamorous! She wears straight simple dresses with only one plain color, blue or pink or black or cream, and a string of pearls whose color coordinates with her dress. She wears simple shoes with a sensible one-inch heel. She has sharp features but they all relax when she smiles, which is often. Her skin colour is a light chocolate, and half the class has a crush on her! She is supposed to teach literature, but really, what she teaches us is, well, life.

Miss Sahota's parents come from India, and she herself was born in Canada. She speaks perfect English. Her parents lived in the Punjab, and practice the Sikh religion. She said the Sikhs invented equality among religion. She explained why they carry a dagger called karpan *and why their men wear turbans. You remember those Indians in Manila with turbans on their heads — the Bumbays? How frightened I was of them! "I'll feed you to the Bumbays if you're not good," the maids always threatened us. I can't imagine how Bumbays could have a child as beautiful and kind as Miss Sahota, and if they did, they must be normal people.*

Miss Sahota gives us assignments that make us think. Imagine the colour red on your walk home, and write down all the red things that you see, and write them with your left hand. One rainy day, Miss Sahota closed all the lights and made us put our heads down on our desks, and commanded us to listen to the rain. At every class, she makes us do something special. Sometimes it's jumping up and down and laughing, or pulling a fortune from a jar of fortune cookies. But usually it's writing something special, quick quick, no erasing, for 10 minutes. Then she collects the papers and we all read somebody else's writing. If you were brave, you could volunteer to read what you wrote. The rule is no comments should be given after the reading, no good or bad comments, no clapping, no making fun, and no praising.

One day, the class was about "diversity." Miss Sahota asked each student where we were born, where our parents were born, and marked them on a map. I was surprised to see that there were three of us born in the Philippines. So many pupils had parents born in India, in Hong Kong, in other parts of Canada, in places in Europe unfamiliar to me. Just about every continent had a mark. Miss Sahota gave assignments for everyone to come back next day with a word in the language of the country where our parents or we were born, which meant "Thank You". She also asked us to describe something we ate that was special to that country. Then she gave the special assignment for the day: write ten minutes, no erasing, on the topic: "This I believe with all my heart".

We all crouched on our desks, pushed our pens hard and serious. Then Miss Sahota rang the bell.

"Any volunteers to read?" she asked.

Margaret read first. Hers was hilarious.

"This I believe with all my heart. If I'm good, I will go to heaven. If I'm bad I can make it up in purgatory then I can go to heaven. Because God is good and doesn't have the heart to send us

to hell. But we need hell, because if there was no hell, what's the fun for God that we are good?"

Is that weird or what? After the murmurings subsided, Jorge read next, something like:

"This, I believe with all my heart. She is the most beautiful girl I have ever met. She read the letter I sent her. She is only pretending that she does not notice me. I know because I saw her look my way and she blushed. She's an angel and she likes me. And I promise not to tell who she is."

That got us all laughing, and wondering who it might be!

"One more volunteer?" asked Miss Sahota. I raised my hand.

I stood up, blinked and shrugged my shoulders, blinked and shrugged, blinked again and shrugged again. Which I do when I'm nervous. A small giggle in the back started up. Miss Sahota scowled and held up her open palm, motioning them to stop.

I read.

"This I believe.

There are friends waiting for my brother and me, calling our names.

There are hungry stomachs waiting for my mother's food, so good.

There are buildings waiting for my father to build, so tall and beautiful and erect.

And best of all, they will never fall.

We're only stumbling in Paradise after all.

With all my heart, I believe."

The room was quiet when I sat down. The bell rang. I sat on my chair, my head bowed, feeling embarrassed for the sadness beneath the cheery words. Miss Sahota lifted my chin, wiped my tears, and hugged me. Breaking her own rule, she said, "That's beautiful."

I couldn't sleep all night wondering what Miss. Sahota found beautiful in my poem, and relishing her praise. I wonder what assignment she will give next time. Stay tuned!

I love you very much and miss you!

Sonia

PS. Lola, I'm really more happy than sad most days, ok? The poem just came out that way.

* * *

CHAPTER 9

Canada
Manuel, 1982–1983

In the beginning, I enjoyed meeting people, regaling them with stories 'back home' and the fabulous buildings I designed. I always skipped the Film Centre building. By then, everybody knew of the collapse. It wasn't my fault, but it's natural for people to be suspicious, after all, I was the engineer. I should know what happened. The truth was, I didn't have a good explanation. I just know it wasn't my fault.

I told them of my friends the generals, my contacts with the First Lady, my famous stepmother the *artista*, the developments Dad built. I showed pictures of our family home in Bel Air, Makati. Later, it depressed me to talk about our life in the Philippines, when I continued to be unemployed. It seemed I talked of nothing else but the past. Nothing in the present was worth talking about.

After a while, the things to buy at Safeway, Woodward's, Zellers and how cheap or expensive they were held no interest for me anymore. I was bored with the uneventful lives of my new Filipino friends like Paquito. I developed the habit of drinking beer and Johnny Walker with Paquito and his friends, snacking on *pulutan* Josie or Ludy served: crackling pork rinds, garlic nuts, squid *adobo*. I became the group's hero of sorts, the rich engineer who designed buildings, whereas they, in Vancouver, held down lowly jobs.

Hanging out at Paquito's, I got a lot of advice.

"You don't have to hurry up and get any job. Your family's rich. You're lucky. I have to slave it out in the kitchen," said someone who was a dishwasher in a hotel restaurant.

"Come and be a salesman at the Bay," said another. "I can speak to my boss about you. Employees get a discount on all the things you buy there," he said.

"School Board employees get good benefits, even if it's just janitor. Better than the Bay," offered another.

"Carpenters get good money. And more than that, plumbers. And electricians. Bus drivers. Have you applied for any of these jobs?" asked someone.

"They all require certificates and special credentials. I have to go back to school, and then apprentice. It's like starting all over again. I may as well start all over as an engineer," I said.

"But it takes much longer to study as engineer. It's quicker to study as a plumber, and in the end, the pay is the same anyway," said another.

"Plumber? Carpenter? Electrician? I did not come here to be a labourer. Just because you have decided to become labourers does not mean I have to do it too," I said.

"You are too proud," interrupted Josie. "We can't eat pride," she added.

"Just give me more time, Josie. I'm not the same as you. Teaching is not much to give up for cooking," I said.

"You think I'm only a teacher so I can give it up for anything? Who do you think you are, engineer that can't get a job, refusing to take lowly jobs. Insulting other people who at least pay for their drinks. At least my cooking pays for our bills!" Josie cried, and stormed out of the room.

"She has changed. She's so proud now. She can just raise her voice to me and run out, just because she is bringing in money and I'm not," I complained to my buddies.

"Don't worry, you'll find a job. Here, drink some more," said someone.

"There's a picnic of domestic workers in the park day after tomorrow. Why don't you come, since you're not working anyway? It's my day off, I'll take you there," said someone.

"Sure, why not? Why do I have to make *pandesal* anyway? She can make them herself," I said. I drank down a shot, and signalled for another one.

* * *

Josie's insult stung. She wasn't like that in Manila, when I was earning a lot of money as an engineer. She's changing. Who can blame her though? I have to pull my own weight.

I decided to try walking into an engineering company, and applying directly. What's the harm in that?

I sat down with the phone book and marked some engineering companies, and their addresses. I targeted the ones in Surrey. Ferringham and Associates was an engineering company specializing in commercial and institutional buildings, the ad said.

The next day, when no one was home, I dressed up in my good suit, folded my resume and stuck it in the inside coat pocket of my suit. I was going to apply for a job at Ferringham, but I did not want anyone to know in case I didn't get the job. I did not want to raise my family's expectations.

The office was a stand-alone building three storeys high with the name of the firm on the building facade. They are doing well to have their own building. The receptionist was busy. I stood by her desk a while before she looked up.

"Can I help you?" she said. She looked somewhat annoyed for being disturbed.

"Yes, you can," I said.

"Yes?" she added. I guess that's my cue.

"I'm here to apply for an engineering job," I said in my most correct English.

"Sure. Why don't you leave us your resume," she offered, and began scanning the paper on her desk.

I thought of how much time I spent dressing up and preparing what to say to get the job, and I did not want to just leave my resume.

"I have designed many buildings in the past and would like to talk to someone about a job," I said.

"I'm sure you do. Our process is for applicants to leave their resume with us. Someone will then review it and call the candidate for an interview appointment if the company is interested," the receptionist said with what I thought was a patronizing air.

"Isn't someone available right now? I came all the way. Even just five minutes?" I did not like that I seemed to be begging, but I thought I had to press or get nowhere. In the Philippines, I would drop someone's name at right about now.

"Sorry, they're all at a meeting," she said.

"You didn't even check. I saw someone at his desk right now," I said rather loudly.

A door opened from behind. "Is anything the matter?" asked a tall white-haired man in a shirt and tie.

"Uhmm...this gentleman wants to apply for a job and wants to see someone now. I said everyone's busy and to leave his resume for us to review," the receptionist said defensively.

"No, you said everyone's in a meeting, and clearly you lied. Someone is not at a meeting," I said, with a hint of victory.

I addressed the gentleman who may be a hiring engineer. Who knows? I may be lucky. "I was hoping to see someone, even just for five minutes, as I came all the way," I said boldly.

The gentleman may have been somewhat embarrassed by the receptionist being caught in a lie. "Well, alright," he said. "Why don't you come into my office?"

As I walked into his office, I noticed from my peripheral vision the receptionist making hand signs to the gentleman.

"So how can I help you, Mr...," began the gentleman.

"Del Mundo, Manuel del Mundo," I said.

"Andrew Jackson," said the gentleman and we shook hands.

"Well, Mr. Jackson. I have designed many commercial and institutional buildings in the past, like the University of Los Banos Annex, the Philippine General Hospital emergency wing." As I was not getting any reaction from Mr. Jackson, I added "And the International Film Centre, that's a big project of our First Lady," I said.

"Oh, is that the building that collapsed?" Mr. Jackson came alive with the name. "Workers trapped in the wet cement and paved over to rush the job? I heard about that in the news. Is that the same one?" he asked.

I panicked. I hadn't thought this through. I didn't imagine they would know here, and certainly I didn't mean to mention it.

"Uhmm...yes, the same one. But that was because of some drunk workers who caused the scaffolding to collapse," I rushed to explain.

"What happened?" asked Mr. Jackson, now intensely interested.

"We really don't know what happened because there was a blackout on the news right away. Even I, the building engineer, wasn't told until much later, and when I found out what they did — going ahead and paving over the bodies — I quit the job!" I exclaimed.

"Really? That's odd that they won't even talk to the engineer in charge?" he said.

"Well, I was not really the engineer in charge of the whole thing. I was an engineer in the team," I clarified.

"Oh, but you said earlier..." Mr. Jackson stopped, looking somewhat embarrassed.

"I meant I was an engineer for the Film Centre," I said.

"And for the other two buildings you mentioned?" Mr. Jackson queried.

I felt trapped. "It's alright, Mr. Jackson. Everything is in this resume." I handed him the resume from my pocket. I continued, "I believe my five minutes is over. Thank you for your time," I stood up, trying to salvage some dignity.

"Thank you, Mr. del Mundo," Mr. Jackson said without a smile. I turned to walk away as fast as I could.

* * *

Bear Creek Park is a lovely piece of forest in Surrey. A stream runs through it, and you can cross over the stream from the parking lot on a wooden bridge. Down by the stream, on a patch of grass under the shade of a willow tree, a checkered blanket sat, its corners ruffling in the wind. Several women were busily hovering about, bringing food onto the blanket, unfolding plastic chairs, setting up drinks, cutting up a watermelon, hanging a plastic garbage bag by a branch. The gurgling of the stream competed with the sound of the women happily chatting and birds chirping. Farther down the stream, two kids sloshed about in the water with a puppy. The brilliant sun created a halo around the scene. I stood on the bridge taking it all in. I felt a lump in my throat, wishing it was my family waiting for me down there by the stream. Next time, I must bring Josie and the kids here.

"*Kuya*, you aren't eating my *guinatan*," teased Carla, one of the women at the picnic. Carla was a petite beauty, what they called *morena*, for her dark looks.

Paquito said that Carla is a caregiver working two jobs. One was working for her cousin who sponsored her, advanced her airfare to Canada, and for whom she works for free to pay for it all. The other was working for a regular employer who pays her wages. With her two jobs, she hardly had time off, and today she was liberated from work, as both her employer and cousin were away on holidays the same day.

"I'm so full now I can't eat a thing anymore or I will explode," I said, holding my belly.

"But you ate *Ate*'s watermelon," Carla said with a pretend pout.

"That's only fruit; it's mostly water," I said.

"So what, you ate what she brought and not what I brought. Maybe you don't like me," she continued. I think she likes me.

"Okay then. Let me have a little of your *guinatan*," I said.

"Good, you won't regret it," Carla said.

I took a spoonful of the warm fruit stewed in coconut milk.

"Uuum, yummy." It was good.

"See, I told you. Have some more. In fact, I can pack some for you to take home. There's lots of it," said Carla.

"Careful, Manuel, that *guinatan* may have some *gayuma* in it," said one of the men. Everyone laughed.

For the boys more than anything else, I put my arm around Carla and kissed her cheek quickly.

"See, it's working already," I said, referring to the aphrodisiac that someone said was in the *guinatan*.

Carla, blushing, but obviously enjoying the teasing, took my arm off her shoulder.

"*Kuya*, your wife might take it the wrong way," Carla said.

"No she won't. She won't even know, will she?" I said, winking to my buddies.

They all laughed.

Embarrassed, Carla stood up and ran towards the shallow stream. As she put out her hands to scoop water to wash her hot face, she slipped on a stone and fell into the water. I ran and tried to catch her, but I too fell in, and landed on her.

More laughter. I stood up on my feet, all wet. Looking at Carla wet and dishevelled and confused, I felt a warm feeling towards her — part pity, part wanting to help her, part attracted to her. I swooped her up in my arms, walked a few steps with her arms around my neck, and deposited her on the ground. I made a grand bow to Carla as she found her footing. The audience clapped in unison.

"Uuuuy. Just like a newly married couple," teased one of the girls.

"Kiss the bride, kiss the bride!" shouted someone.

I looked at Carla, held her face, and gave her a long kiss on the mouth.

When I let Carla go, everybody had become quiet. Carla stared at me shocked. She slapped me.

Then I kissed her again. Longer.

When I let her go, I said, "You started it." I walked away.

Later, Carla told me that she wanted to run after me and slap me again, but she wasn't sure whether that was to get even with me for disrespecting her, or so that I would kiss her again, longer.

*   *   *

I felt victorious somehow. My manhood was reclaimed with the Carla episode. I walked more straight that day, smiled confidently and was patient with Bobby. I even baked *pandesal* that night for the whole family, when I usually only bake in the morning.

Manolita squealed for the first *pandesal*. I split open the *pandesal* with my fingers and spooned *adobo* pieces inside it like a sandwich, and gave it to Manolita. *Adobo* sandwich was Manolita's favourite. Sonia, whose favourite was *pancit*, sliced her *pandesal* open, letting the steam out, then stuffed two big spoonfuls of the noodles into the *pandesal*. Bobby dipped a corner of his *pandesal* in the runny egg of his plate of *longsilog*, his favourite dish. Josie watched over her brood contentedly, as she drank leftover green papaya *tinola* soup from a cup. She tore a piece of *pandesal*, dropped it in the soup, and ate the soaked bread.

"You're happy. Did you have good job prospects today?" asked Josie.

"No, not that. I discovered a beautiful place — Bear Creek Park. Let's go this weekend," I said.

"I've been there! Miss Sahota took us. It's beautiful!" said Sonia.

"Can we go swimming?" asked Manolita.

"Yes, and the stream is especially shallow just so my Manolita won't drown," said Manuel.

"Are there bears?" asked Manolita.

"Yes, lots and lots of them. Big black bears hungry to eat little girls like you," said Bobby, crawling after Manolita, and biting her leg. Manolita squealed.

"Stop scaring her," I said, kicking Bobby gently.

"He's just teasing," said Josie.

"I know, I was just teasing too," I said. I ruffled Bobby's hair. "How's school, Bobby?" I felt like really knowing.

"Okay. I've a whole bunch of friends now," Bobby answered.

"Yeah, the Diablos Gang," said Sonia.

"A gang? *Tinamaan ng lintik!* Are you involved in a gang?" I slapped Bobby on the side of the head.

Bobby stood up and sat by his mom.

"For heaven's sake Manuel. Can't you listen to his answer first before judging him?" said Josie. I breathed slowly, trying to control my temper.

"What is this gang thing, Bobby?" asked Josie.

"Nothing, ma. Just a group of Filipinos getting together so other boys don't bully us. Ever since I joined the group, no one calls me Flip anymore or make fun of me," Bobby said.

"And why not? Because you carry weapons? Why are they afraid of you?" I interrogated him.

"Because. They know they can't fool around with us," Bobby said.

"Why can't they fool around with you, hot shot? What do you do with them?" I do not trust him.

"Nothing. They just know not to cross us," said Bobby.

"Or else?" asked Josie.

"They'll fight. And they're good. Better than any other gang. They do karate," said Sonia.

"Fighting? Is that what you do in school now? Is that what you're proud of?" I knew it.

Stumbling Through Paradise

"I've never fought. I just learn karate, just in case. When they know you know karate, they are careful. They can't bully us *Pinoys* anymore," said Bobby, demonstrating a kick.

"Just use it for self defense. Don't show it off, or that will get you into trouble." He is such a showboat.

"At least he has a way of protecting himself," cried Josie, always on his side.

"And me too! A boy whistled at me, and I told him to scram, or I'll get my brother to beat him up. He asked who's my brother. I told him that Bobby's with the Diablos. He never bothered me again," said Sonia.

"Hmmm." I watched Bobby, looking strong and confident. He's not so bad really. A feeling of pride along with a feeling of envy crept inside me. When was the last time I felt that invulnerable?

"Just watch it that you don't show off, okay?" I said, giving Bobby a nod of approval.

"And don't start anything. Just for self-defence, okay?" said Josie. "Thank you for looking after you sister," Josie gave Bobby a hug.

Sonia came and hugged Bobby too, and Manolita joined the group hug. I wrapped my arms around my family, feeling guilty about my little boy doing the protecting, when I should be the protector. Instead, I was at home, *palamunin*, fed by my wife, protected by my son. What am I good for? And now thinking thoughts about Carla as well.

* * *

CHAPTER 10

Canada
Manuel, 1982–1984

She is very good, I have to say. I didn't think Josie was a business whiz when I married her. She's good not only with the cooking, but also managing her sub-contractors, and securing orders. Her catering business flourished. Lily referred all parish events now to Josie.

As business grew, I hardly saw Josie. She seemed to have become a new person. She was constantly busy with the orders, harried and short-tempered. She transformed the apartment into one giant kitchen. She acquired a second used fridge, and a used deep freezer, which occupied the kitchen and dining areas. The living room became a kitchen extension with long tables laid out for cutting ingredients and for assembling food onto large trays. She found cheap open shelving to stack food supplies and the shelves lined the living room. Her catering crew expanded to a team of four: Rosie, Carmen, Anita and Mario for deliveries. Sonia helped after her homework was done. She was keen to learn how the dishes were cooked, and had an eye for presentation. Manolita hang around, playing amongst the cooking. Bobby no longer helped. He said he was busy at school, and Josie could not be bothered with checking up on him.

Josie and I just grew farther and farther apart.

"You check up on Bobby," Josie told me, as I was suspicious of his activities. "You have too little to do, imagining all these bad things about Bobby. Follow him. Find out what he's up to. Don't ask me. I'm busy making money to feed our family," she continued.

I wanted to slap her mouth when she acted like that. I had lost authority over my family. I felt like a ghost in the house. I began to hate the smell of frying garlic and fish. I tried escaping from the smells by showering constantly, but even the towels smelled of cooking. I saw oily stains on the ceiling and walls, so thick you could scrape them off with a knife.

"How about the *pandesal*? We need 100 pieces by tomorrow morning. If you can't do even that, I'll subcontract it out to someone else," Josie demanded.

"I'm going out to see Paquito. I'll make the *pandesal* tonight when you're all finished here. Don't worry, it'll be ready for the delivery," I said on my way out.

Out on the street, I could finally breathe. Summer in Canada was like Baguio in the Philippines without the smell of the pines. All I needed was a light jacket on top of a sweater. I should really play tennis again. I did not know where I was going. I just wanted to get out of the cookhouse. I thought I'd cross the big King George Highway and walk the other side of town today. Traffic was light. I kept walking down the highway, and found the same park of the recent picnic. My heart, or is it my loins, must be guiding my feet. I paused by the small wooden bridge and watched the gurgling stream, imagining Carla all wet, remembering the kiss, the slap, the red face. My face felt hot. I walked to the stream and washed my face to cool off. I heard cooing sounds, looked up and saw birds flying between the trees. There was no one in the park except the birds. The water flowed by and the sun shone gently. I felt a delicious sensation of solitude, of being complete, not needing anything. I remembered my life back home in Manila. The beautiful home in Bel Air, the maids, my big building projects, my friends and *compadres.* What would they say if they see me now? Jobless. A house taken over by cooking. A wife who had become a monster. Bobby going farther away, into bad company. Sonia's ticks were lessening, but she was not the lively fun girl she used to be. Something is wrong with Sonia. I have to remember to talk to her. Thank God for Manolita, who seemed to be the only one unaffected.

Suddenly, the decision was clear to me. I will return home. I will pick up from where I left. The Film Centre story should be forgotten now. There are other buildings I designed. They will remember me for those other buildings. I will get my old job back, and get my family back. Fuelled by hope, I began to walk out of the park, shoulders erect, head held high, a light spring in my step. I thought I'd walk farther, saw the tall Pattullo Bridge, wondered about its design, and decided to explore.

As I walked up and down the hill of the winding King George Highway, I felt lost amidst the wide roadway, the traffic zooming at high speeds. I walked by the vacant lots, auto body shops, wreck car lots, dump sites, dilapidated housing, and imagined that this must be the older part of town, so different from the ritzy subdivisions in other parts of Surrey.

It had become overcast, cooler. Standing on the bridge, I looked below, at the voluminous waters of the Fraser River. Tugs pulled barges loaded with logs and gravel. Up and down the river, fishing boats sailed by. An emergency boat with a large red cross sped along. I noticed a small figure in the distance, standing by the bridge rail, looking down at the water. Coming closer, I recognized Carla. What is she doing here? I saw that her feet were bare, her shoes sat by the side of her feet, and her coat was folded beside her shoes. Carla seemed entranced, staring down at the river.

Something very dangerous flashed in my mind and I ran. I grabbed Carla from behind and pulled her away from the rail.

I held her a long time. I felt her body shivering with cold. I held her tight and still, until I felt it was safe to release her. She felt limp in my arms. She did not struggle. After some time, I turned her to me.

"What are you doing? Were you planning to jump?"

"It's no use. I've nothing to live for. Everything's gone. Why did you pull me back?" Carla asked in a resigned tone.

Carla slumped onto the ground and covered her face with her hands. The bridge shook with the vehicles rumbling by. She started to cry. I sat down beside her, and took her in my arms. I let her cry on my shoulders, till all the crying was done. I noticed the clouds move and the sun peek through the clouds. Carla felt warm in my arms and her sobbing had stopped. I felt my own heart throbbing. I came just in time. What would have happened if I did not walk this way, if I stayed home that morning? Is this what destiny means? That I was meant to be here, in Surrey, on this bridge, at this time and day, or a woman would be dead? I felt a feeling so clear and filled with light. Did destiny also mean I am responsible for this life I saved? I hugged the precious bundle in my arms.

Carla broke away, and began to put her coat back on. She slipped her feet into her sneakers. She looked at me with a sadness I'd never seen before on a face, grey and heavy like a stone. Gone was the flirtatious face in the picnic. "I'm sorry," she said, and stood up.

"I won't tell anyone. Would you like to talk?" I asked.

She did not answer. We walked away from the bridge. When I hooked her arm under mine, she did not take it away.

We walked through the same hill of King George Highway, but somehow it did not seem as oppressive as before. As I sought to console Carla, this time I saw the greenness of the mountain by the roadside, the houses high on top of the hills which must have beautiful views, the pretty flower shop and corner grocery store at the bend of the road.

The Roundhouse Cafe was a quiet place at 3 pm. We took a table far to the corner where we would not be disturbed or seen. She ordered coke; I ordered coffee. The waitress seemed to understand and left us alone.

"I can't even do it right. You of all people had to see me, and save me." Carla pulled her coat around her as though she felt cold.

"Why? How bad can it be?"

"How bad? My husband has been seeing another woman. I caught them in the act. I threw acid on the woman's face. He said it was over. I believed him. I even gave him money to buy a tricycle so he could make extra money. Last night, a neighbour called. She said my husband went out partying with his mistress, the same woman I caught him with. They took my daughter along in the tricycle. He must have been drunk. They hit a tree and fell off a cliff. The tricycle exploded. Everyone's dead. Burnt."

Carla took a sip of coke.

I reached over the table and put my hand over Carla's.

I was stunned.

"I have no one left. My parents died a long time ago. I was raised by my grandmother. She has passed away too. My husband was my childhood friend. I loved him very much. He said he'd wait for me to get him. I never thought he would betray me, and I believed him when he said he would stop seeing her. He said he missed me too much and that he had to have an outlet. He said he loved me. So I believed him. And now it seemed he lied. The minute I left, he went right back to her. Why did they have to take my daughter?"

Carla could not continue and began to cry. I came over to her side, feeling a mixture of anger, disbelief and compassion for Carla.

"To complicate it all, I don't want to return to my cousin's house. Her husband pushed me into the bathroom last night, cornered me against the wall with his body, and tried to kiss me. I fought him back and escaped, and didn't tell anyone. Now, I'm afraid to go back there."

Carla looked straight into my face, as though accusing me.

"What's wrong with me? Why do bad things follow me around? Why am I being punished? What did I do wrong?" Carla cried.

"It's not your fault," said Manuel. "Don't blame yourself. Sometimes we don't know why bad things happen. They just do."

"It's hopeless," said Carla, looking outside the window. The clouds had returned, heavy with rain. A few drops of rain hit the glass window at a slant like needles.

"I have no one left. What's the point of going on?"

"You have me. I'll help you. I'll look after you." What was I saying?

"Help? How? You have a family yourself to look after," she said.

"I don't know. We'll find a way," I said.

That day, I took Carla to our home. Carla told her story again. Josie felt sorry for her and offered that Carla stay in our home until we could figure out what to do. We planned that Carla would still report to his employer where she got paid, but would not return to her cousin's place with the excuse that the other employer requested her service for a few days.

* * *

"We cannot have her here for too long. We're already cramped here. What can we do, really?" Josie said.

"She cannot return to the cousin's house and be raped," I said.

"Is she asking for it maybe? Sometimes, I wonder. She acts a little...you know...the way she dresses in short skirts and her hair all sexy. I mean. Sometimes, men think you're asking for it when you dress like that. And maybe she wouldn't mind having a rich boyfriend. I was not born yesterday," Josie said. I had never seen this cold cynical side of Josie.

"How can you say that? She lost her child and her husband to a violent end. How can you be so...harsh, Josie? What's happened to you?" I said.

"Whatever. I'm sorry. You're right. It's not her fault her daughter and husband were killed. It's not her fault that the husband of her employer wants to molest her. So, what do we do?" Ever -practical Josie.

"I don't know. I don't know yet. I'll ask around tomorrow about how to deal with the cousin's husband. Carla has to be able to return to that home without fear of being molested, or not return at all. Maybe we can help her find another employer," I suggested.

"She already has another employer. Why not just make that employment full time, and pay back the cousin faster because she has no one to send the money back home now?" Makes sense, but I remembered another thing.

"Carla needs to look after her cousin's kids. She owes the cousin," I said.

"Too bad. Carla should just tell her cousin all about the husband," said Josie.

"She won't believe her of course," I said.

"Hmmm. I don't know. Sounds like you want to keep her here. Is there something else going on here?" She accused me.

"How can you be so cruel?" I exploded. "I can't believe you're the same Josie I courted and married. How could you think this?" I raged with righteousness. "How would you like it if this happened to you, and instead of being helped, you got blamed? And the person who helps you is suspected of bad intentions?"

"I'm sorry. Sorry. I'm not thinking. I'm tired. This has been an exhausting day. You have been a good Samaritan," Josie said. She kissed me quickly. "Carla should be so lucky you were there on the bridge."

Somewhat appeased, I calmed down.

"My head hurts from all this. It's too much. I can't imagine such a tragedy, all of her family, in one swoop, gone?" asked Josie.

"Are you saying she's lying?" I was still in a fighting mood.

"No, no. I didn't mean that. It's just that I can't imagine such a string of catastrophes on one person. I only meant that I'm so glad our problems are so small in comparison." Josie came close to me and placed her hand on my chest.

I let Josie embrace me, but I could not somehow embrace her back.

"I know. We're still blessed. Let's try to sleep now. It will be better in the morning," I said.

But it didn't feel better at all in the next days, in fact just the opposite.

* * *

CHAPTER 11

Canada
Josie, 1984

The next days were difficult for all of us. Bobby and Sonia were not happy about having another person sleeping on the living room floor with them. Manuel was looking after Carla like she was a child. Carla kept offering her services to help with the cooking and cleaning, while Manuel kept wanting to do the chores himself so Carla could rest. I could sense that while Sonia and Bobby felt sorry for Carla, they wondered how long she would stay. Fair enough. They seemed confused about why we should be nice to Carla. Manuel said that this is the problem with our children who have experienced nothing but abundance, not enough compassion for the unfortunate.

"Is she here because we're related?" asked Sonia. Manuel glared at her.

"She has no relations, that's why we're helping," I whispered, not wanting Carla to hear.

Manuel threw himself to the task of helping Carla. He called around to lawyers, and found out how expensive they were. He offered to pay for a lawyer. I was adamant not to use our precious funds. Carla overheard our loud voices from the kitchen.

"You are having too much trouble over me," Carla said, slipping into the conversation. "I can just go back and tell my cousin about her husband and hope she believes me," she said.

"Ching told me about a lawyer who helped a caregiver against an abusive employer. She said the service was free. I'll call her in the morning and find out," Manuel offered.

"No, I'll go home tonight and make an appointment with the lawyer sometime soon," said Carla.

"No, you won't. You'll go back when it's safe," Manuel insisted.

"She keeps my passport. She might do something with it if I don't show up soon," said Carla.

"Why does she keep your passport?" I was surprised. So was Manuel.

"I don't know. She just said that's how it's done. Since she sponsored me, I guess she could keep my passport," said Carla.

"I've never heard anything like that. Mario never kept our passports. We should tell the lawyer about that too," Manuel said.

"*Ate* might say I seduced her husband and that it's my fault. Or that I am just making it up so I won't have to pay her back and look after her kids," Carla explained.

"Stop worrying, and let's just see what the lawyer says," Manuel said.

* * *

At the Surrey Memorial Hospital cafeteria, Lily and I sat having coffee.

"Well, at least she cooks well. Her spicy *Bicol* dish was a hit at last night's event," said Lily. Lily had become my best friend since she commissioned my first catering event. Since then, Lily referred many parish events to me. I had become a popular caterer for private parties with parishioners at Holy Rosary. Lily was a nurse at the Surrey Memorial Hospital.

"Manuel seems to like spicy coconut dishes all of a sudden. That's all he eats nowadays," I said.

"Don't go there, *hija*. She's no competition for you. Jealousy will eat you up. A damsel in distress is a most irresistible seducer, but that will be only for a while, while the novelty lasts. In the end, your strength will keep him, better than her weakness," said Lily.

"I wonder if it's the other way around? Weakness is strength. With men, anyway."

"Men aren't worth the worry, Josie. You have to be strong for the kids."

"I hardly see Bobby. He gave me $100 the other day. He said it was to help out."

"Is he working?" Lily the detective.

"He said he does part-time work at McDonalds." I realize I'm not even certain of this.

"How are his grades?"

"I haven't seen them. He says they're good." I can't believe I have not seen his report card.

Lily looked quietly at me. I'm sure that whatever admiration she must have had for me was gone that instant.

"Sounds like you're not sure. Why don't you call his teacher and find out how he's doing?" offered Lily.

I didn't answer.

"Sometimes our kids are more important than our husband," said Lily. "Bobby sounds like he needs someone who loves him to remind him about that."

"I told Manuel he needs to do that, I'm so busy. He's the father." My defense.

"You're the one that can see what's happening. You can't wait for him. Bobby may be into drugs, or something. He's with the Diablos," said Lily.

"He said it's not a gang, just a group of Filipinos." Do I really believe this?

"Don't underestimate them. Filipinos can do a gang just like any ethnic group." Lily comforted me with her knowledge. "It starts simple enough, they feel protected in the group, and then they follow whatever the leader says. You know, there are telling signs of drug use."

"Yeah? Like what?" I exclaimed.

"They keep to themselves. They don't bring friends home. Bloodshot eyes. They begin to be unkempt. They seem to have a lot of money, spending on things." I guess nurses know these things.

"Well, he's a bit quieter now, but we do talk. That's true, I have not met any of his friends, but he tells me about them. I should pay attention to his eyes. His clothes? He is well groomed as always. And money. Well, he did give me $100, but he does work and gets paid." I explained.

"Anyway, that's up to you; just a friend's advice. You worked hard to get here. You are too good a person to lose your family now that you've arrived in Paradise."

"Some paradise." I felt paradise betrayed me.

"Come, Josie. I've never seen you this way. Giving up. You're my hero. You can do anything," Lily my faithful champion.

"Where would I be without you, Lily?"

"In God's hands, as you always are. Don't forget that. And don't forget to call the hospital contact I gave you to cater their staff retreat. That will be a good contract. I have to go." Lily took a last sip of coffee.

"It's you who are my angel. I'll check with Bobby's teacher," I promised.

"You do that, and let me know! I'm happy to be wrong! Oh by the way, did you hear about the Mrs. Philippines contest? I think you should run. You're the prettiest Filipina Mrs, hands down. Great way for your business to be known, and great contacts for the business!"

"What?!" I cried, thrilled.

"Think about it," Lily said, laughing, and then blew me a kiss.

* * *

Should I worry about this, or should I not? Is Manuel just being a Good Samaritan, or are they falling in love with each other? Should I tolerate this, Lord? Are you asking that I be compassionate to a suffering woman? If I do, will you promise to keep them away from each other, that way? Please Lord, help Carla's employment situation to settle well so she can leave our house. How perceptive Sonia is in her letter.

Dear Lola Iska and Lolo Lino,

I'm so sorry for not writing often. How are you? How are your eyes, Lola Iska? Hope they are better. Bobby sure is saving up for your cataract operation, he told me not to tell you, because he's still saving up. He is doing very well in school, and he's got a job too! When I'm a little bigger, I can work at McDonalds too and save money for you. Can you believe it? I am tutoring a Chinese classmate in English, and she is paying me $1 for every session. I have now saved $4! That's not much yet for your eye operation, but word's got around, and maybe her other Chinese friend wants *me to teach her too! Manolita is going to kindergarten now, and she is smart just like me! I am liking it at school better now that I have a few friends, and my favourite teacher Miss Sahota, the Indian princess is wonderful as usual.*

We are all cooking here at home for Mommy's catering business, even me and Manolita cutting up carrots, and I get to be tray decorator, and Daddy bakes pandesal. Our business is doing so well and Mom bought a car so we don't have to borrow Uncle Mario's to deliver. It's only used, but it's color red and fun!

We have a new friend whose name is Carla. She is living with us, because she has no home anymore. Her whole family — that's her baby and her husband — died in an accident. And where she lives, there is also another bad man so she can't live there anymore. We are entertaining her so she does not get so sad, with such a life as that! We took her to a swimming pool the other day. She had no swimsuit and Mommy had to lend her one. She looked very pretty, not like a maid, which she is. She has been cooking for us, and cleaning up, and our house doesn't quite smell of cooking as much as before. She boils water and vanilla and it absorbs the smells! But she's not very smart, so Dad and Mom are helping Carla. They got a lawyer to write a letter to the bad man where Carla works, and that did the trick. The man is not bad to Carla anymore. And the lawyer never even asked to be paid. What a great place is Canada! So Carla is leaving soon, and I'll be back with a bigger bed space on the floor! We'll miss her, but I don't think mom will.

You can tell Bekang all my news, and that I will write her a very very long letter soon, including about all my best friends here, but tell her not to worry, because she is still my best best best friend of all.

Ps. I forgot to tell you about cherry blossoms. I can't believe I forgot. That was some time ago. Last April, cherry blossoms bloomed all over the city. They are pink and white and cream, and they are so thick on their branches, and when you walk under them, it feels like heaven. When the wind blows, their little petals fall like snow, so quiet. I'm attaching a picture here from a magazine. Isn't Canada beautiful? And I haven't even seen one tenth of it! I saved another picture for Bekang too.

Luv u and miss you lots,
Your loving and favourite (heh heh) granddaughter
Sonia

* * *

Mario and Ching threw a party for our successful advocacy for Carla with her employer. My catering team was present — Rosie, Carmen and Anita. Lily came by with cake. She said she was late for a meeting and just wanted to drop off something, but everybody knew that Lily was there just to meet Carla. Manuel was flush with victory.

"Congratulations, *utol*!" said Mario. "Maybe you should be a lawyer — that was good advocacy!"

"It was Carla. She told her story well and the lawyer said not to worry. He said he will write a letter that'll scare him, but not too much so that he will still keep her in his employ," said Manuel.

"And the thing about the passport? You should have seen how *Ate* gave me my passport right away. She said 'I just wanted to keep it safe for you,'" said Carla, imitating her cousin's sly tone. Carla has really settled in, no longer the shy flower of the past.

"When Carla returns, she will have her own room with a lock. That's what the lawyer asked, and they agreed," said Manuel.

"I like the way the lawyer turned things around and said that employers have to live up to their obligations or face up to the law. They may be in trouble, not me!" said Carla.

"I don't think he'll try anything nasty now," said Ching.

"Thank you, Ching, for referring this lawyer to us. I can't thank you enough!" I said.

"Don't mention it. Caregivers have to stick together," said Ching.

"And Manuel can be the caregivers' advocate. He's good," said Carla, looking dreamily at Manuel.

"First, he must get an engineering job," I reminded everyone.

"Oh, and that lawyer was really kind. When I told him about my troubles getting work as an engineer, he suggested I speak with someone at the APE, that's the Association of Professional Engineers," said Manuel, reading from a calling card. "He said they are the ones that review foreign engineering credentials. I have an appointment to see someone there next week," Manuel added with a tinge of pride.

"Great, *utol*! Good luck on that!" said Mario.

Manuel beamed with happiness, savouring the thought of the engineering job. Carla served Manuel attentively, refreshing his beer, replenishing his plate. Looking on, I felt there was something wrong in this picture. What was that woman doing, serving my own husband? Ching caught me looking at Carla and Manuel, and I shifted my eyes away, embarrassed at how the truth was so plain to see. I stood up and went to the bedroom to get my purse. Ching followed me.

"It's just a crush, I'm sure. No one pays attention to her, certainly not a nice guy like Manuel. Manuel is just being helpful. You're a good wife to lend your husband like that to somebody who is in need," said Ching.

"I feel so embarrassed, everybody must be talking," I said.

"Let them be. It's only one-way anyway. Manuel knows how valuable you are, she's nothing compared to you. She'll be on her own now, and you'll have Manuel back. The talk will stop. Just don't mind it," assured Ching.

"There's talk?" Now I'm really worried.

"A little, but not to worry. It's just all about her having a crush on her hero, right?" said Ching.

"I don't know."

"How could Manuel even think it? You are the top-ranked candidate for Mrs. Philippines. I'm so proud of you!" said Ching.

"Oh that. It's all about how much funds you raise anyway," I explained.

"Well? That means you're the best fundraiser, the most popular and a great looker too! The winner will be all over the papers, you'll be famous!"

"Well, just in the Philippine community."

"That's still a lot of publicity...for your business!" teased Ching.

"I'm excited for the business, yes. You have been so kind to me. Without your friends, I would have never have been able to start the business."

"You are too much. It's you that did all the work, and your husband does not deserve you. Hang in there, sis," said Ching.

I was confused. I never thought Ching cared for me at all. All the time, I thought Ching was on Manuel's side, Carla's side. I hugged Ching back. I made up my mind to be a better friend to her.

* * *

CHAPTER 12

Canada
Manuel, 1984

It was a beautiful June afternoon. My appointment with APE was for 3 pm. I should have just stuck to that. But instead — it was such a tragic mistake.

I took a shower after lunch, brushed my teeth and rinsed with Listerine to get rid of the garlic smell of the wonderful adobo dish with shrimp paste, coconut milk and chili that Carla had made. Josie was away on delivery, and Carla had just put Manolita to sleep. Bobby and Sonia were at school. Carla and I were the only ones at home.

I put on my best suit, the black one with thin stripes. That should impress those APE officers. Did they think they were dealing with a jungle man? They probably did not own a suit as expensive as this. I brushed the soft silk of the collar. Very nice. I chose a grey tie, looked at myself in the mirror, and liked what I saw. I combed down the unruly waves of my hair. I wish they were straight like Mario's.

"Don't, it's nice that way," said Carla. "You look handsome. You should wear that more often." Carla. So sweet. I wished

Josie were half as sweet. Josie was always cooking, on the phone, ordering everyone around. The big businesswoman.

"With no job to go, what shall I wear it to?" I complained.

"You'll get a job. You're the most intelligent man I know. You'll see, they'll say yes," said Carla.

"I wish they had as much confidence in me as you do," I touched her under the chin. She was so petite. I could lift her with my one hand. Her eyes were so enticing.

"With you dressed like that, they'll surely let you work as an engineer," said Carla, lifting her face to me. I looked down at Carla's adoring eyes and her fresh lips, and kissed her. Her lips were sweet and yielding. I should have stopped there. But her body felt soft. Her thigh urgently brushed against mine.

I decided that they wouldn't mind me being a few minutes late for my appointment.

I lifted Carla and pressed her against the wall. She tore off my coat. I pulled her dress up. She struggled with my pants and I pushed her hand away to do it myself. We were down on the floor. My whole body was exploding. Our bodies were writhing in abandon when suddenly, the door crashed open.

"What's this?" cried Bobby, staring at us half-naked in each other's arms on the floor.

I scrambled to my feet, pulling up my pants. I faced Bobby and said the only thing that came to my head. "You're supposed to be in school!" I said it with as much authority as I could.

"*Putangina!* Is this what you do while my mother works to feed you?" shouted Bobby. He threw a chair at me. The chair fell over and hit Carla who was trying to get up. She fell back on the floor.

I lounged at Bobby with my fist, but I only caught his collar. Something dawned on me. "Who do you think you are? You druggie, look at your blood-shot eyes. Do you think I don't know? You flash your money around, and think you're better than all of us!" I pushed him roughly.

He came back and swung his arm, almost hitting my face with his fist. Missing it, he swung again and connected with his left arm. I fell on the floor, my lips bloodied. It hurt.

"You better leave this house with this whore of yours, or you'll get more of that. I don't want you in this house disrespecting my mother, do you hear? Get out!"

Carla crawled over to my side, wiping the blood on my face with her hand. Bobby lifted Carla and shoved her towards the door. "You. Get out! I don't ever want to see you again in this house! Both of you, out!" he cried, kicking me as well.

Bobby leaned on the table, hair dishevelled, eyes red with fury. "You snake...after all the kindness of my mother, you give her this!" He ran towards us. He looked insane. I scrambled to get away. Carla slipped out the door. I felt Bobby's hard kick on my back.

"*Putangina*! You're no father of mine. Don't ever come back here again!" said Bobby.

I fled.

* * *

CHAPTER 14

Canada
Josie, 1984

I knew something was afoot when I arrived home from delivering orders, to a house that was all cleaned up. The table was set for four. Bobby was home already, and kissed me tenderly, taking my things away. Sonia looked away and did not kiss me as she usually does. Manolita was already seated at her usual place at the table. Bobby led me to my seat, and he sat at the head of the table, Manuel's seat.

The tension in the air was palpable. Sonia's eyes were red. That's what she was hiding from me, why she didn't kiss me.

"What's going on?" I ask. Silence. I address Bobby.

"Where's your dad? And why are you sitting on his chair?" I asked.

"He's gone, with his whore. That *puta* Carla," Bobby spat out the name.

I am stunned.

"I caught them on the floor naked, fucking. No one else was home. I arrived early today. They must have been doing this a long time. He didn't deny it," Bobby said.

I am speechless. I am imagining them on the floor, in the bathroom, on our bed. When? Since when? Why does this not shock me? I must have known it all along. I shut my eyes wishing the images would go away. I feel suddenly dirty. I feel sobs rising from my chest, to my throat, my mouth. I am vomiting dry sobs and I cover my mouth with my hand. I can't breathe.

Bobby is kneeling beside me, comforting me. Sonia on the other side of me, crying. Manolita, seated at her chair, is crying too.

"Why are we crying?" asks Manolita, through her tears.

Sonia shushess her.

"Did somebody die?" Manolita persists.

"No. Just keep quiet," says Sonia, taking Manolita onto her lap.

"Why is everyone sad?" asks Manolita.

"Why is Daddy not here? Where is Daddy?" Manolita insists.

"Your daddy's gone. He's left us," Bobby said.

"No. No. He's not! He lives here. He's my dad," screams Manolita. She starts hitting Sonia.

Bobby takes Manolita from Sonia and sits her on his lap.

"Your daddy doesn't love us. He loves someone else. He has gone to live with someone else," Bobby tells Manolita.

"That's not true! My dad loves me! He loves me!" cries Manolita, kicking Bobby, who tries to hug her.

"Enough," I say. I stand up and take Manolita from Bobby. I sit her on my lap. Somehow, this is comforting. Manuel's favorite child on my lap. He will return. For her.

"It's okay. Everything will be okay. Of course your dad loves you, sweetie. It's me he doesn't love anymore." I wipe Manolita's tears.

Stumbling Through Paradise

"Why?" asks Manolita.

"I don't know," I say.

"What will happen to us Mommy?" asks Manolita.

"We'll be fine. We don't need him. I'll look after us, you'll see. We'll be happier without him," Bobby assures Manolita.

"Will we still see Dad?" asks Sonia.

"I don't know," I say.

"NO! We won't see him anymore! He won't enter this house ever again!" Bobby cries.

Manolita's crying becomes more shrill.

"Stop it Bobby. You're making her more upset," I demand.

"Let's eat, we're all hungry," Bobby says.

"I'm not hungry," says Sonia.

"Me too," says Manolita.

"Okay then, just go to bed, you two," says Bobby.

"Can we sleep with you, Mom?" asks Sonia.

Her offer comforts me.

* * *

That night, and every night after, I lay in the middle of the bed, with Manolita on my right arm, and Sonia on my left. Bobby slept on a blanket at the bottom of the bed. On the dresser, I arranged small crucifixes, pictures of the Virgin Mary, the Sacred Heart of Jesus, the infant Jesus, votive candles and rosaries wrapped around crucifixes. Every night, before going to bed, we all said a prayer, which became the family mantra: "Dear lord, please bring our daddy back home. Make him sleep here, and eat here, and live here like before." Although he was there, Bobby never joined in the prayer, whispering his own.

* * *

Our home was like a tomb. Gone was the happy chattering of the girls as we chopped, mixed, baked and simmered the stews, sauces and pastries. Everyone kept silent in deference to me. I felt strange, numb, out of my body. Whose hands were these cutting the onions? I couldn't hear much. When I looked at someone talking to me, it was like a silent film. I was filled with darkness. I couldn't talk to Jesus. I couldn't pray. I was angry. Betrayed. I was a fool. Here I was slaving away and there they were betraying me. In my own home. While I was helping her. How could Manuel do this to us? We should never have let that tramp into our home. I kept imagining where else they did it. Did Manolita see them? God, why?

I worked like a robot, mixing ingredients together, not bothering to taste the dishes. Sonia worked extra hard to make the fruit platters exceptionally pretty and asked me how I liked it, but I just nodded. Making food at least kept me busy.

I spoke to the homeroom teachers of the kids about the separation. In my own time as a teacher in Manila, I appreciated moms telling me when something significant happened at home. It helped the teacher help the pupils.

I was glad to hear from Miss Eagle, who said that she had noticed a marked improvement in Bobby's attendance and his grades since the separation. Bobby acted as the father of our family, he came home early, gave me his money regularly, explaining his work. I felt happy that the separation's effect on Bobby was incredibly positive. It was the silver lining behind the dark cloud. But I was not comfortable with the enmity between him and Manuel. There was something toxic between them.

I was confused with the many feelings the separation brought. I felt a heavy lump in my chest every time I thought about Manuel and his betrayal. Tears simmered around my eyes and flowed at any thought related to Manuel and Carla. I couldn't bear to think about it. I buried myself in activity. I didn't want to see him, speak to him. When he called, I refused to answer the phone. When he came to the door, I refused to see him. I felt violated. I could not bear to look at him. I went weeks without any communication with Manuel. I believed I was trying to get used to life without him, moving forward with our lives. I believed I was punishing him. Did I need him? I could do without him. We could do without him. I covered the pain with bravado. Going it alone gave me purpose, and I drove myself in the business.

My thoughts were all over the place. I hate him. I try to blot out the scene of him and Carla on the floor, but it looms bigger the more I blot it out. I feel pity for myself. Then I feel thankful for being independent, and doing well. I think of the early courtship years, how madly I fell in love with him, how he defended me to his parents. I remembered Manuel's easy way of laughing and joking. I was always the serious one. I remembered the first time we met at St Theresa's, by the 'cage,' how he enchanted me with his praise. I remembered his clear and fast decision to elope with me, and tell the family later. He seemed so charming and confident — a man of the world. And now, he seemed diminished. I thought about the life we left in Manila: successful, in love. Or were we?

I remembered the last impetus that made us leave: the film centre collapse, how that haunted Manuel professionally, the collapse of our close family ties during that time when everything revolved around money, prestige. I had begun to lose Manuel by that time. Didn't I want the move to Canada to start a new life? Less stress? But it has not been that way at all. Canada is no Paradise. But thinking of the beautiful parks, the mountains, the ocean and the good affordable schools for the kids, I've had a glimpse, a small taste.

I felt guilty. Did I drive him away by pushing him so hard to get a job? Did I demean him, and in so doing push him away? If I didn't push him, he'd never do anything. Was it my fault that I was doing well and he was not? No. I felt convinced that I was the one wronged. They betrayed me, in my own home, and after all I'd done for Carla. The family is better off without him. My thoughts went swirling about until I felt my head could not hold any more thoughts.

I wanted to give up, return to Manila.

I decided to put down the swirling thoughts on paper, lining up the costs and benefits of my life. The list looked like this:

PROS

-I have good business; it's very tiring, but fun overall.

-Kids enjoy the business, friends make money. I can help my friends.

-Good health benefits. Spend only few dollars and doctors' fees are free. In the Philippines, it's very expensive. Have to get a really big job and high income to afford medical care there.

CONS
- Manuel cannot practise engineering.
- He fell in love with someone else, who may be nicer than me.
- Have I become a bad person in trying to succeed in business?
- The kids don't have their dad at home.
- Manolita is upset with me.
- I have lost my husband, and people are talking.
- We have a broken family.

- I miss him.

PROS
- At least, Bobby has become so much better because of the separation.
- The same with Sonia — she is so much more mature.
- Their future is more secure here, with a single-mom salary; the schools are inexpensive, unlike back home, when my in-laws had to subsidize the kids' schooling at exclusive schools.
- I am meeting more people with the Mrs. Philippines victory and I am getting new business from outside the Philippine community, like hospital meetings, business retreats, board meetings.

CON
- I am so far from *inay* and *itay* and the boys.

PRO
- Good thing they can't see me like this. If I were in the Philippines, there would be such a scandal!

CON
- But there is already scandal here!

PRO
- But not as much as if it were in Manila.
- And besides Canada is a beautiful place with free parks, swimming pools, kind people, etc. That can't be quantified.

I counted all the pros: 10.
Then counted all the cons: 9.
More pros than cons! Then stay in Canada!

Who was I kidding? I was sure to come up with more cons if I wanted to, and then again more pros!

I should do this exercise with the kids tonight and see what they come up with.

* * *

That night, I made *tinola* soup with green papaya and chicken. *Tinola* always gave me comfort. The light broth with ginger and garlic, the soft papaya, the wilted greens, slipped into my mouth, warming and soothing me like no other thing in the world, except maybe talking with God.

I overheard Bobby say to Sonia, "*Tinola* again?" "Shh... she's still sad. What do you think?" I pretended I didn't hear. I realized that we'd been having a version of *tinola* almost every day the past week, except the vegetables became spinach or bok choy, sometimes tomatoes were added, and the meat changed to pork. I decided to stop serving up my sadness to the kids. They deserve better. I also realized we've not had *pandesal* in a while. This is stupid. I must get some *pandesal* for breakfast.

After dinner, we created a list of pros and cons to staying in Canada. I came up with new cons and pros right away:

CONS
- The shame of being abandoned by your husband, which Bobby turned into a pro immediately.

PRO
- Bobby offered: family feeling better without the cheating of Manuel and Carla, it's all out in the open now

- I offered: Bobby has been a great brother and father in all this. I kissed Bobby when I pointed this out, and Bobby smiled, pleased with himself.

Manolita was very quiet. She blurted out: "I miss Dad!" Sonia wrote that down under con.

CON
- Manolita misses Dad.

"Why can't he just come home?" continued Manolita, who began to cry.

I held Manolita. Sonia began to cry too.

"We're gonna be okay here, Mom! We're staying, and this game stinks!" cried Bobby.

* * *

CHAPTER 15

Canada
Manuel, 1984

I didn't quite realize what had happened. My son turfed me out of my own home, and I couldn't do anything about it. I did a bad thing, I know. But Carla was so good to me, supportive, needing me, and so thankful to me. She was so attractive, and invited my attention every time. What could I do but yield? I didn't think it did any harm. There had been many kisses by that time: stolen touches, secret torrid skirmishes in the bathroom when no one was around. She was so good to me, made me feel like a man again. I ached at night, wishing it was Carla in bed with me. I was so tempted to make love with her in bed when everyone was away, but I could not bear to do it on the matrimonial bed. We did it on the sofa, the floor, the corridor, anywhere but the bed. Who would have thought Bobby would come home so early? He always came home late. I didn't mean to leave the kids — not Sonia, not Manolita.

Now it's all out. I had to live with the consequences. The first nights, I stayed at Mario's place. Ching was cold as ice to me. Carla's cousin employer was equally cold to Carla, blaming her for the 'problems with our men'. She accused Carla of being a 'husband stealer.' Within days, Carla found a basement bachelor suite where she moved. Then I moved in with her.

In the makeshift home that Carla made for us, I missed my family. What was I doing here, away from my family? Did I love Carla? I liked the way I was with her, I felt easy and relaxed. I liked the way she made me feel important, served my every need. Her dishes were so tasty; I know they were 'cooked with love' just like Josie's dishes when we lived in Manila. It seemed like such a long time ago. Josie had become sour, while Carla was so sweet. Carla needs me so much. I'll not let her down. She makes me want to aspire.

When I thought of Josie, all I could feel was hardness, nagging, scolding and impatience. With Josie, I felt small. She was no longer the sweet girl I knew and courted and loved. I knew she was only being strong for the family, but she had also grown cruel to me. I felt relief being away from those feelings. I missed the kids, especially Manolita and Sonia. I needed to talk to Josie.

I called her on the phone many times. No Josie. One time, Sonia picked up, and said Josie would not come to the phone. The other time, I called and I knew that was Josie on the line, but she hung up.

I visited one afternoon. Sonia and Manolita had just arrived from school. The red Toyota was not parked in the usual location, so I knew Josie was not in. Through Sonia's arrangements, I visited twice a week without Josie or Bobby knowing. That didn't last long, as Manolita one day talked about going to the park with me, and that was the end of the visits.

I sent Josie flowers, which were swiftly returned. I waited for her at the church door on Sunday to talk to her. When she saw me, she turned and walked away in another direction. I sent her a letter. It was returned unopened.

The basement suite had become more and more pleasant, with Carla finding furniture from various places. We had a bed now, a small couch, and a dining table with two chairs. I felt guilty for all the costs she incurred, but Carla insisted that they cost close to nothing, being throwaways from friends, church, and garage sales. I knew my savings would be depleted soon, with a new rental cost to pay, in addition to my family's rent. I decided to get a job, any job would do.

I noticed a sign at the local liquor store, advertising for a "stacker." I inquired at the store about it, and they gave me the job posting. The wage was $10 an hour, which was $1600 a month with benefits. That's like 16,000 pesos a month! Better than my engineering take at the height of my career. I was astounded. And there was no pressure about buildings falling. Not bad. I looked at the store, peeked behind the stacks, and saw where the stackers worked. I liked that they were hidden from view. None of my friends would see me. Why didn't I think about this sooner? I filled in an application form.

"Whatever you do, don't say you have an engineering degree," advised Paquito.

"What then did I finish?" I asked.

"High school," said Paquito.

"What if they ask about his experience?" asked Mario.

"Say you've been doing labour jobs in construction, you know, like the jobs you used to supervise," said Paquito.

"What if they say, 'why aren't you doing construction work?'" asked Mario.

"Then say you're not certified for construction labour. Just say you are strong and healthy and can lift big boxes, and that you are hardworking and reliable. You have a family to feed. Whatever. Just bullshit. Make it sound like you're very excited about this job!" said Paquito.

"And don't wear a suit, for heaven's sake," reminded Paquito.

The interview turned out easier than I anticipated.

Mr. Nesbitt was about the same age as me. What surprised me was his question, "Why do you have such good English if you've been here only less than a year?" I didn't realize that my English was considered very good. I explained that English was the medium of instruction in schools in the Philippines, which impressed Mr. Nesbitt. I had taken my English proficiency completely for granted.

And the other surprise question: How much do you drink? I figured what the desired answer was: not much. "How much," he asked? "Couple beers on the weekend with my friends," was my answer.

"Why would he ask that?" I asked Paquito when we debriefed the interview.

"If you liked your drink too much, you might be tempted to steal a few," he said.

I considered the possibility and understood. The temptation would be great.

When I got the call offering me the job, I was so happy I cried. The job assured me of my manhood, brought back a feeling of self-respect. I celebrated with Carla, Paquito and his wife Ludy over a bucket of Kentucky Fried Chicken. The next day, I visited Sonia and Manolita, and told Sonia the news. I gave Sonia an envelope with cash. I felt like a father again.

That same night, I found the envelope under the door of our basement suite, and scribbled in Bobby's handwriting: "We don't need your money!"

It pained me to see Bobby hate me so much. I wrote a letter to Josie.

* * *

CHAPTER 16

Canada
Josie, 1984

I had not been answering Manuel's phone calls. But Sonia seemed so happy about her dad's getting a job, so I opened the thick envelope. I was pleased that Manuel got a job, and pleased that he cared enough to send us some money. I knew that Bobby would have the money returned. I considered not telling him about the envelope, but he already got the news from Manolita. Bobby insisted on returning the money. "Aren't we making enough money to make ends meet? Does he think he can buy his way back to us?" Bobby took off and personally delivered the envelope.

When a second, thin envelope came next day, I felt tempted to open it. I let it stay in my purse unopened for a day. I did not let Bobby know about it. On the third day, I decided to open it.

My dearest Josie,

I hope you will read this letter. I will not give up. I love you and our children. I made a big mistake. I wish we could get back together again. My feelings for Carla are different than my feelings for you. She is hurt and she needs me. She loves me and I have feelings for her. Our relationship makes me feel worthwhile. I need to continue to support her. But I don't love her the way I love you. What would you like for me to do so you would accept me back?

I'm now working at the liquor store as a stacker. I miss you and the kids.

Loving you always,
Manuel

I wished I didn't read the letter. I couldn't believe it. I was livid with anger, and wrote this:

How dare you have feelings for that woman and expect me to take you back? You are my husband and the father of your children. She needs you? Your kids need you! I need you to help me with our life. We should be the first and only priority for you. You have been cheating with her all this time and lying to me. And there you are living with that woman, and asking to come back to us! What about your vows? Stop writing me, and asking to come back. If you continue to live with that woman, forget seeing the kids again. I will not have you coming here ever again!

I reread the letter and folded it, slipped it inside an envelope, then cried. I decided to sleep on it and send it the next day. I prayed fervently that night. I struggled finding a patron saint to pray to who might bring Manuel back, without Carla. St. Monica was the closest, for she bore the trials of a drunken faithless husband who eventually returned to her. St. Monica's son was St Augustine, who was wayward himself and later converted to Christianity and became a great saint. I thought of Bobby and his conversion to a good father figure, and decided St. Monica would do just fine. I also prayed to St. Joseph, Mary's husband. He was the ideal husband. I prayed to St. Elizabeth, Queen of Portugal who had an unfaithful husband estranged from their son, just like Manuel and Bobby. I ended up praying into the wee hours of the night, what with all the saints to pray to and the novenas in their honour. I wished a live saint like Sr. Redempta were here to talk things over with.

* * *

The next day, I went to Mass early in the morning and prayed for guidance.

I saw a priest enter the confessional box. I could go to confession and seek advice. I opened the door of the confessional and knelt.

"Bless me Father, for I have sinned. My last confession was a month ago."

I saw that the priest was Father Carlos.

"Hello, Josie. God bless you. Please continue," Father Carlos said.

"Father, my husband has left us for another woman. He is living with her. I feel sometimes I drove him to adultery because I was too hard on him to get a job. Maybe I was too proud that I was doing better than him and put him down. Maybe that's why he got attracted to someone else. He says he loves that woman in a different way from how he loves me. He says he wants to continue a relationship with this woman because she needs him, but he also wants to come back to our family. I don't know what to do. I don't feel I can trust him anymore. He has hurt me so much. I don't feel that I love him anymore. My eldest and second children are okay I think, but my little girl misses him very much. What should I do, Father?"

Father Carlos was quiet for a moment.

"Take him back. Didn't he say he loves you, and he loves this woman in another way because this woman needs him? You are blessed with gifts by God. You can afford to share your husband with someone who needs him. You are being selfish to want him all to yourself when he is helping another person. Jealousy is a capital sin. He wants to be with you and his family. He merely wants to help another person along the way," said Father Carlos.

"But Father, he is not just helping her, he is fucking her as well, pardon my language, Father," I cried in frustration.

"Shhh. How do you know that he is…doing that with her?" asked Father Carlos.

"My son caught them in the act!"

"Good God!" said Father Carlos. He continued unperturbed.

"But now that he is asking to return, maybe he will give up that part of the relationship. Maybe you can ask him to promise that, and if he does, give him another chance. We are all human and imperfect, and if God can forgive those who put him to death, how much more for us imperfect beings? We should forgive one another's frailty," said Father Carlos.

I felt a knot in my chest. My body resisted everything Father Carlos was asking.

"Father that's too hard to do! I can't do it!" I said.

"Set aside your pride, Josie and think of your children who need their father. Your forgiveness will soften his heart to you, and maybe even cause him to lose interest in the other woman," said Father Carlos. I felt sick. Defeated.

"I'll think about it, Father," I finally said.

"One Our Father and three Hail Mary's. God be with you, Josie," Father Carlos said and closed the curtain on his side.

I talked to Lily. To Ching. To Mario. To Sonia. Bobby.

I decided to see a lawyer.

* * *

CHAPTER 17

Canada
Manuel, 1984–1990

I was surprised that a week passed, and my letter to Josie was still unreturned. I felt a little hope.

I finally made the appointment to see the Association of Professional Engineers of BC. "Just say APE," I told Carla, who could not say all of it in one go. I had finally assembled my transcript of records from the university, my detailed work experience and my work references.

"You built quite a few buildings within only a year of graduation," said Mr. Bartlett of APE.

"Oh yes, my father is a big contractor in the Philippines and is well known," I confirmed with pride.

"How do you mean? Do you mean that it's your father's contracted buildings that you design?" asked Mr. Bartlett.

"Well, not really, not always. Some yes. But you see, if they know him, I am more likely to get the job," I boasted.

"Do you mean you got the job because they knew your father's work was quality, and therefore your work would be quality too?" Mr. Bartlett asked.

"No, well yes. It just works that way. If you know people, more jobs will come your way, because they know you," I explained.

Mr. Bartlett seemed confused, but let it go.

"How were you able to design a building before you graduated?" Mr. Bartlett asked.

"Well, I was working with my father, and there were many engineers on the job. I worked for them."

"I see, so you were assisting them — you were not the engineer in charge."

"Yes." I was becoming irritated.

"So this statement is incorrect?" Mr. Bartlett crossed out something on my resume and wrote over it.

"Are you saying that I'm lying?" I felt heat at the back of my neck.

"I'm only saying that the way it is written here suggests you were in charge..."

I interrupted. "So how are you supposed to say it then?"

"Mr. del Mundo, please, I don't mean disrespect. I was only clarifying the scope of your work in these projects."

"You're interrogating me like I'm a criminal. Why don't you believe me? Because I'm not white? Because I come from the Philippines? Don't you know I've built buildings bigger than the ones you have in this city?" I cried. I was enraged. I stabbed the desk with my finger to make the point, and started to stand up. Suddenly, my chest tightened and I could barely breathe. I clutched at my shirt and began to fall. Mr. Bartlett came around to my side of the desk and sat me down. He called for help, opened my shirt to let me breathe and fanned me with a magazine.

I felt my breathing come back. Someone came with a glass of water. I took a sip.

"Are you ok? Shall we take you to the hospital?" asked Mr. Bartlett.

"No, no. Just leave me alone please. I'll be fine."

"Are you sure? We can call an ambulance."

"No. Please." I did not want to spend one more second in that room.

"Just get me a taxi, and I'll go home."

"We can do this another time," said Mr. Bartlett.

In the taxi, I felt relief to get away. The refreshing wind from the open window of the taxi contrasted with Mr. Bartlett's claustrophobic office. I still felt the sting of the man's questions. I felt so insulted I swore never to go back there again. Who do they think they are? I massaged my chest, wondering whether I had a heart attack of some kind. I should be more careful.

* * *

I felt excited and nervous about my first day at UBC. I had applied to take one engineering course in the Civil Engineering Program, "just to see what it was like."

I refused to go back to APE to continue discussion of my credentials. I was closed to the idea of re-studying for an engineering degree in Canada. A Filipino engineer, now practising in Canada as an engineer after redoing engineering courses, dropped the suggestion to sample one course. "Just see for yourself, for your own peace of mind, how your knowledge measures up against the Canadian standard," he said. I agreed that one course wouldn't hurt.

Carla urged me to accept her money to help out with tuition, but I would not accept. I used some from my Philippine savings, and some from my salary at the liquor store.

School was not what I expected. I did not feel like I belonged in that class at UBC. My classmates were all young boys and girls who talked strange and partied. They mocked my achievements or didn't believe me when I told them of the buildings I designed. I thought that the professor didn't know what he was talking about. I had no friends there. There was no one worthy. I had already built great institutional buildings and commercial buildings, and they had just started to learn the principles of building.

Every time I opened my mouth to answer a question of the professor, the group of young boys snickered. I knew they called me 'prof' behind my back.

It became so that I hated going to school, and found excuses to miss school. The liquor store asked me to come in earlier today, do different hours, more hours. I already know the course lecture today; why bother to attend.

"If you don't like it, why continue?" asked Carla.

"I've already invested the tuition money, I should at least get the credits," I said.

"Will you pass if you don't attend?"

"I'll attend the exams. I'll pass those for sure." I wondered whether I would in fact.

I kept having dreams of finding out at the end of the term that I had enrolled for courses I never attended. I woke up to realize I had barely attended the one course I enrolled in.

In the end, I felt so unconnected to the course, the university, the classmates and the instructor that I dropped out of the course rather than complete and fail it.

Later on, I avoided meeting Filipino engineers who held engineering jobs. I had no excuse to offer those who went back to school and are now full engineers with prestigious jobs and good pay. I felt embarrassed for giving up so easily, yet I always managed some excuse. "But that engineer was married to a nurse who had a good income," or "that engineer had no kids then, while I have several," I explained to Carla, forgetting that I gave my family no support. I developed more and more reasons to justify the decision to drop out of school, and became more and more convinced of the rightness of my views.

I am a different man now, I convinced myself. A professional job is not the most important thing. After all, in Canada, labour jobs pay well enough. My measure of a man was already established as an engineer. I need not prove that again. A job is a job, and it has dignity if you do it well. I figured I was onto another phase in my life, a more mature phase, one based not on job prestige, but on having a simple life.

* * *

We lived a life of ordinary pleasures and work, Carla and I. But anything set me off; my fuse became increasingly short.

Carla liked to serve the freshest things from the grocery, and grocery shopping was a trip we often did together.

One day, Carla was in the fruit section checking out the green grapes. An older Caucasian woman approached her and said, "You're not supposed to touch the grapes! You should just go back where you belong!" she hissed.

I saw it all and heard the remark.

I came toward the woman and said, "Do you own the grapes? This is where we belong. And you, old lady — are you sure you belong here, or did you skip out of a mental institution?"

I didn't realize that people were beginning to gather around the scene. I felt Carla pull me away saying, "Let's go, she doesn't know what she's talking about."

"No, the trouble with you is you don't stand up for your rights, Carla. That's why they'll always treat us badly. We don't stand up to them," I shouted to the people gathered about.

"Yes, but not this way," said Carla pulling me farther away.

* * *

At the liquor store, I was a diligent worker. Once, my supervisor checked the number of boxes and bottles in the delivery stated in my report, by counting the actual bottles and cartons on the display stands. When I saw what he was doing, I protested. "I can buy my own beer you know. You think I can't buy my own beer?"

"I'm not accusing you. This is my job," said my supervisor. "Are you alright?" he continued.

"No. I'm not alright." I left work early.

At home, I invited Paquito and some other buddies for drinks. We drank *tagay*, each one downing a shot in one gulp, and passing on the glass to the next one, who does the same. Carla prepared our favourite *pulutans*: barbecue on a stick, *chicharron*, dried squid, fried tofu soaked in vinegar and garlic. Everyone was having a great relaxing time, exchanging stories and jokes.

"Hey, did you hear about your ex? Heard she has a new boyfriend," someone said.

I stiffened.

"Yeah?" I asked. "So who?"

"I don't know. Actually, umm... maybe it's just gossip."

"You bet it's just idle gossip," said Paquito.

"Then why did you start the story?" I stood up, bearing down on the guy who began the story.

"Hey, enough of that" said Paquito, pulling me away.

Stumbling Through Paradise

"Here's another drink. Can you bring us more ice, Carla?" continued Paquito, changing the subject.

* * *

CHAPTER 18

Canada
Josie, 1985–1990

I became a minor celebrity in the Filipino community after winning the Mrs. Philippines contest. I graced fiestas wearing Filipino costume dresses such as *patajongs, barong gowns* and *batik sarongs*. A Mrs. Philippines sash hung across my chest, and a small tiara sat on my head. I met all the dignitaries at these events — city councillors, MLAs and MPs, local Filipino businessmen and businesswomen and community leaders. I gave them my business card as catering operator each time. I kept a Rolodex of business cards of people I met, and after the event, I gave them a call to let them know about my business and to offer them a special price. I advertised in the local Filipino community rags — there were at least four of them — and I featured my own picture in Mrs. Philippines costume on my advertisement. The orders I got more than made up for the cost of advertising. Lily made it all happen. She sold so many tickets, which made me win. Bobby too. My shyness about this whole thing disappeared after I won, and after the orders increased by so much, I had to expand my crew.

I subcontracted special dishes to different people so that I only needed to call in orders and the dishes would be ready. I didn't need to cook myself. I planned menus, ordered the different dishes, assembled them in one place, took care to present them beautifully, delivered them and sometimes served them with some help from other subcontractors. I was the face of the operation, the promoter, the organizer and the one who paid everybody else. I felt proud that I was able to give extra income to caregivers who earned very little and had so many mouths to feed back home. Drivers and servers also earned extra incomes from me.

So successful was the business that other caregivers asked me to help them establish their own businesses. I showed them how with a specific project: a cookbook featuring each one of their specialty dishes. Everyone got excited with the project. They came up with titles like "Comfort Food for the *Pinoy* Soul," "*Adobo* Planet," "*Balut* and *Bagoong* and other Brave Acts." I offered: "Cooked with Love." They chose that one.

Our successful advocacy for Carla about her employment rights became well known, and other caregivers came to me with similar cases. I referred them to the same lawyer: Harvey Falcon at the Pro Bono Law Society of BC. One day, Harvey asked me if I would assemble a group of caregivers to take courses about employee rights.

I thought it was brilliant. Put them in one room and give them the information about their rights. That early knowledge will help prevent abuse from happening. But how will they pay for these courses? They don't have much money. They send all of their money home to their families.

Harvey explained, "The Law Society lawyers can give the courses for free. I can assemble a group of lawyers to teach the courses, make a schedule and we can do it here in our office, if you bring in the caregivers."

"Just like that?" I asked. I began to understand the kindness of Canadian society, why they call it Paradise, and for once fully believed it.

In no time, a group of 25 caregivers came to the first course, and the courses became regular. The caregivers organized themselves into a group that eventually became the Caring for Caregivers Society, with myself as one of their advisers. The caregivers assembled often at my home, which became a hub of activity for planning parties, picnics, courses and the place to bring troubles to.

A caregiver had just arrived, and the employer who was supposed to pick her up and give her a job was nowhere in sight. Could she stay somewhere while she looked for her employer?

A caregiver was very ill and on her deathbed, and her mother in the Philippines wanted to be with her in Canada. Could someone help to facilitate the mother's visa?

A caregiver in her first month in Canada was diagnosed with cancer. She had no health benefits, as she was not working. How could she work when she was sick? She would have to go home to the Philippines where she would get even less care. Could they help raise funds for her hospital care?

A caregiver was experiencing abuse, but could not leave the job until she had another one. She didn't want to complain because her employer would not give her a reference, and she would not be able to find another job. Could they help find another job for her quickly?

I was astounded with the amount of troubles caregivers faced. I began to see my troubles as small in comparison. Harvey helped to form the caregivers into a non-profit society so that they could raise funds to provide for some of these needs. I looked about for an office for the group, as our home was no longer adequate. I met Anna, a former caregiver who had now become owner and operator of a successful and popular Filipino retail store. She offered a corner room in the retail store as free office space for the caregivers. The group was delighted and launched the office space and Society with a party. They invited Filipino media. The Society was written up in the Filipino community papers, and pretty soon, many caregivers dropped in for help, so much so that they needed a professional coordinator to be available round the clock. Harvey helped them prepare a grant proposal asking for funds to support a part-time coordinator.

Sonia was privy to all of these activities. She, of all my children, took most interest. She always asked me about their stories, why they had such problems, and saw how some of the problems were solved. She sought Anna, the former caregiver turned successful businesswoman, and asked her how she did it, while so many others had problems. Sonia absorbed everything like a sponge.

Sonia was also our link to Manuel. She brought Manolita to visit Manuel, and accompanied Manolita at home while Manuel visited. She brought us stories of 'the other side.'

"Dad is always angry, and short-tempered. I miss my laughing Dad. It has something to do with his job, no longer being an engineer. When I grow up, I'll find out how to help him." Dear Lord, thank you for Sonia.

I still had not resolved my situation with Manuel. My lawyer advised me to file for divorce, but I could not do it.

The Catholic religion forbids divorce, and I could not imagine asking to sever the ties that bound Manuel and me, even if he was already living with someone else. Annulment? That meant our kids are bastards. I shuddered at the thought. I did not miss Manuel much anymore, having developed a full and busy life. As for Father Carlos's advice, I just could not execute it. I prayed for grace that one day I might be the saint Father Carlos wanted me to be.

I left things as they were. I turned a blind eye to the kids seeing Manuel from time to time. Bobby himself had become busy with his schoolwork and business of landscaping maintenance that he did not pay too much attention to the Manuel issue so long as he did not hear about it.

In this state, life rolled along.

* * *

Several years passed. My business prospered. I expanded to packaging food products that were popular and difficult to make at home: *tocino, longganisa, hamonado, achara*. I created my own brand "Plates of Paradise" with the Mrs. Philippines image in the corner of every package. I gave my full attention to marketing, something I realized that I enjoyed. My business expanded to other cities in Canada and the US.

With Bobby's business growing as well, we bought a comfortable three-bedroom house in Vancouver.

I began to mentor other caregivers on how to set up their own businesses — how to secure cleaning contracts, how to market their talent such as sewing dresses, and even for Mario, his singing talent. I saw the power of being connected with a broader network of people beyond the Filipino community, and urged my friends to open their eyes, expand and connect with their neighborhoods and businesses, not stick to Filipinos only.

I felt for the caregivers who helped me in the business, and often thought of Carla, and her loss of family to a violent end. I almost felt ready to forgive her in my heart, but something always pulled me back. Carla may be in need, but she stole my husband. I had to remind myself.

As for Manuel, I felt torn. I had no feelings left for him, and never spoke to him again since the letter. But something hung over my head: our good times together, the fact that he fathered our children. Do I still love him? My bitterness had begun to fade. Prayers helped create an absence of hate, but was there a presence of love? Had I maybe forgiven him in my heart? Lord, show me the way. When it is time, when he is over her, when he is the same Manuel I knew, I will let him come back to us. I promise.

The children had grown used to the situation. I felt sadness about it all, but in the end knew it was better this way, peaceful and uncomplicated.

Various men courted me, but I was not interested. The thrill of romance was replaced by the thrill of chasing success. I felt content with the satisfaction of a peaceful home, a hearth full of the warmth of my children growing up well.

Bobby flourished in his landscaping maintenance business and expanded into development. With the help of Ken Davidson, president of Westcan Development Company, one of the biggest land developers in Surrey, Bobby learned the business. They met at an event I catered. Ken was very impressed by Bobby, took him under his wing and introduced him around. Bobby learned to buy fixer-uppers, renovate them and sell for a profit. Later, he learned to buy land cheap, subdivide them into smaller lots, and then sell them for a profit.

But there was always an air of mystery around Bobby. There was just too much money it seems. How could a landscaping business allow him to buy whole properties? The math didn't seem to add up. But I was too comfortable to pay attention.

Manolita, now 15 years old, had become a popular singer in Philippine community circles. She was in grade 10, having skipped grades two times. She spoke no Tagalog and held no interest in learning it. She played soccer, joined the drama club, and was star debater at the forensics club. She was already curious about politics since the class played roles as City Councillors and Mayor once. She planned to take up law and become "the first woman anything" — Mayor, Premier or Prime Minister of Canada.

Sonia, on the other hand, had become an activist. She believed "partisan politics was the barrier to real social change." As far as she was concerned, "skilled immigrants continue to be underutilized," their skills wasted — just like her Dad's. None of the parties offered any real solutions to curtail the power of professional associations and the "systemic discrimination within the system." Sonia took up communication and cross-cultural diversity courses at UBC. She held symposiums to highlight business strategies and communication styles of different cultures, and the issues of immigrants. Sonia believed intensely, and there was not much that she had no strong opinion about. I worry about her.

Manuel and Carla continued to live together, Manuel working with the liquor store, and Carla continued caregiving. I didn't care. I was busy. I had grown used to my independent life.

* * *

CHAPTER 19

Canada
Josie, 1991

It had been 10 years since we arrived in Canada. It was Mario who later told me about Manuel's birthday party, which brought the disaster to my doorstep.

A party was held in honour of Manuel's 46th birthday at Paquito's house. The table was laid with all of Manuel s favourites: chicken BBQ with *achara*, fried tofu in garlic vinegar, adobo with coconut, chilli and shrimp paste and *guinatan*. Carla and Manuel were encircled by happy well wishers.

"A toast for 46-year-old man who drinks like he's 36!"

"And fucks like one too!" Roars of laughter.

"A toast for 10 years in Canada!"

"In Paradise!"

"A toast to my beautiful sweet darling," Manuel, already inebriated, kissed Carla.

"And a new baby!" Manuel rubbed Carla's tummy.

"Congrats, *utol*," beamed Mario.

"Well, it's good you can start again with another boy, one who's not a criminal," said someone.

Manuel was surprised. "What did you say?"

"Bobby's into drugs big time. I know. My nephew said he worked for him. Apparently, started a long time ago, with the Diablos."

"What? *Putangina!* That *putangina* forced me out of my own home when he was drug dealer? He had no right! All this time, a drug dealer, and he pushed me out of my house?" Manuel started laughing and suddenly stopped, like a bulb lit up in his mind. He ran inside, and when he came out, he was holding a gun.

"Where are you going? Give me that gun," cried Carla, but Manuel had already pocketed it.

He climbed behind the wheel of his Ford Taurus. Mario and Paquito ran behind and jumped into the car.

"Where are we going?" asked Mario.

"I'll show that bastard. Who's the big hero now?" Manuel muttered, speeding away.

It was almost midnight when I heard the doorbell continuously ring and someone was banging on the door. I felt alarmed. When I opened the door, there was Manuel with Mario and Paquito.

"What's the matter?" I cried.

"Where's your son? Our son?" Manuel demanded with a crazed look.

"Upstairs sleeping. Why, what's wrong?" I asked.

Manuel pushed me away and ran upstairs followed by Mario and Paquito. I heard him opening and closing doors. I caught up with him in Bobby's room.

Manuel shook Bobby from his sleep and said, "Hey druggie, wake up. How many injections did you have today ha? Wake up!" Manuel pulled him down onto the floor, and kicked him. "Wake up, druggie!"

Stumbling Through Paradise

Mario and Paquito restrained Manuel. I put myself between Manuel and Bobby.

"What are you doing, mad man?" I cried.

"Don't you know? This great big hero son of yours is a drug pusher? And a drug user, since all the way when he was 15. All that time, making me look like the devil, but he, he was the devil. Such a big shot, ha? All the time. Dirty money."

Manuel kicked and screamed while Bobby began to back away from an uncontrolled Manuel.

"What else could I do? You left us. And even when you were here, you were useless! We had to fend for ourselves. So I dealt in drugs. It kept us alive while you went fucking around!" screamed Bobby.

Suddenly Manuel had the gun in his raised hand. Hands reached over trying to grab the gun. Then he started to choke. The gun fell on the bed. He held his chest with both hands, not able to breathe. He fell back, caught by Mario and Paquito. His eyes looked ahead unseeing, his body stopped struggling, and he became still.

The house broke into chaos. The ambulance came and rushed Manuel to the hospital. But it was no use. Manuel suffered a massive fatal heart attack.

* * *

I stared at the stranger in the coffin. Poor Manuel, how time ravaged you. Are you listening to me Manuel? I know your spirit is alive and listening.

Manuel it's me, Josie. Can you hear me? You're the only man I loved: did you know that?

Did his head move imperceptibly? Did he nod? Was that a hot expulsion of a breath?

I wished his eyes would open to see me say: "I've always loved only you."

I could almost hear the words from his cracked entombed lips: Forgive. Is that what he said?

"Yes, yes," I said. "And me. Can you forgive me?" I felt long unshed tears running down my face.

But there was no movement on the grey face. No answer. The connection was dead.

"I forgive you, Manuel. Please forgive me," I implored.

My tears rushed out like waters from a broken dam. I could not see his face through my tears.

* * *

At the funeral, the audience was hushed, the room full. On the first row sat our family, including Ben and Lolita del Mundo, who had flown from the Philippines to attend the funeral.

Manolita stood erect and sang Manuel's favourite song.

> *Somewhere over the rainbow, way up high*
> *There's a land that I've heard of once in a lullaby.*
> *Somewhere over the rainbow, skies are blue*
> *And the dreams that you dare to dream,*
> *Really do come true.*

* * *

When everybody left, I sat on the front pew, exhausted. I heard the door behind the hall open. Sonia let Carla in, and together they walked towards the coffin. In profile, Carla's protruding stomach was much more visible.

I discovered only then that she was pregnant.

Sonia and Carla stood beside the coffin in the dim light.

I stood up and walked towards them.

I stood beside Carla who was now weeping.

I whispered in Carla's ear a consolation I wished someone could say to me: "Thank you for making him happy."

"What will I do now, *Ate*?" cried Carla.

"Don't worry," I said. "It'll be okay." The words just came out of me. Were they there all this time? It felt good to let them out.

Carla looked up at me.

"Yes. I'll help you," I said.

Carla embraced me, weeping.

I felt her tears rain upon my parched earth.

I looked down on the peace of Manuel's body, the unspoken gratitude, the mercy.

I prayed for strength to make good my own.

* * *

PART 2
SONIA AND BOBBY'S SEARCH:

The Scent of Black Cigarettes and Money

CHAPTER 1

Canada
Sonia, 2001

As I begin to tell this, the sky is cold blue and white, the sun a pale blurred circle underneath the clouds. It looks crisp out there on this typical October day in Vancouver, and the waters of False Creek are placid. The geodesic dome of Science World welcomes everyone to Vancouver's City Centre with its winking lights. Inside the condo, the artificial fireplace is burning off real heat. I can hear the whirring of grilling tools in the background, another kind of whirring from the SkyTrain rolling below me, and still another from the trucks lumbering by. I hear a more shrill type of whirring, from yet another part of the building under renovation. It seems the air around me is full of sounds, yet it is so silent in the room. I just finished reading Alistair MacLeod's *No Great Mischief*. The last line rings in my head: "All of us are better when we're loved."

Could my brother have lived a different life if he were loved by my father? When did Bobby know that he was not loved by my father? Did my father always not love Bobby, or did it happen years later when he became disconsolate and a failure? Did he always fear that Bobby would take his place, did he always know that in his bones, when Bobby grew up so handsome, so confident and cocky, so laughing in his face? Did my father not love him on the first sign that my mother loved Bobby more than him? Or believed more in Bobby? Could my father have been looking for love from Bobby? Fathers need to be loved too.

My father must have felt invisible — to employers of engineers, that official who evaluated his credentials, and his young classmates in the lone engineering class he attempted to attend. It ate him up, so that every time, he saw it in people's eyes, that non-recognition, that demeaning look. When he did not get quite what he wanted, his explanation was that they considered him not a man, less than a man. They did not see him, the real him, the bright engineer from an affluent Manila family, with important influential friends in society. What did he think people saw then? An insignificant, poor, uneducated immigrant, who considered himself better than others for no reason. The thing is, obsessed by how people saw him, did my father become that person eventually?

I will always remember the way Mom's face changed. The way her face looked, seeing my father no longer breathing in that coffin. It was the face of someone who realized that all was in fact lost forever. With his last breath, he took away something she was still hoping for, and now was no longer possible. Did she mean to, want to, or hope to get back together with my father? Or did she only want his apology, maybe a declaration of love from him? She too must have needed his love. I always asked her why she did not remarry. She just shrugged, waving me away as though it was the least important thing to worry about. Did she want his forgiveness, and now that was no longer possible? Forgiveness for what?

For denying him a life with his children, I suppose, for not giving him another chance? I remember how she fell into a silence for days after his death. She lay on the bed, her arm on her forehead, staring into the ceiling. In the middle of dinner, I remember how she would stop chewing her food, her hands suddenly still with the spoon and fork, like a film tape that has been stopped, her eyes trained on a spot that was not in front of her but somewhere perhaps in the back of her mind, in a place she is searching for, as though she was almost there, but that it slipped away.

I remember how confusing it was for me who thought my mother crossed my father from our lives for good all these years. How admirably she forged onward with our lives. Why would his death affect her so? I didn't know very much then I guess; 23 is such a foolish age, anyway. Hurtling into anything, everything, mindlessly, seeing but not really seeing, except oneself at the centre of the world. I remember feeling relief about my father's death, who had become for me almost an embarrassment.

I hated having to be with my father and Carla in their house full of crocheted doilies, artificial roses dusty with time, velvet paintings of sunsets with carabao silhouettes in the foreground. Not my father's taste for sure. Manolita and I came for the obligatory second Thanksgiving dinner, or Christmas dinner, or Easter. They always made a big effort preparing the dinner, making a great feast of *lechon, hamonado, pancit*, grilled *bangus*, fruit salad, *kinilaw* and coconut chicken with chili, even for just the four of us. I remember how little got eaten, for Manolita only really cared for hamburgers, fried chicken and steaks, and I could not handle too much spicy foods and fatty, oily foods. How Carla insisted on wrapping the leftovers for us, saying, "For your mom, so she does not have to cook. Isn't it enough that she cooks for others all the time?" Or, "For Bobby, doesn't he miss *lechon*?" Or, "For you, because you are getting too skinny, so you don't have to buy your lunch at work. Do you even have lunch? Maybe you are working too hard? Your mother doesn't feed you much, does she? She is too busy, is she?" Or, "For Manolita, how can you not eat *bangus*? Have you forgotten you're a Filipina? You're not a Filipino if you don't eat *bangus* and *lechon*." We came home with a big bag of food that would stay a long time in the fridge, until Bobby invited his friends and had a party on the food, with beer and vodka.

In a way, I miss those dinners. Seeing my father look after Carla like a child, and Carla looking after my father like her prized guest, felt new, refreshing in its own way. It was so unlike any relationships I knew among our family or friends. How she treated him never changed, from when they started to live together, until he died. She treated him with the dedicated and unquestioning service a maid gives a hotel customer, or a rich employer. But he never demeaned her like a rich employer would a maid, but rather like a teacher to a pupil. He held her ignorance, or lack of taste or knowledge of things as merely opportunities to educate her more. I think that in Carla, my father found the person who needed him, with all his imperfections, needed him just the same. A man is better when he is needed.

Stephen said to me once, "That's what I like about you: you are so complete, so independent, never needing anyone, so strong." He loved me because I didn't need him. That was our first month together. Last week, he said, "That's the problem with you: you are so complete, so right in everything, you don't need anyone, everyone's just in your way, I'm in your way." Then he left, because I didn't need him. It wasn't me that changed — only his attitude to my not needing him. Before, it was attractive; now, it is repulsive. I'm sorry for not needing you, Stephen.

The phone is ringing, but I feel weary and do not feel like answering it. It will only be Mom asking how I am. Or Bobby. Or another emergency from work. I let it ring until I hear the message.

"Sonia. We have a situation. A big group of Filipino seniors are here waiting for you. Seems like they're farm workers, and they haven't been paid for months. Come right away. Oh, and a call from CBC. They want to interview you about Bamboo Network. Where are you anyway?" Marietta. No one better to hold the fort. Lucky for us.

I should call Stephen. The farm workers sound like they'll need a lawyer. I have no energy to talk to him. I drag myself from the sofa and pick up the phone. "Mariets. I'm on my way. Call Stephen. Ask him to join us with the farm workers. I'll be there in 30 minutes."

I make my way to the bathroom to shower, get dressed, go to work and face the day. The Immigrant Communities Collective. How far we have come. Seems the more programs we offer, the more problems come out of the woodwork. Before ICC, where did they go? My own father went nowhere. At least they've got ICC now.

* * *

I am sitting behind my desk at the ICC, the phone tucked against my right shoulder, talking to the CBC interviewer as I watch the street outside. It is overcast but dry, and few people are walking the street.

"So why Bamboo Network?" asks the interviewer.

"Bamboo is a plant that survives the strongest storms because it bends with the wind. It grows profusely in Asia where many immigrants to Canada come from. Immigrants succeed when they are like the bamboo — resilient, flexible and connected to each other and Canadians in a helping network," I answer.

"How is it a helping network?"

"We have so many skilled immigrants arriving in Canada, yet very few of them are able to practise their professions. The engineer from India ends up driving taxis, the nurse from the Philippines works as a cleaner in hospitals or a caregiver. Why? Many reasons. But one of them is the lack of understanding of how professions are regulated in Canada, and not knowing how to look for jobs here. Newcomers apply for jobs in their field, but no one responds to their applications. For many of them, it's a mystery how to get jobs in their field. So, running out of savings, they take the first job that is offered, usually an unskilled labour job. Nothing wrong with these jobs, except newcomers are not utilizing their full potential, nor is Canada utilizing the full potential of skilled immigrants.

"Enter the Bamboo Network. We provide newcomers with mentors, people in various professions, many of them immigrants themselves who are now practicing their professions. Or they may be professionals who have lived in Canada all their lives and wish to help immigrants practise their professions."

"Mentors? What do they do?"

"Mentors work with newly arrived immigrants. Mentors explain the types of jobs available in the newcomer's profession, where you can apply for them, who regulates the profession and how. Mentors refer jobs to their mentees, coach them on their resumes, practise interviews with them, and sometimes provide them a personal reference. Often, mentors and mentees become friends for life."

"And what are your results so far?"

"We now have engineer newcomers getting entry-level engineering jobs at companies where the mentor works, for example. The mentor's introduction, referral and coaching help the newcomers get the job. The job may not be at the newcomer's level, but it is at least in his field, where he can have the chance to show his full abilities and work his way up.

"Sometimes, the newcomer may not yet get a job in his profession, but with the friendly coaching of the mentor, he begins to understand how foreign credentials get evaluated, and why the process is needed. Accepting and cooperating with the process helps him a lot, psychologically. Pretty soon, the newcomer decides to take courses which would lead him to practise his profession, or volunteer at a civic committee which engages his professional skill as a volunteer. For us, this embarking on a process to practise one's profession is in itself a positive result, even without an actual, paying job in the field. The process will get him there eventually."

"Bamboo Network sounds like a great idea. What inspired you to create this program?"

"My father was a successful engineer in Manila, but could not practise engineering here. It broke his confidence, it tore our family apart, and in the end, he died broken because of it. I was only 13 when we arrived in Vancouver and saw my father change from a successful and confident man to a failed, angry, and bitter man, and I promised myself that I would do something about this." My voice started to break.

"You are an inspiration yourself, and I'm sure your father would be very proud of you now. How can people use this wonderful program?"

"All they need to do is drop by our office at the Immigrant Communities Collective in Vancouver, or call for an appointment."

"Is there anything you want to say to our audience before we say goodbye?"

"To skilled immigrants, don't give up hope. There is a way to realize your dreams in Canada, learn it and implement it. We can help. And for everyone else, we invite you to be mentors in the Bamboo Network. Call us or drop by. It's easy to be a mentor, and satisfying. You can help make a difference in someone's life, build friendships, and contribute to a strong Canada."

"That was excellent Sonia. It's a wrap. It'll air tomorrow. This ICC sounds like a great organization. Congratulations!" says the interviewer, and hangs up.

I look around me, at the small, improvised office of ICC. A great organization, he said. Music to my ears. It took a great deal of stumbling around to get here.

* * *

CHAPTER 2

Venice, Italy and Vancouver, Canada
Sonia, 1991

Venice is like no other city: a fantasy land that is real. The city is filled with black canals with putrid water and sleek gondolas with comical singing gondoliers winding their way throughout the city. As a result, Venice has a lot of bridges, which I love. Venetian bridges have beautiful intricate designs. Some streets are so narrow that when you open your umbrella, the tips touch the buildings that form the walls of the street. Because of the narrow streets lined by three- and four-story buildings, it is usually dark in the streets, and with so many tourists travelling through, the air is heavy with sweat. So much so that when you finally reach San Marco Square, you can finally breathe. The sky is suddenly wide and blue, the quadrangle huge and solid with not a canal in sight. The pigeons are everywhere, as ubiquitous as the sidewalk cafe chairs and tables scattered about. The square is anchored by the San Marco Cathedral on one end, with its facade of midnight blue studded with golden stars guarded by lions, and elsewhere, a perimeter of arcaded buildings frame the plaza. Every hour, the bells of San Marco ring throughout the city, a sound I have forgotten that I loved.

I am sitting in one of the sidewalk cafes sipping a cup of cappuccino, taking it all in, the beauty of Venice. I am watching out for my two other friends who were supposed to meet me here. The man wearing a hat across from me has his arms flung open, his bread-crumb-loaded palms facing the sky. Shortly, pigeons and crows hover about and descend on his palm and on top of his hat, devouring the breadcrumbs. He looks like a scarecrow, except the reverse: he attracts crows. The orchestra is about to start. The handsome waiter wearing a starched white shirt and tie, and elegant black pants approaches me once again. *Mas cafe, signorina*? *No mas*, I say, with a sweet smile. I need to nurse this cup of coffee until my friends come, and then it will be time to order wine, or I'll have to leave this cafe, that's what they tell me. You need to keep ordering or give up the seat.

Why don't we have more plazas like this in Vancouver? I look again at the scarecrow man who is replenishing his palms and hat with more breadcrumbs. When he stands up and faces me with his arms flung wide open, I am surprised: it's my dad looking at me, a sad expression on his face. I blink several times and lean closer to see. No, it's not him. I could have sworn.

My friends arrive. I look back at scarecrow man, but he is leaving now. The handsome waiter is back and is taking my friends' orders. When it is my turn, he asks, *mas cafe*? I look at him to give my order, and surprise! It is my father's face looking sadly at me. Dad? I ask incredulously. He looks down to pick up my empty cup of coffee, and then looks at me again. No, not my dad. What is wrong with me?

On the walk back to our pension, I decide to call home. No one is answering. Well it's midnight there. I cannot sleep for a long time, thinking of my father. Finally I doze off.

I have a vivid dream. Bobby is rising from underneath the concrete of a collapsed building, and when he does, the chaos of the building sets itself straight like a reverse hurricane. His figure floats above the building, then the figure turns his face to me, and suddenly it is the face of my father, with the same sad look of the scarecrow and the waiter, pointing his finger straight at me, but instead of a finger, it is an injection needle.

I am unnerved and I wake up.

I call home again, and that's when I learn that my father died in the night from a heart attack when he confronted Bobby about being a drug dealer.

* * *

In the airplane flying back to Vancouver, I go over that dream many times figuring out what it could possibly mean. What was my father trying to tell me? Bobby is rehabilitating my father's career, making up for him. He seems to be doing exactly that, with his successful development business. But why point to me? Does he want me to rehabilitate his career? I'm not a builder like Bobby, not interested in architecture, engineering, or development. The only thing that remotely makes sense to me is if he meant for me to do something so that immigrants like him can get to practise their professions in Canada. But why the injection needle? Drugs. Is he accusing me of using drugs? That should be more in reference to Bobby. Does he mean that I should do something about Bobby's drugs? That I should do something about immigrants AND Bobby's drugs?

Mom thinks I'm taking the dream way too seriously, and that my father was merely saying goodbye to me.

Bobby thinks my dream was hilarious.

"He means for you to stop dealing and doing drugs, and that I should bug you about it," I insist.

"I have stopped dealing and doing drugs, a long time ago! It was just a little thing to help out when we had no money, and I just did it for Dante. No one believes me, but everyone believes some stupid boy who says he works for me. I don't need drug money. I'm doing fine with the landscaping and the subdivisions. Do you want me to show you our books, how I invest?" cried Bobby.

He's convincing. I will take him up on his dare.

As to the other message — do something about immigrants — I have a mind to do that. I was thinking of that anyway.

What steps might I take? I'm a graduate of a general Bachelor of Arts Degree, doing this and that. Nothing much yet. Waitering, travelling and writing about my travels, volunteering here and there for the church, the English conversation club for immigrants, helping with Mom's business sometimes. I have to get more involved with immigrants somehow, maybe find a job, or volunteer where skilled immigrant newcomers go. I draw a blank. I have a lot of research to do.

* * *

Lolo Ben has got to be the youngest looking 71-year-old grandfather in the world. He is full of energy, and wants to see everything of Vancouver since the funeral. Tito Mario and all of us can't keep up with him. Lola Lita, who is ten years his junior, has given up on him. His development businesses in the Philippines continue to be successful, and he wants to compare them with Vancouver subdivisions, houses, condos and commercial buildings. Bobby and he are tight. They found in each other a business soul mate.

"Why didn't I come here earlier? You boys kept this secret from me," Lolo Ben says.

Tito Mario moves closer to the window and looks out on the street. He doesn't answer. I know what he's thinking, the same thing Dad was thinking: that was the whole idea, to get away from you.

"Come if you want. You can come through the investors' category. Put in $250,000 worth of investment in a Canadian venture, or your own business, and you're in," offers Tito Mario.

"I don't know about you Ben, but I'm not about to slave in a house like all these kids cleaning after you, keeping house. I can't do without maids. I'm too old for this change, my dear. You'll just have to do this without me, and fly back and forth between Vancouver and Manila," says Lola Lita, looking as beautiful as ever.

Lolo Ben becomes silent. He looks thoughtful, as though it never occurred to him that his wife could refuse joining him wherever he went.

"Bobby and I will do business together, yes Bobby? Subdivisions in Surrey look like a great market," Lolo Ben slaps Bobby on the back fondly.

"Ken is thrilled that you're interested, Lolo. But heads up, Lolo. There's so much development cost here, you might be shocked. If we make 15 percent, we're lucky," says Bobby.

"What's wrong with 15 percent?" I interrupt. "That's better than what any hard-working labourer makes. Bobby, ugghhh, why do you have to have so much? It's never enough!" I am exasperated, thinking of the measly incomes of the construction workers who work for Bobby.

"Why do you get upset with me? Don't I put up the capital and risk my money never knowing whether it will all work out? And if it doesn't, who's out? My workers? No, it's yours truly. They get their salary whether I make it or not. I don't set the minimum wages. I only follow them," Bobby argues.

"Your workers are engineers and architects back home. They are capable of much more. In fact, they do so much better in their work for you because they are more skilled, and you pay them only so much," I counter.

"Is it my fault if they are not certified engineers and architects here? At least they are in the building business with me, and I give them good bonuses. We will beat those East Indian construction workers and be known as the best *Pinoy* contracting team in BC. They like working with me. They know they'll go places with me," boasts Bobby.

I didn't imagine Bobby would ever get like this: so materialistic, a crass capitalist. Yet, I can't help but admire his entrepreneurship. He was always good in business.

"Nothing wrong with making money," says Mom, carrying a golden roasted turkey on a silver tray. "Dinner is served!" she says, as everyone cheers the turkey.

The table is set in such finery. We are using the formal dining table in the formal dining room. Mom outdid herself for Lolo Ben and Lola Lita. She must be so proud of herself, achieving all this with little help from their son, she whom they demeaned as being unworthy of the del Mundos. All the silver is out, and crystal glasses for red wine, white wine, champagne, even if we don't drink wine much. Large water goblets crowd the table. Our best plates — the gold-rimmed ones which we never use — are laid out on leather place mats. Turkey and all the trims, *hamonado*, roast beef, baked whole salmon, seafood *paella*, a medley of roasted vegetables — asparagus, peppers, tomatoes and artichokes. It is actually all a little too much, and I feel embarrassed once again for my over-aspiring Mom.

The candelabra are also out. Mom lights the candles and dims the chandelier. In that light, the fireplace glowing behind us, the crystals on the table reflecting the lights, our whole family around the table — Mom at one end, Bobby on the other — my grandparents from back home here with us, Uncle Mario and Ching, the vacant seat for the always-late Manolita, I feel so happy and full. The only thing that would make it more perfect is my father at the table.

Mom recites the prayers before the meal. Then in comes Manolita.

"Sorry, I'm late!" Manolita says while kissing in turn all the people around the table. Dinner begins in earnest. Food and drinks are passed around. There is much joking, teasing and gastronomical noises of appreciation and delight.

I love my family. I love them especially when we are all together like this and everything well among us. No one is angry at someone, not really anyway. Everyone is here that should be, except for my father, whose absence now is at least legitimate. It's a different feeling, his absence now, compared to his absence before. It's as though when he died, he became more acceptable to us, than when he was alive and living with someone else. Now, we can imagine him as we want to, simply our loving father who died, and he would not be alive to contradict it.

We must have gone on for hours at the table eating and chatting, until finally Lola Lita raises her glass: "That was a beautiful dinner, Josie. A toast to you!"

Mom stands up to receive the toast. Just when she is raising her glass, she drops it, and she falls back unconscious into her chair. We all run to her. Bobby starts fanning her, while I open her blouse at the neck. She looks so pale, her hands feel cold, but she is breathing.

Tita Ching gives me an alcohol-drenched cotton ball and I put it under Mom's nostrils. She coughs and wakes up. She is fine. We are all relieved. I forget that Tita Ching was a nurse in the Philippines, even if she's been a caregiver in Canada all this time.

"I must be tired, that's all," Mom says, and starts to get up.

"No stay put. You've been under a lot of stress, plus this big dinner. Time to rest now. We will clean up. You relax," Tita Ching orders.

We move Mom to the sofa in the living room, and everybody follows suit. Tita Ching calls Manolita to help her clean up. Manolita grumbles but Tita Ching glares at her.

I sit on the floor beside Mom's chair while Bobby keeps fanning her.

"When was your last vacation, Josie?" asks Tito Mario.

Mom doesn't answer.

"See? You haven't had a holiday for a long time. You've been working too hard, sis," says Tito Mario.

I agree. "You need a break, Mom."

"Maybe it's time for you to visit the Philippines, take a long vacation. You haven't seen Lolo Iska and Lolo Lino for such a long time," says Bobby.

"We should all go!" says Manolita from the dining room.

"About time!" said Lolo Ben.

We are all looking at Mom who looks shy with all the attention on her.

"So?" I press.

"I don't know. Can we afford all of us going? We just had a lot of expenses for the funeral, and no business coming in when I go away?" Mom. Always worried about money.

"Don't worry, I'll look after it," says Bobby. Good ol' Bobby. My mysteriously rich brother Bobby, who insists he does no drug business. It's the landscape maintenance and the subdivisions he says, over and over.

I feel complicit as I agree to his offer. We prepare for our first grand holiday back home.

* * *

I loved summers back home because that meant I was going to stay with Lola Iska in Pililla for one whole month. Bobby and I finished all our chores with no complaints for weeks, knowing we could leave early if we behaved. Pililla was our hometown, where Mom was born and grew up, and where Mom's mother Lola Iska, and her father Lolo Lino, and all manner of cousins and second cousins lived. Bobby and I went there in a great big bus, travelling out of busy Manila, along long stretches of country roads marked by towns, markets, churches, plazas, basketball courts, schools, wooden houses with galvanized iron roofs, rice fields with isolated nipa huts, mountains, then towns again and markets and churches and plazas, and on and on like that for about two-and-a-half hours, until we reached Pililla.

I knew we were getting close because the vendors who stopped by the bus windows began to speak in bobbing accents, up and down their intonations went. I knew we were really close when I saw the biggest market in the journey, and the cabaret beside it, which everyone in Pililla gossiped about. The fanciest church had huge acacia trees sheltering the front gate where sat vendors selling rosaries, rice cakes, magic herbs and lotions, little crucifixes and stampitas of various saints, dried ayungin, squids on a stick grilling over a fire, and stacks of bamboo baskets. Then came the wide open rice fields and soon, soon, the corner with the thick mango groves on the right side, the path from the river across from it, tin houses, and wooden houses, and after about 20 of them, there it was, on the right side, Lola Iska's house. Para! *I shouted. The bus rolled to a halt. Bobby and I dislodged ourselves from the bus, the conductor following with our bags. We jumped over the low bamboo gate that separated Lola Iska's house from the road, and ran up the steps to her waiting arms.*

Even in old age, you could see how Lola Iska could be a beauty queen in her time. She had a small frail body, and her face was slim with well-sculpted features: thin, moderately high nose, smiling almond eyes and high cheekbones. Her wispy hair was gathered up in a bun, showing her Castilian face. Her mother was rumoured to have been the girlfriend of the local parish priest, a Spanish friar. Lolo Lino was a big bronze man with large kind eyes, thick wavy hair, and a prominent Adam's apple. He looked like a movie star. He was not native to Pililla, but came from a town in Cavite where it is said that a group of Indians lived, and his tall dark looks may have come from that.

Lola Iska let the kids do anything we liked. As soon as we arrived, I ran down the house to the backfields, to see my best friend Bekang. Bekang was the same age as me, and lived in a tiny hut at the back of Lola Iska's house. She was the eldest of a family of five, and I helped her look after the kids. Their house consisted of one room, which served as living room, dining room, kitchen and bedroom. They cooked with coal on the banggerahan, *a ledge protruding from one wall, with an overhanging roof. An open veranda stood outside the one room of their house, and this is where we played with the kids, and where Bekang's mother prepared food.*

There was a duyan *in the middle of their living room, a bamboo hammock that hung from the ceiling. I loved to lie down in the hammock, cradling the latest baby, and singing her to sleep. Bekang's family had one appliance: a radio with earplugs. I couldn't remember how they got this equipment, as Bekang's dad was a farmer, and her mother stayed home or sold the farm produce by walking throughout the village with a basket of fruits and vegetables on top of her head. None of Lola Iska's relations ever had a radio like this. I loved wearing the earplugs even if they smelled like old unwashed blankets, and listening to radio music as I swung slowly in the hammock.*

That day we arrived from Manila, I found Bekang and a troop of kids gathered around their mother in the veranda, intently watching her cut open a pineapple on a newspaper laid out on the floor.

"Sonia! When did you arrive!" exclaimed Bekang.

"Just now, let's go and play," I said.

"Not until you eat a pineapple," said Bekang's mother, whom everybody called Ate Pining. Ate Pining was a tiny dark woman with small diamond-shaped eyes and black lips. She was crouched on the floor, half mouthing the words as her lips held on to a black cigarette with the flaming portion inside her mouth. I could never figure out how she did that. So many women of Pililla smoked cigarettes this way, including Lola Iska.

I sat down on the cool bamboo slats and watched Ate Pining use the knife deftly. She cut away the porcupine skin very thinly so as to keep as much of the golden flesh intact. Then she cut wedges all around the pineapple in spirals to get rid of the eyes. She cut very close to the eyes so as not to waste any of the flesh. As the long slivers came away, the kids grabbed them and sucked on the flesh.

"Oy, careful with the eyes, or you'll get itchy stomach," Ate Pining said.

One of the babies wandered off close to the stairs, and Bekang grabbed her legs. Another sat gobbling up pineapple slivers — I lifted her up, away from the pineapple, and onto my lap to get the baby to stop.

The pineapple shorn of eyes looked so pretty with its perfect spirals. Ate Pining rubbed it all around with coarse salt, then bathed it in cool clean water in a basin on the floor. Then she cut it in the middle, sliced long thin wedges along the hard core, and gave me the first cut. It was the sweetest juiciest pineapple I ever tasted. Ate Pining cut a few other wedges in quarters and gave everyone else a quarter of a wedge, and kept the rest on a plate. I always got special treatment in their house, and felt a little guilty depriving them who had so little. I gave away half of my slice to Bekang who happily devoured it.

"Go on you two, I'll look after the kids," said Ate Pining.

Off we went running down the bamboo steps, to the back of their house, where the sun now sat huge like a fireball. We ran towards our favourite kamachile tree beside the shallow narrow stream, and sat on the bank with our feet in the cool water, watching the great big ball of fire. There was nothing else to do but sink into that wonderful feeling of happiness.

Bekang snapped some branches from a kakawate shrub behind us, and gave me a few. We broke the soft stems at intervals, then peeled the stem like a banana, careful not to cut the stem completely, until the stem hung like a necklace with a pretty leaf as its medallion. I hung mine around my neck and Bekang placed hers on her head, like a tiara, the greens glinting like jewels on her thick jet-black hair. As she laughed, Bekang's eyes twinkled. Dimples appeared on her cheeks, and her brilliant white teeth flashed. I secretly envied those teeth that Bekang swore were cleaned by nothing else than water and salt.

"Sonia, supper time!" came a call from behind.

"Patintero after supper?" I asked. I loved the rough and tumble of that game.

"Meet me in front of your house. I'll draw the markings on the street, and get the others over. Don't take too long, or we'll start without you," warned Bekang.

"No you won't or I'll never talk to you again," I lied, for I could not envision not ever talking to Bekang.

"And I'll not let you listen to my radio again," Bekang taunted and began splashing cold water with her legs towards me. I did the same. We stood in the stream, splashing each other fiercely till we were soaked.

"Sonia, supper!" came the call again.

We scrambled up from the bank. Bekang ran back to her house, while I ran off to supper, wondering whether that half of a pineapple was all the supper Bekang will have tonight.

* * *

We did not play patintero *that night, because Bekang's little sister got a stomach ache. The local 'doctor' or* herbolario *was fetched, and it did not look good.*

The doctor, who looked more like a witch, did not think it was the pineapple at all, but said a spirit gave the child the stomach ache because it was not pleased with something the child had done. Maybe she picked fruit from a tree where the spirit lived, without asking permission, the doctor surmised. Bekang and I saw what the spirit looked like from the tawas *— something like hot candle wax — which the doctor dropped into the basin of cold water: it had the shape of a dwarf. The dwarf had a sinister look, misshapen legs, and only one arm. It was a mean spirit.*

"So you better ask permission from the spirit of any tree before picking fruits," the witch doctor warned.

"But she's too little to know," I said.

"Then whoever is looking after her should do it," the witch doctor continued.

"What about branches and leaves?" I asked, worried about the garlands we made that afternoon from the kakawate shrub.

"Yes, that too, because you never know," said the witch doctor.

I could see us taking forever talking to trees what with all the picking we do. "But we have been picking without permission all this time and I haven't got a stomach ache!" I countered.

The witch doctor looked directly into my eyes: "Not yet."

I shivered, and imagined how the spirit of the huge kamachile tree might look like.

The witch doctor episode made us miss playing patintero, and almost made me miss my favourite part of the day. Before tucking in to sleep in Lola Iska's house, everyone gathered around the veranda, sitting on the benches and chairs, watching the village night. There were no streetlights, and the only lights came from the occasional bus that rumbled by. It was the time for telling stories, catching up on village news. Lola Iska sat on the bamboo floor, leaning against the door, and the kids competed for who gets to lie down on her lap. Bobby and I had priority as we were from out of town and bumped out the local cousins.

I lay my head on Lola Iska's soft lap. Lola Iska's one hand held a fan that she continuously waved above me, causing a cool light breeze over my body. Lola Iska's other hand scratched my back, and then ran fingers through my hair. Sometimes Lola Iska smoked a black cigarette with the flaming tip inside her mouth, and sometimes she chewed red betel nut.

"This time next year, they will be in Canada. How cold it must be! Snow everyday. Frozen lakes. How do they fish?" said a cousin.

"Silly, they do not fish in Canada. They're rich!" another said.

I scrambled up and protested: "No. They said it would take five years for our papers to get approved!"

"You wish," Uncle Terio said. "Your papers got approved and you're going away next month!" Uncle Terio was mom's younger brother.

"That's not true! Dad's too busy and we're not going anymore. And besides I'm not going anyway. I'm only grade 5 and it's not good to interrupt my studies said Sister Carina. I can stay with you instead, right Lola Iska?" I asked.

"Of course, my dear," Lola Iska said.

"See? I don't have to go to freezing Canada," I buried my face in Lola Iska's lap.

"Why did Manuel change his mind? I thought he put that whole thing off, now that he's making so much money now with the government?" asked Lolo Lino.

"Haven't you heard? The accident on the Film Centre building construction?" said Uncle Terio.

"The latest project of the First Lady? The one he's engineering?" asked Lolo Lino.

"Yup. Beam holding construction workers collapsed. Workers fell into the wet cement and sunk to their death," he continued.

"Susmaryosep!"

"They did not stop construction so as not to delay the International Film Festival opening. They just continued building over the cement rather than stop and recover the bodies," he said.

"Santisima!"

"When the contractors continued working, Manuel resigned. He said he cannot stomach it," Uncle Terio finished.

"Well, he better leave fast," said Lolo Lino with a worried look. "In fact, all of you should leave fast," addressing me and Bobby, who had just snuck in from the street.

"Leave for where?" Bobby asked slumping onto the floor with Lola Iska.

"Canada! Where have you been?" I said.

"I thought we're not leaving anymore?" asked Bobby.

"Construction workers died, and no one fished them out of the wet cement, and Dad quit his job and now we have to go away," I explained.

"Silly girl," Bobby said. "Is that true Lola Iska?" he continued.

"Your Lolo Lino will tell you. Siya, let's sleep now," Lola Iska said.

I stood up with Lola Iska, and moved the door to get at the mats stored behind it. I rolled out the mats on the living room floor, and then laid out the pillows and blankets in a long line on the floor for all the people in the house. Lola Iska lay down in the middle, and I lay on one side of her.

Bobby, who usually took the other side of Lola Iska, instead went all the way skipping over the cousins to the other end beside Lolo Lino, and I heard him say, "Is it true?"

I hugged Lola Iska tight, wishing Canada would go away, and the First Lady, and construction workers dying. I imagined how it felt to be dead under wet cement, with posts and beams and nails and hammers, whole floors and movie houses on top of your dead body. I wondered how people could watch movies and eat popcorn with dead bodies underneath them. I imagined ghosts of construction workers sitting on the empty seats in the dark beside Bekang and me, and I swore never to watch a movie in that Film Centre ever!

* * *

Ten years is a long time. I wonder what they all look like now.

I can never understand why we have to bring so much presents for our family in the Philippines — soap, shampoo, shaving cream, toothpaste, bath towels, dishtowels, lipsticks, perfumes, makeup, boxes of chocolates, gummy bears, jelly beans, grapes, apples and pears.

"But they have lots of food there, why all this?" I ask in exasperation looking at the great big boxes of *pasalubong* we are packing.

"Everything is expensive in the Philippines," Mom says.

"Even toothpaste?" I ask incredulously.

"Of course, especially in Pililla. Chocolates are not available there, and these fruits."

"Dishtowels?"

"Yes, real dishtowels are expensive there and your Lolo and Lola in Pililla don't have much money at all."

"So, what do they use for dishtowels?"

"Old torn up T-shirts. You know, anything. So a real dishtowel is a treat," she says.

"Flashlight? Batteries?" I look inside the *pasalubong* box. "Canned peaches. Canned tuna. Canned sausages. Cheese. Vitamin C. Multiple Vitamins. Sneakers. Handbag. Marlboro. All expensive over there?" I am figuring this out.

"Uhumm." Mom nods as she continues inserting things in the box.

"So what can I bring Bekang and her family?"

"Money. Just give them money. Pesos. They'll appreciate that more. These fruits, they might not even know how to eat these. They've probably never eaten peaches."

I remember the pineapple Bekang's mom so carefully prepared for us.

"I'll bring them fresh peaches. That's like our mango. They'll like that."

"Up to you. Wrap them in a box or they'll get squished, won't taste good."

"What do we have for Lola Iska?"

"Vitamins, towels, canned fruits so they are soft," she says. "Bobby will look after her cataract operation."

"And Lolo Lino?"

"Chivas Regal. The sausages for *pulutan*. He'll love that," she chuckles.

"Isn't he too old to drink?" I ask.

"More and more I hear, the older he gets. Oh well, at least an imported drink will be special."

"Who are the transistor radios for?"

"Your uncles."

"So many sunglasses and compact powders?"

"For their wives."

"Why so many chocolate boxes and little towels and soaps?"

"For kids, or just for give away to neighbors and friends who come by. You never know."

"Why does everybody have to have a present?"

"That's just how it is. You go abroad. You bring things home. That's expected. It's how we say we love each other. I don't know."

"I thought that was food. We cook and eat so much because that's how we show our love," I say.

"That too. There are many things we do to show our love for each other, because we'd rather not say it. So, shut up and pack," Mom replies.

I hug my mom, and shut up. We are true hardworking Filipinos, mom and I. Too busy loving to say it. Don't need to say it. I get it.

* * *

CHAPTER 3

Philippines
Sonia, 1991

It is April in the Philippines, the time of Holy Week. I want to go to Pililla right away, to help Lola Iska decorate our family statue of Jesus in the Agony in the Garden for the annual *Pabasa*, an all day chanting of the bible by the community. I want to catch all the preparations: the making of paper flowers from multi-coloured crèche paper, the laying of satin skirts around the carriage where the statue will be paraded, the making of the arc from thin bamboo strips under which the statue will rest while people sit around tables laid in front of it, singing the bible verses. I want to be there to watch the teenage boys and girls of Pililla flirt and court each other right under their parents' noses as they hammer the nails into the arc, twist the flowers into shape, drape the pale blue satin robe over the Jesus statue and wipe away the yearlong dust over his bleeding brow. I want to hear the grinding of the rice for the *puto* and *bibingka* late into the night, help the ladies catch the rice juice in *kacha* cloth to screen out remaining coarse kernels, and squeeze out the creamy juice. And I want to catch up with Bekang.

But we have to stay first in Makati with Lolo Ben and Lola Lita and party with the del Mundo clan before we do anything. I am anxious to meet Tita Marites, father's younger sister. I brought her a fancy lipstick as they say she is a sophisticated beauty and a high-flying television producer. I feel ridiculous worrying over my *pasalubong* for my aunt. I realize I feel insecure around the del Mundo wealth, feeling I don't belong. I am definitely a Pililla girl.

I have forgotten the life of luxury. At Lolo Ben's place, everything is done for us by maids, it seems there are maids for everything: for cooking, for serving and cleaning up after dinner, for cleaning up different parts of the house, for keeping up the gardens, for washing clothes and for ironing them, for driving Lolo Ben or Lola Lita or Marites or us. Lola Lita brings in a *masahista* who stays in the house for several days massaging each of us in turn. When she is done with that, she offers to give us manicure, pedicure, and hair treatment, whatever and whenever we want. Lola Lita insists I get the full treatment as "What would your *titas* and cousins say? They'll say my *apos* are *siyanas* from Canada?" She brings us to Rustan's and buys us clothes and shoes and bags to match, so we wouldn't look like country bumpkins. They have beautiful clothes here, and after converting the pesos to dollars, I realize how inexpensive the clothes are in dollars. I could get used to this. We are driven around in one of seven cars in their driveway, by one of three drivers on stand by for anyone.

The thing that bothers me though is driving through the streets of Manila, seeing the real Manila of poverty and slums. I see shacks made of cardboard, coca cola posters, pieces of patched up plywood and sheets of rusted corrugated iron.

There are whole communities of them crowded under bridges, along busy roads, and in vacant lots. Along Roxas Boulevard, by the beautiful sunset over Manila Bay, children lie on the sidewalks at night all in a row. This is where they sleep and live. Boys dive down the stinking polluted waters of the bay, looking for crab and fish to eat. Vendors approach my window selling all manner of things: cigarettes by the stick, samaguita garlands, coffee in muddy glasses, green mangoes, *chicharron*, wet towels, regular towels, hub caps, radios, birds in cages, even once, a snake. I'm just so surprised with how everyone is so used to poverty including the poor people themselves. Am I the only one who feels bad about it? Perhaps if I lived here, and saw this everyday I'd get immune to it all like everyone else.

"So where do you live, Pepe?" I ask the driver assigned to me today.

"Just around," he hedges.

I learn that Pepe is 60 years old, has five kids and that he lives in one of the shantytowns in Tondo. He has to start leaving his house at 5 am to make it to my grandpa's house by 7 am to be on standby for anything. He has worked for my grandpa all his adult life.

"What do your kids do?"

"Two of my boys are in Saudi, in construction," he says proudly. "My other boy drives a taxi."

"Any girls?"

"Two. A daughter is in Japan, my youngest works in the office of your Lolo."

"What does your daughter do in Japan?"

He hesitates. "She sings in clubs."

"Nice."

"I'm very lucky, your grandpa is a good boss, and my kids are all doing well."

I find out later from Tita Marites that singing in clubs in Japan is code for *"japayuki,"* a call girl for Japanese businessmen, and that Pepe's daughter is a *japayuki*.

* * *

It is foggy out there. The fog is a thick blanket covering the world. I know there is a street there, Science World, False Creek, the SkyTrain line, cars and bicycles, but they are totally hidden from view. The grey-white fog is a solid wall. I suddenly feel claustrophobic, but there is nowhere to turn. All around the windows of my condo, 180 degrees, is a wall of fog.

* * *

In Pililla, I seek Bekang. She is always out. Doesn't she want to see me? Has she changed? We have lost touch. I have not written her in years. I keep walking by her house in the backfield, now a concrete house with iron grill windows. The setting sun is as large as before, but not as orange, and the stream is down to a trickle. I hear she's the toast of the town, the most popular and champion majorette at the fiesta. They call her Becky now. I want to see what she looks like, how my old friend has changed. So I go to the plaza one day when I hear that she is practising with the band for the competition.

There is Bekang, in the middle of the quadrangle, twirling her baton, throwing it high up in the air, catching it from behind, then twirling it around her knees. Her jet-black hair is short and curled close to her face. Her face is fair, her lips red. When did she become a *mestisa*? She is wearing high black boots up to her knees, and her thighs are white and plump, shiny with sheer stockings. She is wearing something like a ballerina's tutu, a short white skirt that stops at the base of her buttocks, and a long-sleeved satin white blouse tight around her body, studded with metal buttons and blue and red stripes. She wears a sailor's cap tied around her chin with a red sequined string. The band plays to a crescendo and she throws the baton higher than ever before, then dives to the ground, face to the sky, one leg flat on the ground, the other in a sexy triangle, hands behind and cradling her head, as she catches the baton with her mouth.

The bandleader walks towards Bekang and helps her to her feet. Hugs her.

"You are the best! We will be champion again this year!"

I approach Bekang. I feel shy. She looks like a star.

"Bekang. It's me, Sonia," I say.

"I know," she smiles.

I feel awkward. I want to hug her, but she shows no signs of moving toward me. I look closer to see signs of the friend I had before, and my arms cannot seem to wrap themselves around a virtual stranger. I feel betrayed. Where is my old friend? I think she understood that, which is why she kept away from me since I arrived. We walk through the streets of Pililla together, the silence trying to catch up with our thoughts and feelings. At a corner, some boys are hooting and whistling at us, but she just waves at them with a familiar smile, like a tired prima donna. Little boys trail after us, touching the satin tassels of her baton dangling by her side as we walk.

We reach her house. There is no veranda anywhere. A shiny mahogany door is unlocked by her key. The floor is a red painted concrete, shiny from floor wax. I survey the contents of Bekang's house. A living room furniture set made of shiny rattan, with seats of woven bamboo. A television set by the wall. A white plastic dining table with four white plastic chairs. A single gas burner, a sink, a small fridge. I peer into the inner room; I see the traditional coal/wood burning stove and *banggerahan*. We laugh. Our first laugh. The dirty kitchen is still where they cook and eat even with the modern appliances in the clean kitchen, which are there for show.

She shows me a bare room with no windows. "*Inay* and *Itay* sleep here, and my brothers and sisters." She shows me the bathroom. The floor is cemented. A toilet seat with no flushing mechanism. A drum of water under a faucet, a plastic tub with a long handle floating on top of the water. An empty pail beside it. A small window high up on a wall. A great improvement from the outhouse of before. She shows me her bedroom. A double bed draped with a crocheted coverlet. A side table with a pleated lampshade, a small window overlooking the backfield.

"Nice," I say.

She shakes her boots off and jumps on the bed bouncing herself, giggling. I jump in myself, and we laugh, bouncing about on the bed. Relief floods through me. I have my old friend back.

It's true that when two people have not spoken with each other a long time, they need a third something to focus on, a common thing between them to get the feeling of sharing going, to prime the pump and fetch more water from the well of their long-time shared experiences. So we talk about anything in front of us.

I notice a lizard on the ceiling. It has a pretty green tail. She throws her baton aiming at the lizard, and I scream and avoid the falling steel baton, but it only thunks me on the head. It is plastic after all, not heavy metal as I thought. She laughs at me. I twirl the baton about with my right hand.

"How did you learn all this anyway?" I ask.

"I was so eager to be like Conching the majorette, you remember her? So I watched her every time she practiced, copied the moves, and practiced every day in the backfield with a stick until I learned. Then I added my own moves, like this." She takes the baton from me, stands on the floor at the foot of the bed and gives me a demonstration.

"You look so different," I comment.

"So do you," she says as she twirls the baton.

"Have a boyfriend?" I ask.

"Uhumm," she says, twirling the baton behind her back.

"Someone I know?" I probe.

"No one you know," she catches the baton, and faces me. "Anyway, he's married. But he's nice." She continues to twirl the baton, and then throws it to me. I catch it.

"But why? You're so pretty. You can get someone who's not married," I say.

"He's rich. That's why I have this," Bekang waves her hand over her head, meaning the house. "And this," she says, pointing to her fancy hair. "And this," pointing to her made-up face, making a funny face at me. I did the same and we both laughed.

"Who is he? Is he cute at least?" I ask.

"He's powerful, anyway. He's the mayor around here," she says.

"Since when did you..."

"Since I came home from Japan, I got tired of that... singing," she says.

"O Bekang." I fall silent.

"We were so poor. I could see nothing for me here. So when somebody said they would pay for my tickets and everything else in Japan, and all I had to do was serve and sing, I said why not?" Bekang looks out the window into the backfield. I see her brown complexion underneath the thick white makeup, a redness in her eyes peeking through the thick-layered mascara.

"I didn't know," she continues. "I was lucky I got away from there." Bekang is quiet. She lays down the baton on the bed. "They wanted me to pay them back for the airfare. He protected me from those guys. So, I stay with him. He's good enough to me. But everybody talks about me. No one would want to marry me now. And as soon as he is no longer mayor, who knows what will happen to me?"

I hold her hand. She hugs me, a long time.

"Could you just sponsor me to Canada? I can be a caregiver, anything," says Bekang.

I look at my dear friend, the desperation on her face. I imagine her life in Canada. She is beautiful, and helpless and desperate. All the right ingredients to be abused by an employer. I could check and recheck her employer, find someone I know to hire her, a friend with a baby or an elderly parent. At least she'll earn in dollars. At least there is no family to leave behind, other than a married man whom she's better off without anyway. And after three years with an employer, she can apply to be an immigrant, do other work and support her parents and siblings much better. Maybe marry a nice Canadian man.

"Would you? Please?" she pleads.

"I'll see what I can do," I say cautiously, not wanting to raise expectations. "You'll need to take the caregiving course." As soon as I said that, I tried to take it back, but it was too late.

"Oh thank you! Thank you! Thank you!" she says hugging me.

"I can't promise, ok, I'll have to find the right employer. Who knows, they might not approve. There are many requirements. I'll have to ask Mom. It might take a long time," I say.

"Thank you! Thank you! You are an angel from heaven! Thank God, bless you, bless you, Sonia," she says with tears in her eyes.

* * *

Tita Marites is a big woman who couldn't care less. She is 5-foot-5 in 3-inch heels, weighs about 170 lbs, and she wears fancy tight clothes that reveal every pound of her body. She colours her hair a deep burgundy-black, and, with a very fair *mestisa* face, dusky brown and blue eyeshadows and strawberry-red lipstick, she looks so striking you forget that each feature is actually nondescript. Her clothes are always flowing or trailing with big butterfly sleeves or draped over with shawls, and when she walks, she trails rich smelling fragrances along her path. She smokes dark Virginia Slims, which she holds elegantly between with her plump fingers lengthened by painted fingernails. She speaks with a honeyed assurance that everything she says will be followed, a voice full of power. She is some corporate bigwig at ABS television. She is almost always away. She is 36 and unmarried because "all Filipino men are philanderers, and none is worth marrying." I am totally awed by her, and Manolita simply adores her.

"You have to tell me what happened. No one talks about it here," she says in one of our few moments alone. We are in the car, she asks to be dropped off somewhere on my way to the shopping centre. I do not know where to begin.

"What do you know?" I ask, looking for somewhere to start.

"Just about zero," she settles in, pulls out a long Virginia Slim, rolls down the window and smokes while I talk. The traffic is thick as our conversation, and I end up not going shopping, and she ends up missing her appointment.

When I am finished and have nothing else to say, I look up at Tita Marites, to see this big beautiful powerful woman weeping unashamedly.

"It's not right...not fair..." she says, shaking her head, sobbing."He should have never left," she continues, as she dabs the side of her eyes. "He should have just come home. He is so proud. All of them. It's ridiculous." She bursts into another round of crying. I hold her.

"Why did they want to leave anyway? Dad, Uncle Mario? They have everything here," I ask.

"Everything and nothing. Ever since Mom died, this place has been unbearable. Papa has no time for anyone except his business and that witch, and who knows how many *queridas*. He demeans the boys specially, almost pushing them away. I think they, we, remind him of Mom," she says.

"Why should reminding him of his wife, make him bad towards you?" I ask.

"Don't you know?" she asks.

"What don't I know?" I am surprised.

"How she died? How mom died?" she says.

I'm suddenly afraid. I'm not sure I want to know how my Dad's mom died.

"She died running away from him. They were having dinner in a restaurant, when she found out that he was living with that witch on the side, your Lola Lita. She ran out of the restaurant and a truck ran over her. She died instantly."

"I thought it was just an accident."

"More than an accident, don't you think? Like he killed her. Mario saw it all, he was just a kid then, 12 maybe. He was with them in the restaurant, heard their fight, saw Mom run out, saw the truck, the blood, everything." Tita Marites stops, trying to control her anger.

"The boys can't forgive Papa. I was just an infant then. I don't think Papa's forgiven himself either," she says.

I imagine my Dad, 10 years old, losing his mom. I feel his grief. Then having to live with a new 'mom' who caused the death of his mom. I feel his anger. I imagine my Dad's mom, hearing about her husband's betrayal, her husband who fathered her three children. I feel her hurt, her blood rising up to her head, face flushed with anger, no words coming out of her mouth, just her feet moving on their own, running away, away from that deep hurt, anywhere. Then as though to give her quick respite, a truck mercifully ends her agony, and starts the long agony of two little boys, and their hapless father.

I wish I knew all this when my father was alive. I could have loved him a little more. I can still do that now, imagining my dream of him. Yes, Dad, I will do as you ask.

I snuggle up with Tita Marites who puts her arm around me. We travel the rest of the trip in silence.

* * *

The morning sun is brilliant. Up in my condo, I see the waters of False Creek quietly shimmering, cars obediently lined up in traffic, now slowly moving. I hear the sirens of ambulances and police cars, and the dull roar of trucks. I see a single golden tree among a line of evergreens in the middle of the road, little ant-like cyclists rolling along the sidewalk. The SkyTrain is like a white caterpillar moving quietly along the rails, another one moving the opposite way on the track beside it. Everybody's busy going somewhere, and me? Where am I going?

* * *

It's not the same anymore. Not how I remember it. They have done up something like a stage in the middle of the compound, and two tables in front for the chanters. There are only three chanters, one of whom is singing through a microphone. Their chanting is thin and flat like modern singing, unlike the deep nasal wailing I remember from before, when several groups sang a verse in turn, then the next group chanted the next verse, overlapping a little each time, the next group's voices increasing in volume as the other group receded, like waves of chanting. Now, there are more eaters and talkers than chanters. A long buffet table is laid out on one side of the quadrangle, loaded with rice cakes and pastries. Benches are lined up like bleachers on the other side of the compound where people sit, eating and chatting or watching the singing.

People I don't know pull in some plastic chairs for Mom and me to sit on. It's just us, since Manolita and Bobby had things to do in Makati and didn't come with us to Pililla.

Lola Iska looks well except she now has a pronounced hunch on her back, and she seems thinner than before. Lolo Lino, whom I always imagined to be huge and tall, seems to have shrunk in size and weight, but still very much in control of the large household. The handsomeness of my Lola and Lolo is very much intact with the years, but maybe I'm so much their champion because of my attachment to them. This is what Manolita tells me anyway, who thinks Lola Iska and Lolo Lino are on the decline, and we better be ready to say our goodbyes.

There are now new aunts and cousins to know as Mom's brothers have married, and have had children. Strewn about the compound are little boys and girls who are the sons and daughters of this uncle, and that aunt, or various neighbours. Lolo Lino is introducing each one to my Mom, explaining who this is a child of, making them *mano* to my mom, that is, touching their foreheads to my mom's outstretched hand. I see my mom smiling her high-cheek-bones-bugs-bunny smile, and notice her discreetly pushing a folded bill in each kid's hand. They are all happy with their presents, and proud of us, the successful relatives from Canada.

There is a small excitement at the gate. Uncle Terio rushes in.

"*Alkalde* is here," Uncle Terio says, waving to someone to bring out another chair.

A well-dressed, distinguished-looking man walks in with a huge smile, shaking people's hands as he walks in.

"Mayor!" welcomes Lolo Lino, and shakes the Mayor's hand. "Thank you for the honour of your visit," Lolo Lino says with no patronizing hint whatsoever.

I freeze, realizing this is the married lover of my dear friend.

"No, it's my honour. I have to meet the lovely Rose of Pililla who was kidnapped by Canada. Do you even remember me, Josie?" he says, taking my Mom's hand.

"Is it you, Sendong?" my mom says, crinkling her eyes and nose.

"Mayor Rosendo Sales now," says Uncle Terio, grinning.

"No, just good old Sendong," says the Mayor, smiling from ear to ear.

"I would never have thought," my mom says, teasing.

"Neither did any of us. Sendong was the black sheep of my class," Lolo Lino says as though that was a point of pride.

"It's only now that I'm reforming, yes Prof? It took being a Mayor to become a good boy, I have to, for our *Kababayans*, no?" He thinks he is charming, and I already can't stand him.

"So what has our beautiful valedictorian become in Canada? I hear only good things!" I feel like retching.

"This and that. It's okay. We're doing okay," says my Mom.

"And is this one of your children?" He turns to me. I instinctively move away to not be touched by his outstretched slimy hand.

"Yes, this is Sonia, my second," Mom looks at me urging me to smile.

I make an obviously forced smile, and hold that for a half a minute on my face. He seems to be disconcerted, and pulls his hand away.

"My eldest is now 25, and my youngest is now 15. And you, how many kids?" Mom continues gaily.

"Two, both married and with kids. I'm now a *Lolo*," he beams.

"You don't look like a grandfather! You had an early start. Who did you marry?" asked my flirtatious mom.

"You don't know her. She's not from here. Ever since you left, there was no one that could match you. I had to get one all the way from Manila, a Tupas," he says with a lowered voice of respect for the famous family name. Uncle Terio looks at me, rubbing the fingers of his hand, the sign for "lots of money." The snake. I am not impressed. But it makes sense. He would try to marry up, to get into politics — he's the sort. Then have *queridas,* mistresses like Bekang, on the side. I have him all figured out. What did he say about 'since you left'? Were he and my mom an item before? I shudder at the thought.

"May I invite you and your daughter to dinner at my place, and visit my *pabasa*?" The snake has pounced.

"Oh you don't have to," says my coquettish mother who has just lost a husband.

"But I do. We have a lot to talk about since our elementary days, catch up on everybody's lives. You have to meet my wife.

She would be delighted to meet you," the snake says. And how about your *querida*, will you introduce her too?

"Then okay," says my mother, too quickly. "Coming?" she looks at me, eyes gleaming.

I shake my head. She shrugs.

"Let's go then before the *Pabasa* finishes!" says the Mayor, touching my mother's elbow to guide her.

* * *

Lola Iska hardly does anything now. The daughters-in-law do all the cooking and cleaning and looking after the children now, and she mostly sits in her chair on the veranda smoking her black cigarettes. She now wears very thick glasses, but soon, after the cataract operation, she will not need to wear those. She enjoyed the peaches I brought her, ate a piece and gave the rest away.

"Don't you like it?" I ask.

"Delicious. Must be very expensive?" she says.

"No. Not expensive at all. Eat more." I insist.

"Expensive here. Give to the kids," she smiles.

Her grandchildren come to her and she puts them on her lap and brushes their hair. She hardly speaks now. I want to know what she is thinking. What does a 75-year-old woman who raised a huge family do after all that? I hardly know what to say to her too, so much time has passed, where to start? So I just sit beside her and hold her hand, and put my head on her lap like the old days, and she brushes my hair as she smokes her black cigarette. It is the most soothing, comforting thing I know, how I know I am loved unconditionally. I wrap my arms around her bony waist, close my eyes to feel the warmth of her lap, smell the scent of her black cigarette, enjoy the tender soft brushing of my hair by her hand, and remember it all vividly, packing it all in a bottle, the precious essence of love.

* * *

We decide to stay a few days in Pililla, for me to watch the full splendour of the Holy Week festivities, and for my mom to catch up on family and her old friends. I have not seen my mother so lively and animated. She is constantly surrounded by people, old classmates and their children, if they had any, second and third cousins and other distant relatives, old neighbours, old teachers. She is always dressed up, her hair coiffed or up in a bun, face made up as though she was going somewhere, but it is only to 'receive guests.'

When I asked her why, she said, "They need to see me successful, so that they'll have hope...for themselves." Really? "They need to see us successful to counter all that talk about your dad leaving us for another woman." I see, but I don't really see. What do they care? They're so far away. What do we care what they think? I am just only now seeing a new side of my mom, what she had to grow up with, how it is really like here. I do not see myself being part of this competition, so I dress up in my jean shorts and t-shirts and sneakers. "You should dress up a little you know," my mom says weakly. She knows I'll not listen to her anyway.

It is the early evening, and the stars are beginning to light the night sky. Imagine a moving 'stations of the cross.' Instead of paintings of the journey of Jesus to his death on the cross hung up on the pillars of a church, there are life-size statues depicting these scenes set up on carriages or carried on the shoulders of men in the middle of the street. The statues are accompanied by two lines of candle-bearing people, in a procession that moves through the streets of town, ending in the church. Ours is "Agony in the Garden," where Jesus is kneeling in a garden, his hands extended forward and open, showing blood on his palms. His sad eyes are looking upward to his father, agreeing to his part of the bargain that is dreadfully coming to pass soon enough. There's another one: "Veronica and Jesus," where Veronica is holding up a handkerchief that she just wiped Jesus' face with. The handkerchief bears the image of Jesus. And another one: Jesus fallen on the ground with a heavy cross on his shoulder. There are many, maybe 20 statues throughout the procession. The last one is a gloriously decorated coffin with the dead Jesus in it. The procession ends up in the Church where a 'dead mass' is held — that's a shortened version of the mass, because Jesus is dead.

Lola Iska's family is very proud of the way our Jesus is decorated and the grand setting made for him on the carriage. "The others are only carried on the shoulders, with no decoration. Ours is the best, isn't it?" whispers Uncle Terio to me. Everyone is so excited at home because Uncle Terio's little girl Maya is the angel for the *Salubungan*, a ritual commemorating the meeting of the risen Jesus and Mary. Maya has been practicing her poem for so long now, and even mom has got into the action herself, teaching Maya where to pause, and where it has to be louder. "My niece must be the best angel Pililla has ever seen," I catch her saying to Lola Iska. Uncle Terio and his brothers Uncle Eddie and Uncle Danny Boy are busy all day setting up the bamboo trellis to make sure it will be strong to carry Maya safely.

On Easter Sunday, at the break of dawn, the whole town converges around an intersection in the middle of town, where a trellis has been set up. Waiting on one corner is a carriage with the statue of Mary, and on the other corner is another carriage with the statue of the risen Jesus. To commemorate the resurrection of Jesus and his meeting Mary, the two statues are made to meet underneath the trellis, where, lo and behold, an angel is lowered from a hole in the trellis. This angel is a live little girl dressed in white, bearing angel wings. She is tied to a pole by strings running across her breasts and tied at the back, and her feet rest on a little platform attached to the pole. When she is at the same level as the Jesus and Mary statues perched on their carriages, she waves a veil between Jesus and Mary while the band plays and the people sing a rousing song as Jesus is now resurrected. When the singing stops, the angel recites her poem, an ode to Jesus the resurrected, a poem of thanks and joy on behalf of all humankind. Then the band plays again and the procession moves to the church where Easter Mass is held.

At the moment of the lowering of the angel, there is a little tension in the air as there is always a fear that the construction may give, that the pole may break, or that the little girl angel may fall from the pole; any accident may happen. But mostly, the tension is from the angel's family, worried that their little girl may forget her lines, speak too soft, or lose composure up there on the pole and shame her family. Maya does nothing of the sort. When she is lowered, she is even smiling. She recites her lines with a ringing voice, just like how an angelic herald of good tidings would. When the band plays and the procession moves along, I hear sighs of relief, and pride, from the corner where our family stands. I see many hands reaching out to untie Maya from the pole, lift her and carry her into the waiting arms of grandmas and aunts and cousins eager to hug and kiss their angel of the *Salubungan*.

* * *

It is time to go. Bekang makes me promise one more time that I will sponsor her, and I promise.

There is much talk about sponsoring my uncles and aunts, but they seem to be uncertain of wanting to come to Canada, just as mom seems also uncertain that it is a good idea to sponsor them. At their late age and having their own families and all, they can no longer be sponsored. They would have to apply through the business category, as skilled immigrants.

Uncle Terio at age 44, a teacher, will certainly not be able to teach in Canada, what can he do instead? Uncle Eddie, a year younger than Uncle Terio runs a small business of making shoe heels and sends them to Marikina, the shoe centre of Metro Manila. And my youngest uncle, Uncle Danny Boy, drives a jeepney. He didn't finish high school. Their incomes here are so small compared to the incomes they will make in Canada even from the lowest labour jobs there. So yes, it makes economic sense to go to Canada, even I agree.

"Won't you miss all this? This family, this village, the processions, the fiestas, this big community life?" I ask.

"Sure, we are happy being together. But we're poor. What about the kids? If we stay here, they will remain poor. If we go to Canada, they will have a chance for a better future," says Uncle Eddie. "I can run a business just like *Ate* Josie. Maybe instead of making heels for shoes and bringing them to Marikina, I can bring the shoes from Marikina to sell in Canada? How much did you buy your shoes, *Ate*?" Uncle Eddie asks my mom.

"About 30, 40 dollars maybe?" she replies.

"That's the equivalent of 800 pesos here. You buy that in Marikina for only 50 pesos! I can make a lot of money," says Uncle Eddie. "Never mind the processions," he grins. "I can always see them again when I come back to visit or do business," he says, ruffling my hair.

"How will you meet the economic class? You need to be skilled," I say.

"How's that?" asks Uncle Eddie.

"You need a good education, to have a skill, work experience and to speak English to adapt to Canada," I rattle them off.

"Business is my skill! And I have a business degree. The Macomber shoe storeowner thinks I speak good English, and I have a sister in Vancouver who will help me adapt, right *Ate*? Whatever that means, I'll do it. I should pass the test, I think," Uncle Eddie says. I nod in agreement.

"What about me, *kuya*?" asks Uncle Danny Boy.

"I don't know about you. You didn't finish high school. No degree," says Uncle Eddie.

"But I have a skill! I can drive jeepneys, tricycles," says Uncle Danny Boy.

"There are no jeepneys and tricycles there," I laugh.

"Well then, I can drive buses, and trucks and taxis, whatever! They're all the same anyway," says Uncle Danny Boy.

"You can't speak English," says Uncle Terio.

"Say you? My inglis no good to you? I speak da inglis op the green buck dollar!" jokes Uncle Danny. Everyody laughs.

"*Tarantado!*" teases Uncle Terio, slapping Uncle Danny's back affectionately.

"How about you Terio?" asks Uncle Eddie.

"I don't know. I like it here. I'll be principal here one day I hope, and that's good enough for me," says Uncle Terio. I am surprised, but not really.

"I belong here. I'm relaxed here. I know everyone and they know me. Simple life, humble, but happy. Now the kids may be different. Maya, if she likes, one day, when she grows up, she might like to go. That's her decision," Uncle Terio says. "Besides, someone has to look after *Inay* and *Itay*," he finishes. What a good man is my Uncle Terio. I decide that he is my favourite Uncle.

So we leave it at that. Uncle Eddie and Uncle Danny Boy will apply in the economic class as skilled immigrants. And I will look around for an employer who will sponsor Bekang as caregiver.

I am the only one going home to Manila, as Mom decides she wants to stay around another day or so to catch up with friends. I am a little annoyed.

"So how will you get to Manila?" I ask.

"Don't worry about me. Sendong will drive me home as he's going to Manila anyway in a couple of days," says my Mom. I am suddenly terrified at the thought of my mom and that man. I shove my mom aside.

"Mom, can I speak to you alone?"

"What's wrong?"

"That Mayor Sendong of yours. Do you know? Mom. This married man has a mistress. Bekang. He keeps her in a house he built for her in the backfield over there. Wake up, Mom. He's not for you. Let's go home," I beg.

"Oh that. I know. He told me. Poor Bekang. She was a *japayuki* who escaped and her recruiters threatened to take her back to Japan if she didn't pay them back for her airfare. Bekang asked for Sendong's help, and he protected her. And out of the kindness of his heart, he had a small house built for her so she need not go back and be a prostitute. Isn't that generous? What's wrong with that?" says my poor ignorant blinded mom.

"Mom, she is his mistress. Do you think he will build her a house and expect nothing in return? I know, Bekang told me. She's my friend."

"And I have heard about your friend. Tsk tsk. Don't you think you should choose your friends more wisely?" says my Mom, disapproval on her face.

"It's not her fault, Mom!" I protest, but I could see that she had made up her mind about what this was all about.

I am wondering how one obviously bad man can put my best friend and my mother under his spell. I suppose, with the same charm that got the whole town of Pililla voting for him. I wonder about the judgment of my best friend and my mom, in fact that of the whole Pililla. For once, I am eager to leave Pililla for Manila.

I hug my Lola Iska hard and long, thinking this may be the last time I will see her. I put in her hand what I think is a lot of pesos, and whisper in her ear as I hug her goodbye, "For yourself or the kids". She gives me a weak smile, and wipes a tear from under her thick glasses. I stifle my own sob, hug her tight again, and run to the waiting van. In the cool air-conditioned van, I wave goodbye to all of them standing by the gate: Lola Iska, Lolo Lino, Uncle Terio, Uncle Eddie, Uncle Danny Boy, their wives, their children, Bekang. Mom waving from the window. All waving, smiling, the kids jumping up and down, hollering. "Bye *Tita*! Bye *Tita*! Come back again *Tita*!" My people, here, living their lives, while I am over there, living mine. Here they are, loving me, while I have almost forgotten them in my life in Canada. I must remember them always, remember that they love me, that they are my people. I am part of them and they are part of me, and I must never forget them.

* * *

CHAPTER 4

Canada
Sonia, 1991

False Creek is quiet. Not a ripple, not a boat in sight. Over the Cambie Bridge, cars stream along in both directions, like busy ants. The sky is almost evenly grey, shades of white on the far horizon. On the eastern side of my view, a SkyTrain is parked on the rails, like a white caterpillar sitting on a branch. It finally moves. Then along comes a longer grey caterpillar, it disappears into the VanCity building. I wonder how it feels like to have an office in a building where a train keeps coming through the building? Constant rumbling? Or maybe nothing, like it is here, so quiet with all the action around the city. A bevy of swallows suddenly flies from one of the buildings. They fly around briefly and settle back onto the same roof, all lined up in a row. What are they thinking? A lone bird joins them, perches away from the group. A few of the swallows sidle along towards the newcomer, closing the gap a little. Now they are four on one side and the rest on the other. I watch that gap between the swallows on the roof, will it close soon enough?

* * *

When we return from the Philippines, we are all inspired with new projects. Mom is busy expanding her business with a classy Filipino restaurant. Bobby is connecting with Lolo's contacts for development plans in Vancouver and in the Philippines. It seems like an explosion of possibilities. Manolita is talking about starring in a new show on ABSCBN, should it materialize. My head is wandering about, unable to wrap my head around what I saw in the Philippines. Such a big gap between the rich and the poor, the city and the village. My families — how different on each side: my mom's side, my dad's side. I am anchored by my immediate projects: to find an employer for Bekang, and of course, to keep my promise to my dad in my dream.

I decide to volunteer with an immigrant-serving agency during my days off waitering. At Cross Currents Society, the lobby is filled with welcome signs in all languages. When I walk the corridor to the office of the volunteer coordinator, I see on the doors of offices, titles referring to different countries: Hispanic coordinator, East European coordinator, Middle East Coordinator.

"Why would you like to volunteer here?" says the friendly woman who is the volunteer coordinator. I cannot place her cultural roots. Probably one of those rare Caucasians born in Canada.

"I'd like to learn about immigrant needs, and to help somehow. My family immigrated here from Manila over 10 years ago, and my dad had...problems finding work in his field. He was an engineer, but never practiced engineering here. He's dead now. Anyway, I'd like to know how to help newcomers like him," I explain.

"So sorry about your dad. It's a tall order, what you want to do. It's a big problem for newcomers. Your dad's not the only one. We have a group here that does employment counselling for newcomers. Maybe that's a place you might be interested in?"

"Yes, that sounds just about right. But I don't know what I can do for them."

"What's your background?"

"I have a general BA from UBC, and I've been well...taking it easy. Doing lots of travelling with friends. Writing about it. Waitering. I know it's not much. At UBC, I took some cross-cultural courses, organized workshops to talk about how different cultures communicate, do business, things like that. I was part of an English conversation club for newcomers. I have an interest in these things but don't quite know how to go farther with it, career wise." I feel miserable about my paltry achievements.

"Sounds like the life of a normal young woman," she smiles, and I relax a little. "I think your experience with newcomers' communication needs and business ways is really interesting. That should be helpful to the employment counselling team. No promises, but I'll talk with their manager, and see how you can help there. Besides, there are more and more immigrants coming from the Philippines, and we currently don't have anyone on staff that is a Filipino. That could be another angle. Do you speak Philippine?" she asks.

"Pilipino is the name of the language, which is based on the Tagalog dialect, the dialect of the main region in the Philippines. I speak Tagalog okay, but not as good as I used to," I say.

"Sorry about that. When you refer to Philippine things and people, do you say Philippine or Philipino, and is it spelled with Ph or F?" she asks.

"Everybody has the same problem. For the country, it's Philippines with a ph, one l and two p's. The people are called Filipinos and Filipinas with an F, one l, and one p. But when you refer to objects, say, mangoes, you say Philippine mangoes, with the ph, ending in e. Beats me why it has to be so complicated. I think it all started with King Philip the II who was the Spanish King when Magellan "discovered" the Philippines on behalf of Spain and named the islands after him. I think the F replaced the ph when the Americans took over the Philippines and they anglicized the language, simplifying the ph's to the more phonetic F." I'm not so sure about the last part, and realize how little I know about my language and history.

"Isn't that interesting? I didn't know that. Anyway, it's great you speak Tagalog too. That helps a lot. How much time can you volunteer?" she asks.

I think about that and surprise myself. "You know what? As much as is needed."

"Really? Aren't you working at the…a fancy restaurant, or something?" she thumbs through my resume.

"If it's really interesting work here, I can reduce my hours there, whatever. I'm flexible."

"Wow, that's great. We should be so lucky. Thank you, Sonia! I'll be in touch soon." We shake hands and I walk the long corridor back to the lobby and the elevator, imagining another door with a new title "Filipino coordinator," or should it be "Philippine coordinator"? I must really check that out.

* * *

I am an assistant for anything and anyone with the employment-counselling group at Cross Currents Society. I am happy to do anything. It is my first day on the job, and I am to observe and take notes, while an employment counsellor interviews a newcomer from the Philippines. Fernando Borja is a PhD in Environmental Assessment, and was a professor at the Asian Institute of Management. He took other courses in the Netherlands, Paris, and Brussels. His resume is littered with places in the world I'd like to go to. What is he doing here?

"When did you arrive in Vancouver?"

"About six months ago."

"And who did you come with?"

"My wife, and my son and daughter. My son is 15 and my daughter is 13." The same age as Bobby and myself when we arrived in Vancouver.

"And your wife, how is she?"

"She's fine. She's not able to work yet. She's …ill, one reason we really wanted to come here."

"I'm sorry. And under what category did you come to Canada?"

"Economic class, as skilled immigrants."

"Great, and how are things with you?"

"Well, not so good I guess," he smiled with some embarrassment, shifting his weight on the seat. "That's why I'm here. I've not been able to find a job, and I'm starting to worry. I'm studying to get into insurance, just to do something, but I don't really like it."

"You've come to the right place. We will help you help yourself to find a job."

"What does that mean: 'help me help myself find a job'? I've been working at finding a job. Why do I need you to help me find a job? I thought you'd find a job for me?"

"No. I mean yes. We will help you find the job, but it is you who will work to find the job, not us. We will teach you how to find that job."

"Oh, I need to learn how to find a job? I've been filling job application forms! Isn't that what you do? What else is involved? Is there a secret we don't know about?" Mr. Borja is starting to get upset. How tautly stretched he is, he could break any time. I see my own father.

"No, I don't mean there is secrecy involved." The counsellor is losing it. I am bold and care for nothing, and I intervene.

"You know, you are right Mr. Borja. There are secrets to effective job search in Canada, and we didn't know about them when we arrived as newcomers. They were never taught to us. We think it's just a matter of submitting job applications? But it's not at all like that. There is a special way of doing it, and here in this agency, we will teach you those secrets." I say.

"Yes, and 80 percent of people we help, find a job that they targeted. We also help them figure out what job is a reasonable target for them so that they don't get frustrated." The counsellor has recovered.

"So what's reasonable for me? I'm a PhD. I teach, I do environmental assessments. Can I not expect to get a job as a teacher or an environmental assessor?" asks Fernando.

"Maybe you can, but maybe not right away. That depends on your background and credentials, and the available jobs in your field. We have to review all that, and your career goals, then we can help you make a realistic career plan. We can help you write resumes fit for different jobs. We can teach you how to write forwarding letters that make hirers pay attention and short-list you for an interview. We will give you mock interviews to practise your responses to questions interviewers are likely to ask. There are a lot of things to learn," says the counsellor.

"Wow. You can teach me all that? How much will it cost me?" asks Fernando.

"Nothing. Just your time and commitment over two to six months. It depends on you. We are funded by government to help newcomers like you."

"Really? How much time is required?"

"We'll need an hour intake interview. Then, if it's appropriate, we suggest you take our four-week career orientation course. As part of the course, we provide background on the labour market in Vancouver, and help you with your career plan, resumes and interviews. After that, you're on your own, doing weekly check-ups with us. Some find a job in a month, some in six months, or longer. It depends. You could use our career centre to make calls, and our computers to write your resumes. We are available for coaching or questions you may have."

"Okay! When can I start?"

"How about now? Do you have an hour for an intake interview?"

"I have all the time in the world," Fernando smiles for the first time in the meeting. "So you're a Filipina too," he turns to me. "Where do you come from in the Philippines?"

"Manila mostly, and Pililla in Rizal," I say.

"Is that near Antipolo?"

"Near enough, but you have to go through several towns like Morong, Tanay, before you get there. It's the last town before you hit Laguna. It's really a small town," I say. "How about you, where do you come from?"

"Pangasinan, and my Mrs. is from Cagayan," he says.

"Great." I press no further so as not to expose my lack of knowledge of the country's geography.

"When did you come to Canada?" he asks, as though he and I are now the best of friends.

"About 10 years ago," I say.

"You are doing well for yourself!"

"Thank you, I'm getting by okay."

"They must pay you well here. How much do you make?" he asks. This is one thing I can't figure out with Filipinos. Why absolute strangers feel entitled to know how much one makes.

"I'm actually a volunteer here. I work here, but don't get paid. I work somewhere else where I get paid."

"Really! You must make a lot of money where you work so that you can work here with no pay?"

"No, not really. I just want to help out here, with newcomers, because I was a newcomer myself once," I say.

"We can start with your intake interview when you're ready," says the counsellor, rescuing me from the interrogation.

* * *

I feel like I understand a little bit better what my father went through. If he was able to find Cross Currents Society and attend the career orientation course, if he got coaching from a counsellor, could he have secured a job in engineering? I want to observe someone who is an engineer, and I specifically ask the counsellor to include me when there is an engineer newcomer. The opportunity came soon enough.

Santosh is an engineer from Nepal. He is tall and slim and dark in a coal-grey kind of way. His curly hair is silver grey and his bushy moustache is the same. When he speaks, the Adam's apple under his chin travels up and down. Santosh has the same exact problem as my dad, probably the same age. He had been building commercial and institutional buildings in Nepal for over 20 years, and cannot find work here. He is different from my dad in that he has more difficulty with the English language. He has a pronounced accent that makes it difficult to understand him. It doesn't help that he speaks fast. The counsellor asks him several times for clarification on what he is saying, to which his response is to speak louder. As a result, it's hard talking to him, or rather, listening to him. His suit carries a powerful fragrance of curry, and I wonder whether my father's suits carried a similar cooking smell from all the cooking in the house, and whether that worked against him just as it seems to be working against Santosh, where I am concerned. Am I being racist, thinking these thoughts?

"Have you connected with the Association of Professional Engineers?" the counsellor asks. Coreen Douglas is one of the members of the employment-counselling program of Cross Currents Society.

"What's that?" he asks.

Coreen explains that it is the institution that certifies engineers.

"Where have you applied?" Coreen asks.

"Construction companies, development companies."

"Have you tried Government? Crown Corporations? Consulting firms?"

"No? Do they have my type of engineering jobs?"

Coreen explains.

It is obvious that the Nepalese engineer needs to learn a whole lot more to find a job, and he readily agrees to join the four-week course.

Later, I ask Coreen about the racist thoughts I had. I am surprised with her answer.

"Do you know? People make first impressions on others first through how they look, then how they smell, then how they speak. People pay attention to the intonation, the facial expressions, body language like gestures, posture, eye contact, then only what they say. Words are the last thing that make an impression."

As I seem reticent, Coreen continues.

"Your body betrays you, how you really feel. Despite the nice words you say, the way you feel inside will show: your lack of self-esteem, your resentment, or your feeling that this job is beneath you, your lack of faith in this whole process, your desperation. Whatever, it will show. Desperation specially, you cannot be desperate. That's one thing I have learned," she emphasized.

I am thinking about people asking for loans in the bank. Banks don't give loans to people who need it, they give it to those who don't need it — it's less risky. I'm beginning to see the light.

Coreen is on a roll. "People cannot stand desperate people — it's too much responsibility, too much trouble. People want it easy, and they will hire the person who will make things easy for them, not trouble them with their desperateness." It makes sense.

She continues, "And because people want it easy, they want to hire someone that they understand. If you are too different — speak different, look and smell different from them — they think it may be difficult to work with you, as they don't understand you. Why hire someone who is different, and therefore risky, when there's someone else who is like themselves and the others in the team? You will go for the less risky candidate, right? And guess who that is?" she asks, her eyes widening, a smug smile on her face.

"Not the newcomer," I answer.

"You got it," she says.

"Are you saying it's human nature to discriminate against newcomers?" I ask.

"It's human nature to go with people like ourselves, to avoid people we don't understand, as people we don't understand pose a threat to us. It's the law of self-preservation," she says.

"But that means it's okay to discriminate against newcomers!" I ask, getting flustered and puzzled and a bit angry with Coreen.

"I'm not saying it's okay to discriminate against newcomers. Just that it is understandable. People need to accept that first, before we can get to a solution." she says.

"And what's that?" I ask.

"Have many more hirers from different cultural groups. Educate hirers about different cultures, so that they will understand the newcomers they are interviewing. Let newcomers know about this 'secret', that they can make themselves 'more like their hirers' when they apply for jobs. How? Dress like them, smell like them, look them in the eye like they look you in the eye. Learn to speak like them by learning idioms and by knowing more about the industry, so they can converse with hirers like an equal in the interview." Coreen pauses. "The solution has to come from both sides: the employers looking to fill jobs, and the job applicants themselves."

"That's a lot to ask of newcomers. You're saying they have to change themselves to make themselves more acceptable?" I ask, feeling somewhat disgusted. "That guy can't help it if he smells of curry. That's what he always eats!"

"Hold it there. I'm not saying he should stop eating curry, just that when he comes to the interview, he should wear clothes that smell fresh and do not smell of anything, including curry. Gurgle Listerine before the interview, whatever. Know something about the engineering regulatory body, so that at the interview, he at least knows about this organization and its role. Even if he has not passed the organization's criteria, just the fact that he knows about the group raises the level of comfort of the hirer, and makes the hirer think that he is in tune with the industry. Accent is hard to change, but perhaps he could speak more slowly, not loudly, so he could be understood. I know he is likely not aware of any of these impressions he is making. It is our job to tell him, so he can work on them and increase his chances of success."

Coreen leans back on her chair, resigned.

"You bet it's a lot to ask newcomers. For newcomers, it's a job to find a job. The sooner they accept that reality, the sooner they will get the job they want," she finishes.

I cannot deny her powerful logic.

"But it's not just the applicants. The employers have to change too," Coreen continues.

"How so? They have a right to hire who they want, correct?" I ask, now uncertain of my beliefs.

"Sure they do, at their own risk, I must say. So, they hire only candidates whose credentials they know, such as graduates of local universities they know. They hire those candidates who have no accents, and on and on. But they are missing out on the extremely good skills of these newcomers!"

"What would compel employers to hire skilled newcomers?"

"Their own bottom line. Their competition. The marketplace in the end is what will compel them. When they see that they are no longer competitive as other employers are getting ahead financially with skilled employees from diverse cultures, they will smarten up. Look at the banks which hire people of diverse cultures in front-line operations. They understand that clients and customers are more comfortable talking to people of their own culture, who understand them, who will help them manage their funds and invest. So these banks mirror the community's culture in the way they hire employees. Given so many newcomers coming in to Vancouver, think of how many new accounts that would create! Hiring for diversity pays off for the banks, and other employers need to learn from them," Coreen explains.

"It's not as compelling for construction companies, is it? Or government?" I am still thinking of my dad.

"It should be, but they are not as aware of the benefits of hiring skilled newcomers. The obvious advantage is that the newcomers are skilled and usually have long years of experience. Also, research is showing that companies that hire skilled newcomers find them loyal, and stable employees. Because they speak a language other than English, and have knowledge of another country and culture, they become a valuable resource to increase customer base locally, and helpful in global expansion." Coreen is making so much sense, but I still don't understand.

"So how will employers become aware of these benefits so that they'll hire skilled newcomers?" I ask.

"Someone has to do an awareness raising campaign with employers. Get progressive employers talking to other employers and share their knowledge."

"And who should do that?"

"Government, after all they are the ones bringing in the skilled immigrants ostensibly to help the economy. Non-profit organizations that work with immigrants, like our agency, can advocate and lobby for change. Someone also has to lobby those professional accrediting bodies. Many of them are very restrictive, and for many skilled immigrants, these bodies are the stumbling block to moving forward."

"Like the APE, for engineers, right?" I say, happy to contribute one bit of information.

"You bet. With their rules, the only way for a foreign-trained engineer to practise engineering in Canada, is to study in Canada all over again. For many newcomers with limited savings, they can't afford to do this."

"So how can we change APE and other bodies like them?"

"I really don't know. You see, they have the authority to make their own rules. Even Government cannot make them do otherwise. These bodies were given the legal mandate to regulate their respective professions. The College of Physicians and Surgeons regulates the medical doctors. Licensed Registered Nurses Association regulates the registered nurses, etc. How to change them? Maybe just through persuasion. Make them see the wisdom and benefits of being flexible in the way they recognize credentials. I don't know. This is a big barrier to skilled immigrants practicing their professions in Canada." It looks complicated.

"How do other countries do it?" I ask.

"That's a good question, and a good area for research. I know for example in other countries, the people who regulate the profession are not the professionals themselves, but an independent Regulatory Office, like an Ombudsman. The idea is to avoid conflict of interest. For example, when medical doctors control the registration of other medical doctors, that action has the effect of reducing the competition for doctors. It protects the wages of existing doctors. That's not fair. That's why the independent body or Ombudsman gets to regulate professions, not the professionals themselves."

"Makes sense. So why doesn't Canada do that?"

"Beats me. Regulatory bodies are powerful. They would not want to give up control. What politician would like to fight with powerful bodies like these who have a legitimate mandate of protecting the safety of Canadians by guarding against any 'substandard' education and skills of people applying to be certified in the professions?"

"Then we have to prove that the education and skills and experience of skilled immigrants from other countries are just as good, or better, than in Canada!" I am convinced of it.

"Good luck! That's an excellent idea. And a lot of work! Maybe you can convince government to undertake this massive study comparing credentials all over the world, and present that to all the regulatory bodies of Canada?" she says tongue in cheek.

"How about just start with engineering, like a pilot study?" I ask, only semi-seriously.

"Actually...that's very practical! Even our agency might be able to do it with some sympathetic partners in this field, who would help make the study credible." She is thinking, and looking at me, and now smiling. "Why don't I raise it at our next managers meeting, and see what happens?" says Coreen.

I feel so hopeful. "Good luck! And let me know how I can help on anything," I offer.

"Of course, you're in on this, it's your idea! Let's go for coffee, my treat!" she says happily, but not as happy as me.

* * *

The sun is brilliant, its heat muted and soft on this November morning. I can look at it without squinting, and its thin rays emanate from a glowing centre, quivering like cat's whiskers. A patch of dark cloud sits ominously underneath the sun and I hope it moves away soon. It's been raining steady the past days, and today is the first day the sun has come out. My fireplace is on, and the combination of sunshine and fireplace soothes my weary heart. The sunlight wreaks havoc on the tiled floors of my living room, casting playful shadows in rectangles, triangles, stripes on the walls, the sofa, and the tables. The boats are out today, trailing v's all over the shimmering waters of False Creek. A stab of happiness hits me, and I remember the first time I met Stephen.

* * *

It's Remembrance Day and the restaurant is predictably busy for brunch. The sun is out and customers are choosing to sit on the patio by False Creek. It is nippy, but the heaters are on and the sun is ablaze. In other places in Canada, they call this weather Indian Summer. The customers are arriving in large groups, and everybody seems thirsty, hungry, and demanding variations on everything: orange slice not lemon in the water, can I exchange the fries for fried tomatoes, make sure the egg is still runny on the benny, just semi-toasted bread please. I am not having a good day. In the corner table, I am serving a group of young men in animated conversation. I am grateful, as they don't seem to be too interested in the food, just coffee and eggs benedict for everybody.

"That's a human rights violation, and I think he should sue," says one of them.

"That should teach those regulatory bodies to discriminate against foreign-trained engineers," says another.

My ears perk.

"What's the precedent for it?" says someone.

"I don't know yet, but I'm sure I can find something," says the first one.

"If we win, that will make regulatory bodies open their doors to accepting foreign credentials, or risk more lawsuits," he continues.

"Yeah, better than any policy," says one.

"The thing is to find a live case, a winnable one," says another.

I am so excited that I knock over one of the glasses, and the water splashes all over the table and the lap of one of them.

"I'm so sorry, so sorry," I say, flustered and embarrassed. "Are you okay?" I ask the man who is now standing, wiping his pants with his napkin. I am also wiping his pants, and his front begins to bulge up slightly. When I realize what I'm doing, I feel even more embarrassed.

"I'm so sorry," I continue to say. He laughs, takes my wiping hand to stop me and says, "It's okay. It'll dry. It's only water." He looks into my eyes with the sweetest smile that makes me relax.

"I couldn't help but overhear," I say. "If you're looking for cases of skilled immigrants not able to work in their field, I know a place where they have lots."

"Really? Where?" asks the man whose drink I knocked over.

"At Cross Currents Society, they have a program of helping skilled newcomers find work in their field, and almost all their clients have this problem. I volunteer with that program. You should be able to find a suitable case there," I suggest.

"I heard about them. Yes, we should try them," he says.

We exchange names and contact information. "Stephen Lee, Advocate, Human Rights BC," says his business card.

"Is an 'advocate' a lawyer?" I ask.

"Yes," he says smiling.

I smile at my new ally. What a great godsend, a lawyer to help our cause. In fact, a whole group of lawyers. And a huge tip for me as well.

The next day, Stephen phones me. We meet for coffee that same afternoon, just before I start work at the restaurant. He is charming, funny and bright. He is a recent graduate of law at Simon Fraser University. His parents come from China, and he was born in Vancouver. He speaks a little mandarin. Some of his ancestors worked building the rails, and their maltreatment is part of why he pursued human rights advocacy in his legal studies. I am fascinated by his story, as he is by mine. He is an avid backpack traveller too and we compare places we've visited. We meet again next day for dinner, and again, and again, even before we meet with Cross Currents Society on the project. By then, we are fast friends, and I am already mildly in love.

* * *

CHAPTER 5

Canada
Bobby, 1992

It's a beautiful fall day, and here I am sitting outside the Surrey Mayor's office, with Jim Purdy our engineer, and Ken Davidson my boss, waiting for our appointment with the Mayor. We'll be telling him all about our plans for a subdivision in South Surrey. How did I, little old me, without a degree, get to do this anyway? Dad was a fool. All this land was just waiting for someone like him to subdivide and make pots of money. Here's Ken and I doing it, not one of us an engineer. So, we hire one. Didn't Dad even think of it? What was on his mind? Fucking Carla. I shut out the scene on the floor, throwing them out. I remember feeling so lost after all that. Not knowing what to do, I ran to my buddies.

* * *

"Ding, got anything on you?"
"Just some weed...Hey, what's up, Bro?"
"Nothing. Roll me a couple."
"That bad, eh?"

I took a drag. "Your worst nightmare man. This is gooood."

"So..."

"My Dad's fucked. Fucked that whore. Caught them right in the act. In my house. Man. We're fucked. I'm fucked. My whole family's fucked."

"Who's the chick?"

"That caregiver we were helping. Employer was abusing her. Mom and Dad sheltered her. She was living with us."

"Fuck."

"Man. Could have been going on all that time. Maybe even before. Maybe that's how she came to live with us. We were all duped. Fuck!"

"What d'you do?"

"Kicked the asses out."

"Good for you. That's good man."

"Hey, what's up?"

"Dante. Bobby's got trouble. Dad trouble."

"Ya?"

"Caught his Dad fucking some chick in their own house."

"Shit. What's the deal?"

"A caregiver. Said she was abused by her employer so my mom took her in. Then this. No, my Dad was the one who took her in. Maybe they've been carrying on even before. Maybe that's why he took her in. What a play. Fuck."

"Man, that sucks. So, what happens next?"

"I kicked them out. Told Dad never to come back. Who needs him? I'll look after us. Fuck! And to think he always belittled me. Nothing I did was ever any good. The snake. Poor Mom. She works so hard. To get this."

"Take it easy, man. You can handle it. We'll help you. Here... It'll take you away from all this. Make you feel strong, bro."

"What's that?"

"Here's what you do...snort in one nostril, then the other. Not a sudden inhale, just...you know...relaxed inhale. Like that. Your turn."

"Not that way, man!

"Achoo!"

"Shit!"

The snow powder scattered about. Ding crawled and sniffed up whatever he could get from the floor. Dante laughed watching Ding sprawled out on the floor laughing, covered with white powder. I laughed, and then cried. I didn't care if they saw me crying. I cried for my mom, and my sisters. I cried for what we left behind. I cried for my grandparents, our big home, my buddies at Ateneo. I cried for the joke of Canada as paradise. I cried for my fucked-up drughead friends who love me. I cried for me and what I'd become. I cried for my hatred for my dad, bigger than my fear of what I've done. Cast him away. Be the father to my family. I cried for the man I must be now. Drugs and all. Whatever it takes. So be it. My dad is now dead to me. We will make our paradise here, without him. I swear it.

When I came home, Sonia was already putting things away. Manolita was asleep in the room.

"Such a mess, what happened here?" she asked.

I told her.

She was shocked, and then angry. Then she started crying. I let her cry on my shoulders for a long time. My tears had all dried up. I assured her everything would be all right. I told her to rest. I cleaned the pots and pans, the trays, the chopping blocks and the knives and put them away. I boiled vanilla and water, like what I've seen Sonia do, opened the windows and doors to freshen the air. I saw that supper was ready on the stove. I arranged four place settings on the table.

Stumbling Through Paradise

Mom arrived from delivering orders just when the house was all cleaned up. I kissed her and called everyone to dinner. I told them about what I discovered. I told them Dad was never coming back. I told them I will look after the family, and that we will be better off.

After the separation, I felt I grew up incredibly fast. It seemed I aged instantly from my meager 15 years, becoming the father of our family. I semi-dropped out of the Diablos to take care of the family. Dante offered me a job maintaining landscaping and painting, his own sideline with some members of the group. I happily took it and learned the business. I also worked part-time at McDonald's. I still did weed from time to time, but stayed away from cocaine. Dante told me about the incredible income from dealing coke, and I was tempted. I guess I was too afraid of it then.

I still did karate and got better. When a competition was announced, I joined a team and earned a red belt. My teacher taught me to meditate as part of the practice. I liked that.

In time, I formed my own group with my karate buddies, called Desiderata. We started our own businesses including cutting grass, building fences, easy painting jobs. And I still worked at McDonald's, while managing to keep up my grades.

I came home early whenever I could, and gave my money to Mom regularly. I felt a sense of victory over my dad and over fate, realizing that we could live adequately on our own, despite my worst fears. The only thing I wished for that seemed to be out of my hands was to break Mom's perpetual sadness with a smile, a laugh. And for that I needed to be happy myself. My teacher said not to rush it. "Let grief work itself through you, and her. The cloud will lift before you know it," he said.

* * *

"The Mayor's ready to see you now." I straighten up, button up my jacket and set my bitter memories aside. Ken slaps me on the knee and stands up.

"Nervous? Just relax and enjoy." He winks.

The new Mayor is a big guy. They say he played football. He won the elections by a big margin. Popular guy. They say he's in nobody's pocket. His handshake is strong. I like him already.

"Thanks for seeing us, Mr. Mayor." Ken passes his card, Jim's and mine to the Mayor.

"No, it's my honour. My staff tell me you've been doing good work here in Surrey."

"Thank you sir. We do our best. I'm glad your staff think so. How are you enjoying your new job, sir?"

"Love it. Have a great team on staff and Council, and just raring to go."

"Yes, congratulations, your party won a strong majority!"

"I feel humbled by the people's faith in me and my party. I promise to deserve it. With the help of developers like you, we'll have a Surrey that rivals Vancouver. So, Ken, what can I help you with?"

"We've plans for a new subdivision in South Surrey. We haven't submitted anything yet. It will require a rezoning but the new zone is all in accordance with the Official Community Plan. At this time, we just wanted to introduce ourselves to you, and see what you think of the idea."

"It's a good start that the zoning is in accordance with the plan. Where in South Surrey?"

"Near the border crossing."

"What zone?"

"We are thinking half acre or half acre gross."

"Hmm...in the farmlands?"

"Just outside. It's in the acreage areas."

"Might be too early...talk to the community. They have an active ratepayers group there. Check them out before you go too far. And talk to the staff, of course. There are only wells there, isn't it? Utilities may be an issue. Anyway, you know all that more than me."

The secretary opens the door. "Mr. Mayor, your next appointment is here. For the fundraiser?"

"Oh yes, we'll be finished shortly. By the way, Ken, our group is holding a fundraiser. May I invite you?"

"Absolutely, we'll be honoured."

"Great! Well, got to go. Great to meet you. Keep it up." We shake hands all around, and then the Mayor speaks to me directly.

"Nice to meet young businessmen in our City! Which country did you originally come from...let's see, Filipino?"

"Yes, sir." I'm pleased he got me right.

"We've lots of Filipinos now living in Surrey...good people, hardworking. Where in Surrey do you live?"

"Sorry, sir. I live in Vancouver. "

"Well then, when are you planning to move to Surrey? All the others will beat you to it!"

He laughs amiably, and shakes my hand again.

Ken moves to the door, which is now opened by the secretary.

"Thank you Mr. Mayor for your advice and time."

In the car, Ken is very pleased with the meeting.

"Why? He didn't promise anything," I say.

"He said we do good work. So we have a good reputation with staff, that's important. Also, he invited us to the fundraiser. That means we will donate, and not only he, but also his group of Councillors, who form the majority, will know that we have donated to their cause. That makes us 'friends.'"

"Does that mean they will approve our development?"

"Not necessarily. But they will be predisposed to voting for it if all other things are addressed. He mentioned what those issues are: the neighborhood, that it might be too 'advanced,' and the utilities. So we have the clues that, if we address, will get his and his group's support. That's a lot."

"I see. We have our work cut out for us."

"Who said this thing was easy? But it gets easier when you make strategic moves, like this." He winked.

"Got a date for the party?" I asked.

"No. Got someone for me?"

"Maybe."

Ken is really smart. I'm so lucky to have him for my mentor. He'd be great for Mom. But she spurns everyone who courts her. What did she see in my good for nothing Dad anyway? Ken's so much better. If Dad met someone like Ken at that time to show him the ropes, we would have a different life. Then Mom would be really happy. Maybe she can still be happy.

* * *

Mom didn't agree. She even got upset at my trying to matchmake. Sonia liked Ken, and so did Manolita. "Will you please all leave me alone?" Mom cried. So be it.

I went to the party in my best suit. It was a glittering affair held at the Hazelmere Golf and Country Club. I met so many people I could not remember their names. But as Ken advised, I made sure to take the business card of everyone I met, as I was supposed to email each one next day, say I was glad to meet them, and leave them my business coordinates. If it was a Surrey City Hall staff member, I made sure to talk with them longer, find out their department and what they do, and let them know what I do. In our business, it helps that the person on the other side of the counter knows you, according to Ken.

The hors d'ourves were exceptional, beautifully crafted morsels of seafood, little rolls filled with mysterious and delectable spreads, bright-coloured fruits shining on top of little piles of cream. I had my fill of champagne.

It was a stand up affair, and only one speech — just the Mayor introducing all the Councillors, and the main entertainment: a pianist. Her name was Nicole McIsaac. She walked to the piano, a vision of beauty. An ivory goddess in a black flowing gown. Her blonde hair was parted on one side, and the rest of her hair was curled up against the nape of her neck, like a Hollywood diva. Her long neck was emphasized by her off-shoulder gown, which swayed gently as she walked. She sat at the piano, placed her hands on her lap for a moment, then played. She started with something thunderous, which shifted to something playful and fast, then again rolling thunder. The audience loved it. She bowed, and then started another piece, slow and sweet and flowing, ending in a very long trill that had her fingers going from one end of the piano to the other. She bowed again. For the third piece, I could not hear the music anymore, as I was completely enchanted by her intense face, the delicate paleness of her skin, the grace of her body moving along with her hands. She was incredibly beautiful. When she stood up and smiled, I was already in love with her. I asked Ken to get someone to introduce us. He got the Mayor. Lucky me.

"Nicole, you have to meet this young man. He is our future in Surrey. The best looking, too. Bobby del Mundo."

The Mayor paused. He looked at me, then Nicole.

"I see, that I'm no longer needed here." He coughed and pulled Ken away, leaving Nicole and me alone.

I can't remember all that we said to each other. I seemed to be in a trance, my nerves all jangled up. All I remember was that she kept laughing. I wasn't even trying to be funny. I just managed to drop one, or was it two, hors d'oeurves on my jacket, and then I spilled champagne when I tried to drink it with my nose, and then I stepped on her foot trying to save the glass, which happily did not break on the thick carpet. I remember that she took my hand and led me outside to the garden and sat us down on a quiet bench. She wiped my jacket with a napkin, and then she said, "Now, we can start over." I looked at her lovely understanding eyes, and I felt like crying for I had met the woman of my life. I asked her with my eyes, and she answered by pressing her lips softly against mine. It felt right and good. We talked for I don't know how long, until someone found Nicole.

"There you are! They are asking for another piece or two. Will you?"

"Of course." Then she stood up, naughtily blew me a kiss, and disappeared.

I was still wondering whether it all happened, when I felt a tap on my shoulder.

"Bobby old boy! I wasn't sure. Is it really you?"

"Dante?" He had long hair, wore a white tux that hung around a lean body, a sort of brown Mick Jagger.

"Hey man!" We hugged roughly.

"You look great, bro!" he said.

"What you doin' here?" We asked at the same time, and hugged some more.

"I'm developing in Surrey now. How about you?"

"Same old. Same old. Just bigger and better," he said. "Hey, something big's happening. Want in on it?"

"Man. I don't do that anymore. Not since my Dad passed. It just was too close for comfort. Getting fingered. I'm legit now. Not as much dough but it's good. I'm good."

"Well...I'm happy for you man. But if you ever want to, uh... make gazillions, you know who to call. You don't even need to do anything. I'm raising capital for this move. So, you just provide...an investment. Silent partner, you know?" He inserted a card in my hand. "Got to go, kid."

I looked at the card. Gold embossed print. "Dante Salvador." Underneath that: "President, Paradise Incorporated." On the corner, the image of a globe. Underneath that: "All the world's a paradise." I thought of how much Dante must be making. I thought of how nice it would be to marry Nicole. I fantasized a million-dollar wedding, building her a beautiful home in West Vancouver, having a baby with her, vacations in the Bahamas. A future secure, never to worry for Mom, Sonia, Manolita. It's just a silent investor. It's like buying stocks, only, double figure rate of return. The idea wouldn't leave me.

When I met up with Nicole again after her performance, she seemed livelier, her cheeks flushed. I wanted to take her home, but suddenly felt embarrassed about my homely Honda. If I went in with Dante, I could take her home in a... Porsche? As it turned out, the organizers had a limo for her. She had donated her concert after all. I met the woman of my dreams tonight, but something spoiled it. The wish for something more, when what I received tonight was a treasure. What was wrong with me? I put it out of my mind and focused on Nicole. She was everything I knew she was going to be: wonderful.

After a week, I still had not removed Dante's card from my wallet. Every time I opened it, the card was there, luring me. I debated pros and cons. But then in the end, who would know? No one. I trust Dante. He would never betray me. I finally called the number.

* * *

CHAPTER 6

Canada
Sonia, 1992–1993

I never know about Carla, how I feel about her. She is a tangle of tragedies, the victim of poverty and unfortunate circumstances, yet she always seems to come out on top. Either she is a very lucky person, a person with engaging qualities I don't see, or a very manipulative person, or perhaps a combination.

I take Stephen with me when I visit Carla and the baby. Carla has named the baby Manuel Junior, or Jun Jun for short.

They have moved to a basement home off of Kingsway in East Vancouver. It is a pleasant neighbourhood, with a park across the street. The basement suite is accessed from the side of the main house. The door to their suite is off a big backyard. Inside, the house is surprisingly bright from one big window overlooking the backyard. The house is stuffed with things: small appliances, flower vases with artificial flowers on crocheted doilies, crucifixes and images of saints carved from bamboo, pictures in frames on the tables, a mosaic of pictures on the wall, posters of Philippine beaches and jeepneys.

A crib sits in the middle of the living room, like a throne. Baby Jun Jun is a few weeks old. He has my father's thick eyebrows and his dark colour. He has Carla's fine features. His fingers are enclosed in little white gloves, as are his feet.

"So that he does not scratch his face," Carla says.

"Can you not cut his nails?" I ask.

"I'm afraid to cut his nails. They are too soft."

I see a white band around the baby's tummy. "Why's that?"

"Where the umbilical chord was cut is a wound. The *bigkis* wrapped tight around the belly will help protect and heal it. Also, to keep the belly button down. If not, the belly button might stick out. When he's grown up, not nice to see." I didn't know that.

Carla is small and slim, but large in the middle, as though she might still be pregnant. Her long curly hair is tied in a pony tail, and her face is the kind that does not need much make up as the features are fine in themselves: almond eyes, pert nose, high cheekbones.

"Would you like a beer, Stephen? Have some *palitaw*. Sorry, I have not prepared anything. If I had known you were coming, I would have made something."

"Oh no, thank you. I'm full. We just had lunch."

"Or maybe some peanuts? Or apples?" Carla insists.

"No thank you, really. May I use your washroom?" Stephen asks.

"It's over here. But let me tidy it up a little first, you should have told me you were coming, Sonia. The house is a mess."

"It's okay, you don't have to. I'm sure it's fine," Stephen says.

"He's a nice man, isn't he? Chinese?" asks Carla when Stephen was gone.

"Yes, Chinese, second generation," I say. Seeing the blank look on Carla's face, I explain. "His parents come from China, but he was already born here."

"Ah, must be rich! You know. Chinese. He's handsome. You're lucky." Carla winks at me. Seeing him come out of the bathroom, she says, "*Pasensiya na* for our humble house. I can't afford much, but I try to keep it clean always."

"And good thing for the generosity of your mom, we have a little more each month," Carla continues. "I offer to help her with the house, but she says no. She is kind, your mom. And you too, thank you for the present for Jun Jun. So kind."

I feel awkward and decide it's time to go.

I take one last look at the baby in the cradle.

"Want to carry him?" Carla asks. I nod. She picks up the baby and places him on my waiting arms.

It is so small, so hairy and so light in my arms. My father's son, my little half-brother. I bring my face to his face to kiss him, smelling the coconut oil on his hair. His eyes are closed in sleep. His tiny lips pucker and break into a smile at the touch of my kiss.

"An angel is passing," Carla says. I look at Carla, not knowing what that meant. "That's what they say. When a baby smiles in his sleep, it's because an angel is passing," she explains. I like that.

After the visit, Stephen tells me to quit feeling sorry for Carla.

"She'll be fine. I can see how she...well...got your father. Tragedy is seductive. It can be used as a weapon of power, and she sure knows how. And she's not bad looking. Some men like being fawned over. She does that well. Doesn't work for me though." Stephen chuckles.

Stephen has the same clarity about the problem of under-utilized skilled newcomers.

"Skilled newcomers from all over the world are coming to Canada on Canada's invitation, with hopes of practicing those skills in Canada. Regulatory bodies do not recognize their credentials, companies do not hire them, and Canada looks the other way. Whose fault is it, that we now have underutilized skilled newcomers, and continuing shortage of skilled labor in Canada?"

He answers his own question, "Canadian Government, end of story".

He continues. "In any problem, I always look for the one with the power. They should be accountable; they are the ones through whose use, misuse, or lack of use of power, the problem happened in the first place. And they have the power to make it better." I mull that over.

Carla had the power over my father, the power of her tragedy, of her need for him. Or was it my father who had the power over Carla, the power of wealth, status and education? Seeing relationships as an exercise of power is new to me, and I wonder who is exercising what power where it comes to Stephen and me.

"She'll be fine. She'll always come out fine, you'll see," Stephen says. I don't feel right about that somehow, realizing this is the first time I doubt Stephen's judgment.

* * *

My back hurts, the left side of my shoulder. I can't even reach out for my glass of water with my left hand. I must have sprained it sleeping on my left side, the one towards the window, and the side away from Stephen. I must sleep on the right side tonight, against the blank space where he used to sleep. I can never sprawl all over the bed. I must be waiting for him still.

Outside, the sky is a grey bowl covering the city. It is absolutely still at dawn, even the flags of Science World are silent. A tow truck is parked by the side of the road, and its blinking lights alerting traffic are the only movement on the street. I am piled up with comforters, yet I feel cold.

Touching the coldness of the vacant space on my bed, I think of all the things Stephen was right about, including about Carla.

* * *

We are celebrating Bobby's birthday at a restaurant. Bobby has not yet arrived. I confront Manolita about her telling Bobby about Mom's support for Carla and Jun Jun, something that was supposed to be kept secret from Bobby.

"What's the harm? He'll find out about it anyway, sooner or later. And what could he do? It's not his money!" cries Manolita. "This secrecy in the family is so...overdramatic." *You are the overdramatic one.*

"Do you know what Bobby said, when he found out?" I say to Manolita. She smirks, waiting for me to answer my own question.

"'I'm leaving the family', that's what he said."

"So how can he leave the family? That's just his drama," says Manolita.

"Oh yes, I can," says a voice from behind. It's Bobby arriving with his girlfriend, Nicole.

We stop the conversation, and kiss Bobby and Nicole. They settle in their chairs, Bobby solicitously helping Nicole from her coat, holding her scarf and gloves as she takes her seat. Nicole is a delicate beauty, reserved and proper. Bobby treats her as carefully as a doll. I watch her fingers as the gloves come off, so smooth and slender, the precious fine fingers of a concert pianist. Her blonde hair is gathered up in a French twist, and a band of hair crosses her forehead at an angle. She gives a sweet smile to everyone, with her big blue eyes and cherry-red lips. She is too good for my brother.

Stephen arrives next, and we all do the kissing round again. Stephen is already cracking a joke, and everybody's laughing and gay, and I am pleased he is the man I love. I cuddle up to him, and forget all about Carla. Mom arrives in a huff.

"So sorry kids, we got delayed," she says. Behind her, Tita Lily, Mom's best friend, is following. We all rise again and kiss the new arrivals, settle in and chitchat.

Everything is going well, everyone having a good laughing time, when Carla, looking elegant in a flowing pink dress appears. She is bearing a gift-wrapped box. She stands beside Bobby who is sitting at the head of the rectangular table, and extends the box towards him.

"Happy birthday, Bobby," she says shyly.

We are all stunned. Bobby looks at her and then unseeingly at others around the table. An ominous silence descends on the party. All I can remember is Mom standing up from the other head of the table and walking towards Carla. She takes the present from her hand. "Why thank you, Carla. You didn't have to," she says.

"Oh, Manuel would have remembered and would have wanted to give Bobby a present," Carla says.

Silence again.

"Uhh, why don't you...join us for dinner?" says my Mom.

"No, no, that's not necessary," Carla says.

"Why not? You're already here?" says my Mom.

"Well..." Carla is not sure what to do.

In the uncertainty of that moment, Bobby stands up. He helps Nicole from her chair, picks up their things and leaves the table. We all look at each other. I feel helpless.

Carla says, "No, I'm going. I'm sorry to have come. So sorry." She walks away, fast, toward the door she came from, almost knocking over a waiter.

"She has nerve," I hear Stephen say under his breath.

Mom sits on Bobby's chair, looking at the present on the table.

Manolita announces, "Well, I'm not wasting my dinner," picking up the half-eaten burger, and biting into it.

"Bobby knows about the support you send Carla," I say. "Manolita told him."

Mom shakes her head as she looks at Manolita chomping her food down. We all eat in silence.

I later understand what Bobby meant when he threatened to leave the family if Mom continued the support for Carla. After the birthday dinner, he stops coming home. He doesn't return my calls, nor Mom's, nor Manolita's. It's like he dropped off from our lives. It goes on like this for a week, until finally, Mom leaves him a message on his phone to say that she will stop the support for Carla.

Bobby calls back later and says, "If you're lying to me, and I find that you are still sending her money, forget you have a son."

This is never mentioned again in our home. Nobody can mention Carla or Jun Jun's names in Bobby's presence.

He seems to have so much hate for them, and I cannot understand where this comes from. Or I do, but not its intensity. The way it never goes away for Bobby. I cannot hold a grudge as long as that, or perhaps I have not been as wronged. I do not know of a hurt so deep it cannot be healed. I think of my own feelings of abandonment, and I know the feelings of insecurity lurk around in my heart when I see other people's families so happy with their doting fathers. I know the sadness will always be there, but it does not grip me in a vise that I cannot move forward, the way it grips my brother.

Bobby becomes more distant from everybody after the birthday dinner, as though we all betrayed him. Soon after the reconciliation, Bobby rents a condo, saying that it would be his business office as well. Thankfully, it is near our own house in Vancouver, and the separation doesn't seem as painful.

Bobby immerses himself in his business and to my eyes, rapidly grows older than his years. It seems like he is in a terrible hurry to succeed. He busies himself so that he does not have to think of whatever it is that resides in him that he wants to forget.

He begins making plans for marrying Nicole. We learn this the night we surprise him with a housewarming party for his new apartment.

"Nicole's father is a judge, and her mother is a university professor. I have met them. The McIsaacs are rich — old money from mining. They are nice. I'd like to marry Nicole, maybe next year," he says.

"Are they good to you? Are we...good enough for them?" asks Mom.

"Why shouldn't we be good enough for them?!" explodes Bobby.

"Sorry *anak*, I didn't mean to upset you. What's wrong, Bobby? Why are you so uptight? You've been so...distant lately. Is something troubling you?" Mom asks, touching Bobby's cheek with her hand.

Bobby turns his face away. "No, nothing's wrong. It's just that...why must you think we are...never good enough? As though there's something deficient with us. We are the del Mundos, an important family in the Philippines. We are educated, and own good successful businesses in Canada. We are good people. I could have my pick of women, and I choose their daughter. Maybe they should ask if they are good enough for us!"

"*Anak*, it's just that...well, you know...It's alright. You're right. We shouldn't feel lower than them. I shouldn't feel lower than them. It's me only who feels this way. You kids are all right. You're all okay," says Mom apologetically. I go to her and hug her.

"Don't say that, Mom. You're very okay." I see that her eyes are moist.

"Sometimes I wish I had your father here. Maybe we could invite your Lolo to come and ask for Nicole's hand in marriage!" Mom brightens up at her idea.

"Or maybe we could all go to Manila with Nicole's family for the engagement party!" says Manolita. "That'll impress them!"

Bobby smiles for the first time. "I'll call Lolo, he'll be delighted!"

The marriage becomes a big project, a show of force by the del Mundos to impress the McIsaacs. Bobby wants entry into Canadian society, if it means reaching out across the oceans for the lustre of the del Mundos. The McIsaacs accept the invitation to come to Manila for the official asking of the hand in marriage. A February date is selected for reasons of benign climate at that time of year in the Philippines, and February is the month of lovers, says Bobby. Bobby is so sentimental and romantic about this marriage Manolita and I can't stand it. Lolo Ben is paying for the trip and hosting all of us.

If Dad were alive, he would oppose all this. He would not want his father messing with his family, the more distance the better. With Tita Marites' revelation, I now understand why. Father's death is getting us back with the del Mundos. I don't mind that. We needn't be so alone. I look forward to coming home again, and spending more time with Tita Marites. I still do not have an employer for Bekang, and I am getting anxious. I better have one to report by the time we go to Manila. Stephen wants to come too, and I am pleased for him to know my people.

* * *

Stopping the support for Carla turns out to be a bigger deal than expected. It means Carla needs to go back to work. But what about the baby? Care for infants being so expensive and pay for domestic workers being so low, it doesn't make sense for Carla to work. Unless, she could look after the baby while she worked. Perhaps if she looked after kids in her own home while she looked after her own — that might work. And she can continue taking food orders from Mom to add to her income.

Carla takes in two children to look after in her home. For a while, things go well, but soon enough, it is all too much for Carla. One of the kids hurts himself when Carla was not looking and the parent takes him out of her care. The *kakanins* she bakes are not as good as before and the customers complain. Carla falls ill with a long bout of flu, which means she could not take the other child.

It is lucky for Carla that one of Mom's clients, a Canadian couple, who are both professors, with only one five-year-old child, lose their caregiver to marriage. They are delighted to have Carla and her baby stay with them in their large home to look after their child. It works out very well: everyone is happy, including their child, who is delighted to have a baby to look after. Carla is ecstatic with the arrangement and profusely thanks Mom for getting her the job. Mom and I are relieved.

It didn't take very long for Stephen's prophecy to come true. Within six months of Carla's hiring, Mom comes home very angry one night.

"She's done it again. That...woman...broke another family. My client told me that she found out her husband and Carla were having an affair. She is filing for a divorce. Her husband has accepted it. He, Carla and baby Jun Jun have moved out. My client is upset at me for bringing Carla into her family. I dare not tell her that Carla did the same thing to me," says Mom.

I am beyond anger. I feel like a fool. Mom and I and my Dad. We all fell for it.

"Well at least the baby will be well looked after. He's got a future now. You don't have to worry," says Stephen, always the pragmatic one.

Stephen is right. Now we don't have to worry about Jun Jun, or Carla. She's with a wealthy professor now, set up for life. I should be happy. But I feel used. I try to understand. She is impoverished. She is just trying to survive, using what wiles she has to do so, and doing it very well. I feel old and betrayed. I taste bitterness in my mouth. I feel bad for my Dad. She used you too Dad. Did you even know that? Did you mind it, and not care, so long as she made you feel good? She must be very good at it. Damn.

* * *

I hear Carla is now called "Dona Carla" by the caregivers' circle. She is now resident queen of her own mansion. I hear she doesn't know what to do with her newfound money. She has opened up a karaoke bar, which is now the hangout of her caregiver friends. I hear she has started to promote herself as a singer. She was the main singer at a concert whose proceeds went to her church.

Mom asks me to pick up some dishes ordered from Rosie, Anita and Tita Ching. They must have had a cookout at Tita Ching's based on the mess in the kitchen when I get there.

"*Susmaryosep*! She has a thick face! How bold to try and sing such a grand song as 'The Rose'. Her voice could not sustain the long notes and her voice cracked. It was so embarrassing," says Tita Ching.

"Who are you talking about?" I ask. It sounded like juicy gossip.

"Who else, but your friend, Dona Carla?" says Rosie.

"If it were me, I would have just stopped singing. But she just continued on as though nothing happened. Just before the song ended, she went out of tune on the last notes! But did you think she was ashamed? No way, she kept smiling, and bowing, and throwing kisses in the air as though she was a superstar," Rosie says, acting it all out.

"What did the audience do? Did they boo her?"

"No. Some people still clapped, mostly the friends she invited. The clapping came mostly from the front where her friends and her husband sat. But you could hear murmuring from the audience. Some clapped weakly in sympathy I think."

"I hear she has opened up a school too," Anita pipes in.

"A school? What does she know to run a school!" exclaims Rosie.

"A school for nannies — cooking the Canadian way, Canadian child-rearing tips, things like that," explains Anita.

"Huh? How would she know to do that? What she should really teach is 'how to steal a rich Canadian husband,'" offers Rosie. Laughter all around.

"Anita, you should enroll for that course!" suggests Tita Ching. More laughter.

"Ha! Then I can hire all of you to clean my mansion in Shaughnessey!" jokes Anita.

"But you know, it won't last long, I hear. The husband and she are fighting because of the money. Apparently, there isn't as much as she thought, and he wants to put a lid on her. I see a divorce on the horizon…" warns Rosie naughtily.

Rosie pauses for effect. "And do you know what the real trouble is?"

We all await the answer.

"It's not about the money. I hear she's got a close friend now who encourages her on the businesses. And I hear she is really not just a friend, but her girlfriend, if you know what I mean?" whispers Rosie.

"Really!" Tita Ching, Anita and I exclaim in unison.

"No way! They're probably just friends," I say.

"If you don't want to believe me, you can ask around," says Rosie.

"If she doesn't watch it, she'll lose everything," says Tita Ching.

"As they say, easy come, easy go," says Rosie.

I'm not exactly enjoying this as I think of baby Jun Jun, my little half-brother, wondering how this all would affect him. I prepare to leave and think of a reason to visit Carla. I realize I don't even know where she lives anymore.

"So where is that karaoke bar anyway?" I ask.

"Why? You want to tell your friend we are gossiping about her?" asks Rosie.

"Lay off her, Rosie," warns Tita Ching.

"I want to see the baby. I haven't seen him in a long time. He's my half brother, after all," I say.

"You be careful, she'll use you too if you don't watch out. Hang on to your Stephen, he looks like a good catch," Rosie warns.

I don't like this conversation. "Stephen's not like that," I say defensively.

"Uuuy, she's jealous," teases Rosie.

"Stop that, Rosie," says Tita Ching.

"I'm late. Got to go now." I leave abruptly, wondering why I feel a ring of truth in what Rosie said. Yet I know that there's no way Carla and Stephen... She's so much older than him. And she's not his type. Stephen said so. And he's too smart to get played, a lawyer. Yet the men she got — my father's an engineer, the Canadian professor. She has maybe a 'girlfriend' now too? Na, couldn't be. They're surely just good friends. How cruel gossip can be. I feel more curious to locate not the baby, but Carla.

* * *

The pilot project to research engineering foreign credentials compared with Canadian credentials is growing by leaps and bounds. It now includes research into how other countries regulate the engineering profession compared with Canada. A Federal Government agency is interested to fund the research, and I am offered a paid job as researcher in the team if I want to. I am thrilled to be on the team.

As to finding a case for Stephen's group to litigate, it is a more challenging task than I thought. They need a case where the skilled immigrant is prepared to come forward and litigate. Most newcomers simply want to get on with their lives, work, earn and support their families. Also, many are afraid of repercussions on their future careers, preferring to cooperate with authorities rather than fighting them. You need someone who is also very confident, of his or her credentials and experience. In other words, a highly experienced foreign-trained professional, who has been denied certification by a regulatory body and unable to work in his profession, with sufficient funds to withstand trial. Tough to find.

At a meeting with Coreen Douglas and the employment program team at Cross Currents Society, a different approach develops.

"If we can't file a lawsuit, we can mount a campaign — an information awareness campaign telling stories of the waste of human talent. Foreign-trained immigrants, highly skilled doctors and engineers, working as taxi drivers, cleaners, clerks," explains Stephen.

"Sure, newcomers will share their stories. There is minimal risk to them. But don't give up the search for a case for the lawsuit. Keep up the pressure on these regulatory bodies. Maybe just the knowledge that a group is preparing to litigate against them has made APE more interested in reforming. They have agreed to participate in our study."

I agree with Coreen.

"Hah! They're clever. They get into the tent so they can give it their spin," says Stephen. "You watch them. Don't let them get away with their excuses. Put their feet to the fire," Stephen warns.

"Don't worry, Sonia will be there, right Sonia?" Coreen smiles at me.

"Of course I'll be there. But I'm going to need more help from you to stand up to those officials. Could we make the Human Rights BC another partner in the research? That would balance them out. Human Rights BC is a legitimate stakeholder," I offer.

Stephen is looking at me strangely. Is the smile on his face one of admiration?

"Genius! I'll arrange it so I'll represent the Human Rights BC," Stephen says.

"Great idea. Let's propose that at the next meeting," says Coreen.

* * *

CHAPTER 7

Canada
Sonia, 1993

I have a runny nose, my bones are achy, my arms and hands sore from kneading the green papaya for the *achara*. My eyes feel hot, and I don't know whether the tingling inside me is a chill or a fever. I walked from downtown yesterday in the rain, with an umbrella but no toque, and mom says *"nahamugan ka, anak."* A cold draft must have hit you, daughter. I like it when she calls me *anak*. My child. Sickness brings the term on. I feel closer to her, which is a difficult thing to do with mom. She is always busy, and a bit harsh, trying to be perfect — a perfect businesswoman, a perfect mom. The real Josie is tough to pry lose. It must be hard parenting in her generation, having to be perfect for your kids. It's an impossible thing to be. I know I'll not even try to be a parent. It's difficult enough to lead one's own life well, let alone raise children and help them lead good lives.

I got close to Mom once at a retreat we attended at Bowen Island, a small island community 10 minutes by ferry from Vancouver. There is a spirit lodge there called Mountain Glen where an ecumenical group holds spiritual retreats from time to time. Mom went by herself once, and came back so peaceful and rejuvenated that I decided to go with her next time.

The lodge is situated up on a hill overlooking the village of Bowen Island. On a clear day, you see the mountains forming a backdrop for Bowen Bay. Beside the lodge is an outdoor storage building, and farther, a small cabin for small groups. A few steps away is a forest with many paths and special viewing spots. It's a wonderful place to be still. You hear a lot of sounds — the rushing of wind, the crackle of dry leaves you step on. You see tiny things — a drop of rain at the tip of a branch that looks like a star in the early morning light.

The lodge itself is a solid three-level wood and glass structure atop a hill. Mom and I are sharing a room, located on the second floor. The room has two beds, and a bathroom. Each bed has a night table and lamp beside it. A shared closet. The fresh sheets are laid out folded on the bed, and the first thing you do is to make up the bed and pillows. Later, when you leave, you are asked to peel off the sheets and pillowcases you used and stuff them in a laundry bag out on the corridor. There are detergents underneath the bathroom sink and you are expected to clean the bathroom lightly before you go. Pay what you can afford. There is something convent-like about it all, clean and comfortable but spartan, that makes me think of the nuns at St. Theresa's College. This is probably the kind of rooms they had, and the way they operate. On one wall is an abstract crucifix, and on another wall, a small high window that lets you see the tops of trees and the sky.

I have forgotten how fastidious Mom is, how organized with her things. She has a container for everything: for soap, for teeth things, for hair things, for make up, for vitamins, for first aid, and sometimes containers within containers within containers. She could be a nun. She brought out a beautifully covered journal from her suitcase.

"I didn't know you write," I say.

"No, I don't. But last time, I found myself writing things I never thought I would, and liked it. It's nothing for you. You write all the time. I'm shy, but so long as I know no one will read it, I feel free to write the worst junk!" she laughs.

"What do you write about?"

"What I wish I did. Things I could have done better. What I still can do better. Writing to Jesus. Is that weird, *anak*? Then I let him write me back. I let his spirit write the words in reply, using my hand and my pen."

"How...?" I am beginning to feel weird.

"Well Jesus is not really writing, but my best self, inspired by God's grace, is writing the reply to my regular self. Anyway, maybe it's just a game I play with myself, but I get such clear responses from him. I guess it's true that we have all the answers within us; our divine self just needs to be listened to. We need to get quiet to hear the whisper. That's why the silent retreat." I am amazed at my mom, God's secret correspondent.

"I don't have to...write to God?" I ask.

"Of course not. Each to her own journey."

"Do we need to be silent ALL the time?"

"After the orientation and dinner tonight, yes."

"Can I pass notes?"

"It's the spirit of silence we aim to observe. Inner silence. We are in communion with God, so try and remember that. Sure you can pass notes saying what a lovely sunset this is, but the point is, just watch the sunset by yourself and see what truths are revealed to you by that beautiful sunset. That's God communicating something to you. If you try to share that sunset with someone, you may not hear what your own divine self, or God, is telling you. We even try not to look at each other's eyes as we pass, to respect each other's private inner journey. Of course, if you have a stomach ache and need something for it, talk to one of the staff, don't need to write it."

"Silent for five days?"

"You'll be surprised how easy it is to keep the lips silent. It's the thoughts that are hard to quiet down. We'll be given some tools to help us with that, passages we can focus on. Each one of us is assigned a spiritual director or guide. We get to talk with her every day for 15 minutes or so. She helps us plan our day and our journey through the retreat."

"But how can they advise us, when they don't know us?" I am wondering whether this retreat was a good idea. I don't want to be in a cult!

"Give it a try. You'll see what I mean. She is more like a spiritual facilitator. She helps you understand what you want to get out of this journey, and depending on your answer, she will give you some questions to ask yourself during the day. No, I'm telling you too much now. This might ruin it for you. Just listen with an open heart throughout the retreat. No one can make you do something you don't believe in. You can always leave. Okay?" Yes, I can always leave.

One thing I notice is a preponderance of women. A few older men. Different ages. A bell is rung to summon everyone to the dining room. A prayer is said and a welcome to all. The household rules are described, and it is announced that silence begins after dinner. I make myself talk over dinner even if I don't want to just because it's the last time in a long while. At my table, everyone has been to this retreat at least once. I'm the only newbie. I see another woman of my same age. I'd say the average age of the group is 50. The food is incredibly healthy, delicious, and abundant. People speak in hushed tones as though we were already in retreat. I watch my mother socialize. She brags about her children mostly, and then complains tongue in cheek about her obviously successful catering business, and anything about the Philippines, in that order.

The woman beside her says "Your daughter? How nice to have a mother and daughter in the retreat. We don't usually get that."

"I was surprised myself," says my mother, winking at me.

I smile my dutiful daughterly smile, and wonder about the expectation behind that comment. I don't know why I'm here, why I should want so much of that same peace I saw on my mother's face after her retreat. I'm not even troubled in the way others get when they need a retreat. Stephen and I are enjoying each other, even thinking of moving in together, and my project at Cross Currents Society is moving along with more success than I ever imagined. With advice from my team, the APE is now an enthusiastic member of my project. Maybe that's just it, things seem too pat, too easy. I feel a restlessness as though everything's been too good, or not good enough. Maybe it's easy because I'm only scratching the surface and I haven't reached the core. I feel suspended, wanting to be grounded. I feel hollow.

That night, I snuggle up with Mom in her bed and we make up our own rules. Can we at least have a chat before going to bed, I ask? No, she says. It will not be the same, she insists. We discuss lights out: anytime. We discuss how independent of each other we will be in terms of activities: entirely independent. Okay, I get it. And with that, I accept and start my silent retreat.

I decide to walk around the lodge, as it is too early, only 8:30 pm. It is early February and I wear a coat and scarf over my sweater, tucking gloves and toque in my pocket. I walk lightly along the corridor where the lights are dimmed. I pass the rooms labelled Goldenrod, Hyacinth, Azalea. There is a light in the library. A woman is reading by the fireplace. I walk all the way to the end of the corridor where a perfect window seat is framed by a pitched gable roof. Soft light streams in through the window from the street lamp of the driveway. I sit for a moment and relish my solitude. I decide to sit awhile and get comfortable, watching the dim corridor, the softly lit night outside. A van drives up the driveway, and I hear the crunch of gravel as it drives towards the parking lot. The driver carries a big sack of something towards the kitchen. The motion-sensitive light from the outdoor storage building turns on and off as he walks by. I decide that it is safe enough to walk the grounds. I walk down the steps to the main floor, the lobby, the chapel, and walk out. The night is cold. I put on my toque and gloves, and tie my scarf around my neck. The stars are out. I walk towards the garden outside the kitchen and see work going on inside. Kitchen work is never over. I should know. The village lights are out except for a few streetlights. The waters of the bay are still, a band of shimmering silver light cast upon it by the full moon. The sky is glowing with numerous little stars. I hear a rush of wind and the rustle of leaves. All the trees are swaying in the breeze. I smile and hug myself for warmth. I walk towards the forest debating whether I should go in. It looks so dark. But the moon lights the entry path. I decide to enter.

The pathway is narrow, uphill, and lined with trees whose branches and leaves brush against me. At the end of the path is a lookout, brightly lit by the moon. There is a log seat so inviting in the moonlight that I decide to sit and stay. I look around and see a circle of stones on the ground, with burnt ashes in the middle of it. Across from where I sit is another lookout facing the direction towards the village. A tangle of logs is perched at the edge of the lookout. The moonlight casts a light over the logs. The clearing created by both lookouts is bathed in soft silver light like a magical place. Suddenly, I hear footfall over by the logs, and I see what looks like a deer with antlers. He stands there quietly, at a distance of maybe 10 feet, watching me. I've never been that close to a deer. He has great big almond shaped eyes and huge antlers. His skin is tight and golden in the evening light. The silent magnificence of this huge creature hypnotizes me, I become still, entranced by the deer's nobility. I feel his fear as he must feel mine. We sense each other's mystery, and that of the dark forest. I feel swallowed up. I don't even know how long it lasted. Maybe a few seconds, maybe half an hour? I lose track of time. Is that how eternity feels? When he leaves, it seems he just vanished.

The next day, I share my magical experience of the deer with my spiritual facilitator who says that a family of deer lives in the forest, that a fawn was recently born, and my presence must have brought out the parent who was concerned over his child. The appearance of wildlife, says my spiritual facilitator, is one of the ways God talks to us, and she invites me to meditate that day on what could be God's message to me in that encounter. At the communal gathering in the late afternoon, the prayer leader asks for anyone to share one thing they are grateful for. I am the last one to say anything. I say that I am grateful for my mother, for being both mother and father to me all these years with the fierce vigilance of the deer I met in the forest.

That night Mom kisses me before going to bed, and says, "I love you very much," breaking our rule. I hug her back and make her climb into my bed.

"It must have been hard for you, knowing Dad was out there living with someone else, you looking after us by yourself," I say.

"The hardest thing is feeling rejected, not good enough. I had to pretend it didn't hurt. I had to show him, everyone, that I am better than both of them. It's made me hard and cynical about love, marriage, commitments and men. Business or work is more dependable. It gives you what you give it, in equal measure. People, not so."

"The Canadian men are different. Why not give them a chance?"

"It's not about whether they are Canadian or Filipino. I just can't seem to trust anymore."

"But you like Sendong though?"

"Sendong is different. He has no pretensions to faithfulness, love, and commitment. He is a purely pragmatic person living every opportunity that comes his way day by day. He says I am his only love, since we were kids. When I married, he couldn't love anybody else he said, instead marrying for gain. He is in a loveless but friendly marriage and the problems of the community keep him occupied. I admire his intentions with the community, and feel a little envious actually, of his ability to help Pililla. Oddly enough, I trust him. I feel comfortable with him, safe. He has no pretensions about himself, and I don't feel I have to pretend with him. I feel loved by him and I'm not asked anything in return."

"Do you really think so, he does not expect anything in return? Watch it Mom, you are vulnerable. He is a user, see what he does with Bekang, exploiting her need of protection, then making her his mistress?"

"Bekang is like him, *anak*, don't worry. She needed something and she knew what was asked for in return. It was a business transaction. They are both getting what they wanted. If anyone is using anybody, then both are using each other."

"But it's not a transaction of equals. One is using his power over the other who is without power."

"Without power? Bekang has a lot of power — her beauty, her youth. She knows it, and used it to her advantage. What's the advantage? She figured it would be better to be the mistress of one and live like a queen, than be a sex slave to many and be a pauper." The truth freezes me.

Mom continues. "We all have power. Even absence of power is powerful. Weakness can be a power. It's how we use what we have that anything becomes powerful. Look at Carla: she used her weakness and neediness to gain power over your Dad, and me, us. I was too innocent then to play this power game. I could have used you, my children, as my power, my leverage. But I just folded. You see, power is a state of mind. And it's neutral. It can be used for good or bad. I could have prevented you, especially Manolita, from seeing him, and he might have returned to us. But that's no good for me. I needed to be loved too, not just win over Carla. It would be a hollow marriage, as he would still love her. But maybe you kids might have been happier. Father Carlos says my pride is my sin, and my broken family is my punishment forever. He is probably right, but I cannot sacrifice my life that way even for my kids. I am no saint, and I accept my punishment. God, you my kids, will forgive me in time, I hope."

"No, Mom. There is nothing to forgive. You made the right decision. You have to be happy first before you can help others be happy. I am stronger because you have been strong for us. So is Bobby. And Manolita, well, as a matter of fact, she is probably as selfish as she is because she was the one most exposed to Dad and Carla. I don't know. Mom, you can't be thinking you are the one to blame for our broken family? He started it, it's his fault."

"Is it? Maybe it's me that started it, not paying attention to him, not supporting him through his struggles, and instead focusing on mine. It made him easy prey for Carla."

"Maybe it's everybody's fault? Does it matter who started it?" I ask, backtracking on myself.

"You're right, who started it doesn't really matter. We were all to blame: I, him, Carla."

"And maybe it's not about blaming. It's just the way things are. We all behave in accordance with how we were brought up, and our circumstances," I venture.

"You mean that we don't have power over our will? I don't think so, Sonia. Or where will our world be? Someone can murder another person because his parents maltreated him?"

"I don't mean the murderer is not to blame. He did the act, and he still needs to be punished. But the bad act is caused not only by him, but also by a whole lot of other things: his parents, his parents' parents likely, and the society in general that deprived them of opportunity. It's not a question of blame because that assumes one intentionally and fully knew something was bad, had control, and did it anyway. No one is purely to 'blame' because everything affects everyone," I suggest.

"That does not absolve one of one's share of the blame," says Mom.

"No, it doesn't. But you are taking more blame than you should. You were responsible for only a little miniscule bit. So stop punishing yourself. You are a great mom! And besides, 'everything affects everyone' applies to the good as well. Someone's good act helps someone else become better. Look, our family may be 'broken', but we are happy and successful, aren't we? That's because of you. You already helped Carla by giving her support, and now she doesn't need it anymore. And you are helping other caregivers by giving them cooking contracts. You mentor them on how to set up businesses. What else do you need to do? All your good balances whatever blame you are responsible for with Dad. You are too harsh on yourself. You just need to forgive yourself now, Mom."

"Thank you, *anak*. How did you get so wise?"

"The benefit of growing up in a 'broken family'?" We laugh. I hug my mom tight. With my head against her chest, I smell her sweet lavender scent, feel the surrender in her bones, her vulnerability in her soft breast, making me feel strong. I remember this moment and pour it in my bottle of precious essence.

I can't sleep. A soft snore is coming from mom's bed, but that is not what's keeping me awake. It's just a feeling of restlessness, a disquiet. I breathe in and out slowly and visualize calming each part of my body from my scalp to my chest to my tummy and I lose it. I try visualizing a light coming into my body from the top of my head through to my throat then my spine, then down through my legs through to the floor down to the earth to anchor me, when my mind flies somewhere else. To Stephen, to my work, to the meeting coming up for my project, which I realize is something I am anxious about. What do I know of the labour market, the skills shortage, the goings-on among the regulatory bodies, the immigration policies? How did I get this job to coordinate the Immigrant Engineers pilot project? How shall I handle the meeting with all the stakeholders next week?

I see the pad of paper on the desk, a ballpoint pen, some crayons. I pick up the pad and pen, turn on the lamp to the lowest illumination, and let my hand write.

Dear Jesus,

I don't know why I'm writing you. I don't even know you really. I hope you don't mind hearing from a stranger. It's just that I am afraid. I don't know how to handle those important experts next week. I don't know how to do my job. Where to even begin. Would you help me please?

Yours sincerely,

Sonia

I don't know what gets over me, but I transfer the pen to my left hand, and it starts to make a scrawl. I watch my left hand write painstakingly slow.

Trust. U have answer.

Then my left hand stopped.

Then it started again.

I luv u.

Huh?

I drop the pen. No. I throw it away, part in disgust at my own game playing, part in surprise. Myself likes to write shorthand. Myself luvs myself?

My left hand reaches for the pen, and seeks the paper.

It writes: *all want to help remember*.

My left hand stops. It puts the pen down. I read the scrawl again.

All want to help. Remember.

All those stakeholders want to help? They do?

I turn off the light and think about how those stakeholders could help if they cared. I draw blanks. They are faceless people, the stakeholders. I can't even imagine them. I see only my father in my head, his intense gaze, his gaunt face, his dark wavy hair, and his sad eyes. I want to tell him that Jesus said the stakeholders want to help him, but I don't want raise his expectations. I tell him about my meeting coming up and who all will be there, naming each person, each agency. I fall asleep along the way.

Next days, I walk the labyrinth, around the lake, around the village. I walk everywhere. I feel light-headed, my heart unburdened, as though I had no care in the world, as though I needed nothing. The trees, the ocean, the birds, the moss on the ground, the light shower of rain, the brilliant sun, the ever-changing clouds. Everything nourished me, slaked my thirst, embraced me, making me feel loved. I fell in love with Stephen all over again without him doing anything. In fact it's as if I fell in love with everyone and everything.

* * *

The project is growing wings. Around the board room table at Cross Currents are seated the representatives from Human Resources Canada (HRC), Immigration Canada, University of British Columbia (UBC) Engineering Department, Association of Professional Engineers of BC (APE), Stephen representing Human Rights BC (HRBC), and the Director of the Task Force for Inter Provincial Professional Regulatory Bodies of Canada. The last one is someone I flushed out through my research. I found out that there is already an initiative to get regulatory bodies of the same professions in different provinces to harmonize their regulations. Yes, that's true. Even among the different provinces of Canada, the rules for practising the professions are not the same: an engineer in BC cannot necessarily practise in Ontario. That's how bad it is. From Cross Currents Society, there is Lawrence Ho, Director of the employment program, and then there's me, now the paid manager of the project.

"I want to thank you all for coming to this meeting," says Lawrence. "We have the agenda in front of us, so let's begin with the first item. Let's introduce ourselves briefly, and our roles." Lawrence starts off by introducing himself, and each one around the room in turn rattles off his or her name and position at what agency, ending with me. I have also circulated a piece of paper for people to write their names, position and agency, phone numbers and email address.

"Sonia will present the status of the project, and what we hope to accomplish with this meeting," Lawrence turns to me.

I am ready with my power point presentation and begin by displaying faces of immigrants.

I click on the first slide. "This is Zhang Wei. She has an architectural degree from China with over 10 years professional experience in commercial buildings. She now works as a laundry woman at the Mr. Clean Laundromat in Vancouver.

I click on the second slide. "This is Maria Soledad. She is a medical doctor from the Philippines, with over fifteen years experience as pediatrician in numerous hospitals. She is now working as a care aid in a seniors facility in Richmond."

I click on the third slide: "This is Santosh. He is an environmental engineer from Nepal, with post-graduate degrees from Amsterdam, London and Tokyo and over 18 years advising governments in environmental assessments. He now works as a cashier in 7-Eleven in Burnaby.

"As you all know, they are only a few of the growing number of underutilized foreign-trained talent who came to Canada at the invitation of our government to fill the looming skilled labour shortage in our country. They are unable to practise their skills when they get here. What seems to be the problem? There are several."

I click on the next slide, showing several bullet points.

"On the immigrants' side — Lack of preparation and knowledge about the job search process here and about the rules to practise their professions. Lack of sufficient English. Lack of money to persist until the right job is found.

On the employers' side — Impatience with the inadequate English of immigrants. Lack of understanding of the culture of immigrants, their educational and work backgrounds. Faced with too much difference, employer would rather hire people from cultures they understand.

On the side of the regulatory bodies — Non-recognition of foreign degrees. Difficult and complicated application processes that do not give much opportunity for foreign-trained professionals to become accepted.

On the side of Government — Not providing sufficient information to applicants abroad about what to expect when they apply for skilled work in Canada. Not providing sufficient help to immigrants when they arrive here about how to find work in their field. Not providing sufficient motivation to regulatory bodies to make their processes more open and accessible to immigrants, and to employers to hire skilled immigrants."

I click the next slide in. It shows a tangled knot.

"The issues are complicated and interrelated like a tight knot. We thought a good way to start unravelling the knot is by unravelling one thread: the engineering profession. Follow it to where it is tangled up, untangle it, and as we are able to unravel one thread or one profession, that might lead us to untangle the rest of the knot for the skilled immigrant labour market."

I click the next slide, a close up of the end of a thread sticking out of the knot.

"You each have an important role to play in untangling the knot. Can you help us free up the talents of immigrants, for Canada?"

I hold out a string and give it to the person closest to me, Stephen. "If you are willing to help, take this string, and pass the end of the string to the person next to you while holding the rest of the string loosely with your other hand."

Stephen takes the string quickly as we had rehearsed, holds the rest of the string with his left hand, and passes the end of the string to the person on his right. The next person isn't quite sure what to do. She hesitates, then accepts the string, holds it in her left hand, and gives the end of the string to the next person on her right. Each one in turn does the same, until the end of the string returns to me, and we see that we are all holding the string in a circle.

I continue. "Thank you for your commitment and your courage. We will be doing new things in this Initiative that may not be popular with our own agencies, and we will need to be imaginative and persistent to find effective solutions. Today, we start the journey with a brainstorming on what each one of us can do. Not anyone else, but you yourself. What can you do in your role in your respective agencies, even a small step, so that the engineering thread will be untangled like the string we hold in our hand? Who would like to start with an idea?" I ask.

"I can try to propose that information about how to job search in Canada be provided at the source countries themselves. I can have some articles written which can be viewed on the website, or a brochure they can pick up. I can look into a seminar they can attend before they even apply, so that they have full knowledge and are prepared when they arrive," said the HRC representative.

I draw a large circle on the flip chart, mark one point in the circle with a big dot, and write beside it: "early job search info to source countries — HRC".

"Oh, and I can try to propose a new program for employment counselling specifically for skilled engineers as a pilot," the HRC representative adds. I hear murmurs as I write beside the dot a new line: "new program employment counselling for skilled engineers — HRC." The HRC staff continues, "I'll try anyway. No expectations yet, okay? As it is end of the fiscal year, we may be able to pick up some remainder unused funds from this year." I see heads nodding.

"Would it be better to increase the English language proficiency standard for skilled immigrants?" asks the immigration representative.

"I'm not sure it's the English proficiency standard that needs to change, but more the attitude of the employers, the hirers, and the regulatory bodies," says Lawrence. "Does a person have to speak with no accent? Is that possible even? If people pass the necessary TOFEL level, isn't that enough? Or we may end up not having anyone pass. Even English language speakers from Australia or Britain have an accent."

"Yes, we may be encouraging racial discrimination," Stephen chimes in.

"So how do you address the concerns of hirers who have a right to ensure their employees can communicate adequately in their jobs?" asks the immigration representative.

"They are getting a very skilled employee. Why doesn't the employer provide English courses as part of orientation and ongoing employee training?" Stephen replies.

"That would be a disincentive because of the training cost. If he hired someone whose English is completely on par, he would not have to provide for English retraining," says somebody else.

"Can the Government make English retraining a tax benefit for the employer?" asks another. As there was silence after this,

I chime in. "Maybe we can park this idea out here in the circle, and check later on, as to who might be able to follow up on it."

"I'll look into it," said the HRC representative. I write another line for the HRC representative: "explore tax benefits for employers, English retraining skilled immigrant employees". I speak, looking at the APE representative, "Other ideas?"

The Director of Interprovincial Regulatory Bodies Task Force speaks. "I know of an Engineering regulatory body in another country that provides what's called a 'Provisional Engineering Certificate'. That's for foreign-trained engineers with lots of experience in another country. He has to work under supervision of a certified engineer for a period of time, then takes a challenge exam at the end of the period, and if he passes, he gets the full engineering certificate."

"How about the engineering law, contracts in Canada. How could they know about these essential matters just by working at a job?" asks the APE representative.

"Make them go through a course and pass it, as another prerequisite," offers the UBC representative.

"Hmm," nods the APE representative. "I'll look into this. I'll discuss the provisional certificate idea with my folks, and maybe consult with you on this idea of a legal engineering course." I can't believe what I am hearing, and I write it down fast before anyone takes it back. I draw a big dot on another part of the circle and write "explore provisional engineering certificate for foreign-trained immigrants — APE". I draw another dot close to it and write "explore legal course prerequisite for foreign-trained engineers — APE and UBC".

"How about making the engineering regulations more accessible to foreign-trained engineers — simplify them, explain them better, including how foreign credentials are evaluated. All these rules are mystifying to newcomers. They feel their integrity is being questioned when they are asked to explain their resumes." I address the APE representative.

"I know what you mean," said the APE representative. "Yes we need to do something about that. There is one case I know when a foreign-trained engineer had a heart attack during an interview reviewing his credentials. It was some time ago. Apparently he felt his integrity was being challenged."

I am stunned. That was my father. If they knew it, why didn't they do something about it? I am getting tense.

"So why didn't you do something about it then?" I challenge the APE representative. My voice is raised.

"We did. We tried to give the man a ride, but he refused the ride. He never came back."

"Yes. But what did you do after, about your policies, your regulations? Why didn't you make the process better then?" I feel my face reddening.

Stephen intervenes saying, "Sonia, are you okay?"

"No, I'm not okay," I say. "Excuse me." I rush out to the washroom. I throw up in the toilet. I sit on it for a while until I am breathing more normally. What got over me? I am too emotional. I cannot do this job while also blaming our partners. If they knew that their practise was making people ill, why haven't they done anything about it? Why does it take someone like me who knows nothing, a victim of injustice, to make them do anything? I try to calm myself. It's not the man's fault. It's his whole institution, the whole system that is too complacent, and uninformed. That is the problem. It can only be changed slowly. One change at a time. And this man representing APE in the room may be our answer. So why am I fighting with him? I should befriend him. All want to help, said my left hand. Remember. I stood up and went to the sink, splashing my face with cold water.

Coreen walks in. "How are you? What happened? Can you continue?" she asks.

I nod.

I return to the room, take my place in front. "I'm sorry for that. I apologize to all of you, especially to our friend from APE. I didn't mean to be rude. I just realized that it may have been my father you were talking about, the man who had a heart attack defending his credentials," I say.

"My God, I'm so sorry," said the APE representative.

"No, it's not your fault, not anybody's fault. It's just the system, people are simply not aware that a good thing like inviting skilled immigrants to Canada needs a whole bunch of supportive measures to make it work, or else, it's self-defeating. And the good thing is that now, we are all trying to change the system, with all your help. So thank you so much. Can we continue? Where did we leave off?"

The meeting goes on for another hour, with many more ideas coming out. In the end, the flip chart paper is loaded with notes of actions to take, connected around a circle. We agree to meet again in a month to report on progress of our various actions.

After the meeting, the APE representative shakes my hand. "How's your father?" he asks.

"He died recently," I say.

"I'm so sorry." He is obviously taken aback.

"It's okay. The point is we're doing something about it now."

"I want to help. I'll make every effort to do our part. I promise."

"Thank you. I know you will."

* * *

CHAPTER 8

Canada and Philippines
Bobby, 1993–1994

It's Christmas Eve. I'm sitting on the deck of the McIsaacs' beach house on Galiano Island. Wow. I estimate the value of the property alone. They're rich. I could get used to this.

It's blowy and grey, the waves of the Straight of Georgia are crawling toward the beach. The air is full of sounds: the surfing waves, the rustling maple tree branches, the rumbling of the ocean waves from far in the horizon. A dash of rain sprinkles on my head. The gulls are flying low, close to the water, hunting for food. The waves are bigger farther to the east, dashing against the large rocks and the cliffside. I like this wildness.

The McIsaacs have owned this house since Nicole was a little girl, her dad said. It was a cottage when grandfather McIsaac owned it. Mr. McIsaac expanded it by surrounding it with verandas and building a second floor, cascading decks and garden, and the footbridge connecting to the beach. Now it's a beautiful two-level home with golden oak panels around the windows, doors and dormers. From the street, you can't see the house. You have to drive through a winding driveway lined with arbutus trees. You would never know about the ocean until you walk around the veranda, then there it is: the ocean in great splendor. The house is much like the McIsaacs: modest on the outside, their affluence discretely hidden.

The house has floor-to-ceiling glass windows bringing the outdoors in. A high ceiling roofs a great open space consisting of living areas, dining area, and kitchen all flowing into each other with only tall ornamental plants creating the separation between spaces. The floors are made of blonde maple wood, covered with occasional area rugs. Instead of paintings, the walls are covered with stained glass artwork. The centre of the house is a baby grand piano, and a huge Christmas tree. The bedrooms are located on the mezzanine, opening into a corridor, which overlooks the open space below. Sonia occupies one room with Stephen, Mom shares a room with Manolita, and Nicole and I are in the third room. The McIsaacs have the master bedroom located on the main floor opposite the kitchen, in a room jutting out toward the ocean.

The McIsaacs invited us to their country home in the Island for the families to get to know one another. Theirs is a tiny family consisting only of one child: Nicole.

"Mrs. McIsaac, whose crib is the one in our room?" Manolita asks.

"Please call me Catherine," Mrs. McIsaac replies. "We had a second child who died in childbirth. We keep his crib in the house. I was told I couldn't have any more children after." Mrs. McIsaac falls silent for a moment, and then continues, "Angus and I are blessed to have Nicole."

"Why don't you play for us, dear?" asked Mr. McIsaac. "Nicole is the first concert pianist in our family, although there is much music in our blood. Mostly fiddlers and bagpipe players. Miners and classical music don't mix. When Nicole became a concert pianist, I knew that our grandparents' sacrifice in immigrating to Canada, doing hard mining work at that time, has paid off. When a family can afford, and welcome, an arts career in the family, they have arrived. Right, mom? As for me, I wish I could have learned some music. But listening is enough. I like to listen to Nicole before I write a difficult judgment. It relaxes me and clears my mind."

"'The Nicole Judgment', they say," Mrs. McIsaac chimes in. "Depending on which side they're on, some lawyers have asked Nicole to play for Angus after a hearing is done, because they say he makes softer judgments after hearing Nicole play."

"They say it's what I play too that makes the difference, right Dad?" Nicole laughs.

"These lawyers. They don't know me. No amount of Chopin can make a guilty offender go off with a light sentence in my books," says Mr. McIsaac.

"Chopin it is," says Nicole. She kisses her father on the head. Nicole sits on the piano bench, breathes deeply, and places her hands on her thighs. She raises her hands above the keys flexing her fingers in the air, then sets them down gently on top of the keys. She plays. The notes fall like little raindrops tinkling on a roof. No wonder that the piece is called "The Raindrop Prelude," Nicole explains when she finishes.

"How about one for Bobby?" ask Mrs. McIsaac.

"I don't know what I want." I feel embarrassed with my lack of knowledge of classical music.

"I know what you'd like," says Nicole, and plays again. This time she plays a piece with a force and vigor like a big battle, with a rousing victory in the end.

"Why did you think I'd like that?" I ask.

"Well, didn't you?"

"Yes, but it makes me feel like a...unrefined."

"But you ARE unrefined! What else do you think?" Manolita laughs.

I knock Manolita on the head, laughing.

"I love you not because you are an expert in classical music," teases Nicole who comes and wraps her arms around me. "It's precisely because you're not. And I like how you like the music despite not being familiar with it. You enjoy music more emotionally than many classical music experts I know. I like that." She kisses me warmly.

I nuzzle Nicole and kiss her ear. "And I love you because you always make me look good, even if I don't deserve it."

"You are good and you deserve every good thing said about you, my dear," says Mrs. McIsaac. "I've never seen a more hardworking businessman as you. Nicole is very lucky. You spoil her. We are very lucky to have you, and your family, in our family," she adds.

"I'm the lucky one," I say, embracing Nicole.

"How about some Christmas songs? Manolita, can you sing for us?" Mom asks. Manolita leaps to her feet and sits beside Nicole discussing what songs to sing. Manolita starts with "It Came Upon a Midnight Clear" her voice soaring like an angel.

Mom's face is transported as she watches the scene. I've never seen her so happy. The light of the sun reflects the colors of the stained glass, catches the leaves of the tall plants and the glittering Christmas lights, and on Mom's face, the light casts a glow. The glow moves in a stream toward Mr. and Mrs. McIsaac and wraps around them, and then flows through the Christmas tree and around the piano, embracing Nicole and Manolita. It moves to Sonia and Stephen and Manolita, encircling them. Then the glow reaches me, enveloping me. The glow feels warm and moist like a soft rain. It flows away towards the door, towards a man standing there. It is my Dad. In his hand is a glowing gun. He fires it at me in an explosion of light, and I am struck by a sharp pain and joy, both. An ecstasy. My body feels like it's melting, and I feel light as a feather, like I'm floating on wings, like I've been forgiven.

"Bobby? You're crying?" Nicole.

"I just love you very much." I hug her. I watch the now empty doorway still glowing with light. I remember my promise that we would succeed without you Dad. Isn't that enough? Do I also have to forgive?

* * *

It is decided to hold a wedding in Manila rather than just asking for Nicole's hand in marriage. As it turns out, Nicole is pregnant by the time February 1992 rolls along, and everybody agrees that a del Mundo wedding would be good for the family still suffering the unspoken pains of Dad's death. We plan a grand wedding at the historic San Agustin Church, a reception at the luxurious Intercontinental Hotel, and a honeymoon at the Camp John Hay in Baguio, the summer capital of the Philippines.

The Manila society columns are full of the news, and Lolo Ben and Lola Lita bask in the attention. Tita Marites is pulling out all her connections to "make it up" to my dad, including TV news coverage of the wedding. The McIsaacs are overwhelmed at every turn: the press interest, the grandeur of the church ceremony, the lavishness of the reception, the chauffeurs and maids that wait on them, the attention of so many relatives and friends. Lolo Ben insists on the best of everything for his new granddaughter-in-law and family, "to show them who are the del Mundos," to the point of embarrassment, even for me.

* * *

After the short honeymoon in Baguio, and before everyone goes back to Canada, Mayor Sendong insists on hosting a reception for us in Pililla. It was to be held at the town square, to celebrate, in the words of a press release from the Mayor's office, "the co-joining of Vancouver and Pililla symbolized by the marriage of Bobby del Mundo, a favored Pililla son, to Nicole McIsaac, a precious Vancouver daughter." I hear that Sendong is personally looking after the preparations. Ten pigs are being killed and roasted for *lechon* for the whole village, and two bands are playing at the dance.

We have agreed to sponsor Bekang as our baby's caregiver. Bekang is giddy with happiness, and keeps thanking Nicole and me and Sonia.

The party is held at the quadrangle in front of the Pililla *municipyo*. The festivities started at about 7 pm. They have gone to a lot of trouble for this! The quadrangle is decorated with lights and banners. A stage covered by a canvas roof is set up at one end of the open space. On the stage sits a rectangular table draped with white tablecloth, a bouquet of red roses in the centre, and swags of ribbons decorating the tablecloth skirt. Our whole family, along with Mayor Sendong, sits at the table on stage facing the audience. Behind us is a large white banner showing a red heart pierced by cupid's arrow. Printed in the area on the top left side of the heart, are the words

"Pililla's Bobby del Mundo," and on the lower right side, the words "Vancouver's Nicole McIsaac." Underneath the heart are big bold letters: "Pililla and Mayor Sendong wish you a long prosperous life!" A drawing of cupid, looking like Mayor Sendong, appears beside Mayor Sendong's name. Nicole and I have a good laugh.

A microphone stands on the stage, the right side. On the floor of the quadrangle, rectangular tables are arranged in rows facing the stage. They are arranged along two columns, separated by a wide corridor, which turns out to be the dance area. A dais is set up on the floor of the quadrangle below the stage, where the band plays. At the other end of the quadrangle facing the stage is a long table with food containers, watched over by women dressed in colourful *patajongs*. A waist-high fence of wire with overhanging banana leaves surrounds the party area. On-lookers gather beyond the fence to see and enjoy the festivities. A reception line of men and women dressed in *barong tagalog* stand at the entry way, greeting the visitors who were more dressed up than the on-lookers, but not as fancied up as the reception line or the food women. Mayor Sendong must have made his Council and employees dress up for the occasion. We heard that the guest list was well picked, representing the elite of Pililla. I wonder how much this affair cost, knowing Pililla taxes are probably funding this affair, while down there and outside the fence stood the poor folks of Pililla. I must remember to make a donation to help cover the cost.

I see how happy everyone is, including people outside the fence. They are chatting, laughing and enjoying their own food from carts selling banana barbecue, cotton candy, *gulaman* juice and corn. The feeling is like a carnival. I see that

Nicole and her parents are enjoying every bit of it. Good on Mayor Sendong for putting this all up for us.

The Mayor is at his best hosting us all at the head table on stage. Nicole looks radiant, if a little anxious. We sit at the middle of the table. To our left sit Mayor Sendong and the First Lady Mrs. Sendong, then Mom, then McIsaacs, then Lola Lita and Lolo Ben. To our right sit Lolo Lino and Lola Iska, Sonia and Stephen, Tito Mario and Tita Ching, Manolita and Tita Marites. Mayor Sendong had already given his opening remarks, punctuated with a lot of jokes, which put everyone in a jolly festive mood. He had already introduced each of us in a grand way, spending the most time with Mom, who he introduced as the Rose of Pililla. The band had been playing background music for a while as we ate. The *patajong* ladies are beginning to gather the plates from the tables. A sense of excitement could be felt in the air, in anticipation of the next part of the program, which is everybody's favourite: dancing.

When most plates are cleared, the Mayor goes to the microphone and asks if everybody was full. "YESS!" is the response. Then he asks if everybody was ready to dance, a bigger "YESS!" He then asks the band to play *"Dahil sa Iyo"*. I whisper to Nicole that the title means 'because of you'. Then Mayor Sendong invites Nicole and me to centre stage for the first dance.

Nicole and I begin a slow dance while the audience cheers. Nicole giggles. I tell her to wave to the audience, which she does. The audience cheers even more loudly. I am so proud of Nicole, her beauty and her sweetness, and imagine our beautiful *mestiza* child, the best of east and west. I hold her closer, feeling protective, and the audience cheers again. Then Mayor Sendong stands up and leads his wife to the centre stage and dances with her. He raises his hands to the crowd to cheer them on. He gestures to the rest of the table, inviting all to dance.

By the time all are up dancing, I see that Mayor Sendong's partner is now Mom, looking flushed, and Mrs. Sendong is seated back in her chair looking bored. The wide corridor in the middle of the quadrangle is now beginning to fill with people dancing. The band changes to a fast tune, and the action picks up on the floor where even more people rise from their seats to dance. With the faster tune, the oldies start to return to their seats, and there is much movement on the stage.

Which is how I didn't see it coming. Right there. On the stage. In front of everyone. I saw a half-naked man slashing a long thick bloodied knife in the air. Mayor Sendong falling on the floor bloodied. Nicole standing beside the body, screaming, her white dress splattered with red blood. A screaming Mom kneeling on the floor beside the body. I rush the half-naked man, pushing him down. I grab the wrist that held the knife and press it down hard on the floor to release the knife. My other hand pushes the man's face down and I kneel on his chest, to keep him still. The man is remarkably weak, as though he was finished, having done the damage. I kick the knife away, and turn the man on his back. I hold his wrists together, shouting for help to tie the man up. Mayor Sendong is lying still on the floor, his eyes closed, blood all over his chest. Not sure if he's breathing. Finally someone comes to pick up the half-naked man from my hands. He doesn't struggle as though he didn't care anymore. I kneel beside Sendong and feel a pulse. I make a decision right there. I lift him up and shout for the people on stage to clear the way. I am shouting 'get a car ready' or something like that as I run like mad, carrying the

Mayor's body, down the stairs of the stage, along the path that cleared up, and into a jeepney.

I do not hear the people screaming, women crying, the crowd praying. I do not see the half-naked man being led to the *munisipyo*, to be held in a temporary jail there. I do not see what's happening to Nicole or Mr. and Mrs. McIsaac or Mom, or anyone. I do not even think of how my wedding party has turned into a nightmare. I just hold the Mayor in my arms on the floor of the jeepney, hoping to God we get to the hospital in time.

* * *

Lolo Ben decides to transport everyone to the del Mundo home in Makati, and not stay one moment longer in Pililla.

I stay in the hospital with Mrs. Sendong. Mom arrives shortly after we did. The doctor does not hold any promise of hope. Later in the night, he declares Mayor Sendong dead.

It turns out that the *huramentado* was a farmer who owned the pigs slaughtered for the party. Sendong ordered the pigs taken from the man's farm, in payment for a debt that the farmer owed Sendong, and which had been unpaid for some time. In subsequent press reports, we learn that the farmer could no longer hold his hatred for Sendong, lost his sanity, and like a *huramentado*, went berserk. He ran to kill the Mayor in front of everybody to "show up that oppressor."

Lolo Ben apologizes profusely to the McIsaacs for the terrifying experience, noting specifically that the Pililla reception was not the responsibility of the del Mundos, but in fact was from the side of the de Jesus', my mother's side. Sonia tries her best to explain the class structure of the Philippines, and the internal violence it breeds. The McIsaacs are very good about it, including Nicole who worried for the *huramentado's* family. We all mercifully return to Vancouver, hoping the joys of the trip would last longer in the McIsaacs' memory than the nightmare at the end.

I wish I saw the *huramentado* earlier and prevented the blow. I wish I ran faster to the waiting vehicle. I despair that my wedding in Manila, supposedly the redemption of the del Mundos, would always be remembered alongside with another catastrophe: the hacking death of Mayor Sendong.

"No, Bobby. We'll all remember it as your heroic moment. How proud we were of you, your courage and strength. How you risked your life to try and save another, and now everyone knows what a good man you are. Not the drug king they gossip about." Sonia, my champion.

"If Dad were here, he'd be proud of you, bro," says Manolita.

"He was always proud of you. He just didn't know how to show it," says Mom.

* * *

I don't know if this event triggered Mom's strange decision to run for Mayor of Pililla. She said people begged her to run for Mayor, that they needed someone "good," someone "bright," "who understands Pilillans," and who is wealthy enough that she would not need the office of Mayor to try to get rich. They said that the Vice Mayor was corrupt. Luckily, the elections were coming up in a few months, and the Vice Mayor would be acting mayor only for a few months. The town had a chance to elect a new Mayor soon. Pilillans wanted the Rose of Pililla, my mother, as their Mayor.

"My problem is, can I leave you by yourselves now?" she asks my sisters and me.

"Why not?" the three of us say, almost in unison. We laugh.

"Seriously," I say. "It's your life. We can look after ourselves. I'll look after these girls." I realize how deeply I care for my sisters, despite how much I tease them.

"Stephen and I are just about ready to move in together anyway," says Sonia.

"Then Manolita can stay with Nicole and me. Simple! Next question?" I offer.

"What about my business? I'd like it to stay alive until I know if I get elected anyway," Mom says.

"I can look after it, if you show me how," says Sonia.

"You need campaign money. Where will you get that?" asks Manolita, herself already volunteering with local electoral campaigns in Vancouver.

"I don't know yet. That may be what will kill this idea. They say it requires a lot of money," Mom suggests.

"How about Lolo Ben?" I suggest.

"I don't know. I don't want to owe him development favours. I don't want to start that way," Mom says.

"How else can you get money? Anyone who donates to your campaign will want something in return, some favor," says Manolita.

Sonia looks at Manolita in a strange way. Manolita opens her hands in front of her to emphasize the point, and shrugs.

"Don't accept too much donation from anyone person or group. Just a little from many, that way they don't expect too much. How much does it take to win the mayor seat of such a small town anyway?" Sonia adds.

"I can give you some," I offer.

Mom looks grateful.

"And I can raise a few from my developer friends," I add.

Mom nods slowly, stands up and says, "Let's sleep on it some more. This will disrupt our lives. I have to know that it's really what I want to do."

"Why, Mom? Why do you want to do it?" Sonia asks.

"Because Pilillans deserve a chance to have better lives. Without having to go abroad. They are so backward here. It's worth a try. I think I want to help. I think it may be hard, I don't know how the job works, but the people said they would help me. I'm prepared to try. A few years of my life. And if it doesn't work, well, I still have Canada, right?" she asks.

"That's good enough for me. Go for it, Mom! You'll do great," I say.

"Knock 'em dead," says Manolita.

I stare at her. Manolita truly is a surprise.

* * *

CHAPTER 9

Philippines and Canada
Sonia, 1994-1996

A line of young bamboo trees is rustling in the wind. Farther, a lone banana tree stands swaying in the breeze, heavy with fruit. The wind blows harder and a great rustle stirs in the field, and even the door to the washroom beside my bed starts banging lightly. The early afternoon sun of Pililla casts a bright light on the verdant field, against a baby blue sky. Not a hint of brown in the air as in Manila. Red and orange bougainvilleas creep over the sides of the field, and the kamachile tree is still standing by the dry creek. The air feels pure and innocent, not a trace of the evil that just happened in the town. I am sitting propped on a cushion on Bekang's bed, while she goes and gets us cold San Miguel beers.

"Poor Sendong, he would never have thought Mang Tibo the farmer could ever do that. They said Mang Tibo had been drinking Tanduay rum since sundown, and must have been blind drunk by the time he ran out with the *bolo*. So were his friends. No one stopped him," says Bekang, her eyes still red from the crying.

"Will you miss him?"

"Of course. He was good enough to me. Now, I don't know what will happen to me. This house — I hear his wife wants to claim it. I will fight her for it. I don't know how. It's all we have, where will my family live?" Bekang fills my glass with frothy beer.

"I'll ask Mom to talk to Sendong's wife to let you stay here, until at least when you get to Canada. When you work for Bobby, you can send money to pay her back. She won't be so cruel as to just kick you out, will she?" I take a long swallow of the cold beer that Filipinos love.

"She's very rich and does not need this house. She's just being vengeful. She doesn't even know me. Doesn't care. She knows I'm no competition. Still, it's her pride that may make her do it."

"I'll talk to Mom. She's staying a little while here in Pililla to explore running for Mayor."

"I heard. That will be good for us in Pililla. She is kind and not corrupt, but can she fight dirty? Politics here is so mean. She might be eaten up alive. Can she buy votes? Can she take cruel untrue gossip about her? Can she spread bad rumours about the other candidate? Can she stomach all that?"

"I don't know. She hopes she can win without having to play dirty."

"Good luck to her!" Bekang raises her glass in salute.

"Help her with your contacts, okay? Who she should talk to. Who can tell her about what's needed by Pilillans. People like those."

"She should speak to Father Bautista. He knows everyone and helps everyone. People run to him about their problems."

"I'll tell her. If you think of anyone else, let her know, okay?"

"I can do more than that, I can help her in the campaign if she doesn't mind me helping."

"Why wouldn't she want your help? Of course, she'd love your help." But I know what Bekang means.

The big ball of sun is setting. I have to go.

"Good luck on your caregiver application. And make sure you refresh your caregiving course okay? Maybe get some experience looking after young children, so you can say you've done that for at least a year. You'll be lucky to get approval within a year, or if not, in two years. Bobby will press for it because of the baby coming soon. Hopefully that works," I say.

"Your family is my lifesaver! Where will I be without you?" Bekang hugs me tight. I hug her back.

I am happy that Bekang has been freed of that man, that she'll have a future in Canada, that Bobby will have someone to look after his child, and my friend and I can be together again. We clink our glasses and finish the now watered down but still ice cold beer.

* * *

The McIsaacs left with Bobby and Nicole and Manolita, while Stephen and I hang out for a couple of days in Metro Manila, Mom in Pililla.

Tita Martites has taken us to her beachside condominium at the Los Palmas Resort in Nasugbu, Batangas. The water is blue and the beach sandy brown, the sun brilliant and hot. We are having mango margaritas by the pool overlooking the beach.

"Why this political aspiration all of a sudden?" asks Tita Marites about my mom. "What's going on? Was she having a relationship with that Sendong fellow that she has to stay behind for the funeral, and even run for his seat as though wanting to continue his work?"

I have wondered about this myself. "I don't think so. Although I always wonder why she doesn't go with these nice Canadian men who are courting her. She said that since Dad left, that she finds it hard to trust men. She said Sendong is just a friend whom she trusts because she knows him from childhood and has no agenda with her. He says Mom was his only love. I think Mom truly believes she could do some good in Pililla, and to continue the work of Sendong whom she says was misunderstood by people."

"No kidding. She may be in over her head. She doesn't know what politics is like here," says Tita Marites.

"She's made up her mind. Can you help her?"

"And how about you?" asks Tita Marites, not answering my question.

"We'll be fine. I'll look after the catering and the restaurant businesses."

"No, I mean, you and Stephen?"

I smile and shrug. I look at Stephen, who smiles shyly.

"We'd like to live together soon," Stephen says, taking my hand. "My parents have yet to meet Sonia. We'll do that soon, right Sonia?"

"Sure." But really, I am unsure. I know Stephen's parents are very conservative and do not believe in living together outside of marriage. If we should live together, they want us to get married first, and I'm not sure whether I want to go there yet. I've been postponing the eventual meeting with his parents, and now I guess I can't postpone things anymore. But I say none of these things to Tita Marites. Stephen offers to explain, and his explanation surprises me somewhat.

"My parents are quite old fashioned. They speak little English. I am their only child, and...they are rather possessive." I thought it was a question of getting married first. It seems it's something else, not wanting to part with their only child. I look at Stephen quizzically, and he looks down at his drink, which he carries to his lips.

Tita Marites looks at me in that way, which means, 'you and I have to talk, girl.'

"They are from the old world, and always thought I would marry a Chinese girl. But no worries, in time, they will come around and see how wonderful Sonia is and will love her as I do," Stephen says.

Another surprise. I didn't know they wanted him to marry within their culture. "You never told me." I accuse Stephen.

"I didn't want you to worry. I know that as soon as they meet you, you will change their minds."

I suddenly feel hot in the face. I head off towards the beach.

"Sonia," Stephen calls to me, but I am running towards the beach. The fine sand is scorching the bottom of my feet, but I don't care so long as I get to the cool blue water, dip my head under it, and let it wash my angry tears away.

* * *

When I arrive back from holidays at my office, I am told that a special announcement is coming at 10 am. I get the feeling of good news about our project because of the way Coreen smiled at me, and how Lawrence was unavailable and closeted with management right until 10 am. My *pasalubongs* for them would have to wait till after the announcement. Everyone's commenting on my tan, snacking on Philippine *hopia* and mango tarts I brought, to go with tea and coffee. I am explaining what's in the pastries and showing pictures of Bobby's wedding. The Executive Director and the Board Chair walk in to the room, followed by Lawrence and other managers. They are all smiling, and we all await the news with excitement.

"As you know, our skilled immigrant pilot project for engineers has resulted in such positive results. In conjunction with our project, APE has now passed provisional certification for foreign-trained engineers, so that foreign-trained engineers can have an opportunity to practise their skills in Canada, something we have all been fighting for. Now an Indian engineer need not drive a taxi for a living. He now has a choice to apply for provisional engineering certificate with APE, work with a certified engineer for a year, and upon passing an exam at the end of the year and an ethics course, he can be licensed as a certified engineer, and work and be paid as a full-fledged engineer," the Executive Director announced.

Applause. I am thrilled. I knew this was happening, but didn't realize it came to fruition while I was away on holidays.

"Let us congratulate our hardworking team led by Lawrence Ho and Sonia del Mundo, who have done incredible work on this ground-breaking issue, working hard with so many stakeholders." The Executive Director beams at Lawrence and me. I am so thrilled I don't know what to do. Everybody looks at Lawrence and me, smiling, applauding.

"We are very pleased to announce that our skilled immigrant pilot project for engineers has so impressed stakeholders that the Federal and Provincial governments have approved in principle the creation of an initiative that will extend this kind of help to all immigrant skilled professionals to better utilize their skills in Canada."

Applause again, oohs and aahs. The Executive Director waves his hand to indicate more is coming.

"To this end, the Federal and Provincial Governments have approved funding in principle for a three-year multi-stakeholder program, called Looking Forward Initiative, to be led by our agency, with the purpose of making recommendations to improve the labour market integration of skilled immigrants in BC. A task force will be created to develop the terms of reference and budget of this program, and this task force will start work today," continues the Executive Director.

I am shocked. This is all too much. Staff break into applause, as do I.

"I am pleased to announce that this Initiative will work under the able management of Lawrence Ho and the Employment Department."

Applause again. The Executive Director, raises his arm again to signal quiet and that there is more to come.

"I am pleased to appoint as Director of this Initiative, someone whom you will all agree with me has shown tremendous passion and results in this work: our very own Sonia del Mundo."

I cannot hear the applause. I can just see my father's sad face nodding to me seriously, the injection needle pointing to me, reminding me that I am a long ways yet to making him happy.

Coreen shoves me, and I wake up from my temporary reverie. Everybody is applauding me and smiling, and I smile back shyly. Coreen hugs me. Hands around me seeking my hand in congratulations. I am asked to join the group in front, where the Board Chair, the Executive Director, Lawrence, and other managers shake my hand. I cannot believe this is happening. How do I know to be a Director? When Lawrence hugs me, I whisper to him," I don't know how to do this, you have to help me."

"Don't worry. You can do this. You've already shown you can. Everyone will help you," Lawrence assures me.

Stephen and I celebrate that night, and I feel so happy and invulnerable that I agree to invite his parents for dinner despite how they feel about me. Stephen suggests a restaurant, 'neutral territory' he says, so that 'you don't have the extra stress of selecting and cooking something they would like, and just focus on getting to know one another.' I should have got the hint right then, but I am distracted with my good news.

The next Saturday, we arrive at the Pearl Chinese Restaurant, one of the oldest Chinese restaurants in Vancouver, and Mr. and Mrs. Lee are already seated at the table. Mrs. Lee is a pale-faced, small, wiry woman, with pin-size eyes that pierce with their sharpness. Her hair is gathered in a neat bun on top of her head and she wears a stunning green *chiongsam* with a golden dragon embroidered throughout the dress. You would not call it a smile that emanates from her face when we are introduced, but more like the acknowledgment of royalty to a vassal. Mr. Lee is a quiet man with tussled grey hair, and the eyes behind his thick eyeglasses are stretched wide open, the better to see I suppose, but they make him seem always surprised. He is wearing a dark suit and tie, and stands from his seat like a soldier with a forward stoop when we are introduced. No one shakes hands or hugs each other, so different from my own family. We all sit, and I am at a loss to say anything, so I stretch my face and lips to the warmest smile I could muster, to try and hook a smile from them. They do not even see it, as they are looking at Stephen, expecting something from him.

"Sonia is a big chief in her office," Stephen starts. "She is in charge of helping engineers and doctors and nurses from different countries to practise their professions in Canada," he explains. Mr. Lee nods his head in seeming understanding, while Mrs. Lee reads the menu.

"Mother, did you hear what I said about Sonia?" asks Stephen.

"Yes, big chief office. Big chief home," she whispers the last phrase, and continues reading the menu.

The sarcasm is thick and unmistakeable and I glance at Stephen with some frustration.

"My pay is more, don't worry," says Stephen.

"Should be. Expensive law school," Mrs. Lee says squeezing her lips together, while still scanning the menu.

"Sonia cooks very well. Her mother cooks very well too," Stephen offers.

"But eat no good," she paints me briskly with her pinpoint eyes and adds, "Too thin. No good for baby." Mrs. Lee frowns.

I somehow like that. She seems to consider me in the running for a wife to Stephen, by already assessing my baby-making capacities so early in the game. I believe that was unintended, but a slip tells you something. I decide that two can play this game.

"No plan baby. Not good marry. Too young. Work more," I say. Stephen looks surprised.

"Is that how they teach English in the Philippines?" says Mr. Lee. Is he making fun of me? Or is he offended?

"Dad briefly taught acupuncture medicine in Manila. He is impressed with the English of Filipinos. He just means you don't have to speak pidgin English. Regular English would do," says Stephen.

"How about...," I look towards Mrs. Lee.

"She understands proper English even if she can't speak it," says Mr. Lee. I feel embarrassed.

"I'm so sorry," I say.

Stumbling Through Paradise

"Stop talking. Eat is better," Mrs. Lee says as she taps a finger at a line item on the menu.

I feel like a child that's been reprimanded, and decide to just go with the flow. From this dinner, I will at least attempt to take away the experience of eating the best Chinese food. Mr. Lee orders a string of dishes all in Chinese, and we await the food in silence. I cannot bear it for too long.

"When did you come to Canada, Mr. Lee?" I ask.

"Long time, before you born," answers Mrs. Lee.

She really does not like me. I give up, and rise. "Excuse me, I'm going to the washroom." I sense Stephen following me.

"She really doesn't mean it," he whispers. "It's just... how she is. Give it some time," he continues.

"You mean she's just rude. Or is she just rude to me?" I say angrily before entering the washroom. I sit it out on the toilet wondering what to do. Do I love Stephen enough to take his mom? Will she ever change towards me? Can I change her? Is it worth trying? My stomach rumbles. I guess I'm hungry. I decide to at least have my dinner.

Back at the table, Stephen pulls my chair for me, and I sit down with a weak smile. The soup mercifully comes, and we are all preoccupied watching the waiter serve the soup adroitly. His left hand is tucked behind him, his right hand stirs the soup gently with the ladle, and then he swiftly scoops the soup into four bowls. He turns the lazy Susan to let each of us pick a bowl. It is delicious. Sharks fin soup. Must cost a fortune nowadays. The dishes come one after the other: ostrich salad, crab in ginger sauce, whole steamed cod with its head on, glistening with a transparent sauce, crispy duck with jellyfish on the side, beef with mushrooms and broccoli, and lastly a noodle dish. Hardly anything is said as we eat, except for a few Chinese words exchanged between Mr. and Mrs.

Lee. There is so much food left over. The waiter takes them away and returns with several plastic bags of leftovers. Mr. Lee seems to have taken care of the bill, from his nod to the waiter. They must be regulars here.

"That was delicious. Thank you so much," I say to Mr. Lee and then to Mrs. Lee.

"You not like Chinese food? Eat so little," says Mrs. Lee.

I can't believe her. I defend myself. "I ate enough." Then I feel food rising up my throat and a great vomit comes out of my mouth. It pours out on the table despite my trying to catch it with my hands. A river of stinking soup, noodles, bits of fish and greens are flowing freely on the table, making its way to Mrs. Lee's lap. She shrieks. I run to the washroom with Stephen following, the waiters running to our table to see what it's all about. In the washroom, I am retching more into the toilet till all that beautiful food on the table is swishing around in the toilet water, and my stomach is finally empty. I wash my face in the sink and gurgle. I see that my makeup is all smudged up from my tears. I really blew it. Strangely enough, I feel better. We're even. I threw up on her. I fix up my face and go out. Stephen is waiting at the door.

"Are you okay?" he asks.

I nod. I see that our table is empty.

"They decided to go. They thought it might be better for you that way." I am relieved.

* * *

What a good thing that Tito Mario agreed to help me manage Mom's restaurant and catering business. With my new job, I have little time left for other things, and Tito Mario turns out to be an able manager. He is now almost full time on it while Tita Ching is reviewing to challenge the nursing exams.

She has decided to go back to nursing, after we had a long chat and I introduced her to my contact at the registered nurses association.

It is a slow process with Looking Forward Initiative, so much research to be done, so much connecting up and engaging various groups, before seeing any real action and change. I am meeting many people, regulatory bodies of various professions, funders, government representatives, immigrant-serving non-profit organizations, leaders of cultural communities and immigrant professionals from different countries. I love what I'm doing even as I am impatient for results.

I am invited to attend a major consultation organized by the City of Vancouver, Heritage Canada and my agency. The purpose is to ask the neighborhoods of the City what they think are the barriers to the full integration of different cultures into society, and what could be solutions or bridges to bring people together. I am curious to see if my hunches about racism are real, and if multiculturalism is reachable, or if it's only a myth.

At the workshop I attend, the participants say things like:

"I hate that when I take my baby for a stroll in his carriage, I am always mistaken for my baby's nanny," says a Filipina who lives in Kerrisdale, one of the ritzy neighborhoods of Vancouver.

"There are ethnic gangs in school, and you feel pressured to join one or you're not safe in school," says a Korean teen.

"If I knew I could not practise as a doctor here, I would not have come. It's for the kids, their future, that's why we continue to stay," says a South Asian man.

"Our children no longer obey us, they do whatever they want because they have their own money. It's like Canada has changed them. We may have a nice house, but our family is farther apart," says a Chinese lady.

I chime in my input: "My boyfriend is Chinese, and his mother is so rude to me. I don't know if it's because she doesn't like to share her son with anybody, or because I am not Chinese. My boyfriend told me that she wanted a Chinese daughter-in-law."

Everybody is sympathetic. The second round of workshops seeks to identify solutions: "More education about different cultures. More neighbourhood parties to get to know each other. More effort to recognize credentials of foreign trained professionals. Systemic discrimination prevents foreign-trained professionals from practising their professions in Canada. More family conversation about family values." As for me, what's the solution for me? "Learn some Chinese to soften her up," offers someone. "Get another boyfriend," offers another and we all laugh.

That is not so far-fetched, as Stephen and I are growing apart. I know he's not to blame for his mother. I've told him that if it were me, I'd make my mom be nice to my boyfriend. Stephen doesn't seem to try. Instead he makes excuses for her. I try to convince myself that Mrs. Lee is not racist towards me, just being a normal possessive mother who does not like competition with her only son's affections. If Stephen's girlfriend were Chinese, would Mrs. Lee be as rude to her? Mr. Lee seems nice enough, but he doesn't do anything to curtail her rudeness. Should I try to learn some Chinese? Why shouldn't she try to speak Pilipino?

"There is no racism, only ignorance," says one of the participants. "With education, there will be no racism," she adds.

"I don't think that's enough," says another. "There needs to be an interest to open up. Education about other cultures may result in understanding, but with no reaching out, people will stay within their enclaves," he says.

"What makes people reach out?" I ask.

"Need," says one. "Willingness to risk," says another. "Compassion," says a third.

I challenge them. "I reached out to my boyfriend's mom. She shunned me. It seems the effort should be both ways for multiculturalism to happen."

"So what can she do if the boyfriend's mom keeps shunning her?" asked the facilitator on my behalf.

"Persist. With your genuine efforts, she will eventually open up, you'll see," said someone.

I feel depressed. Multiculturalism is easy if it's not you that's being discriminated against.

* * *

The Bridging Cultures consultation feeds my work with the Looking Forward Initiative. The notion of systemic discrimination is tempting as the discrimination against so many immigrant professional groups is obvious. But it's not as easy as that.

I find out that foreign-trained doctors cannot ever practise as doctors in Canada as there is such a limited amount of residency opportunities in Canada, not even enough for local medical graduates. If you cannot do a residency, you cannot practise as a medical doctor.

"So why are there such limited residencies?" I ask the representative from the regulatory body for medical doctors.

"Each residency costs one million dollars, and the government does not have enough funds," she says.

"But there is such a shortage of skilled doctors in Canada, which is why the government invites skilled doctor immigrants into the country. So why not allocate funds for more residencies?" I ask in frustration.

"Don't know. Competing government priorities?" she offers.

It seems to me not at all a question of systemic discrimination, but one of gross incompetence, the right hand of government not knowing what the left hand is doing.

I share these frustrations with Manolita who studies law. Her answer frustrates me even more. "Government is the last place to look for coordination between 'left and right hand'. It is such a big bureaucracy that moves so slow, that if an elected Member of Parliament or a Member of the Legislature is able to push one little change in law forward during his term of office, he is to be congratulated."

"So where should we start?" I ask.

"Present your findings and recommendations to the key Ministers. In this case, the Minister of Health and the Minister of Immigration. Talk to their staff deputy ministers beforehand and bring them onside. Take along community leaders with you who represent voters. Ultimately, votes and election campaign donations are what motivates elected officials."

I am so impressed with how practical Manolita is. She has been working on political campaigns on the youth arm, for different parties, and is becoming a formidable political analyst. I suggest her ideas to my team.

* * *

Bobby's development business is thriving. He is growing his subdivision business into the farther suburbs of the Fraser Valley — in Maple Ridge and Abbotsford. "Raw land is cheaper farther out, and they are hungry for development. I don't have as much trouble getting approval. In Surrey, the current Council is not too friendly to development." Bobby has also become adept at networking with civic politicians. His daughter Sarina was christened with several municipal Councillors as godparents.

Nicole is totally preoccupied with Sarina, a beautiful little girl with the Filipino and Canadian mix, a classic *mestisa*. Nicole is eagerly awaiting the arrival of Bekang to help her with Sarina and a ridiculously huge house recently acquired by Bobby located in Coquitlam's ritzy Westwood Plateau. I have not forgotten about my promise to my father's ghost, to shut down Bobby's drug involvement. I begin to think of my promise as being non-committal, and wonder whether my dream was even real. I convince myself that development makes sufficient money for Bobby's lifestyle, and forget all about drugs.

Bekang arrives in March of 1994, not quite a year from the start of Bobby's sponsorship. She has gained weight and looks absolutely happy and excited about everything. I am delighted, but I feel odd about seeing her in a Canadian setting, as Baby Sarina's nanny. I don't feel exactly the same best friend to her when Nicole calls her to put baby Sarina to sleep in the room while we all chat in the living room, or when she cooks and washes dishes while the family has a leisurely dinner. She has developed a set of friends among caregivers through Church, and spends her day off in the mall with them. She looks like she is adjusting well to life in Canada, and I feel less guilty about not showing her around.

One day, I invite Bekang and baby Sarina to Vancouver to take a stroll under the cherry trees with me. Her eyes leap with joy, and for a minute, she and I seemed to be the same best friends as before in Pililla. But she thinks Nicole might not agree. I assure her it would be okay. I ask Nicole who surprisingly complains to me about Bekang.

"I know she is new to Canada, and doesn't know all the ways we look after children. So I teach her. She was very attentive in the beginning, but lately she's distracted. Baby's diaper is all soiled while she is on the phone. She forgets to put the timer on so the chicken got burned. It's happened several times. I know she speaks English well, so when she says that she does not understand my instruction, I don't believe her. Maybe she does not like her job anymore?" Nicole says, a frown on her usually smiling face.

"Why not ask Bobby's help to translate, just to be sure?" I offer.

"Translate? Bobby's always away on business."

I am not surprised. Bobby's been absent at family dinners as well. Time for a long talk with him.

"I'll talk to Bobby. And I'll talk to Bekang. She may still be adjusting. I feel guilty that I have not helped her get used to Canada. I was thinking of taking her and Sarina with me to Vancouver tomorrow, stroll in Stanley Park, have a long chat."

"That's kind of you. Yes, that will be good," Nicole says, but she is already lost in thought.

* * *

We walk along the Burrard Station pathway, my favourite cherry blossom garden, Bekang pushing Sarina in her carriage. Bekang is so excited about the cherry blossoms that she keeps taking pictures of them, of the baby and me against the cherry blossoms, of her and the baby against the cherry blossoms, of her against cherry blossoms. She snaps a few branches too fast before I could warn her not to, as these are public trees.

"It's only a few branches. Surely they won't miss that?" she asks gaily.

"I know, but the..." I give up, as Bekang snaps off a cluster. She inserts a blossom in the buttonhole of Sarina's coat, and another one behind her own ear. They both look lovely.

"So how are you liking Canada?" I ask.

"I love it! Everything is so clean, pretty, everyone so nice. Such big houses! Malls everywhere. No traffic," she gushes.

I interrupt. "How about work. How's that?"

"It's okay...umm...but I have to learn how to operate so many appliances. I broke the vacuum cleaner. I said to take away from my salary. But Mam Nicole is nice, she said no. But so many rules from Mam Nicole with baby! Let her crawl around, it's good for her. But no, she says, crawl only in the crib. It's too small; she won't be strong! And cooking and cleaning and watching baby. Too much to do! Sometimes, I get confused. I burned the chicken again. And so much waste, throwing away perfectly good skin of the chicken? And head of the fish? Canadians are too rich for their own good," Bekang says.

"But you're not supposed to cook or clean, just look after the baby, right?" I ask.

"Yes, but who will cook and who will clean? Mam Nicole hardly cooks, only sandwiches or salad. I offer to cook simple things. And I clean when I can. She likes to just play the piano."

"So don't clean, don't cook. Your first priority is the baby. The rest can wait."

"Well, they're used to it now, and I like to do it, because poor Mam Nicole..."

"What do you mean?"

"Don't tell her I told you?"

I nod and brace myself for very bad news.

"She and Sir Bobby are always fighting. I hear from the room. Sir Bobby's always away until late. I make dinner, but no one eats dinner. Still on the table in the morning. Mam Nicole is always looking sad." Bekang looks sad herself reporting this.

I feel uncomfortable eavesdropping this way on Bobby's life. I change the topic. I really have to see Bobby.

"Good thing you are helping them. Are you missing your family?" I ask.

"A little. I have new friends from church. We meet on Saturdays at the mall. Is Oakridge mall far from here? They say there's another group that hangs out there? Can we maybe drop by there?" Bekang is lively again.

"Sure, we can pass by briefly," I say. I never had to worry about Bekang, I guess.

At the mall, we easily find a cluster of Filipinas sitting on the benches outside the White Spot area. Bekang excitedly breaks away from me and Sarina, and starts talking to one of them. It seems she already knows them. They are cackling away excitedly. I look at them all and wonder what their occupations were back in the Philippines? Who was a nurse, a teacher? They all seem happy. Why should I care that they are not practicing their professions here? I see someone familiar — it looks like Carla. She is also looking at me. Bekang approaches me with some friends.

"This is my friend Sonia, and my little *alaga*, Sarina." They ooh and aah at Sarina.

"So why don't you join us, Bekang. We're watching a movie just there. It's about to start," says someone, pointing to the cinema at the corner.

Bekang looks at me shyly. I look at my watch. I have nothing else planned today. I have to do something about Stephen and me. Either we're together or we're not. This being in limbo is unbearable. Oh well, I can spend quality time with my niece.

"Okay," I smile. "I'll watch Sarina while you see the movie."

Bekang thanks me profusely, and hugs me. For a fleeting moment, I remember that she's my best friend. Carla walks by and says hello to me. I feel strange, trying to remember how close this woman was to my father. She looks older, haggard. She introduces me to the woman beside her, Norma. Now I remember. I smile.

"How is Jun Jun?" I ask.

"Fine," she says, "You should come and visit." She slips a business card in my hand.

"Yes, I should," I say, and off they go. I look at the card: Immigration Consultant, a phone number and an email address. Her new racket?

Carla and Norma join Bekang and the others who are walking towards the cinema ticket booth, where I see a cluster of men — a couple of Filipinos and several Caucasians — looking at the approaching girls. One of the men hands each of the girls a ticket, including Bekang. They walk towards the open cinema doors. I notice Bekang holding the hand of one of the Caucasian men. My friend does not lose time.

I have to warn Bekang about Carla. About what, I'm not sure. Just give her the whole story before she gets poisoned by any other story. I have to see Jun Jun, he's my half-brother after all. He must be what, six or seven years old now? I look at Sarina wrapped cozily in her carriage, Bobby's daughter, my niece, my father's granddaughter, my Lolo Ben's great granddaughter, the McIsaacs' granddaughter. She has a good future. What about Jun Jun? A hazy past, a chaotic present, what will his future be like?

* * *

CHAPTER 10

Canada
Bobby, 1996

I'm worried about my project in South Surrey. It could go sideways. Even my friends in Council won't approve it if the entire neighbourhood's in opposition. I talked to Sonia about it, not really knowing what she could do. I thought she might attend a presentation of the project to Surrey Municipal Council, to observe and give me her thoughts.

"Why me?" Sonia asks.

"The subdivision is just beside farmland, and the owners of the farmlands are opposing my project. They don't like my single-family residences, even if right next door to my land is another single-family subdivision. This is the last remaining property that's on the official community plan as single-family residential, but the zoning is still farmland, and so it needs a change in zoning. When there's a change in zoning, nearby property owners get to have a say about the project before Council makes a decision. My consultant says the neighbors are complaining that we're building 'monster houses,'" I explain.

"Monster houses?"

"It's very popular nowadays, especially with South Asians who have big families. They are large houses with four bedrooms on two levels. They usually have attractive red tiled roofs, and round protrusions in front for living rooms. A family can live upstairs, and two more families can live downstairs; for example, the elderly parents, or a brother's family who have just been sponsored and recently arrived in Canada."

"Sounds good. What's monstrous about that?"

"Some people think the houses are too big and ugly and different from the typical existing houses on the farms." I lay down some pictures.

"These are grand houses. Couldn't afford one." She's not taking me seriously.

"They also say it's 'against the plan' for several families to live in one lot. The zoning bylaw says only a single-family should occupy a lot."

"We lived with Tito Mario and Tita Ching the first time we arrived in Vancouver: two families upstairs, and another one downstairs. That made a lot of sense. We shared space. Everyone must have saved rent money. Were we living illegally at that time?" I ask.

"Seems like. I think these people are being racists. They are discriminating against South Asians, and Filipinos, and other newcomers who come to Canada that have large extended families. The thing is, this kind of house meets their needs."

"I agree. But I can see the problems. You remember the constant complaints from the neighbors downstairs? How crowded I felt in the house, how relieved I felt moving to our own place, even if it was just a basement suite."

"Sonia, you're an expert with immigrants. Maybe you can advise me on how I can counter the opposition."

"No way I'm an expert," she says.

But I managed to convince her to attend the public hearing.

* * *

The public hearing is held in the Council Chambers of Surrey City Hall. On stage, arranged in a semicircle are the seats of the Councillors with their own microphones. In the middle seat is the Mayor who chairs the hearing. Behind him is a huge coat of arms of the City of Surrey. Downstage of them is another microphone and podium where my architect makes his presentation, pointing to the plans mounted on flip chart stands behind him. The audience sits theatre style behind the presenter. My team and I sit on the front row. I look behind me, and I see that the room is packed, and the table for journalists is full. A cameraman is panning the audience with a video camera set up on a platform on the side. My architect finishes talking. The Mayor looks at the sheet in front of him and calls out a name.

Someone from the audience approaches the podium.

"My name is Frank Hortens, and I am the president of the East Semiahmoo Ratepayers Association. I read this petition to you, signed by over 200 members!" He pauses for effect, and reads.

"We welcome development, good development. This project will destroy our quiet neighbourhood and farms. This subdivision will bring more traffic to our streets and make the streets unsafe for our children. More monster houses, like the ones next door to it, will be built. These houses are too big for the lots, they have too many families on them, too many vehicles parked on the road, too much garbage, and our schools will be inundated with too many kids. These lots are not meant for multiple families. These lots are for single families! They will destroy our neighborhood, and lower our land values! Councillors, save Surrey from these monster houses, and do not approve this project!"

He finishes, causing the audience to break out into a great applause. He then opens up the rolled paper he was reading. He shakes it open with a flourish, unrolling a long trail of paper about 5 feet long on the floor like a carpet, filled with what looks like signatures. Cameras click to record the dramatic gesture. More applause.

I am tensing up. Will it all be like this? After the applause, the presenter rolls the paper back, and gives it to a clerk. He looks victoriously at our team in the front row, and then returns to his seat, shaking the hands of some people along the way. I am feeling sick to my stomach, thinking what I have to do to make a living.

The Mayor calls another name. An elderly man wearing dungarees and Stetson hat comes forward.

"Mr. Mayor and Councillors. You all know me. I have lived on this farm all my life, and my father before me, and his father before him. We bought this farm because the plan assured us this would be a quiet farm area. And now, greedy developers want to build more units, for more profits, for what? To house more and more newcomers who don't care for our quality of life!" The applause interrupts his flow.

The elderly farmer continues. "When we invite people to Canada, should they not follow our rules? What's wrong with the nice small houses we have? Why do they have to build these monster houses? Say no to this project, or you will never get my vote again." Another round of applause.

It goes on and on like this. More commentary on the "ugly bulky design," the lack of landscaping in front yards, the many cars parked on the street, the overcrowding of Surrey schools and how children from these subdivisions will overcrowd the schools even more.

One brave South Asian man wearing a white turban takes a turn at the podium.

"My name is Parminder Dhaliwal. I came to Canada with my family from India over 30 years ago, and we are grateful for the opportunity that Canada has given us. I have conducted business in Surrey for many years now. This city has been good to me. In turn, I give back to my community by serving on the Board of the Surrey Chamber of Commerce for many years now. I am also on the multicultural advisory committee of the City of Surrey. My daughter is a girl scout, and my son is goalie on the school hockey team. My wife volunteers with the women's shelter. Like many other South Asian Canadians, we are upstanding members of the Surrey community and proud of it!" A handful of applause from one corner of the room. I look to see a cluster of South Asians clapping.

The South Asian man continues. "It is true we like big houses if we can afford it, because we have big families, unlike Canadians who have only two or four members in a family. We look after our old parents in our house if we can help it, rather than send them to a care facility. When our kids grow up, we prefer that they live with us until they are married, or even after they are married if they can't afford their own place. And when our sponsored brother and his family arrives, we let them stay with us for a while until they find a job and can move to their own place. There is nothing in the zoning bylaw that our large houses are violating: they follow the density limit, the height limit, the front yards, side yards, everything. And this property is planned for urban single family anyway. We are a single family, a different kind of family as you know it, but one family nevertheless. All the other complaints I hear are not in the law. Is Council going to make one law for Canadians and another law for South Asians? That sounds like a racist policy, and I know Canada is not racist. Canada invited us to come, promising a multicultural society. South Asian Canadians supported all of you Councillors. Are you going to disappoint us? Like other Canadians, we work and contribute to Surrey, pay taxes, help build our wonderful community. Let us have the kind of housing that we need! Prove to us and the world, that you are really a multicultural city, and approve this project." There is silence as the South Asian man walks to the corner where a small applause welcomes him.

The next person gives a brief speech.

"If it were really just large extended families living here, we would not mind. But how do you explain the 'suites for rent' we see advertised in the paper for these kinds of homes? Isn't that abuse of the existing rules?" More applause.

More people speak opposing the project. One different voice speaks. It is a young man with blonde hair wearing jeans and a fancy leather jacket.

"My name is Patrick O'Casey and I am an architectural student at UBC. I've been listening to the comments of everybody, and would like to offer my suggestions. Perhaps these large houses could be redesigned to reduce their bulk, provide front landscaping and more on-site parking spaces. Then most of the concerns of neighbours could be met while still allowing the large house these people need. The Official Community Plan permits urban single family on this property," O'Casey states. Some Councillors begin to nod.

The next person gives a rebuttal. "Even if the plan calls for urban single family on this property, the plan also has a policy of providing buffers between farmland and urban single family. Councillors, you should follow your own policy and make this property the buffer. Instead of allowing 8 units to the acre, maybe it should have only 2 units to the acre," the speaker says. Some Councillors look thoughtful. I am mentally calculating, and the answer is not good.

It took three hours. One of the longest public hearings on record, they say.

In the car, we debrief. "What are you going to do?" asks Sonia.

"Call some of my Councillor friends. See what they think. What can be salvaged. Don't worry. It'll be ok," I say absentmindedly.

I feel stressed and do not want to share that with my team. I let them go, and tell them I'll see them in the morning after talking with some Councillors.

I invite Sonia to dinner at home.

"It's late, and I have an early morning at work."

"Sleep over, then you can leave early in the morning. Sis, have I ever asked you to sleep over? I really need your help."

"Ok, I did want to chat with Nicole anyway."

I have several drinks before, during and after dinner as we talk about the project. Nicole tries to dissuade me from the brandy. I ignore her and she says goodnight early. Sonia is giving me warning looks. I don't care.

"If they shoot this down, I lose close to a million. If they let me build a quarter of the density, I lose a quarter of a million anyway. I'm bankrupt. I thought I had both camps of Council supporting me, but none of the Councillors cared to look at me after the public hearing. Bad sign." I go to the washroom and take a line of cocaine. A small one won't harm.

The phone rings. Sonia calls me to the phone. It's Manolita.

I hurry up and wash my face. Outside, Sonia is looking at me strangely. I tell Manolita briefly about the disaster at the public hearing. Manolita talks non-stop. She finally finishes, and I put the phone down.

"What does she think?" Sonia asks.

"Says to ask your immigrant leader friends to raise a stink in the papers about the racism in Surrey."

"How?"

"Get them to write letters to the editor. Talk to columnists. Raise a rally if you can."

"But that would really fan the flames of racism. Make the sides grow even more strident."

I shrug. I look at the half-eaten steak before me. I have lost my appetite. I sip the last bit of brandy. "I'm pooped. See you in the morning, Sis. Bekang will look after your room. Sorry to be such bad company." I give Sonia a kiss on the forehead and go to my room.

I fall asleep quickly. I am awakened by a pounding headache. I look at the clock: already 5 am. I go to the washroom. The light is on and the door is ajar. There's Sonia in the middle of the washroom staring down at the counter. She looks up at me, a ghostly look on her face. I see that she was looking at my drug paraphernalia. I had not cleaned up. Damn.

"You have to stop this Bobby, or you'll lose everything you've worked for."

"It's only every now and then. Last night was too tough. I needed it."

"So you've always used drugs. Have you also been dealing all this time? Don't lie to me!"

I take Sonia out to the dining room so we don't wake Nicole.

"What's it to you? It doesn't affect you, except you never had to worry about your education. You and Manolita. And your lifestyle. Who do you think gives Mom money for all the expenses? You think the catering makes all that much?"

"We don't need the money. Stop using us as your excuse for dealing drugs. Does Nicole know?"

"She knows now. Recently anyway. She saw the stuff in the bathroom one night I neglected to clean up."

"What does she say?"

"She says she'll divorce me if I don't stop."

"So?"

"I said yes. I'll stop drugs. I don't do it much anyway. I can stop it anytime. It's just I have so much pressure with this development."

"What's the worst thing that could happen? Lose a million dollars? Then declare bankruptcy and start all over! Live with us at Mom's house. There's enough room. Nicole can go back to work now that Bekang is here. Or, why not just concentrate on building houses on zoned property, less risk there. Take it one house at a time. Or property maintenance, what you used to do."

"Hah! One house at a time? Property maintenance? You don't know what you're talking about. I'm not going to work for peanuts."

"You'd rather deal in drugs, rake in money, and risk imprisonment, lose your wife and your baby. Where's your head Bobby?"

"So, are you going to do it?"

"Do what?"

"Help me. Get the articles written."

Sonia does not answer.

"You disgu…disappoint me. I don't feel like helping you. So fail. Maybe bankruptcy will make you see the light. Maybe it's good for you to start over."

"Thanks, sis. I knew I could always count on you after all I've done for you." I turn my back and walk away.

"If I help you, will you promise to stop using and dealing?"

"Sure!" I answer without even thinking.

"Really? How will I know?"

"I'll go to drug rehab. After the campaign. And after we get a positive decision."

"No dice. Council is too unpredictable. It has to be sooner."

"How about after a few articles are published."

"How many?"

"I don't know. Three or four?"

"Okay, but not just in Surrey papers, *Vancouver Sun* okay? And TV. Can you get TV?"

"I don't have that much clout!"

"What about the rally?" I remind her.

"NO!!!" She screams.

"Okay, okay, just articles. Four."

"Then you go to rehab?"

"Yes."

"Whatever Council decides?"

"Yes," I breathe more freely. "Whatever Council decides, I promise."

"Including stopping drug dealing?"

"Yes."

"How do I know?"

"You'll just have to take my word on that!"

I'm not sure about this. "I want us to talk more about this one later."

"Okay," I can do this. I put out my hand.

"Deal?"

Sonia put her hand in mine, but she did not look happy.

"Have I made a deal with the devil?" she asks.

"No, you have not. You are an angel! Thank you sis!" I leave to take a shower before she changes her mind. When I come out of the shower, Sonia is gone.

* * *

CHAPTER 11

Canada
Sonia, 1996–2000

Have I made a deal with the devil? At least he has acknowledged his problem and even agreed to go for rehab. That's a start. I'll nag him. He won't get away without going to rehab. And the drug dealing. How does one even check that he's no longer doing that? I'll need help.

As to my part, it's true the neighborhood members who came out in the public hearing sounded racist. They just about came out and said so. Why shouldn't we call it for what it is? Let the community have a debate. Why should I be so worried about fanning the flames of racism? We're not calling for violence, just discussion and awareness of what's happening. How bad can that be? We need to remind Councillors of the implications of their vote on multiculturalism in the community. It's more than approving or rejecting a project. It's about whether Surrey is a multicultural city or a racist one.

I do not have to do much to raise awareness in media about it. In fact, the very next day after the public hearing, articles are already out in two local community papers linking monster houses to racism. I just show my colleagues these articles, and word spreads out. The Vancouver Saturday paper Letters to the Editor section is full of letters pro and con megahouses, pro and con extended immigrant families. Through my influence, three South Asian organizations, a multicultural organization, and Cross Currents Society write letters to the editor. The letters are published prominently under big headlines like "Racism by Zoning?" and "Megahouses Teach Cultural Values". Righteous indignation from church groups about "acceptance of people different from us." Righteous indignation from individuals about newcomers not playing by Canadian rules, and exploiting Canada's hospitality. Some mediating voices suggesting acceptance of mega houses but with design control, no-rent regulations, additional fees for garbage, and increased parking requirements.

In the end, the City of Surrey commissions its staff to develop guidelines to 'tame the monster house.' It takes a year for the regulations to be finished and approved. By then, Bobby takes a financial loss anyway for the amount of time he has had to hold on to the property. The project was approved for half the number of lots than the usual single-family density. It is not a total loss and Bobby does not declare bankruptcy. But he does not develop in Surrey for a long time after that.

Bobby tries to wriggle out of his promise to me saying it was not I that caused the furor in the media. But I insist that I got the major leaders to write the biggest most credible articles on behalf of multiculturalism. He enrols in a drug rehab centre and is pronounced clean after two weeks. Nicole seems happier, as does Bobby. As to his promise to stop drug dealing, he says he has stopped. For proof he says: "I could never deal drugs and not use. If I don't use, I don't deal. I don't want to be around it. Do you want urine tests?"

In fact I do. We arrange for weekly tests when he attends the follow up sessions at the drug rehab centre. After seven weeks of this testing, I agree with his mentor that Bobby can look after his own commitment without testing so long as he continues to attend the weekly sessions. Nicole lets me know about Bobby's attendance at these sessions, and she too is satisfied that Bobby has become truly drug free. But Stephen is doubtful.

* * *

My father too is not satisfied. That night, my old dream returns: Dad pointing the injection needle at me. It's a curious injection needle, something longer and thicker like a ruler, the point also thicker like a compass point. A slide rule maybe? He is reminding me of the engineering part of my promise. But haven't I delivered on that with the new APE provisional certification for engineers? What more do you want of me dad? More help for engineers? Like what?

Next day, I review the various reports and proceedings of conferences and consultations about skilled immigrants. I don't know what I am looking for. A clue that a ghost might suggest to me. Mentoring is mentioned in a lot of the recommendations. Early information to skilled immigrants about what's required. Canadian-style career coaching and counseling. Credential recognition. Professional technical English. I ask myself what can be done now? What does not need a lot of money? What can be done for all, not just for Filipinos or not just for engineers? What of these ideas do I know to do?

I sift through each of the recommendations and how they answer my questions. Mentoring seems to be the best fit. I can organize that. I can start with my friends who are engineers and nurses and doctors. It does not have to be a lot, just enough to try it out. I make a list of professionals I know, and their phone numbers. I call each one.

The first is an Engineer from BC Hydro. I am concerned that he might not be prepared to help because he's a busy man. He is not involved in the Filipino community that I was aware of. He made it in engineering easy. I thought he might say, "I did it. Why can't they?" But as soon as I tell him what the program is all about, he warms to it right away.

"I'd be happy to help. I went through such a hard time. I didn't know what to do then. If I can help to make it easier for someone..." he says.

"What did you do at that time?" I ask.

"I worked during the day on some job, then studied at night. I have kids; I had to keep supporting them. I did that for at least four years. It's about time something like this happened," he says.

I speak to a nurse, and she offers to bring the president of a nursing association she was a member of. "It's something our group wants to do something about. Providing mentors to newcomer nurses would be a good start," she says.

The responses are all like this — positive, eager and enthusiastic. I feel inspired and uplifted. If only this was all in place when my father was alive. If only he met my BC hydro engineer friend.

Over 20 Filipino professionals come out to the meeting held next week. The engineer mentor hosts the meeting at his home, with the usual feast. The feast provided by our long-term Canadian engineer is a mix of Canadian and Filipino dishes: a tender beef roast, baked salmon and *pancit*. His success is evident in his three-level home with a gorgeous view. His children are all in college. His wife is a noted artist.

The first mentors who attend are engineers, nurses, dentists and bank managers. We agree on a few guidelines. Mentors are to inform newcomers about the profession, and are not expected to find a job for the newcomers. Mentors would provide coaching for resumes and job interviews. We set the minimum and maximum length of mentorship period and the hours per month.

In fact, the mentors are so enthusiastic that they are later instrumental in newcomers landing jobs within the mentors' companies. The mentor-mentee pairings become so successful. Nobody pays attention to the maximum length of mentorships. Mentors and mentees become friends.

The name Bamboo Network comes easily. Bamboo is a plant that grows profusely in Asia where most immigrants come from. It is hardy, strong and tall, and the reason it survives strong winds is because of its flexibility and resilience, traits that will help immigrants succeed.

We decide to increase the diversity of the mentors to include mentors in other fields, and mentors other than Filipinos. We document everything so that we could use the information for securing funding in the future and make the project an on-going program with stability.

Stephen suggests we establish our own non-profit organization and run the program through the new organization. We decide to call it the Immigrant Communities Collective or ICC. Our first Board includes some of the early mentors. Stephen and I perform all the staff roles needed to be done, with the help of some volunteers. Work is done outside office hours, out of borrowed spaces like library meeting rooms and our own kitchens. Whenever an immigrant client gets a job related to his profession, we celebrate! A bright Filipina engineer lands an engineering technician position at BC Hydro, the first success story of the Bamboo Network. Her mentor is an engineer at BC Hydro who helped her get the job. She is also set to apply for the provisional engineering certificate with the Association of Professional Engineers. Pretty soon, we have enough success stories and I begin to shop the program around for funding.

I submit a proposal to a Provincial Government's "Request for Proposal." When the fax comes in stating we are being awarded a contract, we are overjoyed. We're now able to hire staff to coordinate the project on a regular basis, recruit more mentors, and expand the service to more immigrants. We can rent an office where all the activities could happen. We begin partnering with organizations and recruiting mentors from corporations, the first one being BC Hydro.

* * *

Stephen and I grow closer working together on the Bamboo Network, and for a while, I think it will work out after all. We are living together in some way: he sleeps over at my family's place after long nights on the project, or I sleep over at his place. We finally decide to live together, with or without his parents' consent. We rent a one-bedroom condo in downtown at Citygate, overlooking False Creek. Because Manolita is now living by herself at our family home in Vancouver, we ask Tito Mario and Tita Ching to take up residence with her in Vancouver, as the family business is mostly in Vancouver now. Tito Mario rents out their place in Surrey.

Stephen and I enjoy choosing the condo and decorating it. We have the same taste: minimal, open, bright, simple. I have not seen his parents since the infamous dinner. Stephen says that he has told them about our move together, and that he does not care about their opinion on the matter. Stephen disappears every Sunday to spend time with his parents. I do the same, visiting Manolita or Nicole and Bobby. I count my little family, all incomplete sets of us: Mom in the Philippines, Stephen's parents invisible, Dad's son — my half-brother Jun Jun — out there somewhere unconnected with us. Bobby's family is complete as could be. I only hope he continues to be clean.

Bekang tells me that she is getting Carla to help her sponsor her sisters and brothers, and for 'very cheap'! She says proudly.

"You can't sponsor anyone yet, *loka*, you fool. You have to complete your 24 months of service and then apply to be an immigrant and only then can you sponsor anyone! How much did you pay her?"

"Two thousand for everyone, but I can pay just monthly, $50."

"Did you pay her anything yet?" I ask.

"I paid her one month," she says.

"Ask for your money back. You don't need to hire someone to sponsor your family! I'll help you when it's time!" I am fuming. I decide to see Carla about it. Besides, I wanted to check in on Jun Jun.

* * *

Carla is still a *Dona*, based on her residence. She and the professor are still together, living in a nice house near Oak and 70 Ave, on the edge of Shaughnessey. When I knock on the 10-foot-high oak door, Norma opens it, a toddler straddling her waist.

"She'll be with you shortly, *Ate*," says Norma. Norma is wearing a nanny's uniform. The house is bright and open.

Norma leads me to the living room. I sink into an oversized sofa.

"And who is this?" I ask, looking at the pretty baby.

"Vina. Carla and Victor's daughter," Norma explains.

I didn't know they had a daughter. She has Carla's curls and almond eyes, Victor's pale skin. A *mestisa*.

"Where's Jun Jun?" I ask.

"Carla is bringing him," Norma says stiffly.

So that's how they are so close. Norma is the baby's nanny.

A shiny, just showered, powdered and combed Jun Jun appears with Carla, holding her hand. His other hand is in his mouth. He is wearing a blue sailor shirt and blue shorts. He has the large eyes and dark looks of my dad. He looks at me shyly, twirling his finger in his mouth.

"Take your finger out of your mouth," scolds Carla. "Make *mano* to Tita Sonia". I extend my hand. Jun Jun takes it to his forehead, and quickly hides behind Carla's skirt. He doesn't know me. The last time I visited was when he was an infant. I guess I am his *Ate*, or older sister, not *Tita*, or aunt, but that would require too much explanation. I wonder if Carla has told him?

I bring out my little present from my purse and give it to Jun Jun. He is not sure, and looks at his mom who nods. He opens the present excitedly and squeals when he sees the transformer car. He turns it around, expertly unlocking the joints, converting it into a transformer. He is now on the floor playing with it, totally preoccupied.

"No thank you to Tita?" asked Carla.

Jun Jun rises from the floor, and runs to me, planting a wet kiss on my cheek. "*Salamat* Tita," he says.

I'm glad he still speaks Tagalog.

"Is he going to school yet?" I ask.

"He's in pre-school. He'll be in kindergarten next year. He's very smart, just like his dad," Carla said.

"He could go to a private school, but it's expensive, and Carla can only afford public school," inserts Norma.

I am not certain what I'm being told, so I keep quiet.

"Carla's husband will only spend for public school. Jun is not his son after all," says Norma.

What do they want, that our family pay for his education? Some nerve this Norma. I change topic and take the offensive.

"I hear you've charged Bekang for sponsoring her family? Is that right?" I ask.

"Yes. She sure is eager to get them here, so we said we can help her," Norma explains.

"She is not even a year caregiving. She can't sponsor anyone," I say.

"That's what we said, but she wanted us to move right away," Norma replies.

"You know well enough you can't do anything for her now. Why did you take her money?" I challenge.

"She insisted on it! She said she did not want to spend the money, and that she prefers to pay early, slowly," Norma raises her voice.

"And you took it? You're exploiting her! Because she doesn't know any better and wants to get her family here so much. I could report you for exploiting her." I blurt out.

"Then report us!" dares Norma.

"Norma, just give back the money. It's only one month yet anyway," says Carla.

"No. Bekang asked our help. She should ask for the money back if she wants," Norma insists.

Carla goes to the dining room, and brings back a fifty-dollar bill. "Here." She gives the bill to me. I take it and shove it in my purse.

"You del Mundos. You think you are so high and mighty. Jun Jun's the son of your own father. No support whatsoever, not even a Christmas present. Not even a bit of a shower from the famous del Mundo wealth. I thought you had a heart and came to visit Jun Jun. I guess not. It was to cause trouble for our business, and get that *haliparot's* money back!" Norma says.

"Norma!' cries Carla.

"Well, what do you call someone who has boyfriends right and left, kissing men she's just met?" challenges Norma.

I am confused. They are talking about Bekang.

"What's fifty dollars to her anyway? I'm sure she has no problem earning more than that from her employer given his... you know...his 'business,'" she says emphasizing the "business."

I feel my face getting hot. "What do you mean by that?" I challenge Norma.

"You know what I mean." Norma's tone is menacing.

"Nothing, she means nothing," cries Carla. "She means Bobby is so successful with business, he must be doing very well." Carla insists.

"I'm leaving now," I rise to go.

"Jun Jun, come and say goodbye to Tita," says Carla.

But I don't wait for Jun Jun, and head for the door and away from that hateful Norma as fast as I can.

* * *

"No doubt. She'll go after the del Mundo inheritance," says Stephen.

"What can we do?" I ask.

"I don't know. He does have some entitlement, I think."

"I hate them. Especially that Norma. She's *mukhang kuwarta*."

"What's that?" I often forget Stephen does not speak Tagalog.

"Money hungry. I don't mind Jun Jun getting something, but it's the way that Norma says it, almost with a blackmailing tone. You should hear how she insinuated that Bobby's business is not above board."

"She's trying to tell you she could use something on you if you report their business as not being above board. She's sly."

"Bobby's clean now," I say.

"Is he?" Stephen asks.

"He says so. Nicole says so."

Stephen looks away. "If you say so."

"What does that mean?"

"I hear things."

"What things?"

"I can't prove it. Not yet. I'll tell you when I have proof," says Stephen. He looks dead serious. Now I'm really worried.

* * *

My dear Sonia,

I am so busy here. I didn't know what I was getting in to. After all the good I have done, the opposition is continuing to tell dirty stories about me being disgrasyada *and abandoned by my husband. Also hinting I had an affair with Sendong. They are always finding fault with me, even my accomplishments. Family and friends are telling me to persist, ignore, keep to the high road and keep busy building a future for poor Pilillans.*

I am enjoying meeting so many Pilillans. They need my help. I am staying for them. I am focusing on livelihood improvement, income-generating projects, creating more jobs here, and getting more money for Pililla from national government. I'm also looking at international sources including Canada through CIDA for better infrastructure like roads and such.

Lola Iska is not well. She may be leaving us one of these days. Can you come? Thank you so much for looking after yourself and everyone. Why no Stephen in your letters, how is he?

love u,
mom

Dear Mom,

I want to see Lola Iska before she goes. Leaving work for vacation is tough. We're very busy. ICC is expanding, getting more grants to expand programs. I'm full time executive director now that Looking Forward Initiative is over. ICC is helping Uncle Eddie get settled, and he is getting along well. He has so many business ideas!

You have a good nose, even from far away. Stephen and I are ok, but his mom and dad do not approve of me. We decided to live together anyway. We seem to get along okay on the home front, and working with him is good. Is it possible to have a good marriage when in-laws do not like you? I did nothing to her, she's just hateful to me. Stephen says she's conservative and wants him to marry a Chinese girl. He said not to worry. He promises that his mother will change later, when we have a baby. I don't know. He said his mother threatened to disinherit him if we go ahead and marry. That got Stephen worried. I think it's unacceptable. What should I do?

All good on the restaurant and catering front. Tito Mario expanding the packaged food products line. He said he'll call you this weekend. Bobby and Nicole and Sarina all fine. Liberals wooing Manolita to run for MP. She's thinking about it. Is politics in our blood or what?

Love u,
Sonia

Dear anak,

Do you love Stephen? And does he love you? If yes to both, go ahead and marry with or without his parents' consent and inheritance. If only you love him, and he won't stand by you, stop this relationship now. If his family is making you wonder if you love him or not, then you don't love him. Best to let go now while it's early. Am I too brutal? Politics has made me so practical. There are many other fish in the sea, and you are a great catch! If his family does not appreciate you, sorry for them. Many other parents would die to have you in their family. Your dad stood by me when the del Mundos thought I was too poor for them. In time, they came through especially when Bobby was born, and you and Manolita. Stephen has to stand by you, or no go, okay?

You know, have you ever thought of living in the Philippines, helping out our country? We sure could use the help of someone like you so passionate about helping, so effective in creating good programs and getting funding. Want to give it a try? Let's chat when you get here!

love u,
Mom.

Dear Mom,

Can't wait to get there. Stephen and I had a big fight. I gave him an ultimatum: let's get married now, with or without inheritance, with or without his parents' consent. He said I am being childish to force a decision now. I said if he loves me he will do this. He says, he loves me but can't turn away from his family. He says why not just wait as they will surely change their minds in due course. So I split up with him. He'll be alone in the apartment while I'm in the Philippines. I said that when I return to Vancouver, I'll be living back at our home with Manolita. He said not to make rash decisions. He begged me to think it over.

He said that he'll be waiting for me. He makes me feel as though I'm immature about this, when in fact it's a question of him not standing by me. It's clear he loves his family more than me. I feel so rejected. I'm very busy and stressed at work, plus this. And Lola Iska. I may be having a breakdown. I need this trip very much. As to living in the Philippines and helping out there, it's tempting! See you soon!

love u,
Sonia

* * *

CHAPTER 12

Canada
Sonia, 2001

I'm watching the peaceful waters of False Creek, and my mind swims past it to the big noisy waters of Nasugbu beach at Tita Marites's place in Batangas, Philippines. I look up from the waves and see the sun about to set, the best time to swim, when it has cooled down. I sink into the cool dark-blue water, let it wash over my face and cool my body from the heat of the day. I swim easy strokes effortlessly as the ocean buoys me up. I could swim forever on this ocean. When I get up, the sun has set, leaving only streaks of orange and purple and blue in the sky riotous with wispy clouds. I remember running to this sky the first time I learned that Stephen's parents wanted him to marry within their culture. The salt of the ocean now always makes me think of those tears. Even then, Tita Marites warned me. Mom is right. Stephen and I can't be together, with his parents so much against me, just for my race alone.

I look around our cozy condo at the foot of False Creek, awash in bright white morning light. I'll miss this light. It always lifts me. The play of shadows on the tiled floor. The gleaming chrome framed glass tables. The glass mirrors reflecting the buildings. The geodesic dome blinking light reflections from its triangular glass pieces. The flags playing with the wind. The sailboats gliding on the smooth waters. The seagulls flying past the window to the next building's rooftop. The caterpillar SkyTrain crawling on branches made of steel. Streams of cyclists, skateboarders, joggers, walkers moving along the seawall. You can never be truly lonely here. The city brings you hope. Every morning. The city renews you with its life.

My bag is packed, just one tiny roll-on bag. I don't want to think about what I'll do there. I just want to get away. Lola Lita would love to take me shopping for clothes anyway. That will give her something to fuss about. Stephen and I said our goodbyes last night at the *despedida* farewell party. I insisted on bringing myself to the airport and made him go to work. At my work, they pushed me to go. "You need a break, or you'll not be useful to anyone," they said. "Take as long as you need," said the Chair of the Board. "Don't worry about us, we'll not try to do much while you're away. We could use the break too!" she teased.

Manolita is besieged now with relatives looking after her, what with Uncle Eddie now living in the house, along with Tito Mario and Tita Ching. She is so busy that they hardly see her at home. She has started to complain to me about being over-guarded. "Christ, I'm a grown up! Sometimes they treat me like I'm 11!" Sarina is now in pre-school, and Nicole back to work at the University. Bobby is deep in the development business. Bekang, or Becky as they call her here, is always in love with some Canadian boyfriend. She seems to have a different one whenever I talk with her. "I can't help it. They are all so cute and nice!" she says. I am taking a lot of *pasalubongs* from her to her family; about half my luggage contains her *pasalubongs*. Oh well.

I have nothing for Lola Iska, except a rosary I bought in Rome once. The seller promised it was blessed by the Pope himself. I can't really expect her to live on forever, can I? I have to let her go. I have to let her know how much she means to me. I want to put my head on her lap one last time, and feel her loving fingers brushing my back, my hair. I'm eager to see Mom, she sounds so happy, so fulfilled. Her invitation for me to stay and help her is intriguing. I keep thinking why not? Maybe even just a few months to see what it's like. Will ICC be ok with me gone so long? I try to push Bobby out of my mind, but he continues to worry me, the drug dealing. Stephen has not come up with any proof.

I beg my dad, or his ghost. Dear Dad, your engineering cause is won, your son clear of drugs. Will you let me be in peace now? Last night I dreamt about him again, and instead of the injection needle, he was showing a police badge to me. Take Bobby to the police? My God. Is he warning us that the police are coming after Bobby?

I call Bobby. I don't know why. "Stop dealing drugs if you still are. The police may be after you," I blurt out.

"What are you talking about?" he exclaims.

"That's all I have to say. Now I have said it. Don't ask me how I know. Just know that, and do something." I insist.

"Do what? Have you gone cuckoo, Sonia?"

"I don't know. Maybe. Just be careful. Dad loves you."

"What did you say?"

"Dad loves you."

"He's been dead so long. What brought this on? Sonia. What's going on with you?"

"And I love you too. Kiss Nicole and Sarina for me, okay?"

"Yeah. Are you sure you're okay? I'll take you to the airport."

"No, I'm fine. Go and take care," I say.

"You take care. Love you," says Bobby.

"Love you," I say. I put down the phone.

Everything is quiet: the house, the phone. I wish it would ring, and that Stephen would be at the other end. Multiculturalism — hogwash. And here I am fighting to help make newcomers successful, to prove Canada is truly a home for people of different cultures. But not so with the person you love. In real families, in real life, it doesn't work. Is all my work here in Canada worth it? Is it just a sham, this multiculturalism? Better go home where you belong, immigrants. Isn't that what the old lady said to my dad at the grocery store? Where is my home? Canada? Philippines? Better just help Filipinos in the Philippines so they don't have to go abroad. Isn't that what mom said to me at the retreat? Who is my home?

People are better when they are loved, said my favourite writer. I say people are better when they are recognized. I am better when I am recognized. If I am not recognized, who is there to love or be loved? Home is who recognizes me, and loves me.

As I lock my Vancouver condo door behind me, I feel it so strongly. This time, I am going home.

* * *

PART 3
THE MAKING OF MANOLITA AND JUN JUN:

*Soup or Salad for the
Canadian Soul?*

CHAPTER 1

Canada
Manolita, 2015

Wish you were here, Dad. Everyone laughed at my foolish dream, except you. You always believed in me. Who would have thought I'd go this far in a new riding? In the Canadian federal elections at that. As an Independent to boot. Everyone wrote me off. Now it's so close between the candidates, in fact too close to call. I've stopped feeling nervous and just want to see it finish. My campaign headquarters is abuzz with excitement. An announcement coming up on TV. The decibel level in the room diminishes as Peter Mansbridge appears.

"Good evening, Canada. Welcome back to the Canadian federal elections 2015 Countdown. It's the tightest election in history according to pundits. It looks like the scandal-rocked Conservatives are going down, the NDP and Liberals fighting for a minority government. Let's check in on new polling results. In BC, the tightly contested Vancouver Kingsway riding has a declared winner — NDP by a slim majority over the Liberals..."

A buzz goes up in the room. Good thing I didn't run in that riding.

"The new Vancouver Granville riding is still too tight to call. We'll keep you abreast. Meantime, let's turn to our political panel..."

This tension is killing me. I dare not expect victory. "You've already won," they keep telling me, seeing how far I have come. But is it far enough?

My campaign manager calls. "Manolita. Over on that screen. They're showing that first interview of you with BCTV." I remember that, the one that started it all. I walk over to that screen.

"Tell us a time when you cried in public," says the interviewer Sophie Lee. It's the sort of question they ask of female candidates, never of male candidates. I should have seen that coming, but didn't. What to answer? I cry all the time during a deep massage. But that won't do. Instead, I said something that started a whole debate.

"I remember once. I was introduced, preparatory to giving a talk. The way the audience welcomed me, the way they looked at me, put their unadulterated trust in me. The way the introducer said I was 'the hope of our country'. It was the first time anyone said that of me. I never claimed a home in my ethnic roots. I claim my home as Canada, with its glorious diversity. I suddenly felt they, the audience, together as a group, were my home. And they were claiming me as theirs. I was theirs. I felt choked, and I could not begin my talk. Tears started welling up in my eyes, and someone gave me a glass of water. I drank that, and apologized. I remember saying, 'I feel so moved by your welcome of me. I feel you are my family. No. More than that. You are my home. I am running for public office for you.'"

Stumbling Through Paradise

"Which community was that you were talking to?"

"It was a gathering at a community centre composed of students and their parents, seniors, neighborhood leaders, Caucasians, Chinese, Indians, Filipinos, First Nations."

"Why did you cry?"

"I have been roundly criticized by the Filipino community, and many ethnic communities who say I am turning my back on them when I talk of Canadian values. I am not denying our roots in our original cultures — our roots will always be with us, and we can never forget that. But we are now Canadians and let us not forget that too. This audience embraced me and what I believed in, and implied that they believed in it too. I had been feeling all alone, but with them, it felt like I came home."

The highlights of the campaign flash in my mind. Canadianism: Chicken Soup for the Canadian Soul. They called me the Soup Lady. Debates over soup or salad taking place all over Canada. People excited talking about Canadian values. It made them love Canada, and pay attention to me, the candidate that reminded them to love Canada. It seemed things were in the bag when the scandal hit.

The vicious attacks on my family and me. Then the media conference, how I gave up on everything, and just told the truth. The polls are so close. Can I survive the attacks?

Peter Mansbridge is back on the screen.

"It looks like we are now ready to announce final results of the remaining ridings. Starting with the new riding of Vancouver Granville." A shot of the Election Officer coming to the podium.

Everyone falls silent, waiting for the announcement. It is the longest moment of my life. It all comes to me: all the work, the hours, the sacrifice, the people who helped me, the people who needed me, the people who crucified me, my dear sweet dead father who believed in me, Bobby who supported my campaign and is now dashing my hopes, mom, Sonia, Jun Jun, the house of the Canadian Parliament focusing, then receding, then focusing again.

My heart is in my throat. I can hardly breathe, watching my destiny unfold.

* * *

CHAPTER 2

Canada
Manolita, 1986

When I woke up that morning of February 22, 1986, there were no usual noises and smells in the kitchen, no frying of garlic with the rice, or *longganisa* sausages and egg. Mom, Bobby and Sonia were all glued to the television. I looked to see what was happening. Everyone was quietly seated on the floor in front of the TV, watching intently. Mom made room for me on the floor, without taking her eyes off of the TV screen.

The scene was of thousands of Filipinos on the streets, tanks and machine guns lined up on the streets. The camera focused in on groups of people praying, someone climbing up on a tank giving a rosary to the soldier sitting on top of the tank, a group of women offering yellow flowers to soldiers clutching machine guns, women and children and nuns holding hands around a group of men who turned out to be the leaders of the revolt against President Ferdinand Marcos of the Philippines. The camera panned and showed thousands, maybe millions of people on the street called EDSA, banners telling Marcos to step down, children holding their hands up making the letter L with their forefinger and thumb.

"What is that L they are making with their hands?" I asked Mom.

"That means *Laban*, the name of the party of the Opposition," Mom answered.

"What does *Laban* mean?" I ask.

"Fight. Shhh," says Sonia.

I don't get it. "What?" I ask again.

"Fight! You know!" Bobby boxes me lightly, ruffles my hair and makes a face. I get it.

The camera focused on a banner showing a large picture of a smiling, plain middle-aged woman wearing eyeglasses. "Who's that?" I ask.

"Cory Aquino. That's the widow of Ninoy Aquino, the guy who was assassinated by Marcos people, they said," explained Mom.

"She's the leader of the people's rebellion against the Marcos dictatorship," added Sonia.

Suddenly helicopters hover over the skies. The announcer screams: "Oh my God, will the helicopters shoot on the crowds, oh my God!" People huddle close together, close their eyes, praying. Other people are crying. A tank moves forward. Nuns and women hold their hands together and kneel in front of the tank. The tank stops. The crowds are hushed as we are hushed watching them on TV. Slowly, the sound of helicopters begins to fade; the camera shows the helicopters flying away from the crowds. Cheers from the crowds. "The people have scared away the helicopters! But for how long?" cries the announcer. "What a remarkable stand-off between armies, soldiers and ordinary civilians! Guns stopped by sheer courage, pluck and prayer," the announcer continues.

Mom made us stay home from school that day. She herself stayed home most of the day except to make a delivery. Bobby left in the afternoon on an errand and returned as soon as he could. Sonia cried most of the time, and I was riveted. We stayed in vigil with the Filipino people, and the world, as though our presence too would contribute to stopping the tanks and machine guns and helicopters from firing on the Filipinos. The phone was busy all day, with friends checking in on each other, bringing each other up to date on the latest news or gossip. Mom was at her rosary when she was not cooking. Sonia was busy on the phone. Bobby strode in and out of the house nervously. I was thrilled and excited about the attention the Philippines was getting from the world media. I felt proud to be a Filipina, and very curious indeed about that lady Cory Aquino who made this all happen. What a woman! To be able to inspire millions to sacrifice their lives to depose a dictator. I want to be like that. One day. A leader of a nation.

In the next days, I followed the news about the Philippines closely, remembering the names of leaders mentioned, what they looked like, their roles and their backgrounds. Enrile, the Defense Secretary who turned against his buddy Marcos. Ramos, the Administration's Vice Chief of Staff who turned against his boss, the President. Gringo Honasan the handsome Navy Lieutenant Colonel who encouraged the soldiers to break away and join the rebel troops. Cardinal Jaime Sin, the leader of Catholic Philippines who told the people to go to EDSA and protect the rebel soldiers. June Keithley the announcer on Radio Veritas, who kept the news going and the community informed of developments. I learned of Pepito Laurel, the Vice Presidential running mate of Cory Aquino. I saw the arrival of Cory Aquino at EDSA amidst a sea of yellow ribbons symbolizing the martyrdom of her husband Ninoy Aquino. I watched the separate inauguration of two presidents, as both Marcos and Aquino claimed they won the elections and the other cheated. I researched and found out about the events surrounding the 'snap election' that was 'forced' by the United States on Marcos in the wake of increasing unrest due to the murder of Senator Ninoy Aquino, Marcos' greatest opponent. I read that 29 computer staff members at the Commission on Elections walked out from their jobs because of how they were being required by the administration to cheat and favor Marcos, how COMELEC declared Marcos winner by 52%, while the election watchdog NAMFREL declared Cory the winner by 53%. I found out how US President Reagan was said to have intervened and encouraged Marcos "to go" as the numbers of protestors exploded and the world opinion formed against him and in favor of Cory Aquino. I read about how, when the Marcos family fled Malacanang Palace, the crowds looted the Palace, about the only bit of violence in the whole "revolution". I learned how, much later, when Cory Aquino addressed the joint Congress and Senate of the USA, she proudly claimed, "our revolution was not only the most peaceful, but also the cheapest". It started on February 22, and, in four remarkable days of history, Marcos, his wife Imelda and their three children accompanied by chief of staff Fabian Ver, were out of the country enroute to Hawaii. By February 25, the Philippines, by the force of an unprecedented people power revolution, was freed of a corrupt dictator that controlled the country for over 20 years.

I had long conversations with my dad's sister Tita Marites who was an employee of ABS CBN television station in Manila. Tita Marites was a broadcaster for the station when the Marcos Administration took it over and established Channel 4, the Government's propaganda arm. She was one of the first employees back on the job when ABS CBN was re-established during people power. From Tita Marites, I learned of the scope of Marcos' corruption, how bankrupt the country had become. Tita Marites warned me not to be too impressed with the "heroes you see" as some of them are "opportunists." She said no doubt there was real heroism in the beginning. The fear of being mowed down by the tanks was very real in the first hours. But after a day or two, the fear was off and the fun took over. People power became a fiesta, a picnic, a party. She told me not to expect too much of the new leaders who can only do so much with the depleted resources of the country. "It will be a very long road to recovery. Save the hurrahs for last, my dear niece," is how she ended our conversation.

At the Holy Rosary Catholic School where I was in grade 5, the Social Studies teacher asked me to tell the class about what was going on in the Philippines. I gave a report that impressed my teacher, who shared it with her co-teachers. My report was published in the school paper, and a school forum was created on the topic of "The People Power Revolution in the Philippines: Lessons to Learn for Canada", with essays chosen from a school-wide competition. I was the youngest panel discussant; all the others were high school students. My piece was entitled:

Recipe for a Peaceful Revolution
and Lasting Change

Ingredients

A corrupt dictator

An oppressed people

A triggering injustice

A charismatic leader

Rebel leaders in the armed forces
and civil administration

A martyr

A living symbol of the martyr

A media network

A place of mass assembly

Instructions

Assemble your ingredients:

1. Make sure your dictator is very corrupt — cheated in elections, robbed the country of millions, caused the death of political opponents, and preferably on the decline. For example, popularity on the wane.

2. Make sure the people are sufficiently oppressed — poverty at record levels, country bankrupt, innocent civilians imprisoned.

3. Build up rebel leaders in key places of the armed force: air force, navy, police, and civic administration, the higher up the better, to encourage support from the ranks.

4. Find a leader with moral authority who can raise support from the masses at an instant — for example, a well-loved religious leader.

5. Wait for an injustice so huge it will trigger people's outrage, for example, the murder of a legitimate hero, or massive demonstrated cheating in elections.

6. Raise a living symbol of the martyrdom. The more innocent the better, for example the gentle wife of the slain hero.

When all the above ingredients are in place, cook up people power:

7. Announce over radio so everyone in the country knows, that rebel civil and military leaders have declared against the dictator.

8. Arrange for a location that is easily accessed by the public and large enough to accommodate masses of people, for example, a public street or plaza.

9. Have your charismatic leader announce that the rebels need people's help. State what specific help you want from people. For example, "Go to X place and protect these rebel leaders from the dictator". The action you want has to be specific and with a specific location.

10. Arrange for enough people to start with — the more innocent the better, like nuns and mothers and children who are not associated with violent acts.

11. Keep news flowing. Focus on the successes of the rebellion, the people showing up in the

streets, news of the dictator, especially bad news about him. This media network is very very important; it is the glue to the entire movement.

12. On the streets, make sure there is NO VIOLENCE from the people. Suggest what they can do instead of violence. For example: pray, give food or flowers or rosaries to the soldiers, kneel in front of tanks, hold your ground even if you think the tanks may move forward. People must be kind to the soldiers, win them over to the people side, remembering they are not the enemy. The soldiers' boss — the dictator — is the enemy.

13. Have banners all around the street proclaiming the cause.

14. Use an easy visual symbol for the revolution: a color for example, a sign of the fingers.

As the people power grows, move the action through your leaders:

15. Get your military leaders to instruct their soldiers not to fire on the people; that if they cannot officially defect to the rebels, they should not move on the President's orders.

16. Get your civil leaders to claim power. For example, have your new leader proclaim she is now the president of the country.

17. Get your military leaders to kick out the dictator peacefully. For example, storm

the Presidential Palace, force him out and
arrange for passage out of the country.

18. In all these, keep the media trained
on the heroic people standing in front
of tanks, make sure the international
media sees what's going on.

19. When all is over, ensure that the new leaders
promise the change the people fought for.

20. In the making of lasting change, it is
essential for the people to keep monitor-
ing the new leaders and make sure they
deliver on their promise, because if they
don't, people should start all over again
to cook a new batch of people power!

Enjoy the fruits of your revolution. Serves a whole country.

* * *

CHAPTER 3

Canada
Manolita, 1987–1991

I was inspired by the people power revolution. I decided I was going to change society — that is my destiny. How, I didn't quite know. I was going to be a leader, maybe a mayor or a Premier or a Prime Minister or the head of the United Nations. Like Cory Aquino. Better than Cory Aquino, who was, in a way, an accidental leader. I wanted to be a real leader of something big and important and noble.

Where to start? I knew no one of consequence. How does one get to be a leader?

I harbored my secret dream, and nurtured it. I read about leaders, what they achieved in power, how they became leaders. First, the women leaders: Margaret Thatcher, Indira Gandhi, Golda Meir, Cory Aquino. Next, male leaders like JFK, Abraham Lincoln, Winston Churchill, Gandhi, Pierre Trudeau. I read about leaders during wartime, leaders during peace times, leaders who led and won revolutions, and those who failed. I decided to study political science and law in university and become a lawyer, the path of most of the leaders.

When reading about leaders and political events, I analyzed the strategies behind their success or failure. I learned to make distinctions among causes: what was changeable, what was not, and learned to choose winnable causes. I developed a practical turn of mind with regard to strategy, advising people to choose their battles, "give in and not fight" when it was more to their advantage, even if it might be against their principle. The point is: you get what you want, sooner.

I became a name in Holy Rosary Catholic School. I excelled in class and skipped years two times. I was elected class president each time, and later, president of the student body. I became the go-to person when students had a complaint. I became the students' spokesperson and negotiator; for example, getting better food in the canteen. Later on, my causes became more substantial. I led the students in partnering with teachers to successfully advocate for a new school building to be built when cramped temporary classrooms had become overcrowded.

"Do you want to be 'right,' or do you want to be an engineer?" I asked Dad, who complained about the unfairness of Canadian requirements for foreign-trained engineers. I thought Dad should just go ahead and redo his degree and get on with being an engineer in Canada. "Canada's requirements are set up to safeguard Canadian buildings and lives — what's the injustice in that?" I asked.

"The injustice is that I have completed an engineering degree and built many buildings before — why should Canada not believe I can design buildings here?" Dad was stubborn.

"People have rules for different countries. This is Canada's law. You came to Canada. Follow its law, and you can work as engineer. It's not that they are preventing you from being an engineer. You can be an engineer here, just follow their rules.

How long's that — another three years, four years? Compare that to a lifetime of being an engineer with a good income!" I argued.

"That's not the point. The point is they should accept me for what I am."

"So you prefer to be right, rather than be an engineer." I surrendered to my old relic of a father and his misguided fight for justice. Why not just move forward?

Sonia and I have running battles regarding how to approach problems. She calls me an opportunist. I call her a wimp.

I saw many newcomers missing out on opportunities in Canada, insisting on speaking their own languages, staying within their own culture, not mixing with Canadians, not learning Canadian ways and culture. I saw my own mother sticking to her own kind, being successful in her business within the Filipino community, but not much farther. I encouraged Mom to offer her catering to mainstream offices and consider expanding her menu to more than Filipino dishes, like sandwiches and wraps and salads. She quickly learned and accepted the wisdom of going beyond the Filipino community as a business strategy. The office catering alone expanded Mom's business a hundred percent in a year.

"Sure, it's good to Canadianize quickly. But you are so ready to just integrate and forget what you grew up with," Sonia told me once.

"So what's so special about what we grew up with? It's all the same anyway: shopping centres, English in schools, a western way of life pretty well," I said.

"And what about Pililla, the fiestas, the religious rituals, Lola Iska and all of them?" Sonia's dear backward Pililla.

"What about them? Do you want to relive the Pililla fiestas and processions in Vancouver?" I shoot back. "How about

Canada's Remembrance Day, do you celebrate that? People who died for Canada so we can live here? As to Lola Iska and family, we can always write to them and speak to them on the phone, remember their birthdays, love them in our hearts. But we live here now. Let's be part of Canada. Why waste time on the past?" I said.

"Love her in our hearts? You never even write to Lola Iska. How does she know you love her?" said Sonia.

"You don't write to Lolo Ben or Lola Lita," I said.

"They're different."

"How?"

"They've got money and don't need us."

"That is so wrong-headed. Just because they're rich doesn't mean they don't need our love."

"Yeah, right."

"Why, what's the matter with them?" I ask.

"Nothing. You ask too many questions."

* * *

Sonia is keeping something from me. They all do. I feel like I'm in kindergarten, protected from 'family secrets.' I can't stand how everyone treats me like a child, when I feel older and wiser than all of them. I'm meant for great things, don't they know?

All the book knowledge about leaders and politics made me hungry for real life experience of politics in Canada. I was graduating high school soon and had no idea of how to channel what had become a burdensome dream. I confided in everyone's favourite teacher, Mr. Wilson. After ball practice one day, we talked while he walked his dog.

"You are already a leader, look what you've done here. Don't be too much in a hurry with your big dreams — you're obsessing. Take it slowly, you're only grade 12. Why do want to be a 'big important' leader?" he asked.

"I don't know. I just want to do important things. I want my life to mean something for many people, to make people's lives better."

"In our school, you've already done that."

"I want to do more things."

"Like what?"

"I don't know."

Mr. Wilson was a star athlete in his time. He was captain of his school rugby and soccer teams, until he broke his knee in a bad play, and that was the end of his dream of professional sports. Instead he became sports coach for high school, and surprised himself with how much he enjoyed it. How sports, especially team sports, was a great teaching tool for developing character and leadership. I think I am one of his favourite students. He wrote in my report card that I may not be the star athlete in the team, but I am a 'strategist' and that I 'inspire' the team to win. I would 'go places,' he said. I had 'drive, intellect.' Music to my ears. But there was something lacking in me, he said. 'Heart.' What does that mean? He did not say. He just said to think about it.

"So what do you care about? What keeps you awake at night? What worries you?" asked Mr. Wilson.

"That I haven't got a clue how to be a real leader. I am valedictorian, president of student council, team captain. I'm going to university and become a lawyer. Then one day I'll become the Premier of BC or the Prime Minister of Canada. But there's that big gap between lawyer and Prime Minister. I know I have to do something now to prepare, not just read and study. But I don't know what to do," I admitted.

"Do you really want to know?" asked Mr. Wilson.

I stopped walking and faced Mr. Wilson. "What?" she asked.

"Well, are you ready to hear the truth?" repeated Mr. Wilson.

Suddenly, I felt nervous. "Yes, umm. I guess so."

"Stop obsessing about yourself, and think of other people. Leadership is about caring for others. You may have all the knowledge and skills and intellect to be a leader, but if you don't care for others and do things only to be seen as a leader, you will not be a true leader," Mr. Wilson said. I'm not sure I'm with him.

He continued. "Look around you. What's happening to other people in your world? What is not going well, what could be better? Could you help them with that? Think about it. When you're ready, tell me what you come up with," he said.

I am frustrated with this kind of talk. "What do you mean? Selfish? Uncaring for others? Doing things only to be seen as a leader? All this time, I've been doing things for the student council and getting elected, but I don't care for them? Didn't I spend hours and hours writing that report that went to the School Board, training everybody for the survey, collating the results, and isn't everybody getting a new school building after all that? Uncaring? How about those overcrowded kids now getting a new better classroom? Didn't I care for them?" I cried.

"There you go again. You're too intellectual. Care for people personally, be more of a person and not just a president of student council advocating for causes. Do you know what's going on in the lives of the people around you whom you deal with every day, your Vice President for example?"

"What about her?"

"Do you know why she has not attended meetings in the last month?"

"No. Why?"

"Did you notice anything about her?"

"I know she's been absent-minded, in fact unreliable. She was not helpful in the campaign at all. I warned her that she might have to step aside if she doesn't perform better."

"Shouldn't you try to find out first what's going on with her before doing anything?"

"I've told her she's not meeting expectations. If she's a responsible officer, she should have told me then what her trouble was."

"Well, she didn't. Maybe because she couldn't. Not everyone is like you."

"You mean some people are weak. Well, they are not ready for office then. Better to let them know and we can move forward with the people that fit the role."

"See what I mean? You are so focused on the job, you forget to care for the human beings you work with. Maybe she's having some big problems?"

"Whatever the problem, surely it can be solved! She should just come out and say so."

"She may not feel comfortable to tell you her problem."

"Well, why not?" I asked, feeling defensive.

"If you sound as harsh and judgmental with her as you are now, I am not surprised why she didn't tell you her problem."

"I have to adjust myself to make them tell me their problems? Isn't it their problem if they can't tell me? Why should it be my problem?" I am exasperated.

"It's your problem if you want to be their leader," Mr. Wilson said quietly.

"Huh? She was elected to do a job. She is not doing it well. As a leader I need people who do their jobs or I will not be effective!"

"You will lose her, and maybe others too. I hear something like that is brewing."

"What do you mean?"

"I hear your executive is planning to resign en masse," Mr. Wilson said.

"Whatever for? I've just won the case for the school!"

"Listen to what you said: 'I've just won the case'. Was it only you who worked? Didn't your executives help?"

"They followed what I told them to do, and if I didn't tell them, we'd be nowhere."

"You're probably right."

Mr. Wilson looked me in the eye. "You said you wanted to hear the truth about becoming a real leader. I don't think you're ready."

I fell silent.

"Am I that bad?"

"It's not your fault. Don't beat yourself up. You're still very young and have much to learn. Just think about what I said," said Mr. Wilson. "If you talk to them, you might be surprised about what you find out," he added.

"How do you know all this anyway?"

"They spoke to me about it."

"Why you? Why not talk to me?" This is so unfair!

Mr. Wilson shrugged signifying he didn't know, or it didn't matter.

"I'm going to be late for class. Think about it. Let's talk again," Mr. Wilson said and ran with his dog towards the parking lot.

* * *

So let them all resign. They should be so lucky they have me for President, or how would they achieve anything? It's close to the end of the year, what do they need to resign for? To make a point? To damage my name? What is it that they're so upset about? And how dare they go to Mr. Wilson. How does he fit? He's not even the Council Advisor.

The thoughts kept churning in my mind. If they have a problem, they should come and see me! Why should I now go and see them? Who do they think they are? What could possibly be their problem? I thought of the recent events: the campaign for the new school building, the planning for the last student body program before graduation. Things were going well. What is there to complain about?

I tried to put it all aside, but it constantly preoccupied me. The next day, I saw the three of them: Xenia the vice president, Holly the secretary and Maryann the treasurer, having coffee at the cafeteria. I walked towards them to join them, but they stood up and left. Did they see me and left on purpose to avoid me, or did their departure have anything to do with me? How can I find out what's the trouble if they don't speak to me? Cowards.

Much as I did not want to think more about it, the thoughts wouldn't leave me. I stewed about it all day and could not concentrate in the classroom. I went to see Mr. Wilson at the end of the day. He was putting away the gym equipment. I picked up some of the balls and put them in the large boxes.

"I tried to talk to them today, but they up and left, like kids. What should I do?" I asked.

"Do you really want to talk to them?"

"Yes! What's the point of stewing about it, now that I know about it? Confront their problem and solve it!"

"If that's why you are wanting to talk to them — to confront and solve — it won't work."

"Why not? Isn't that what you suggested, that I talk to them?"

"Yes, but you need to have an open mind when you go to talk to them. You have already decided they are the problem. How can any communication happen if it's so clear that you've made up your mind that they are wrong and you are right? They are the problem, and you will fix them?" He shook his head.

I kept quiet.

"I guess you haven't heard what I said the other day. Care for them as human beings, talk to them as human beings, not as their high and mighty President. Manolita, this is just a student council, but I assure you, the same applies to a Corporate Board or a Cabinet of Government. You need to treat your colleagues as human beings, with respect, even if they may seem wrong or inept to you."

"But that's what you do in our team. You screamed at Marge who kept fumbling the ball. You took her out and put someone else in."

"You didn't see me talk to Marge afterwards. You didn't see me find out that she thinks she's pregnant. You didn't see me refer her to the school nurse, who examined and tested her, found out she's not pregnant after all, and now she's back in play. She was worried and preoccupied at that time and it was affecting her game, so I had to do something fast. But I talked to her afterwards and helped her figure out what to do. In the heat of the game, I may be rough and make abrupt decisions, but afterwards I try to reconnect as a human being to another, and talk it out." He added, "And just because your executive spoke to me about you, doesn't mean I am perfect. I have my own rough patches. The point is not to be perfect, but to be human, including apologizing when you're at fault, or sometimes even when you're not sure you're at fault," he said.

"What should I apologize about?" I really have no idea what I did wrong.

"I'm not asking you to apologize. I'm asking you to be open to whatever they have to say, and not form judgments beforehand. Can you do that?"

"What if they're so unfair and criticize me. Am I to just take it all?"

He nodded. "If you are more comfortable, I can be there."

"To referee?"

"No, you're not battling teams, and I'm not a referee. You are all one team, and I see myself more as a coach to help the team along. I'll be there to help you see each other's points of view. Remind you that you are one team with the same goal. Work together to solve whatever may be the problem."

"Okay. You arrange it. I'll be there," I agree.

"Remember. Keep open, okay?"

"I'll try."

* * *

The meeting was held after a round of basketball. Mr. Wilson organized a four-on-four. He picked four players at random from his class, to play against my executive team. I understood the wisdom of this strategy later, when I asked Mr. Wilson. "Even 20 minutes of playing on the same team and trying to score against another team was better preparation for the meeting than nothing," he said. I saw that it put us all on the same side, even before the discussion began.

After showers, he treated us to sodas in the faculty lounge where we sat around comfortable round lounge tables, and began the meeting.

"Thanks for playing. I'm glad you're on the student executive and not on the school basketball team!" he opened.

Everyone laughed.

"And thanks for playing here, at this table," he said.

I straightened up.

"We are here to open up to each other and tell what's all concerning us about our Executive Team. You have asked me to facilitate this meeting, and I am honoured. I have only one rule for our meeting today: each one of you may speak only about your own experience, not anyone else's. Only your own action, your own feelings, your own opinions and suggestions. Do you have any questions on this?" he asked.

Everyone was quiet. Some shook their head. Some shrugged.

"Great. Then we can begin. As you know, the Executive Team has one goal, and that is?" he paused.

"To be the best advocate for the student body," everyone said, some saying it out loud, some whispering.

"What's that again?" Mr. Wilson asked.

"To be the best advocate for the student body," said everyone, louder.

"That's great!" he said.

"And let me be the first to congratulate you that you are doing a great job," he said.

"If you were to name the four top greatest successes of your Team, what would those be?"

"Getting better food in the cafeteria," said Maryann, the treasurer.

"Jeans on Fridays!" cried Holly, the secretary.

"Camping scholarships," stated Xenia, the Vice-President.

"Getting a new building for the school," I offered.

"That was with the teachers though," said Xenia.

"Yes, but without me, oh, without us, it would not have happened because we rallied students support," I said.

Xenia, Maryann and Holly looked at each other. Mr. Wilson made eye contact with me, recognizing my effort, and reminding me to keep at it.

"Any team, no matter how great, has its strengths and its challenges, and if no problems occurred, it would not be a human organization. It would be a team of robots," he said. "And even then, robots run into mechanical problems as well."

"Right," said Maryann.

"So, tell me, how long have you been together as a team?" he asked.

"Close to a year?" I said.

"Then you must know each other well by now?" said Mr. Wilson.

Nods and smiles from everyone. Xenia rolled her eyes.

"So tell me one thing you like about each one of you. Who would like to start? Manolita?" he prodded.

That's easy. "I like how Maryann is so up to date on our money, how she gives a financial report to all of us on a regular basis, even if we don't ask. Because of it, our executive has been prudent in how we spend, making us the only Executive with a surplus at the end of the school year!" Maryann smiled as everybody cheered.

I continued. "I like how Holly writes concise minutes and gets them to all of us on time, how she prepares a draft agenda for us to go through before a meeting, reminding us of all the outstanding business that have to be dealt with."

"And how she keeps us all on time as well!" added Maryann.

Everyone eagerly took turns, saying good things about each other.

"Now tell us one pet peeve you have about each other. One thing to ask each other to change if they can, something that will make your own personal relationship with that person better," said Mr. Wilson.

An awkward silence filled the room.

"You can start with me. I can handle it," I offered.

"See, you're doing it again!" Xenia exploded. "That's precisely what I can't stand about you, Manolita. You have to start everything, be in charge of everything. Why can't you just wait and see what happens, let other people initiate things. We are capable of being first to say something. Why do you always have to be the big leader?"

"I'm the President, am I not?" I ask.

"That doesn't mean you always have to be first, or have your way. We are all equal here as Executive. All of us have been elected. We have our own opinions and we should all be able to discuss things before decisions are made, not just whatever you say," said Holly.

"I just meant that it's okay for you to say whatever you want about me, in case you felt you couldn't say it," I clarified.

"See how patronizing you are? You said 'in case you felt you couldn't say it'. What do you think of us — weak, afraid, inept? That you have to give us permission to say what's in our minds?" cried Xenia.

"Girls, only your own experience please. Don't speak for others," Mr. Wilson reminded us.

"I felt so humiliated by how you criticized my being away for a month, in front of everybody," said Xenia. "It's true I've not been attending, and I did not give you an explanation, but you didn't have to humiliate me that way! I felt like an insect," Xenia continued.

"And I felt you overstepped your bounds threatening to force her to resign if she didn't improve. That should be an executive team decision, not just one person's decision. It's like I didn't count, that I have no say!" cried Holly.

"Sometimes I feel, that you feel, that you are the only one working, and that our work is unimportant," contributed Maryann.

"Remember, only your own experience. Speak only for yourself," said Mr. Wilson.

"Sorry. I mean sometimes I feel you discount my work, that my work is unimportant, only yours is important," said Maryann. "Even now. You caught yourself saying 'without me the new school building would not have happened'. How about my work in that project? Didn't I collate all the surveys of all the students and teachers? I had to email them through several rounds so we could get a high response rate. You don't even know how many nights I spent on that. All you cared about was getting it on your deadline, while my own paper in geography got late because of it. I got a C for being late. That jeopardizes my grade point average to make it to university," said Maryann. She looked away, wiping a tear?

Holly looked down at her lap, and Xenia looked directly at me, waiting for me to say something.

I looked at them, not knowing what to say. Was I really such a dictator? Was I as bad as what they describe me to be? I watched Maryann wiping her eyes, and felt like a total bully. Maryann is such a sweet girl, and she's so reliable. Maryann wasn't looking at me, while Xenia's accusing eyes were on me. Mr. Wilson's face had no expression. I felt entirely on my own.

"I didn't know...I didn't think...is that how bad...I'm sorry. So sorry. I didn't know what a... monster I've become. I... sometimes. I can't help..." I stopped and covered my face with my hands, feeling so ashamed.

When I opened my eyes, they felt moist. "I'm so sorry.... I feel like... a total idiot," I said shyly, fighting back tears.

"Yeah, you sure are," said Maryann.

I looked across to Maryann. "Can you forgive me? I can try and speak to your geography teacher. Maybe she can give you a make-up test or something, so you can increase your grade point. What a jerk I am," I whispered the last mostly to myself.

I addressed Holly. "I'm offering my resignation." Holly made a gesture meaning I go ask Xenia.

I turned to Xenia. She was watching me closely.

"I know it's not much of a resignation. The term is almost over, but I don't deserve to be President. I'm afraid I got it all wrong. As Vice, you'll be President. I hope you'll be much better than me. I apologize if I humiliated you. What a jerk I was. Feel free to humiliate me back. Anytime," I said, meaning every word of it.

I felt strange, deprecating myself. It felt easy once you got going, and it was actually liberating to mock yourself once in a while. Why take oneself so seriously? I'm a jerk. It felt good to acknowledge that. So, I'm a jerk. I didn't die. I'm just a jerk. And now I can stop being a jerk now that I know I'm one.

To the girls, I said, "I'm so very sorry for what I must have put you through." I turned to Mr. Wilson and said, "Thanks for persisting in letting me know."

Mr. Wilson looked at Xenia, Maryann and Holly in turn. "What do you think, girls?" he asked. Maryann nodded slightly. Holly shrugged. Xenia pursed her lips and nodded.

"Oh alright. Looks like they'll give you another chance," said Mr. Wilson, smiling as well.

Xenia, Holly and Maryann hugged me, as I fought off tears with smiles. As I hugged my teammates, I felt lighter, unburdened. So this is how it feels to share leadership? How much easier it is. And is this is how it is to be human while being a leader? Nothing and no one has to be perfect. Just be prepared to acknowledge when you've made a mistake and try not to do it again. How good my team is — how easy to forgive. I'm so lucky to have them as my team. I might not have been so forgiving myself if someone behaved like that to me. How much more fun it was too, for once feeling my teammates were not just people who did a job, but my friends now as well.

* * *

I would later look on this experience as the start of my apprenticeship in real leadership. Whenever pride got a hold of me, or willfulness, or being a perfectionist, or when the dictator syndrome loomed, I reminded myself to relax and remember that everyone is a human being. Then I would become 'vulnerable', admit to some imperfection or weakness, make fun of myself, crack a joke, do something personal like make the team a meal, even if it was only fried chicken. It always helped.

* * *

When Dad died of a fatal heart failure while attacking Bobby for his drug use, I was stunned. I could not cry for a long time. I felt everything but sadness. I felt angry towards Bobby, towards Mom, towards Carla, towards my whole sorry dysfunctional family. I felt angry towards fate for disturbing my life. I felt deprived of the chance to show my father my dreams fulfilled. I felt cheated of the times we spent together, even if I spent less and less time with him over the last years, and even if I argued with him half the time we were together, trying to bring him out of his funk, because that's exactly what he was in: a grand depressive funk which mom drove him to, and which Carla only encouraged.

Mr. Wilson was a source of strength and sanity for me during these times. One day after school, he chanced upon me sitting alone on a park bench at the edge of the empty basketball field. He sat beside me. He has become kinder to me since Dad's death.

"How are you holding up?' he said.

I blurted out my thoughts. "Who will give me my medal on graduation day? Why bother to be a valedictorian at all? Why bother becoming a leader, a Prime Minister, who will care?"

"He may be physically gone, but his spirit will always be there watching your progress, cheering you on."

"I wish he lived longer to become the hero I knew him to be as a child. He was never the same man in Canada. I know he could have been so much better. It's so unfair to not give him the chance, to cut the life out of him so early. So unfair. "

"If he was suffering, then it is good that he is now at rest, don't you think? He is now in peace."

"Some peace. Knowing he lived an unfulfilled life. How can he be at peace with that?"

"Bitterness doesn't suit you, Manolita," Mr. Wilson said. "Didn't he give a wake-up call to Bobby? Hasn't Bobby sworn off drugs now? That much your father's death has done."

"Some benefit. Couldn't he just tell him and not die? Why have a heart attack just to let him know? Such hatred between those two. Both of them. It poisoned all of us.

"I always felt guilty when I was with Dad, then guilty when I was with Bobby. It was hate that caused his death. And failure. Failure caused his death. He was so stubborn, so unrelenting in his stupid principle. 'They should recognize me', that's all he kept saying."

I kept shaking my head. "He should have just gone to school, just...do whatever. Something. Not wallow in self-pity and foolish pride....He shouldn't have fought. It was a stupid nonsensical unwinnable fight. Then going with that woman. Leaving us. For what? 'Because she needs me,' he said. What about us? Don't we need him? Such a misplaced sense of heroics. I hate him. I hate him,' I said.

I felt exhausted. I started crying, first softly, then in big deep sobs. I felt Mr. Wilson's arms around me. It felt comforting to cry in those arms. When the rush of tears was over, I lifted my head from Mr. Wilson's soaked shirt, my face wet with tears. The breeze blew strands of hair across my face, which he brushed away gently. Something about the way he did that, the way he held me, the way his kind face was so close. I lifted my lips to his, and kissed him, surprised to feel the responding pressure of his lips. We kissed passionately for a minute, or was it many minutes? Someone broke away, whether it was he or I, wasn't clear.

"I'm sorry," said Mr. Wilson abruptly. "I'm sorry, I got carried away." He stood up.

"I'm not," I said, looking up at him.

"This is not good. It's a mistake. I'm so sorry," said Mr. Wilson. All flustered, he walked away from the bench.

I followed him with my eyes. What a strange feeling. I felt happy when I should be sad. It felt all wrong, but remembering his tenderness, it felt all right.

* * *

In the days that followed, I tried to keep thoughts of Mr. Wilson from my mind. I kept myself occupied with the activities around the funeral, concentrating on preparing for my valedictory speech. There was no reason to see Mr. Wilson. School was over. I attempted to call him on the phone several times and stopped myself. I hoped he would come to the funeral as all the teachers were notified.

While not much of an eater, I ate even less now, refusing even the chips I used to love. I began losing weight. I walked around like a wounded bird, my fun and perkiness all gone. Everyone knew how close I was to Dad, his favourite. By the time the funeral service rolled along, I was skinny as a twig. "It's her grief over her father," everyone whispered. But it was also another grief only I knew about.

Mr. Wilson did not turn up at the funeral, sending his regrets that he was going out of town. When I sang for Dad at the funeral service, the words of 'Somewhere over the Rainbow' dripped with a double meaning.

> "Somewhere over the rainbow bluebirds fly.
> Birds fly over the rainbow. Why then, oh why can't I?
> If happy little bluebirds fly beyond the rainbow,
> Why oh why can't I?"

It was a plaintive cry from my young suffering heart. A song of pain and wounded loss, not only for a father that can no longer be with me, but also for a love I knew can never be.

* * *

CHAPTER 4

Canada
Manolita, 1995

In 1995, the City of Richmond, a suburban island community south of the City of Vancouver had become an enclave of Chinese and Hong Kong emigres. The turnover of Hong Kong's ownership from the British to the Chinese government in 1991 caused a wave of immigration to Canada by Hong Kong nationals who were afraid that the new order would negatively impact their way of life. The exodus to Canada formed a concentration in the City of Richmond, which had the appeal of having the word 'rich' in the city's name and therefore provided favourable fengshui. The City of Richmond was also close to the airport, thereby allowing the immigrants to travel back and forth, leaving their children in Canada while they themselves continued businesses in Hong Kong. The Chinese population in the City of Richmond grew from 96,000 in 1981 to 126,624 in 1991, and by the mid '90s, half of its population was of Asian descent, many of which came from Hong Kong, Taiwan and Mainland China. Many of these immigrants came as business class investing $250,000 for the privilege of living in Canada. Many Chinese businesses were established in Richmond, among them Chinese restaurants and shopping centers. The Chinese population explosion in Richmond caused a stir among existing residents of Richmond who were suddenly surrounded by predominantly Chinese immigrants in their neighborhoods and their schools. One of the sore spots of the Chinese-Canadian relations in Richmond was the Chinese-only signage that arose in the shopping centers of the City. Many Richmond residents felt threatened by their exclusion and demanded that authorities require the signs contain English translations. Other residents felt the Chinese were being targeted, and that underneath the complaints against non-English signs simmered racial intolerance against an emerging power group that threatened the status quo.

The Chinese-only signs created a controversy among policy makers. Should Canadian businesses be required to provide English signs, or not? A similar controversy had arisen in Quebec where the Quebec government protected French-only signs. If the French in Quebec were allowed to have French-only signs, why were Chinese-only signs in Richmond not allowed? Nobody wanted to touch this potentially explosive issue. The Liberal federal government of Canada had just won a great margin of victory in the country. Flushed with a sense of invincibility provided by their recent electoral popularity, the Minister of Heritage Canada Kerry Black joined a panel of experts speaking on the topic at a Richmond hotel.

The symposium was well attended. Many sectors were represented heavily including Chinese groups, neighbourhood groups, the government of the City of Richmond, and the legal sector. It was a popular topic in the law school at the University of British Columbia where I was now in fourth year. I was a strong proponent of the "English signs" side of the debate. As far as I was concerned, it was a non-issue. How can a country permit its national language to not be utilized by a segment of its population? The country would fall apart. I attended the symposium. I particularly wanted to meet the charismatic Minister of Heritage Canada who was known to be dynamic and influential in the inner circle of the Prime Minister. I was eager to hear what she had to say.

It was disappointing to see the panelists dance around the issue. I had my question prepared. When the time came for questions and comments from the audience, I requested comments from each of the panelists to my question: "If you were in charge of the signs in Richmond, what would you do and why?" Except for one panelist, everyone came up for English signs, or Chinese signs with English translations.

The panelist who advocated for Chinese-only signs was a recent immigrant and a business owner in one of the Chinese shopping centers. She spoke in broken English, and had to be helped with translations. In a nutshell, her point was that the customer is always right. The customers she caters to are most recently arrived from China, and speak very little English, or no English at all.

"So, talk Chinese to Chinese people. They understand better. It takes much time to learn to speak English," she said.

"Why not provide English translation along with Chinese, so others can understand?" I asked.

"The goods are meant for Chinese anyway," she said.

"You mean, non-Chinese are not allowed to buy?" I asked.

"Allow yes, but not intend for them. Our sizes are small, Canadians big. If they like, go ahead, buy. Country free," she said.

Stumbling Through Paradise

"But if all the time Chinese language only, Chinese never learn English, never mix with Canadians. People speaking differently, do not understand each other. Not good for country," I said. I mirrored the Chinese lady's English, to make sure I was understood.

"Canada multicultural, said Immigration Canada. That's why we come. We can keep culture, Canada good. Let us have our own culture. Other countries no good, have to stop Chinese, be Australian, American. Canada, ok be Chinese in Canada," she said.

"But it's not good long term for Canada if people do not speak English. We have to speak English, or French, our two national official languages," I argued.

"No one French here. Why speak French? Everybody Chinese here, then speak Chinese!" Cheers came up from the many Chinese people in the audience.

It was clear nothing would be solved in this forum. There needs to be a better understanding of what it means to immigrate to Canada, and a better orientation on what we expect of immigrants to Canada. It was useless to explain to the Chinese businesswoman, or the recently arrived Chinese immigrants. They have a misconception of multiculturalism. If this is the way immigrants understand multiculturalism, our country is in trouble.

I looked to the Minister of Heritage Canada and asked her point blank: "Madame Minister, as someone responsible for Canada's cultural heritage, what can you say to these newly arrived Chinese? What does Canada expect of immigrants and the language they speak?"

"First of all, I want to welcome all the Chinese to Canada. We need immigrants like you. Thank you for choosing Canada as your new home. Yes, Canada is a multicultural nation — that's why we invite people of different countries to live here. We know it is difficult to learn a new language, and we understand if immigrants can't speak English right away. It takes time. But they must try. If they don't try, they won't learn, and if they don't learn to speak English, they will not enjoy all the benefits Canada can give them. It's not my call, but I would only encourage the City of Richmond to give some time to the Chinese merchants to get English translations on their signs," she said.

Well put. Still promoting English translations, but sounding as though she was the champion for the Chinese. "Give them time" was her main comment. She also took no responsibility, leaving it squarely on the shoulders of the City to make the final decision, which would certainly be controversial one way or the other. The 'gentle nudge' would not be construed as interference; in fact she seemed magnanimous in not pressing her authority. She came across as having compassion for Chinese immigrants for their difficulty in learning a new language. There was no question that English should be used, but the way she focused her answer was clever: the issue was not what language may be used in the signs, the issue was how much time to give the businesses to provide English translations on the signs. The Chinese audience seemed to relax, the tension diffused with the Minister's message. The Chinese immigrants felt they were understood, even if they were required to provide English translations. I was impressed with the strategy of the Minister.

After the symposium, I waited in line to introduce myself to the Minister, something I had learned to do as a networking strategy.

"Thank you for your comments. That helped a lot. My name is Manolita del Mundo; I'm a law student, and a student of politics. This whole Canadian culture and values interests me very much," I said.

"I remember your comments. We need more people like you who will come out and promote Canadian values, including language. There is a fine point between being multicultural and staying within cultural enclaves. You seem to understand this point. Did you immigrate to Canada, or were you born here?" the Minister asked.

"I was five when my family came to Vancouver from the Philippines. My first taste of Canada was snow, literally. I put out my tongue to taste the snow on a pole when we arrived in the Vancouver airport, and it stuck. I cried till, finally a security guard unstuck it with warm water. My tongue has always been my problem since then, my parents say." We both laughed.

"And it surely is your gift as well. You're very well spoken. Did you say you have an interest in politics?" she asked.

"Yes, very much so."

"Would you be interested to consider volunteering in our party? It might be a good learning experience for you."

"I would love that! What can I do?"

"I'm sure we can come up with something for a talented young woman like you, right, Darcie?" she winked at both me and her own assistant, who right away understood.

Darcie whipped up a calling card from somewhere, gave it to me and asked for my card in exchange. Darcie said she would get in touch with me right away. The Minister had already turned to the next person in line waiting to talk to her.

*   *   *

In the next months, I was caught up in a whirlwind of activities with the Liberal Party. I was so busy I no longer ate meals, surviving on snacks. I felt like a driven woman. When I was called in for something, I made time to attend and help in whatever capacity.

One time, it was to pick up and drive Members of Parliament coming in for a caucus meeting of the Western Region of the Party. I was happy to do so. I looked forward to meeting and talking with leaders from Alberta and Manitoba and Saskatchewan, places I hadn't even been to. I didn't know there was a Filipino Canadian who was a Member of Parliament in Winnipeg. When we met, he encouraged me to run. In fact, any MP whom I met, upon learning of my political interest, encouraged me to run, as though it was the only thing to do if you were interested in politics.

Another time, I was assigned to the reception desk at a major party fundraiser, with Prime Minister Jean Chretien as the special guest. I tried to remember the names of all the Ministers who came, for future reference. I tried to shake the hand of the Prime Minister on his way into the room, but I got pushed away by the crowd that formed around him as the cheering music played. I spotted my friend Heritage Canada Minister Kerry Black. I made my way towards her, pushing myself in between two other people hovering about the Minister.

"Do you remember me?" I asked. "Richmond, Chinese-only signs?"

"Of course, I do! Darcie tells me you've been active volunteering. How are you liking it?" the Minister asked.

"I'm meeting so many people! I wish I could meet the Prime Minister!" I was just about shouting to be heard over the noisy excitement in the room.

"Do you? Well, stick with me. I'm going over there to say hello, since I'm introducing him," she said.

Did I hear right? I felt thrilled. I kept close to the Minister. It was difficult keeping abreast with Ministers in these parties. They are always being stopped by people, so they need an assistant to be around all the time to pull them away when they are monopolized by someone, or to take notes for follow up, or to point the Minister to someone she needs to speak to and block others until that is done. I tagged behind Minister Black, observing her conversations with people, what Darcie was doing, and trying not to lose the Minister in the crowds.

The lights turned on and off to signal the dinner was about to start. Darcie whispered something to the Minister, who then said goodbye to the person she was speaking to. Darcie led the way to the front of the room, with the Minister and myself trailing behind. The Prime Minister was in the middle of a huddle. A tall man whispered something to him, and the Prime Minister peeled away from the group to join Minister Black.

Minister Black and the Prime Minister went off to the side and chatted for about a minute, then came back to where Darcie and I and the tall man who seemed to be the master of ceremonies stood.

Seeing me, Minister Black said: "By the way, Mr. Prime Minister, meet one of our most active party volunteers in Vancouver. From the Philippines, law student, keen about politics," she said.

I extended my hand to the smiling Prime Minister, who said, "We sure could use more involvement from the Filipino community. Especially bright young Filipinas! And what have you been up to in the party?" he said.

"Oh various things sir. Driving MPs, reception work, telephone canvassing," I rattled off my puny assignments.

"Good, good, keep it up. How about helping us with the Filipino community? Can you bring in some Filipino groups to the next convention? Need more Filipinos. Very bright people, and fun," he said.

"Sure, Mr. Prime Minister. Ah...how should I...uhh... work on it?" I felt excited. The Prime Minister is asking me to do something! The tall man took the microphone and announced the national anthem.

"Kerry can look after you," the Prime Minister said, nodding to Minister Black.

The anthem began to play. I was so thrilled with my new assignment that I sang the Canadian national anthem with such fervor and strength.

When it was over, the Prime Minister whispered to me. "You have a beautiful voice. Everyone should sing the Canadian anthem like that!" Then he was shoved into a seat. Minister Black was led to another seat and everyone sat somewhere. Except me. I stood alone in front of the room not knowing what to do next. Minister Black, sitting beside the Prime Minister, motioned to an empty seat across her. For me? I gestured. Minister Black nodded.

And that was how, 19-year-old me, secret aspirant to be world leader, met my first leader of a country: the Prime Minister of Canada. I sat at the head table with him, along with important Ministers and their spouses, listening to their talk and even contributing my own stories, for a whole 2 hours. It seemed that they liked my stories about the Philippines, my law school experience, my keen interest in politics, the stories I knew of the leaders I studied. They all said I would be a great candidate, and encouraged me to keep in touch. I will never forget that evening, when it seemed my dream was, for the first time, becoming real.

* * *

It was all I talked about with mom, Sonia, Stephen, Bobby and my classmates for a whole week. Bobby was so interested in the important people I met. He made me repeat the names, their positions in government, and particularly the Ministers. "You never know when a high up contact would be useful," he said, taking down notes.

I wanted to meet mom's and Sonia's Filipino contacts.

"How can I meet them all? I want to meet them all!" I cried excitedly.

As usual, Sonia mocked me. "And what? Recruit them into the Liberal Party? Oh, my name is Manolita. I'm the sister of Sonia. May I invite you to join the Liberal Party? Oh, here's a membership card, it's only $10. Can you attend the convention?" Sonia mimicked.

"Well, why not?" I said. "How else would you do it?"

"I don't know, but not like that!" Sonia exaggerated my hand gestures.

Stephen offered some ideas. "How about make an event. Have an important Liberal speak on something Filipino Canadians care about. Someone who has the power to do something on that issue. Then let the Filipino media know. There are so many of them now. In fact put out an ad in their papers, so you give them some business too, then they will more likely cover the event. Make personal invitations to a few Filipino community leaders, those who work with this particular issue. Have the letter come from an important Liberal, maybe a Minister. That'll make them come."

"And make sure you provide some food. Free. And say that in the letter," offered Mom.

"Not food again," I winced. I had given up eating virtually.

"Things go so much better in a Filipino meeting when food is provided," Mom insisted. "As a matter of fact, you will be so much better if you ate something. You're skinny as a stick. What's going on with you?"

"Can we just talk about this another time?" I groaned.

Mom scowled at me, shaking her head. Hesitantly, she continued. "Where was I?"

"The consultation," Sonia inserted.

"Yes. Hold it in a place Filipinos are used to coming, not those fancy hotels, or they'll feel out of place and not talk freely. And have a Filipino host, one who will speak both English and Tagalog. There is nothing so off-putting to Filipinos than other Filipinos who seem to not know how to speak Tagalog anymore," she added.

"Really?" I made a face.

"That's what I noticed. They warm to you when you speak Tagalog. People are so homesick. They love being with other Filipinos speaking Tagalog, cracking Filipino jokes, eating Filipino food, telling stories about 'back home' in the Philippines, even if they have been here so long. And sing, someone should sing a Filipino song and also an English song. Why not you, Manolita, or someone." Mom was on a roll.

"Yikes!" exclaimed Sonia. "It should be a discussion, not a party! That's always what Filipinos do: party, eat, sing, laugh!"

"Well, if you want to get them to come, that's the easiest way. The talk by the Minister is good, but let them enjoy themselves, so when you ask, they will say yes," Mom replied.

"So how and what will you ask, after all the eating and the singing? They don't go together!" I protested.

Sonia replied. "I think we should make it a serious event, say a consultation. The Liberal Government wants to know the needs of the Filipino Canadian community. Then you

Stumbling Through Paradise

can invite a cross section of Filipinos who are working on all kinds of issues — caregivers, skilled immigrants issues — and include students and seniors, and…"

I interrupted. "And representatives from different cities. That way, we can hit all ridings, especially those that have a possibility to go Liberal. Identify potential members and campaign leaders in each riding."

Sonia continued, "You should prepare for small group discussions, it's easier for people to talk in small groups. Then have the groups report to the assembly as a whole. The group reporters become your potential leaders, and can be assigned to follow up on their groups for the next actions. The follow-up action not only makes people confident that something fruitful will come of this discussion, but also gives them opportunity to participate in solutions. It makes them feel part of the process. So when you ask them for attendance at a political convention later, they are more likely to attend, as they have already worked with you on common issues. Hopefully, you've given them a good experience so they'd want to attend the convention with you."

I am thrilled. "Great! And we can still have food, say lunch, as this will likely take at least half a day, right? Should we have group leaders pre-assigned? So we'll be sure to have good discussions and reports?"

"Yup, people who are known and liked in the community, and can speak well. You should have enough of those," offered Stephen.

"I can ask my contacts as to who would be good facilitators. How many would you need — about five, seven?" Mom asked.

"Seven's good. How about partnering one of those with a Liberal party member? A Caucasian or someone not Filipino.

You know, mix it up a bit. That way, it's not just a rant. Ensures people have accountability over what they say," said Sonia.

I saw one more benefit. "That also educates mainstream Liberal party members about Filipino issues."

A consultation was called by the Minister of Heritage Canada with the Filipino community. In her letter to the Filipino leaders, she said that, "the Filipino Canadians are a fast- growing sector of Canada's multicultural fabric. We need to know how they are doing, what problems they may be facing and how Government can help." An unprecedented 120 Filipinos came to the community centre. Party volunteers recorded the contact names, phone numbers and emails of attendees, and their roles in the community and at work. The consultation ended up with such a long list of needs, that it was decided to hire someone to follow up on the whole thing with a report and recommendations to Government. The Minister was happy to provide a small fund for the work.

I had my list of Filipino contacts. I came to know the individuals, what issues they were credible on. More importantly, I learned about the problems of the Filipino community in BC. Frankly, I never thought they had many problems, except for Dad's issue — the problem of skilled immigrants not able to practice their professions. I got to know of caregivers getting exploited, caregivers having no one to go to for help because they are isolated and living with their employees. I heard of seniors feeling lonely and isolated at home, not able to go anywhere without their children who were too busy, their grandchildren no longer able to speak Tagalog. I was surprised about some seniors suffering from their Canadian in-laws not tolerating the smell of their favourite foods like adobo or *bagoong*. I heard of racial fights in school, and the unending problem of doctors and engineers and nurses not being able to practice their professions. Did Filipinos get any orientation to life in Canada, or did they just arrive and 'make do'? At the very least, I thought a proper orientation should be provided.

I got to know the quirks of Filipino Canadians. They made fun of me not speaking Tagalog. How important it was for them to talk Tagalog, even if everybody could speak English. Why is it so important to keep speaking Tagalog in a country that speaks English anyway? I noticed very little attendance from young people and students. Perhaps the Filipino contacts we used didn't have good outreach to young people. I thought there might be a generation gap between Filipino parents and their children. I certainly felt funny being treated like a child by them. Perhaps the issues of the second generation are very different from the first generation? I made a mental note of that for a second special consultation. I also made a mental note of the length of time the Filipinos were in Canada. It disturbed me that despite the years of living in Canada, they seemed to be unconnected to Canadian institutions and decision-making.

After the symposium and the lunch, they made me sing. There was a piano in the community centre, and someone offered to play. I sang Dad's favourite song: "Somewhere Over the Rainbow". It's always a hit. Mom told me later, "You see, that's what will make them remember you. In politics — the Filipino way anyway — it's all about making yourself memorable to people. Doing them a personal favor, remembering something for their grandmother, feeding them something wonderful, laughing with them, sometimes just a great song would do. You don't have to try so hard to get the Filipino vote. It's pretty simple for them: be their friend."

I would always remember this advice from mom, as I know nothing about Philippine politics, but also because she rarely gave me advice. Advice to Sonia, yes, or Bobby, but not me. I always held a different opinion. Something about being Dad's favourite kept Mom and me apart. She didn't try to change me or win me over, but she was always distant. I enjoyed getting a little closer to Mom around the political thing. I was pleasantly surprised later by mom's decision to run for Mayor of Pililla. It sure raised my esteem for her by many points.

* * *

In school, I was a law fiend. I argued cases with a passion. I spent nights labouring over precedents. I made my presentations as though I was in a courtroom.

I was pleased with the attention of my professors, especially Prof. Sanjit Ray. Renowned in international law. Middle-aged, second-generation Indo-Canadian. PhD in law with degrees from Dalhousie, Yale and Harvard. Brash and witty. Self-declared atheist. Attractive. Arrogant, but — hey — he deserves to be. Media always called on him to comment on Canadian politics. He took me aside one day after a particularly brilliant debate.

"You should run for politics, del Mundo. Bring some life to those boring and bored legislators," he said.

"I will. I'm on track," I said proudly.

"Really?"

I told him of my dreams, my plans. Of meeting the Prime Minister, many Liberal Ministers. Sanjit Ray was impressed.

"I'd be happy to help if you need me," he offered.

That was the start of a mentorship that became a friendship that became a sexual relationship that scandalized my family.

"He's married, for heaven's sake," said Sonia.

"It's nothing serious. We're just playing. We're more friends than lovers. He's old. But he's brilliant. And cute. And fun," I replied.

"Why do you do this? Why does he? He risks so much in university, and his family. He's an irresponsible goat!" cried Sonia.

"Seems like father, like daughter," smirked Bobby.

"Don't give me that, you drughead! Don't think I don't know." I said.

Bobby rushed to me, but Sonia blocked his way. "Stop you two!" Sonia cried.

I haven't seen Bobby so angry with me. "You are destroying a family. Think. That man has a wife, and maybe kids, whose life you are destroying just like that whore who destroyed ours!"

"Far from it. They are on the verge of divorce and they have no kids involved. In any case, I don't want to marry him! And he knows that."

"If mom ever finds out, she'll...." Bobby started to say.

"She'll what?" I interrupted. "She had it coming. She didn't love dad enough to fight for him. She just let him go. She preferred for us to grow up fatherless. She didn't care for us. She cared more for her wounded pride. She has no moral superiority to waive over me."

"You are some bitch. She sacrificed for us!" said Bobby.

"Enough!" cried Sonia. "I don't want to hear of this guy again. You can carry on however you want, Manolita, but don't ever let me hear about you two again." Is that supposed to be a warning? Or else, what?

"When you run for office, future Honourable Member of Parliament, this thing will come up for sure. Or didn't you even think about that?" mocked Bobby.

"I know…we're careful," I said.

"You think nobody knows? Everybody knows," said Bobby. "Don't say I didn't warn you." Bobby left, slamming the door behind him.

* * *

CHAPTER 5

Canada
Manolita, 1996–2008

I was happy that Minister Black was pleased with the results of the Filipino consultation. She was also impressed with the number of new Filipinos that turned up, just waiting to be converted into party membership at the coming convention. She planned to make a policy change about skilled immigrants before the next elections, to show that Government and the Liberals were serious about solving the problem. The Filipino community was not the only one crying for change in this area. Other ethnic communities were doing the same. Sonia's Looking Forward Initiative, with its senior administrators of government, regulatory bodies and educational institutions were themselves pushing for change. It was ripe to make some changes happen, release some funds for programs, and make an announcement with many ethnic community leaders on hand. The Liberals would look very good.

Minister Black was fast becoming not only my mentor, but also my sponsor within the Liberal Party. She spoke highly of the Filipino consultation, praising me as the main architect behind the influx of good ideas to win over the Filipino vote, and the increased presence of Filipinos in all Greater Vancouver riding activities. My formula worked. The Minister proposed that the same consultation be made with other ethnic groups whose participation in Liberal party affairs was low.

I enjoyed the praise and the name I was making in the Party. But I felt uncomfortable being typecast in the ethnic vote, as though my value to the party was only in my being Filipino. The next federal elections would be about 1997, and I wanted to be taken seriously as a candidate for a winnable riding in Greater Vancouver. I felt strongly about representing not only Filipinos, or ethnic communities, but all Canadians including Caucasians, women, youth, professionals, business groups. I wanted to develop a broad power base.

It was the first time my mentor and I had close to a disagreement.

"We know you have more to offer, but right now, the Party needs to expand its support base in all ethnic communities. This is a rich source of votes because of the increasing numbers of immigrants in Greater Vancouver. We feel our policies are naturally aligned with theirs. We need to consolidate that into a real support base come elections. If you could do with other ethnic groups what you did with Filipinos, think of how many ridings could turn Liberal in 1997? Don't be in such a hurry. Pay your dues to the party. Help us get elected overall, then finding a riding for you will be easy. You'll get a choice riding that fits your support base," said Minister Kerry Black.

"I feel I can get more than an ethnic support base. I don't want to run or win because of my ethnicity. I want to run on Canadian mainstream issues. I want to be supported by all Canadians, not just ethnic Canadians. I want to win because of everything that I am and can do for Canada," I said with a passion.

"Do you really think so? What have you done for women? For seniors? For professionals? For businesses? If you want to get their support, you should be part of their organizations. You should already be working with them, helping them with their problems. You've barely started doing that with the Filipino community, and you want support from other sectors that you've not worked with at all? You will lose. Is that what you want to do — lose?"

"I agree. I haven't done much yet. That's why I need to start building my base with the other groups. I can't do that if I'm pegged to ethnic consultations, spending all my time in this sector, and getting stereotyped in it. Non-ethnic sectors won't take me seriously as someone who represents them. I need to move towards that sector now."

"Can't you do both? Work on the ethnic consultations and also begin approaching women's groups and businesses. You still need to prove your value to the party, if you want a good riding. I sat in the sidelines a long time, believe me, before I got any serious attention. This opportunity may not come again. There are other ethnic candidates who may pick up this role if you don't. Maybe you could lead a team and not have to do all the work. Here's your chance to be seen as a leader within our ethnic initiative, train other volunteers and candidates. Then you can slowly branch out to mainstream groups."

"Sounds like a good compromise, but I don't have that much time. Doing all you suggest will need a lot of time, and I'm studying for the bar. I want to make honours so I can get good internship offers."

"Well, choose your priorities then. Let me know what you decide. Then I can decide too." It sounded like a warning, and I felt a coldness coming on.

I decided to give in for now. I'll top the bar exams and get one more feather in my hat. I'll deliver a couple more ethnic communities — Iranians? Koreans? Then I can make my play. I'll join the biggest and most prestigious law firm in BC. Then I'll begin associating with corporate women's groups, starting with women lawyers. Women in male dominated fields like mining perhaps, construction and engineering. Even Dad would be pleased with that.

* * *

I didn't top the bar. I came in third. Not bad, but not exactly what I hoped for. The lawyer who topped was also a member of the Youth wing of the Liberals, another candidate-in-waiting. The bar topnotcher also had pedigree. His father was a former Liberal Cabinet Minister, whereas mine, well. I counted my pluses: ethnicity, gender and youth. I'm younger than him and can claim to be the youngest Liberal MP when elected, and the first Filipino Canadian MP in British Columbia. I can also put "top three, BC bar" in my candidate portfolio. That should set me apart from all the other lawyer candidates.

I began studying the ridings, figuring out which one to run in. I could choose the Surrey North riding, citing my first residence as my basis for running in the riding. It was never held by a Liberal, alternating between the National Democratic Party (NDP) and the Reform. A low-income riding, high immigrant population, but mostly South Asian.

I could consider Vancouver Quadra, a known Liberal enclave. Wealthy, upper class, professional. But my connections to the riding would be hard to prove. There Vancouver

Centre, with young urban professionals, including downtown. There will be big fights over who gets these ridings, as they are considered soft and winnable for Liberals.

I was being considered for the low-income, immigrant-rich ridings of Vancouver Kingsway and Vancouver East, which were held by Members of Parliament from the NDP in the past. The Liberals believed these ridings should and could be won. The Richmond riding was immigrant-rich, especially Chinese, and several Chinese candidates were in a big nomination fight for this riding.

In the end, these choice ridings went to other candidates, some handpicked by the Prime Minister, and others winning through bloody nomination fights. It was the first time I saw up-close the process for becoming the party candidate for a riding. I knew I was not ready. I will need "soldiers" ready to sign up members who will vote for me at the nomination. The nominations were held many months before the elections. I had just started to work for BCM law firm, the biggest downtown law firm. I had to prove myself on the job, and that took all my time. I also had not consolidated the kind of support base I wanted to get elected. I decided that the best thing to do was to support the party in general in the west. I could help a candidate or two who might win and become cabinet minister. They would in turn help me when I decided to run.

Besides, the atmosphere was not very good for the Liberals these days. The West felt disenfranchised. The Provinces wanted more power. The Liberals stood for a strong central government, but they had almost lost Quebec in the referendum. In the coming 1997 elections, the Liberals looked like they're in danger of losing their majority in Parliament. The Liberals' pitch to the West was: "If you want a voice, vote for a Liberal representative. Liberals will form government, they will be in power, and can therefore help you get what you want in Parliament." The Reformers pitch to the West was similar: "What has the West gained from the Liberals so far? Nothing. If you want a voice in Parliament, vote Reform, the party of the West." The polls showed British Columbians were listening more and more to the Reformers. A Liberal loss was very possible. I did not want to make my entry into politics with a losing party. Nor did I relish the idea of winning a seat, but sit on the backbenches in opposition — another reason to stay back.

I expressed my thoughts to Minister Black, except the last part of not wanting to associate with a losing party. Kerry thought it was a wise move to wait and not just jump into the ring unprepared.

"While you're at it, I think you should sort out your… married professor. It doesn't look good," Minister Black blurted out. How did she know?

"I don't reveal my sources. It doesn't matter anyway. Hear me?" Minister Black insisted.

I had nothing to say.

"Okay, it's your funeral. Don't say I didn't warn you," said Minister Black.

"By the way, something I meant to tell you earlier. See if you can develop a mentor or a sponsor from the West. I'm getting snowed under. I may lose a power fight. I don't know. Just in case. You need other friends, ok?"

Later on, I understood how considerate Minister Black was in advising me to find a new sponsor/mentor. I found out about the troubles Kerry faced within the Caucus, how rapidly she was losing influence in the inner circle.

It turned out that I, along with the political pundits, was right. In June 1997, the Reformers won 24 seats in the west.

The Liberals took only six ridings, cementing the idea that Reform was indeed the West's party of choice. The Liberals also lost the support of the Maritime Provinces to the NDP. Were it not for the Ontario support and five Liberal seats narrowly won, the Liberals would have formed a minority government. It was the first time too that all five parties gained official standing in Parliament: the Reform, Bloc Quebecois, National Democratic Party or NDP, Progressive Conservatives or PC's, and the ruling Liberals. It would have been very challenging to govern a minority government with five parties squabbling! The Liberals had a lot of work to do. I was glad I stayed out of the running in that election.

I was also glad the affair was over. How easy it is to fall out of love. What is it with me? I remembered Mr. Wilson, my first flame. What attracted me to older married men? Was it being married? Or older? Or are older married men just always so much wiser, and gentler, more tender and sweet? I'm looking for another father, isn't that what Sanjit said? When I found out that Sanjit's wife was diagnosed with breast cancer, it spooked me. It was like cold ice on heat. I felt I could not continue a relationship with a man whose wife was suffering. It took all the joy and fun out of the affair. Sanjit did not put up a fight. We remained friends however, and I consulted him every now and then about law or politics.

From 1997 to 1999, I concentrated on my law practice, focusing on corporate law. I networked with other lawyers, got to know corporate leaders, and attended many fundraising events. I networked with women's organizations, business groups, youth groups, and seniors organizations. I got myself on the Board of a select number of carefully chosen organizations to reflect the diverse support base I was developing.

Soon enough, another election was in play. In 1999, Government called an election for 2000. The 2000 federal elections came as a surprise in a way. The Liberals called an election earlier than usual, to prevent the Canadian Alliance, that had just merged with Reform, from getting organized. They had elected a new leader — Stockwell Day — who seemed set to take Liberal votes in Ontario, the Liberal stronghold. I had done my due diligence with the Liberals, developing the ethnic vote by training local candidates in ethnic consultations, expecting a reward of a winnable riding in the next election. In the end, I was offered an unwinnable riding yet again. Minister Black, whose status in the party had declined, suggested that I "run to establish name recognition, then next time, your name will be more recognizable for voters". I never understood that whole philosophy — your name will now be recognized as the one that keeps losing. I was getting frustrated with the Liberals, and with my own political career. I reminded myself to be patient. It was all about "timing" according to the political veterans. You have to be there for the upwave. The Liberals it seems were on a downwave.

* * *

I had no one to consult with about my future. Sonia was away in the Philippines, figuring out what to do with her life. Stephen was left behind, at a loss of what to do about Sonia. To his question, my answers were clear.

"Follow her." Sometimes, men are so dense. In this I idolized Tita Marites who simply decided that men did not deserve her. My own love life seemed doomed, with my penchant for 'forbidden fruit'.

"What do I do about my parents? They're ready to disown me," Stephen said bitterly.

Stumbling Through Paradise

"So, be disowned. If you love Sonia, you have to be with her and support her. This is your life. Your parents do not own you." I thought this was so clear.

"They have no one but me. They're growing old. They are threatening to return to China."

"All the better, isn't it? It seems they've never really adopted Canada as their home. They might be happier there. Anyone in China to look after them?"

"Just neighbours from the old hometown."

"Why not encourage them to visit and see for themselves? If they like it, then your problem is solved. If they don't like it and return to Canada, there's a stronger chance they will make an effort to make the most of Canada, and accept Sonia and you. A child does wonders. My mom was not accepted by my dad's parents for a long time, until they had Bobby. And by the time I came along, they wanted us to live with them. My parents refused, so my grandparents gave them a house in the same neighbourhood."

"Really?" I agreed that it sounded incredulous.

"It's all true." I said.

Stephen flew to the Philippines.

When Stephen and Sonia returned, Sonia was beaming with news that she was pregnant.

* * *

Meantime, the fortunes of the Liberal party improved a little, but not by much.

As it turned out, the Canadian Alliance's leader made so many gaffes during the campaign that ended in no major Canadian Alliance increases in Ontario, and only a few more increases in the West, leaving the Liberals in a narrower majority, but a majority nevertheless. The Liberals, for the time being, were able to stop the upwave of the Canadian Alliance. Perhaps I should have run.

But whatever Liberal force stopped the Canadian Alliance upwave, never came back, especially when the sponsorship scandals began to rock the Liberal Party. It was alleged that special favours were given by the government to a company that was a big donor to the Liberal Party. Starting about 2001, the Liberals experienced a massive downwave that pulled not only the leader Jean Chretien with it, but the whole Party eventually. Even Paul Martin, the architect of Canada's famed fiscal health, could not stop the downwave of sponsorship scandals. In 2003, he replaced Jean Chretien as leader of the Party and Prime Minister. The Conservative Party, along with the other parties, forced a non-confidence vote, on the basis that the Liberals no longer had moral authority to rule. An election was held in 2004, where Paul Martin managed to salvage the Liberal party government, winning the election for the Liberals, but reducing it to a minority. His leadership was short-lived. In 2006, the Liberals finally lost to the Conservative Party of Canada, who by now had united all the right wing parties — Canadian Alliance, Reform and Progressive Conservatives — under Stephen Harper, in a minority government.

It all seemed to go so fast. The Liberal and the Conservative waves exchanged on the beach of Canadian politics with such speed and force, I was happy to have been out of the area of tidal waves when it happened. After the 2006 elections, the Liberals were reduced to 103 MPs (9 in BC), the Conservatives elected 124, Bloc Quebecois 51 and the NDP 29.

In 2006, the Liberals, 'Canada's natural ruling party,' were out of power. What happened? Could 10 years in power make a sitting party take things for granted? Maybe, the sins of politics appear eventually after a long-enough term, in this case, a decade. The Liberal Party called for a leadership convention, and everyone and his brother and sister put forth their names, including Minister Kerry Black. She was removed in the first balloting, which reminded me of how badly my sponsor's fortunes had fallen in the party. I must remember to ask Kerry about that. The leadership convention elected a little known academic as leader. I was not impressed. What had the party become?

For the first time in a long time, my interest in federal politics waned. My political home had been betrayed, and I had no inclination to help in the rebuilding of a spent force. The rightwing party wanted to reduce immigration levels, and various other spooky policy positions that made me cringe. What about the NDP? They were too ideological on the left for me. I am now 30 years old. I will never be able to claim to be the "youngest MP," maybe not even an anything MP.

The decline of my Party was at least balanced by happiness on the family front. Joy, Sonia and Stephen's daughter, brought exactly that to their family. Stephen's parents constantly borrowed her and she was becoming just a little too spoiled. Sonia was so proud of her daughter, a poster girl for Canadian multiculturalism: a trilingual — speaking English, Tagalog and Mandarin. "So when will you contribute to Canada's diversity?" Sonia teased me. "There's enough diverse ideas I contribute to the country, thank you very much," I retorted.

* * *

I began to look at the Provincial political arena. In 2006, the BC Liberals headed the Government of British Columbia. The name of the party was a misnomer actually, because the BC

Liberals were in fact of the conservative persuasion. I was not inspired. I was tempted to consider running for civic elections in the City of Vancouver where the local right wing party was in power. But I must have set my heart on "nation building" and could not transfer that passion to "city building" quite so readily, where the issues seem to be so single-mindedly about development. I decided that city politics was not deep enough to sustain my political interest.

Instead, I decided to focus on building up some issues close to my heart. I got more involved in specific sectors: ethnic communities, seniors, youth, women and business.

In 2007, I met the Conservative government's new Parliamentary Secretary of Western Affairs Minister Jonathan Prett at a consultation he had initiated. The consultation was in fact of a similar format to the one I had developed for the Liberals in consulting with ethnic communities, but smaller in size, and shorter in duration. Someone who attended my sessions must have copied my model. The session surprised me, considering what was known to be the plan of the Conservatives: "reduce immigration, until Canada had no immigration left." I was rather impressed with the Minister, who turned out to be so unlike my idea of the Conservatives. He was open and seemed genuinely concerned to improve life for immigrants and the immigration system of Canada. He was tall with movie-star good looks, spoke well, and seemed thoughtful, definitely no red neck. I wondered if he was married. I made a mental note to research that.

More or less the same Filipino representatives appeared, and more or less the same issues were expressed. I wondered how the Conservatives would respond to the issues — how different, or similar their response would be to that of the Liberals. I thought the response of the Minister was much more guarded than my friend Minister Black. He promised nothing, except to look into the issues carefully. I later understood this stance as a most practical one: the Conservatives had won themselves a very fragile minority and were therefore uncertain of being able to carry votes sufficient to support new laws, policies or programs. They could not promise changes at this time.

What surprised me the most was how the Minister actively sought me as a candidate for Member of Parliament. In fact, he sought candidates from all other ethnic communities. I did not know him personally. They must have a dossier on ethnic community leaders. Apparently the Conservatives came up with a strategy to find, and win over, the conservative elements within the ethnic communities. Until this time, people had assumed that minority groups were natural Liberal supporters because it was the former Prime Minister Pierre Trudeau and the Liberals who were responsible for the multiculturalism policy and bringing immigrants to Canada. The Conservatives came to understand that ethnic groups, just like any society, have their own political diversity: some on the right, some on the left, and others in the centre. The Conservatives wanted to carve out its share of the ethnic vote by identifying and recruiting that right wing conservative element from among ethnic groups, a large portion of which is the religious right, similar to the religious right elements in the mainstream Conservative party. They wanted to prove that immigrants are 'natural Conservatives', and that ethnic communities have a lot in common with Conservatives. The Conservatives wined and dined ethnic community leaders from all over, and by the end of the second year of their term had made connections with all ethnic groups in Greater Vancouver, lining up possible candidates for the 2008 elections.

I did not answer the offer to run for the Conservatives. I said I would think it over. To my reply, Minister Prett responded, "Take your time. Let me know when we can chat again, maybe in a couple of months."

I had a lot to consider about what the Conservative Party stood for and whether I could support that. Their position on abortion was troubling for me. It was very important that women have choice and control over their bodies. I could live with their stance on reducing the role of government in general, and promoting the American style free market economy. I could even live with their more aggressive foreign policy. Their lack of commitment on environment and climate change was a worry. I didn't care one way or the other about gun control; quite frankly, I didn't understand the ramifications of this issue anyway. To me, if a person wanted to commit a crime, he or she would do it with anything, gun or no gun. I doubted whether the forced registration of guns would substantially reduce violence. I looked for evidence in the official Conservative platform and policies, of the spooky stuff I heard lurking around the party when Stockwell Day was its leader, such as homophobia and belief in creationism. I did not find it in the policy books. Stephen Harper had begun to eliminate extreme elements from the Party in an effort to bring it to the political centre. I examined the party's policy on Quebec, and saw that the Conservatives were willing to give Quebec special status within a united Canada. Okay. And as for immigration and multiculturalism, I read that the Conservatives will maintain immigration levels at 1% per annum or 250,000 immigrants a year. I was pleased that they were not reducing the size of immigration as was the popular notion, but maintaining the current levels of immigration.

I would have preferred an increase, but it was not as bad as I thought.

All in all, it was a platform I could mostly support, with the exception of the abortion issue and the stance on environment. I met with Minister Prett when he was next in Vancouver. We met over cocktails at the Four Seasons Hotel where the Minister had a dinner function to attend. He could spare about an hour, said his assistant.

Minister Prett ordered a coke, and I matched him by ordering a soda with a squeeze of lime.

"I have to pace myself. So much temptation in our business," he joked, tapping his flat belly.

"Well, sounds like what you're doing is effective."

"Thank you," the Minister beamed. I didn't mean to flatter him. He *is* lean.

"I'm the same. Got to stay out of the wine. I can never remember much of what I said after one drink. So I stay away from it when talking business."

"Good girl. Hope you have some fun though. All work and no play makes Jill a dull girl," the Minister encouraged.

"I'm a self-declared workaholic, and nothing gives me more fun than work. I admit it. I am dull and boring."

"We'll see," the Minister teased. "So, Miss Dull-and-Boring, what's on your mind?"

"First of all, thank you for your invitation. I feel honoured." I began.

"No, it's our honour to have you," the Minister said magnanimously.

"I have to say, it's the platform that worried me. I've spent the last month reviewing every Conservative document I know."

"Uh oh, I'm afraid to hear what you have to say then," he joked.

"I have to be able to defend my change from the Liberals to the Conservatives. I know I will be challenged on this." In fact, I am worried.

"You saw the light of day finally, what's wrong with that? Better to see it later than never," he smiled.

I ignored the gratuitous remark, meant as a joke, surely. "I can support most of what I've read, and I can certainly see myself working well with the people I've met so far." I smiled. "If this is what the Conservatives stand for, then the Conservatives are most certainly getting a bad rap from media, or...there is a hidden agenda somewhere?"

Minister Prett opened his palms up and shrugged with a smile, suggesting 'nothing hidden here'. "One member in some remote place is quoted as saying something off-colour, and the whole party is painted with it. What can we do?" Minister Prett is so cool.

I nodded. I can understand that.

"If there is anything that worries me as something I could not personally support and defend to the community, it's two things: your position on the environment, which is very little, and abortion. I couldn't be a woman and not support women's choice over their own bodies."

"I know. I agree with you. Many in the party agree with you. It's just that certain elements in our party that brought us to where we are — business on one hand and the religious right on the other — have to be appeased. These issues are important to them. We need to go slow on these issues or lose our friends. At this time when we have only a fragile minority, we need every Conservative MP's support, which means the support of their ridings."

Stumbling Through Paradise

I waited for more explanation.

"We will ask for more time to deliver on Kyoto," he said, referring to the climate change commitments of Canada at an international agreement held in Kyoto, Japan. "We will get to that stage eventually, but we will need more time so that the business community can adjust financially. They say they are being ruined by the competition from other countries who have not made the same commitment to reduce greenhouse gases."

"How long though?" I asked, a little sharply.

"Until we become a majority in the House?" Minister Prett smiled.

I nodded slowly. I was beginning to understand the play. It was all about getting the people — non-Conservatives and Conservatives alike — to trust the ruling Conservatives enough, and then when they did, the Conservatives would push the 'harder stuff' forward. This 'harder stuff' was a two-edged sword. 'Harder stuff' could mean reforms that the Conservative Party had always wanted, but were too extreme and could not be supported by other parties when the Conservatives were in a minority. Or it could mean reforms that the moderating influences within the Conservative Party itself wanted, but would not be supported by the more extreme elements of the party, and could therefore not be brought forward when the Conservatives were in a minority.

"And how would the abortion issue be finessed for the 'extreme elements'? For until we get a majority in the House?" I asked. Did I use the term 'we'?

"The Prime Minister will let the MPs vote their conscience," Minister Prett said.

"Why does he have to put it on the table at all?"

"It's something he has promised the party."

"Couldn't he renege on that promise? Prime Ministers do it all the time to the electorate. Look at Jean Chretien and his promise to overturn the GST?"

"And look where he is now," said Minister Prett with a sly smile.

Yes, of course, I remembered.

He continued. "Don't worry, by then, there will be enough support for pro-choice among the Conservative MPs when they are released from party voting. The polling trends show it. Do you think the PM will do it if he wasn't already assured of an answer favorable to what he wanted?"

I thought the Minister was confiding a lot of information to me. More than I expected. It made me feel I was already part of the inner circle with the Prime Minister.

"Alright," I heard myself saying. "I'm in," I gave a big smile.

"Good decision," said Minister Prett, extending his hand. His handshake was firm and strong. His obviously pleased face showed a big victory was won, making me feel important. Am I that important to the Conservatives? I felt thrilled, and a little bit suspicious and anxious: what do they expect of me?

"We have lots of work to do," the Minister declared.

"Of course. I look forward to it all, even the dull and boring kind," I teased.

"This won't be, I assure you. Can you stay for this function? I have a few people for you to meet," said the Minister.

"I'd be honoured."

With that, the Minister whisked me away into the grand ballroom where I met so many people whose names I couldn't remember. So many people, and not one of them a redneck. I was pleased about my decision, feeling my dream had just risen from the dead. I was floating on air beside the Minister, who introduced me as 'someone to watch'. I felt as special as a sweetheart, until I remembered the researched fact that Jonathan Prett was married and with two small children. Darn.

It was 11:30 pm when Jonathan Prett walked me back to my car in the underground parking lot of the hotel. The party was far from over yet. The car was parked in a dark corner. When Jonathan opened the door for me, I stood still, looked him in the eye and said, "I had a wonderful time. You won't regret…" I did not finish the sentence as Jonathan pressed his lips against mine, enveloping me in his large arms. My lips responded to the urgent kiss and my body surrendered to the embrace. Abruptly, he let me go. We looked into each other's eyes, searching for the answers to the same question. Satisfied, we both chuckled. I entered the car, and just before I drove away, Jonathan blew me a salute.

* * *

In the end, I did not run for the Conservatives in the federal elections of 2008. I was unprepared for the amount of negativity I received about turning Conservative. I committed so many mistakes during this time in my life that I would never repeat again.

For starters, I decided to tell my Liberal mentor Kerry Black of my decision to join the Conservatives, *after* the fact. I didn't think I could get truly unbiased advice from her about joining the Conservatives, given her deep roots in the Liberal party. I told Kerry for her information, not for advice.

On long distance phone, I explained my decision to join the Conservatives and that I was considering running for them.

"You did all that? Without telling me? After all these years? You don't trust me?" Kerry Black cried.

I felt embarrassed. My mentor and sponsor was right to feel upset for not being consulted early in the game.

"What are you doing? Turning from Liberal to Conservative is like… Are you the same person I know? Have you gone totally opportunistic now that we're down in the polls? Is that all you are? I'm sorry, I just…You've totally wasted my time. I totally misplaced my trust in you," said Kerry Black.

"I'm really sorry, Kerry. I didn't think you'd be so upset."

"Not think I'd be upset? I only vouched for you in the party. I only put you in front of every important Liberal. I only taught you everything I know. Now this. I feel offended. You didn't even have the courtesy to let me know when you received the offer, before you made the decision. Del Mundo, you've no idea! You don't even know why I should be upset?" Kerry's voice had risen several decibel levels.

"I'm so sorry, Kerry," I was almost in tears. "I was…I didn't know."

"Well, good luck. I should have known better. The first time I met you, I could sense your hunger for power. You'd do whatever it takes. So why should that surprise me?" Kerry said, the sarcasm thick in her voice. I was silent.

"Can't take it? You'll need a strong belly from now on, kid. What I said is nothing compared to what your opponents will say about your changing parties."

"Please don't think so badly of me. You've helped me so much. I'm eternally grateful, whatever happens."

As the line was silent, I added in earnest, "I hope one day you'll forgive me."

"Well, I got to go," said Kerry Black, and hang up.

I felt like I was kicked and slapped around as I put down the phone. I lost Kerry as a mentor and friend for sure, but hoped she wouldn't be an enemy. Could I have done it differently? Make the change in parties, but somehow still keep her as a friend? Should I have trusted my mentor enough to seek her advice well before making the decision? I thought that being a stalwart Liberal, Kerry Black might try to convince me out of turning Conservative, and I was afraid I might go along with her advice because of her influence. That is really the reason I did not want to consult with my mentor early on, which means it was myself I did not trust. I didn't trust that my hunger for being elected could withstand the good sense Kerry would drill into me, the loyalty, and all that. I needed to be focused and committed to getting elected. Some sacrifices are needed, I convinced myself. This was one of them.

I remembered my goal. It was now alive again. It was one positive thing to offset the pain of losing a friend.

* * *

I was surprised to see where the first attacks came from: my own family. Sonia in particular expressed disgust. At a dinner for Mom who was in town visiting, they had strong words.

"How could you say they're close to being the same anyway? The Conservatives of Stephen Harper are the exact opposites of the Liberals. Don't trust that man. You! Opportunist! That's the only word for you. The Conservatives are now in power, and the Liberals out, so you go and side with the Conservatives after sleeping with the Liberals for 10 years! Where are your principles?" she asked.

Bobby had a different opinion. "What's the point of hanging around with the losers. If you're with the winners, you can always influence things your way. If you're with the losers, you can't. These Conservatives want you, right? You'd be crazy to turn them down."

"If the Liberals and Conservatives are anything like the Nationalistas and Liberals of Philippine politics, there are no differences between them, just the people. So maybe Bobby is right," said Mom, the Mayor of Pililla for some years now.

"It's not the same here in Canada, Mom," said Sonia. "The Liberals and Conservatives have very different views of governing Canada, and different visions of the future of Canada."

I disagreed. "Maybe the old Reform or Canadian Alliance or even the old Progressive Conservative parties were very different from the Liberal party, but not this new Conservative Party under Harper. It's more centrist, or moving towards the centre. He just needs more time to bring it from the right to the centre."

"He's an evangelical fundamentalist, and surrounds himself with other fundamentalists, including that Minister of yours," said Sonia.

"What's so bad about fundamentalists in politics?" asked Mom. "It's good for leaders to be spiritual, whatever their religion. Better than leaders with no gods or no moral values. Those will more likely lead the country to hell."

"It's not that. It's that some fundamentalists who are also political leaders force their spiritual belief on others. Look at the abortion issue," said Sonia.

That fired up Mom. "So what about the abortion issue? It's so clear that a fetus is a living thing; to abort it would be murder. How much clearer can it be! It's not a question of being a fundamentalist or not, it's just basic science. A life is a gift. It should not be killed for any reason."

"This is going nowhere," I said. "I'm sorry I even brought it up."

"Don't expect me to help you with the Filipino community — you're on your own now," said Sonia.

"The multicultural leaders?" I inquired.

"Sorry, that's your problem now."

"What would you do, if you were me?" I pleaded.

"Wait. Wait for your party to rebuild. Help them. Then run when they, and you, are ready," said Sonia.

"This chance may not come again," warned Bobby.

"You have to be comfortable and confident with this change. If you feel it is the best thing for the communities you are serving, go ahead. People will be comfortable if you are yourself comfortable in it. Can you explain it confidently, without apologies?" Mom's words stayed with me.

I undertook a trial balloon.

I issued a media release stating that I had been invited by the Conservative Party to run for them as MP, and that I wanted to hear comments from the community about it. I invited the public to a coffee session at a community centre. Some 50 people came.

To my surprise, everyone who came did not like the idea. They were my loyal Liberal supporters, what did I expect? They were certainly not ready for this, and neither was I ready to provide answers to their questions. I felt defensive as I explained: "That is why I called for this meeting, I wanted to hear your opinions first before I made a decision."

"That you're even considering it, without understanding the Conservative platform, is shocking," said one of my big supporters from the women's groups.

"I could be a strong voice in the party to change their position," I said.

"Why not just join the party who is already supporting the women's position! If you want to switch, why not switch to the NDP? They are strong on pro-choice!" said another.

I knew the answer to that, but of course I did not voice it out. The NDPs will never be in power nationally, not in my lifetime anyway. I want to spend my time in politics in power, doing things, not sitting in opposition.

To my dismay, people who were not my supporters but known supporters of other parties, came in big numbers. They took over the meeting with their negative comments, making it appear that I had already made the decision, that I was a 'flim flam artist', that I had no integrity. They brought opposition media with them. They took advantage of my open meeting to criticize my considering changing parties.

The Conservative friends I brought with me were appalled. Conservatives were not crucified like that, ever, anywhere in the past. The venom and hatred seemed palpable, and finally, I decided to shut the meeting down with only half an hour of discussion. As I did not have well prepared answers and did not wish to be overly defensive, I made up an excuse that I was called to an emergency meeting and had to leave. I thanked those who came with as much grace as I could muster, emphasizing that I had not yet made the decision and that the comments today "are very helpful for me."

* * *

I met up with my Conservative team at a coffee shop to debrief. I felt dirty, as though I had been thrown rotten tomatoes, as though I was the most evil person on earth. The incredible part of it was how I felt I could not reply back in anger no matter how unjust the criticisms were. I remembered what Kerry Black told me: "A hard strong belly is what you need from now on." Fiona, a Conservative strategist, was the first to be positive about it all.

"We can learn many lessons from this," she said. "First off, the invite should only be for known supporters. And maybe just a small group to start off, an intimate gathering, not a publicized event." Everyone nodded.

"If the whole purpose was to get input, helpful input — then yes, I agree," said Harold, who was tentatively assigned to me as my volunteer assistant. "We did want to see the overall reactions. Media should have been screened out."

"As soon as it was publicized as an open event, you couldn't screen out anyone," said Fiona.

"I was not ready with my answers. That's the bottom line, that's why they ate me up. I should have rehearsed the answers, done a mock question and answer with you guys. I feel like a heel. I must have looked like a heel. I had answers in my head, but the audience thoroughly floored me. I felt defeated by their anger, and if I gave in to my own anger at the unfair criticisms, it would have become worse. In accepting their anger though, I must have looked guilty. Did I…look guilty?"

"I'm afraid you did," said Chris, a new Conservative. Like me, Chris was also considering a run.

"I think we need to do some damage control," said Fiona.

"We need to get ahead of their media. We need to publish our own article with our own spin," said Harold.

"Like what do we say?" I asked.

"That you have consulted supporters about your switching parties, and that more people came to it than the Liberal candidate for the riding when he announced his candidacy," said Harold.

"Is that true?" I asked.

"I think so. Word is that only a handful came," said Harold.

"Anyway, check the number," I said.

"Say that Manolita is next set to consult a whole lot more people. Focus on Manolita. Give her a good quote. Something about 'wanting to integrate community grassroots needs into her platform, whatever Party she may choose'. Get her going a step forward from just consulting, but actually including community issues within her platform. Mention one or two "safe" issues she will advocate for: jobs, education," said Fiona.

"And immigration," I added. "Say I'll advocate for improving the criteria for immigration to increase chances of success in Canada, and maintaining immigration levels. There is some thinking among Conservatives to do that anyway, right? I will add my voice to that movement, so when I do announce as a Conservative candidate, I can say that I have already influenced the party in the community's favor. That will also help counter this popular idea that Conservatives will stop immigration."

"Good point," Fiona said. "So when should this come out and what media?"

"I'll look after that. We have some friendly media that we've advertised with. We'll go for different ethnic community media, not just Filipino, and some mainstream community papers," Harold offered.

"We should really push blogging and tweeting. No one's doing much of it. We can get an edge over them there," said Chris.

"I know. I'm on to that. Someone in the party's looking after it. I'll follow up and see if we can use it here," said Harold.

The media interest on my switching parties was intense but happily brief. It was stopped by my announcement that I was not running for a seat in the coming elections as I had been seconded for more work with my law firm.

I decided to stay out of the political radar for a good three years, sit this election out, and see about the next one.

My new mentor and sponsor in the party, Minister Jonathan Prett agreed with my strategy, although he would not promise an easy seat in 2011. I felt awkward facing him across the table in his office after the intimacy of our last meeting. Jonathan seemed to have forgotten everything. He was all business. Did I imagine that night?

"We fight one election at a time. Keep your irons in the fire, and your profile up in your support communities. Get involved with the party now. By the time 2011 rolls around, switching will no longer be an issue. You would be seen as a party stalwart by then, with much achievement under your belt," he said.

As I sat silent, he added, "I back winners or I lose face. You have to do your part or I can't back you. Now you have to get the party, not me, to love you."

I felt blood rushing up to my face. Who does he think he is, suggesting that I wanted to make him love me? Wasn't it him who invited me to run? Wasn't it him who started the kiss?

"Fuck you!" I cried. I leaned forward on the table. "I never asked you to love me! You invited me to run. You made the pass. Now you're dropping me because of a little problem? Watch me!" I said angrily. I banged the door behind me.

* * *

I did not bother to let Jonathan Prett know of my decision. Thinking about him felt distasteful. I felt bile coming up from my stomach. I tasted bitterness in my mouth. I wanted to retch. Did he do that with everybody, or just me? Did I 'ask' for it? I did find him attractive that first night. He was my prince then. I shouldn't take things too seriously. A night of flirtation must not be seen as anything other than that: one night of fun. I must not let it get in the way of business. He flirted. So did I. Now it's over. I must not expect any favours, any special relations. Back to business. What's my business? To get elected. Can Jonathan help me to get elected? He still may. He's influential among the Conservatives. So why make him an enemy? Swallow your pride, Manolita. No one else knows anyway. Be a sport and forget it all happened. How does one get elected? Keep on working the issues. Keep a high profile with the community. Make friends among the influential. I was already feeling much better. There are many more influential people in the Conservative party I could get to know. I'll impress them. By the time 2011 rolls around, "switching parties will no longer be an issue." I'll be "a party stalwart by then, with much achievement under my belt." It's still good advice, even if it comes from that jerk.

As for Jonathan Prett, he can go fuck himself. Who needs him? But he must not know that. He must think that I still admire him. Oh well, will making him think I admire him kill me? No. Will it help me? Yes. But keep a distance from now on. No letting him escort you to your car alone in a parking lot at night. I must not let that happen again. It must be all business from now on. I'll be a star among the Conservatives. And not because of him. I'll do it all on my own. 2011 is not all that far away. I'll show him.

* * *

CHAPTER 6

Canada
Manolita, 2009–2010

One good thing about not running for a seat at all was reclaiming my family, or at least Sonia.

"*Ate*, I learned my lesson," I confessed to her.

"The hard way, I can see. But it's the only way for my hard-headed sister," Sonia replied.

"I just want to focus on communities now. Learn about them, and really help in what way I can. If the politics comes up again as an opportunity later, fine. If not, fine as well. I feel I need grounding. Can I get on the board or volunteer for your agency maybe?"

Sonia was now heading up a new multicultural non-profit agency called Immigrant Communities Collective or ICC, and was still involved with Cross Currents Society's Looking Forward Initiative. By then, Looking Forward caused some substantial improvements for foreign-trained engineers, but it was still a far cry from resolving the complicated issue of skilled immigrants' not being able to practice their professions in Canada. Stephen, her long-time partner and lawyer advocate with the BC Human Rights Commission, was helpful in getting this done.

"Tell me all about it. What can I do on the legal end?" I asked Stephen.

"So long as the professional regulatory bodies have the power to regulate their respective professions, we will never get anywhere. They are acting in a conflict of interest. When they limit the professionals practicing in Canada, they limit their own competition, which works to their advantage. How can they truly serve the interests of the community as a regulatory body? The Act regulating the professions should be changed. That is a Canadian law. You might try to do something about that, with your ambitions in federal politics," said Stephen.

"And replace it with what?" I asked.

"A report has been done about this. Why don't you read it? Then let us know what you can do," Sonia said.

"Okay!" I am happy that my sister is now talking to me like a real person.

I read the report carefully. I was struck by the great injustice and inefficiency of the system. I joined the Board of Cross Currents Society, and led a separate project to review the Professional Regulatory Act. Along the way, I met many ethnic community leaders, and immigrants, heard their stories, so similar to my father's. Somehow, I could no longer tell these people what I used to advise my dad: to 'just get on with it and redo your courses, then you can practise your profession.' It was difficult to tell the head of a family to study, when he had a family to feed. How little savings they had, and how little value were these savings when transposed to Canadian standard of living. Surely, someone with 25 years of experience in senior positions could be allowed to challenge exams and practice if they pass. I studied the health professions given the huge gap in health professionals in the country. I studied the physicians, and how they had another problem: limitations on residencies, caused by government funding limitations. Did it really cost $1 million to fund one residency position? Surely, the money can be found somewhere if we are bothering to import doctors? I met with the Health Minister and laid down these problems. With my contacts in the Conservative Party, I managed to meet with the Labour Minister, the Skills Canada Minister, the Education Minister, the Immigration Minister, and the Multiculturalism Minister. I made a presentation to the Western Caucus of the Conservatives so I could catch all of them in one go. I didn't realize how complicated was the machinery of the federal government. I became keenly interested in learning the levers of power, the role of Deputies and their staff, the role of Ministers and their staff. I learned about the relationship of federal government, with provincial government, and with city governments. How the health issue is sliced up between federal, provincial, and regional bodies. The workings of governance fascinated me as I explored how to solve the problems I met in the communities.

I directed my questions to Sonia and Stephen, now my close advisers. "How does an ordinary citizen even begin to affect change in her life, with such a complicated governance system? Health is provincial responsibility, and now also administered regionally."

Stephen added, "And different levels of government collect different taxes. If you had a problem about something, it would be next to impossible to know who to approach if you were a new resident, or a new citizen."

Sonia offered, "So people usually go to their MP or their MLA whose staff in turn end up referring them to different organizations. Newcomers don't even know they could have a say in many things happening around them, like the closing of their children's school."

"As a matter of fact, immigrants who've been here many years don't know either," added Stephen.

"Is there any education, orientation, or training anywhere that explains how governance works in people's daily lives?" I asked.

"Not that I'm aware of," said Stephen. "Not even in law courses," he added.

Sonia said, "I think it's critical for any citizen, especially new citizens and new residents to Canada."

I agreed. I had been thinking of a program. "Why not a citizenship orientation program that would teach new citizens and Canadian residents how life is governed in Canada, and how they could participate in that process?"

"That's great! I see it: "Maple Bamboo Initiative." Maple to stand for Canada, bamboo to stand for immigrants. Engaging newcomers in Canadian civic affairs," Sonia is really good with this. She has created many programs at ICC.

I felt so excited. We formed a pilot program through ICC.

At ICC, I led a group of volunteers to develop Maple Bamboo Initiative. I connected the program to the offices of political representatives. Newcomers could not believe how easy it was for them to talk with the local MLA or MP or even Minister. How approachable they seemed to be, the students said. Their amazement was an eye opener for me, for whom all this had been accessible.

One participant said, "In India, you can't just speak to elected officials. You have to know them and have deep connections! Government doesn't ask ordinary people for their opinions. They just go ahead and do things on their own.

They figure they've been elected by the people, so they can go ahead and do whatever they want, without consultation."

Another participant was cynical. "Do you really think our saying no to a shopping centre will make the City Council reject a big company's proposal?" she asked.

I delighted in telling them of famous cases where community made a big difference. The community action that stopped a highway from going through the middle of downtown. A petition that stopped giant Walmart. The community consultations that caused the building of a continuous green pathway along the foreshore of the city.

At the graduation, some star students were asked to speak about their experience.

One Filipina immigrant gave a speech. "I had become depressed in Canada, looking after my household, unemployed, and missing my high profile job in Manila. When I took the Maple Bamboo training program, my son's school was about to close due to low enrollment, and the kids and parents were all upset about it. With the help of knowledge gained in the training program, I got involved in the parent school advisory committee. We fought the closure of the school — and won! The school, rather than being closed, will now keep open, integrating students from several schools that had too little enrollment. Maple Bamboo gave me back my confidence, and I felt I had a place in Canada after all".

An immigrant from China said in her speech: "I've not been able to practise as a physician. My civic engagement experience was with Cross Currents Society. If foreign-educated engineers are now able to practise their professions here, why not the doctors? Would you, my dear classmates, work together with me and do something for foreign-educated doctors, like what Looking Forward Initiative did for foreign-trained engineers?" she challenged.

It was a tall order, I knew, and I did not want to raise expectations. But who knows? With a great amount of passion, one can do anything. I raised my hand and promised to help the group. That caused several other participants to join in.

The group grew from medical professional immigrants to all professionals with training and experience from other countries. Some of the immigrants were practising in their field in entry-level positions. Those who worked in entirely unrelated fields and had given up on their professions, now felt they could have another chance. Others were unemployed. They called themselves Internationally Trained Professionals or ITPs and their purpose was to help each other eventually to practise their professions. The first thing I did was to introduce them to Sonia, who, through the Immigrant Communities Collective, had started the Bamboo Network, a mentoring program for skilled immigrants. For a start, each ITP was given a mentor. The rest followed.

Sonia, Stephen and I worked together closely during the following months helping the ITPs organize. It became clear that the group needed to be broad enough to include all kinds of professions, and not just the nurses and doctors and pharmacists. The physicians group could be a special group, as they seemed ready and impassioned. It was decided that the physicians lead the way on advocacy for this group, and I worked with them closely by finding resources for them. My political contacts with government bodies and Sonia's staff contacts with the same bodies helped to facilitate finding the right sources of funds. I applied for non-profit status for the group and took to writing grants easily with coaching from Sonia. Grant writing was so much like legal briefs. It was all about making a case for a cause. Soon, the ITPs had their own non-profit organization called 'ITP Advocates', a coordinator working with them full time, and myself Chair of their Board.

As Chair of the Board of ITP Advocates, I broadened my network among immigrants, but also among corporate, business, academic and government leaders. I learned, probed and attacked the barriers that stood in the way of internationally trained professionals to practise in Canada. I developed a soft spot for immigrant lawyers, especially women immigrant lawyers. I began to understand their problems, but the eye opener for me was the realization that Canadian women lawyers had their own problems as well.

Sara McKinnon, a senior lawyer from another law firm explained it to me. "The problem is we can never get ahead, as most of us take a leave when we have babies. When we come back to the workplace, we have been left behind. Many of us do not go back as we have been seriously de-skilled during the years away from work."

I thought of women in my firm who were in a similar spot.

"Women are not seen as serious partner material unless they are done with family-raising or unless they commit to having no children," said Sara.

I agreed. I may one day encounter these issues, myself. But how will I ever find time for a boyfriend, let alone a family with children? Aloud, I said, "It's unfair that child-bearing professional women are being discriminated against for something that benefits society: providing human resources for the country."

Sara nodded. "The decline in population is already becoming a problem. It's predicted that starting 2011, there will be no more labour force growth in Canada. Where would the future workers come from?"

The irony was obvious and plain to see. "Immigrants are an obvious answer. Yet the country is discriminating against skilled immigrants, the very people they have brought in to solve the problem."

"And the other potential solution — natural growth by births — is also not being facilitated, in fact, is being discouraged," echoed Sara.

I sighed with the sad recognition. The more I thought about it, the more incensed I became. Seeing as I was already doing something about the immigrant side of the solution, I decided to do something about the female lawyers' side. This would be my start on women's issues.

"How would you like to join me in working on this problem?" I asked Sara.

"Would love to! Lead the way, kid," said Sara.

We came up with additional names of lawyers engaged in this issue: someone who wrote an article about it, someone who did a study, a women's association who does advocacy in this field, and on and on.

We held a breakfast meeting and invited a few more people. Fifteen women lawyers came to the breakfast meeting. Hardly any breakfast was eaten because everybody was so engaged in the discussion that cited more and more stories and solutions. The meeting ended with a decision to form an advocacy group, with me as interim chair to convene the next meeting to discuss an action plan. I called for volunteers to work with me on a draft action plan, and 7 hands shot up. I was inspired by the dynamism of the group.

Over the next months, my plate was full.

I drove myself to frenzy, working 20 hours a day, hardly sleeping, hardly eating. My work at BCM no longer held much interest for me, and I worked on my projects even in the office. The managing partner took me aside one day.

"I really don't care what you do after office hours, or your politics. You're here all night, yet your billings are the lowest they've ever been. If they don't improve, I can't help you," she said.

"No worries, I'm working on them. They're a little complicated, but they're closing soon," I assured her.

"You're sure? You don't look good. Looking haggard in fact. What's killing you? Not the cases?" she said.

"Not at all."

"What then?"

I waved my hand in a way that signified 'nothing to worry about'.

"I hate to have you choose between politics and work, and it need not come to that. Your other activities are clearly jeopardizing your job. We're not running a political office here, and the law firm has got bills to pay. Everybody has to hold up their end. If this does not improve, you understand…?" she said.

"I know," I said. When I was on a streak of popularity, you sure didn't mind. I put the company on the map. And now when I'm out of favour and out of the limelight, BCM is suddenly not a political office. But I held my tongue, saying only: "I'll do better."

"Please do," said the Managing Partner.

During the day, my work at the law firm occupied me. The nights I devoted to the ITPs and the women lawyers. Lunches and coffee meetings were all to do with my volunteer activities, establishing connections, pursuing leads. I was enjoying myself thoroughly. Community building was a whole lot more fun than political campaigning — certainly more fun than structuring mergers and acquisitions. I especially liked working with real people, helping solve real problems with concrete solutions.

Most of all, I enjoyed getting closer to Sonia and Stephen. Even Mom whom I used to ignore, I now listened to for her political wisdom.

"You know, I like you so much more now," Sonia said to me after dinner one evening. "You used to be such an arrogant s.o.b. A spoiled brat. Not interested in the family at all. You used to despise everything Filipino, and now you're even eating *longsilog*. Are you running again for MP maybe?"

"No. That's out of my mind right now. If the opportunity comes, I might consider it, but right now, solving problems through people themselves is so much more compelling. Sis, you were doing this all this time! You should run for office. You're an expert at solving community problems!" I said.

"Two in the family is enough, in fact two is too much. No. One is already too much." Sonia laughed. "Seriously, each to her role. You have the gift of politics, my dear sis, and I have a different gift. I think your political leadership is deepening with what you're doing now. It will serve you well whether you run for office or not. You're becoming a better person." Sonia's eyes warmed to me, and I hugged her.

"What's this — a real hug?" Sonia laughed. It's true, I couldn't remember the last time I hugged her. Sonia released me and looked at me in a strange way.

"You're a skeleton! What's going on?" cried Sonia.

"Nothing."

"You're pale. Look at your arms, skin and bones. You hardly have any flesh on you. My god. You have to eat! Or you'll disappear before our eyes. Are you eating anything?" exclaimed Sonia.

"Yup." I turned away.

"Yup what? When did you eat last? What did you eat?" Sonia insisted.

"Juice. I drank juice. And ate chips."

"When?"

"I don't know. Yesterday?"

"What about today? What did you eat today?"

"I don't know. Water. I drank a lot of water. I don't remember. Why should I remember what I drink or eat!" I protested the interrogation. Then I faltered. I held myself against the table. The room was spinning round and round.

Next thing I knew, I was lying in a hospital bed. Plastic tubes ran down from inverted bottles, ending in needles stuck to both my arms. The world was spinning. I closed my eyes again. Then opened them real slowly. A face through the haze slowly cleared. Sonia's face. "Your body's had a breakdown, sis."

* * *

CHAPTER 7

Canada
Jun Jun, 1999–2009

They call me Jun Jun. When I was a child, I wanted it changed to just one Jun. But it wouldn't stick at home. Mom couldn't drop the second Jun. The two Juns were stuck in her tongue the way B's were. She called Victor, my stepdad, Biktor and Vina my stepsister was Bina. Her vowels were short and clipped, so 'fact' comes out 'fuck.' I always tried to trap her to say 'fact' just for the heck of it. Tita Norma smacked me for that. She was always mom's fierce protector against me or my stepdad. But in the never-ending battles between my mom and stepdad for how to raise me, Tita Norma was my champion. She said yes to everything I wanted, while my stepdad said no, and mom was always in the middle vacillating, apologizing for me, apologizing for my stepdad.

I grew up on Tita Norma's *champurrado, lechon kawali, sinigang*. She was more than my nanny, more like a second mom and grandma rolled into one. So with a mom, a stepdad, a second mom and a grandma, a stepsister and a large home in a ritzy neighbourhood, that should have been good enough.

But nothing makes up for a real father, something I never had. He died before I was born. I am his junior, hence Jun Jun, the second Jun for emphasis, or fondness. Whatever.

Even when I was little, I already knew I was different, and that there was something wrong about me. Well, apart from the fact that I liked to steal. Little things, from the store. Candies, gum, magazines. It gave me a thrill. Everybody did it anyway, just for kicks. I knew it was wrong, but that was nothing, compared to what was really wrong. Something bigger, about my past.

"No, there is nothing wrong about you. Your dad and mom loved each other very much. Your dad loved you even before you were born. Unfortunately, he died from a heart attack. Then your mother met Victor, a nice Canadian professor, then they got married," Tita Norma explained.

I know about my Mom's tragedies. Tita Norma has drilled them all into me. Orphaned early. Raised by a poor grandma. Her first husband and child died in an accident in the Philippines. Her second husband, my dad, died early. Tita Norma keeps saying how lucky my mom is. And that I should be thankful.

"After all that suffering, God has finally rewarded your mom. Carla now has everything she never imagined she would ever have in her life — a good rich white husband, a beautiful big house in Canada, two wonderful children, lots of friends. The only problem is you."

I guess I was a handful then. I ignored everything my Mom said. I treated her husband, my stepdad with disrespect. I closeted myself in my room. Mom gave me everything I wanted: toys, games, clothes. But it didn't make up for what I really wanted. My real father.

My stepdad kept telling her to exert some discipline on me. I overheard them.

"Give him some responsibility, then he might just be less selfish," he said.

"He's had no father, he never knew one, poor child," said Mom.

"And what do you call me? Aren't I his stepdad?"

"You're not his dad, and he knows it. Let him come to you when he's ready, don't force him."

"He's not a child anymore. He's eight, for heaven's sake."

Mom had Tita Norma to tell all her troubles to. She was such a good friend. A wall of strength. They were so alike. They had no families back in the Philippines. Like Mom, Norma was orphaned. She never married. She had no one to live for, until they met. Mom was the only one who lent Tita Norma money to get rid of a big gambling debt. Since then, Tita Norma felt indebted to Mom, and swore off gambling forever. In turn, Tita Norma became all the things Mom never had: a sister, a mother and a loyal friend. She asked for nothing back but a place she could call home. We were the only home Tita Norma had.

To my stepdad's argument, I overheard Tita Norma's defense for me. "Canadians. They don't know how to raise kids. Treating them like adults so fast, no wonder they leave the home so early. They don't give a child time to enjoy their childhood. Eight is just a child. He needs love, not responsibilities. What does he want Jun Jun to do, get a job?"

My wondering about my past finally came to an end one day, years later. I remember that morning, in the kitchen, when I confronted Mom.

"What's *anak sa labas*?" I demanded.

"Where did you hear that?" she asked.

"From Tita Norma's friends."

"How? What did they say about *anak sa labas*? Who did they say is *anak sa labas*?" My mom was in a panic.

"It doesn't matter who. What does it mean?" I pressed on. I was angry. I was all of fourteen years then and knew more about life.

"What were you and dad before I was born? Was I a bastard? Is that what *anak sa labas* means? It was me they were talking about, isn't it? I am the *anak sa labas*, isn't it?" I cried. I think I pushed Mom to the wall.

Tita Norma must have heard the noises in the kitchen, and stepped in.

"Lay off your mother, you little fool!" Tita Norma pulled me away and sat me on a chair. "Yes, you were *anak sa labas*," she began quietly. "Born out of wedlock, but only because your father could not divorce his wife. Your father chose you and your mother. Remember that. He chose you over his family. You were the ones he loved. And he did not hide it. He lived openly with your mother, and left his family. He suffered for it, but he stood by her, and by you. He loved you more than all of them, remember that."

"So I'm a bastard. That makes you a whore, doesn't it?" I said sadly to my mother. Tita Norma slapped me.

I walked away feeling somehow liberated, a thorn plucked from my heart, a feeling of relief, of knowing finally the truth about myself. So those stories about another family of del Mundos in Vancouver must be my father's other family. The legitimate one. I was the illegitimate one.

I stormed out of the house and walked towards nowhere and everywhere, oblivious to my surroundings. I crossed traffic. Cars honked at me. I didn't care. I walked through a park and got sprayed by kids playing with water guns. I sat on a bench and felt a warm liquid on my bum, fresh shit from seagulls. Damn. I sprinted, then jogged, and then walked slowly as I ran out of breath. I took off my shirt to feel the cold air on my skin. I felt like crying, hitting something, someone, my dead father, my lying mother. I wept. I saw a 7-Eleven store across the street. I bought a pack of Marlborough cigarettes. When the cashier turned his back to take a pack from the glass case behind the counter, I quickly snatched several M&M's. I stuffed them in my pocket as I fished out my wallet from the same pocket and paid the cashier for the cigarettes. I asked for matches. I tossed another quarter. I walked out calmly and sat back in the park bench. I never smoked before. I put one stick in my mouth, lit the end of it and inhaled. And coughed, and coughed.

"That's not how you do it," said a voice from behind. A guy about the same age as me sat beside me. He took the cigarette from my mouth, and put it in his own mouth. He inhaled, and then exhaled slowly through slightly opened lips, blowing out a thin stream of smoke.

"First time's always a pain," said the boy. "You'll get it fast. The trick is slow. Slow in, slow out, all through the mouth, not the nose. Try it," he said, giving the cigarette back to me.

I tried again, but I still coughed. I threw the cigarette on the grass and ground it up with my foot.

"That bad eh?" I looked at the boy, seeing him for the first time. A friendly white face. "Sorry. Having a bad day. Jun," I said, extending his hand.

"Nate." He shook my hand.

"It's not what it's cut up to be anyway," Nate continued, referring to the cigarette.

I tossed him the pack of Marlboro, "Have it. I never smoked before. Just throwing a tantrum."

"The M&M's part of the tantrum?" Nate asked.

I flushed. So Nate saw.

"No worries. I do that sometimes too," Nate said with a shrug.

We were silent. I didn't know why I said it, only that I felt a kinship with this person.

"I just found out that I'm a bastard. Illegitimate. Born out of wedlock. My mother stole my father away, and my father ran out on his family. They lived happily together and had me. Then he died. My mother remarried a professor bloke. Total square. But I think she carries on with a woman who I consider my real mother. That's my story."

"So? Is that it? What's so bad about your story? Sounds interesting! People would die to be a love child. And have two mothers," Nate said.

"Love child...hmmm... sounds nice," I pondered that. "Yeah, sounds nice. Love child is good," I smiled for the first time and nodded at Nate who was also smiling. We both laughed and high-fived.

"I'm gay," said Nate proudly, and laughed some more.

"No, seriously." I stopped dead in my tracks, shocked.

"Yeah. What's wrong with that? Just a sexual preference after all," Nate said.

"Uh...how did you know?" I asked.

"A classmate kissed me in the men's washroom, and I surprised myself by liking it, then kissing him back."

"Just like that?"

"Uhum..."

"I'm not...you know...not...gay," I said, feeling flustered.

Nate laughed. "Of course not. I'm not...after you," he added.

Then sensing my, embarrassment, Nate continued. "Not yet, anyway," and he laughed some more.

Sensing that it was all a joke, I finally laughed as well.

That was the start of a friendship that lasted many years, and which supported me through my teenage years of turmoil when it seems I rebelled against everything and everyone, until something happened that turned everything around.

* * *

I grew out the lankiness of my teen years, and by the time I was seventeen, I built up some muscles. I worked to get a well-built frame seeing I was only five foot four. I continued to carry a chip on my shoulders — the outsider chip. I took on the attitude of someone who did wrongs as an entitlement, for having been wronged myself. For this, I became even more disrespectful towards my mother, Tita Norma, and my stepfather. I launched into some kind of rebellion, against what, I'm not sure. My grades were not doing well at all. I came home late without telling where I was. I smoked. I did not talk about my friends or my activities. I was in my last year in high school. I didn't think I would pass, and didn't care. I had no idea what to do with my life, and they all nagged me about it, especially my stepdad.

One day, I saw my stepdad's wallet on the credenza amongst the keys. It was fat and bulging. I opened it. I've never seen so many hundred-dollar bills. I counted quickly. Three-thousand dollars. He would surely miss it. But hell. He has so much money anyway. I took it all.

I walked to the nearby 7-Eleven store thrilled with the fat wad of cash in my pocket. I killed time by reading the magazines on the racks. I liked the games magazine and thought I'd poach it. Just when I stuffed it inside my jacket, I felt a hand grip the arm that held the magazine.

"Can you come with me please?" said the man. He looked officious.

"Why, man? Who are you?" I asked.

The man gripped my arm tighter and whispered, "Do you want to come with me quietly or do you want to make a scene with all these people watching?"

"You're hurting me," I cried. People began to huddle around us.

An older fellow said, "What's going on here. You bullying this kid?"

"No sir, just catching him for shoplifting," said the man.

"No way man," I cried, trying to pull my arm away.

"See, here's the magazine he stole," said the man, opening my jacket revealing the rolled up magazine.

"Is this your store's magazine?" the man asked the cashier who has now joined the group.

"Yes, and he's not paid for it. Yup, he's the same one we've been suspecting all along."

The man turned me around and made me put my hands along the wall while he searched my other pockets. His hand came up with the thick wad of cash.

"Holy, man! Where'd this come from?" exclaimed the man. He rifled through it and whistled. "This must be at least three grand, even more. Check the till," said the man to the cashier.

"That's my money," I cried. "Give me back my money." But the man held my hands in a grip.

The cashier ran to the cash box and checked. "No, everything's here," he said.

"Where'd you get this money? Are you a drug dealer? Who did you steal it from?" said the man.

"I'm not a drug dealer. I didn't steal it. My dad gave it to me! He's rich, he gives me money!"

"Really? What's your name? What's your father's name?" the man growled.

"My name is Manuel del Mundo, Jr. My father is Dr. Victor Hellman, the famous science professor at UBC. He's my stepdad. My father's dead," I screamed the last sentence.

"Here, call my stepdad," I challenged the man, giving him my cell.

"And what, talk to your conspirator? Not so fast boy. Show me your ID," said the man.

I gave him my wallet and the man copied something from it. "Fancy address huh? Let's go and see if you're telling the truth," the man pushed me roughly towards the door.

"Pressing charges?" the man asked the cashier.

"I will if his story doesn't stick," said the cashier.

"And what if it does?" the man asked.

I did not hear what the cashier said. The man and I got into a car and sped away.

The man turned out to be a detective hired by the 7-Eleven store. I felt terrified throughout the whole trip, trying to figure out what could happen. My stepdad would surely know now of my stealing, and would have me charged. Three thousand is serious money to steal. But I am his stepson. Surely he will cover for me. But I also knew that my disciplinarian stepdad would gladly have me punished. My only hope was that mom or Tita Norma would be home and would cover for me. And if they were not, could I say that I only borrowed the money? For what? My thoughts were all jumbled up. I came up with the story that I borrowed the money to buy something for mom's birthday, as a surprise. Surely, my stepdad wouldn't mind that. But I realized my stepdad was no fool and would see through it so fast he might get even angrier and make the punishment worse.

I prayed fiercely for mom to be home. I promised God I would never steal again. I promised to be good and study and not talk back to my parents anymore. I promised I would even be a cop myself, to teach boys never to steal.

We had arrived, and the worst of my fears came true. Mom's car was not there. Of course, she was in the coffee shop with Tita Norma. Only my stepdad was home. He was not going to the University until his office was completely renovated, taking some time off for the time being. I did not want to step out of the car. I feared facing my stepdad's wrath alone. My stepdad would be right about everything, including giving me up for prison. What would happen to me now? I didn't relish the thought of prison. I was shaking with fear as the detective pulled me out of the car.

The detective rang the bell. Dad opened the door. One look at us, and it seemed he knew what was going on. I felt like a heel.

"I'm looking for Dr. Victor Hellman," said the detective.

"That's me."

"Is this your son, sir?"

"Yes, of course he is my son. What's going on here? Who are you?" My stepdad was indignant.

"Sir I'm a detective working for 7-Eleven stores where I caught your son shoplifting a magazine. When I looked into his pockets, I saw this," showing the wad of cash in his palm. "He says you gave it to him," said the man.

Right there and then, I fell on my knees crying, trying to explain between sobs. But I had the surprise of my life. My stepdad raised me up and said, "Of course I gave it to him. It's his graduation present from me. He is graduating in a month.

In fact, it's only an advance of his gift. Depending on the grades he gets, I will give him more. He is my son whom I love. Why would you even doubt his word?" he asked the detective.

"I'm...sorry sir. I didn't know...I wasn't sure..." said the detective.

"Why would he steal a magazine when he has so much money to pay for it? Are you sure you have the right boy, young man?" I couldn't believe my ears. I played along.

"I was going to pay for it before I left the store, but he held me right away, like a criminal," I said.

"I'm sure he was just doing his job, weren't you, detective? Even a great detective makes mistakes, yes?"

"Yes. I guess…He could have still paid for it before he left the store. I just saw him stick it in his jacket...and so I thought he...I'm really sorry sir. I didn't mean to..." stammered the detective.

"That's quite alright. Go now young man and thank you for bringing my son home," my stepdad said, waving the detective's apologies away.

When we were alone, I fell on my knees again before my stepdad. "I'm so sorry. I'll never do it again. Thank you so much. I don't deserve you," I cried, all crumpled up on the floor. I couldn't face him. "How can I make it up to you?"

Again, he raised me up. "Just promise me to be a good person, for your Mother's sake and mine, and to honour your father's memory. Will you do that, my son? Don't you know that I love you and cannot bear to see you in prison? I cannot even bear to tell your mother about this," he spoke with so much kindness, I cried again.

"I don't deserve your love. I promise to be good. You have my promise," I said.

"Now get your face in order, your mom will be arriving soon. You have my word, this is our secret," he said.

"Thank you Dad," I said, embracing him tightly, meaning every letter of that three letter word. I pushed the wad of cash into his hand. He closed my fingers over the money.

"Like I said, it is your graduation gift. Use it well my son," he said.

I cried even more, anguished sobs, tears of regret, pain and joy. "You won't regret it, Dad. Thank you. Thank you." I was beside myself. I was on my way to prison and a broken life, but instead, I had three thousand dollars and the inexplicable love of a father I scorned. I felt that the hand of God touched my life and I was never the same again.

* * *

CHAPTER 8

Canada
Manolita, 2010

In the hospital, I was utterly bored. I'd been a week in bed and on intravenous. I felt my energy trapped underneath the white sheets, the white-walled antiseptic room, the purified air laced with the hospital scents of disinfectant, drugs, rubber tubing, slept-in sheets, and urine. I wanted to get back to the real world — work — and to my many community projects.

"I feel fine," I insisted to my doctor, a 50-something gentleman of the old school who lavished so much attention on me, that Sonia and Bobby teased me about it.

"He's a bachelor they say, and is very picky. They've never seen him make so many visits to a patient," said Sonia.

"He could be my dad!" I protested.

"Precisely!" laughed Sonia and Bobby in unison.

Just then, a dark handsome man in a white gown with a stethoscope stuck in his pocket waltzed into the room smiling.

"How's my favourite patient this morning?" The doctor picked up the log at the foot of my bed and read it silently. He had wavy hair, mahogany skin, deep-set eyes, a high and slightly hooked nose and sharp-edged jaws. Dangerously dashing. The only giveaway to his age might have been the white streaks of hair on his sideburns, which made him look even more attractive. South American? Spanish perhaps, maybe Fijian, or Iranian? I wondered. Is he really fifty? He must be only forties. Mid-forties, max.

"Great and dying to rejoin the world, doc," I said with my most winsome smile. "I feel entirely overweight with all the food you've been stuffing me with. Got to run soon," I added, mimicking a jog.

"Not so fast, young lady. You look much better than a week ago sure, but your color is still pale, your eyes..."

"I haven't seen sunlight for a week, doc, why shouldn't I be pale?"

"Your body mass index is better than bordering emaciated when you came in, but it's still in the low underweight level. Everything you take in is through the tubes still. You walk five steps and you get dizzy and need a prop. You can hardly call that ready to return to real life, can you?" asserted the doctor, more seriously this time.

"Perhaps if my prison simulated real life a bit better, I could cope with real life faster? Say, a laptop for a start. A desk so I'm not always horizontal," I suggested.

"Sounds very much like an office to me, wouldn't you say?" said the doctor.

"Office is my real life, doctor."

"So it is. It's what made you sick. Running on blue smoke, hardly any sleep or food. You have to rest from all that. Give your body a break. Or it will break, as you have seen. Another week, and we'll see, alright?" He patted my hand.

"I'll go crazy, doc. A week more in this place, lying here. No way." I challenged and pleaded at the same time. "I'll escape."

"You could do that, and when we pick you up lying unconscious on a street somewhere, you will be returned not to this nice hospital but somewhere you would hate even more. Now be a nice girl and obey your doctor, and he will see how you are in a few days. How's that?" he said.

"Did you say two days?" I negotiated.

The doctor shook his head and sighed, "Alright, I'll see where you are in two days. You drive a hard bargain, young lady. I would not want to tangle with you."

"Tomorrow maybe?" I tried some more.

The doctor let that go with a finger wag. "Keep an eye on this one, will you?" he turned to Bobby who shook his hand.

"Thank you doc. I'm Bobby, her brother. And this is my sister, Sonia."

"Thank you so much, Dr. Madani," said Sonia, reading the name on his lapel.

"Just Armand would be fine," he smiled. Iranian then.

They shook hands all around, and the doctor left.

"You could try and not swoon all over him, you know," I told Sonia.

"Cute. Not so old, but old enough for you. Bright, professional, dark, wavy hair just like you know who. More to the point, single. Slobbering over you. What else do you want?" said Sonia. It was well acknowledged that being my father's favourite, I looked for my father in the men I fell for. My problems with food started when my parents separated, becoming significant when my father died. I always blamed the catering business and food for my parents' separation, the reason mom got so busy and neglected dad until he fell for another woman who paid more attention to him. I developed a phobia for food ever since dad's death. I reasoned that we really don't

Stumbling Through Paradise

need that much food to keep our bodies healthy. And I've too much to do to be bothered.

"I predict a month in the hospital," teased Bobby. "Engagement in the second month, wedding in the third. He's a great catch, sis, don't sleep on it too much. I'd say there's a line-up for him, or there should be," he added.

"No thanks. He's a dictator. I want someone I can twirl around my fingers, remember?" I said.

"Aren't you already doing that?" laughed Sonia.

The two days went by. I continued to stay in the hospital. My condition did not stabilize, as I kept trying to advance my healing prematurely. I walked to the garden, several floors down, and fell in a dizzy spell. In the TV room, I hung out chatting with people until so late to avoid dinners, then I flushed my food in the toilet to make it look like I ate it. My weight fluctuated, because I drank water just before weighing time. I snuck into the nurses' station and accessed the internet to email my friends. I found that even five minutes on the screen made me dizzy. I was found sprawled at the desk.

"What are you so driven about? What's your hurry?" asked the doctor. "Would you like to see a psychiatrist?"

"I just can't keep still here. I have to move. I'd rather move and fall than stay here doing nothing. TV's the pits. Books make me dizzy," I complained.

"How about books on tape? Or I could read to you," he offered seriously.

"Would you really?" I remembered the times when Dad read to me, but only after she sang for him.

The week went by fast with many reading sessions between the doctor and me. We read in the garden under the sun. He had a lamp brought in so we could read at night by a soft lamplight, and not the glaring fluorescent lamp on top of the bed. We talked.

We talked about his family. How they entered Canada as refugees from Iran. Their escape from Khomeini. His father was a businessman associated with the ruling elite and had to leave. Along with his mother and younger sister, he and his father left all their possessions in the middle of the night, smuggled in container trucks to Morocco, where plans got derailed. After more bribing, they somehow landed in Canada. Her mother fell ill along the way, and after a few days in Vancouver, she died of pneumonia. He was only fifteen then and very frightened.

I told him about my life in the Philippines, our arrival in Canada, my parents' difficulties settling in Canada. How my father couldn't get work as an engineer, and how my mother turned to catering to feed us, how our house smelled of food all day long. How busy my mother became, neglecting my father who turned to another woman for love. How my parents separated and how my father abandoned us, except he always saw me. How he died tragically over a broken heart from a failed career and how I will make up for him in Canada as a leader like Cory Aquino. How I blamed food for everything wrong in my life — that's why my problems with food. And that's why I was in a hurry to get elected, and could not be bothered with food.

After a week, I began to eat real food a little at a time. My body mass index rose to near normal levels, and the dizzy spells were gone. Somewhere in this time, I realized what a folly my law career at BCM was, deciding to give up my job there. What exactly I would do for a living, I was not sure yet, but that I would pick up on the volunteer work I had begun before I fell ill. I could ask Sonia's help for a job. Armand would help me with my health. I'd never had a relationship like the one with Armand. We had developed a deep bond that was beyond sex, but also beyond a platonic relationship. I only knew what I felt: that with him, everything would be all right.

* * *

I was pleased with how my respite in the hospital turned things around for my troublesome food problem and my health. More than that, I was thrilled with the relationship that formed between Armand and me, the healthiest romantic relationship I've ever had. Back at home from the hospital, Sonia and I had a talk, this time about her. It seemed that feeling healthy and loved made me care for other people now.

"How are you and Stephen doing?" I asked.

Sonia gave a naughty smile, and patted her belly.

"Another one?!" I hugged her. "You look exhausted. You should take a break from everything here and get yourself and Joy pampered by Mom and the *lolas* back home. Laugh. Enjoy yourself. Hang out with Tita Marites. She's fun. She'll ruin your seriousness. We'll look after things here," I snuggled up to Sonia. I realize how dearly I love my sister, how she looked after everyone.

"And Bobby?" she asked.

"Want me to continue watching his pee? Really, sis," I said.

"He has not been appearing. I haven't looked at his eyes, have you?"

"He's grown up, learned his lesson, or will never learn his lesson. Either way, you can't watch over him all his life. You need to look after yourself. I haven't seen you laugh for a long time. And now that another one is on the way, you have to be more careful and be more fun! Nicole seems to be happy,

Sarina's wonderful, Bekang is working out well with them, and Bobby seems to be doing well. I'll look in on them from time to time. How's that?" I offered.

"And Uncle Eddie?" she asked. Uncle Eddie, mom's younger brother, was successfully accepted into Canada in business class as a skilled immigrant. He was living with Tito Mario and Tita Ching in Surrey and often stayed with me in the Vancouver house when looking after mom's businesses.

"I'll look in on him too. He's doing well on that small business course he's taking. He's gung ho on this shoe importing business, and he's moving fast on it. He met with the Philippine consul staff and they gave him info on establishing the business from the Philippine side."

"I'm worried that he may be lonely, missing his wife and their kids," said Sonia.

"He has classes in the mornings, then works part time at the Bay shoe department in the afternoon. He is busy. He has coworkers and classmates to socialize with. Tito Mario and Tita Ching, Bobby and Nicole, Sarina, Bekang and I — we're all here. Uncle Eddie's happy. Don't worry," I said.

"Yes, I'm very happy here," said Uncle Eddie, walking into the dining room. He gave Sonia and me a hug. "You girls should stop worrying about me. I'm having the time of my life in Paradise," he announced, taking his coat and hat off and sprawling on a chair. "What else do I want? I have a job. I'm building up my business with the help of experts, for free. Wow, Canada is really a great country!"

The phone rang. It was Tita Ching. Sonia picked up the phone. She nodded.

"Crispy *pata* expert, right?" she said. Pause. "Yeah, I know. High school at Tupper Secondary. He's with the ICC youth program, coaching one of our junior basketball teams. Why, what's wrong with him?" Sonia looked worried.

"What's the hospital?" she asked. A pause. "We'll be there!"

"What's that about?" I asked.

"You remember Tita Rose, the one who cooks for mom? Tita Rose's son, Jay, remember him? Jay and his friends were attacked by a gang of South Asian boys just outside Tupper Secondary. His head is badly beat up. In critical condition in the hospital. Tita Rose is crazy upset. Let's go."

I called Armand quickly, left him a message, and asked him to join me as soon as he can.

* * *

When we arrived at St Paul's Hospital, the emergency lobby was already filled with Filipinos: classmates of Jay, parents of classmates, and friends. Some girls were crying. Tita Rose, all one hundred sixty pounds of her, sat on a chair, a lost panicked look on her face, her eyes red and swollen. People surrounded her: one holding her hand, another fanning her, still another massaging her neck.

"Can I request some people to stay outside, please? It's getting too hot and crowded here. We'll let you know as soon as there's news of your friend," said a nurse.

No one moved. No one wanted to move.

The nurse approached Tita Rose. "Could you please speak to your friends?" she asked. Tita Rose stared back with a blank look. Tita Ching entered the lobby from the corridor and took control. She led the people closest to the doors outside, keeping them moving while she held the door open. To the guests, she said, "Thank you. Don't worry, we'll rotate." She walked back to the nurse and apologized for the crowd. Tita

Ching pulled Sonia to the side. I approached Tita Rose and embraced her. "I'm so sorry Tita."

"Manolita, is it you? Thank you for coming." Tita Rose started crying. I held her close until her sobs subsided. "How is he?" I asked.

Tita Rose started crying again. When she stopped, she shook her head. "We don't know. He's such a good boy. He's never in trouble. In fact, he was only accompanying his younger brother home. They were walking at the tail end of a group of Filipino boys who it turns out were a gang. The South Asian gang must have thought he was part of the Filipino gang. He didn't know there was a gang fight on between the South Asians and the Filipinos. They hit him with a broken bottle. He fought so hard. Several ganged up on him and hit him everywhere, and then they fled. My little one got help and that's how we found out. He was all bloodied." Tita Rose was becoming angry as she cried. "He was helpless. They ganged up on him. Those brutes should be hanged!" she cried half screaming, half crying.

I held her, hushed her. I whispered, "We'll find those boys, don't worry. They won't get away with it. How long before Jay got to the hospital?"

"I don't know. Fifteen, twenty minutes, thirty maybe?" said Tita Rose.

I froze. Too long.

Someone dressed in a blue gown came out of the swing doors of the operation room. He removed his mask and asked for Mrs. Ramos. Tita Rose stood up.

"I'm sorry, Mrs. Ramos. Your son…he's gone. He bled too much by the time he got here. It was for the better. If he lived, he would be a vegetable for life. Part of his brain was completely demolished. At least he did not suffer much."

Tita Rose's face crumpled up, and a high hysterical scream came out from her mouth. She lost her balance. I was the closest to Tita Rose, and I fell underneath her, almost suffocating underneath her solid weight. Hands lifted Tita Rose from the floor. I slowly got up to see the weeping and wailing in the emergency lobby. It seemed everyone was crying, if not on someone's shoulder, then against the walls, into their handkerchiefs, or their coats. I sat up, shocked by the suddenness of death. He's only a boy. He was only fetching his brother, taking him home. It's not fair. He wasn't even involved. How could boys do this to each other? Tita Rose had now fainted, and people were busy trying to revive her. I stood up, and let myself be led away by hands that it turns out belonged to Armand who had now arrived, leading me out to the open air.

When things had calmed down, a funeral was arranged. The school got involved, as well as Immigrant Communities Collective. Jay was a well-liked boy. Tita Rose alternated between grief and anger. Her caregiver friends came in full support, including Caring for Caregivers Society.

The Vancouver Police were on the case. Among the Vancouver Police who came to Tita Rosie's house to meet with Jay's friends was a young Filipino officer, by the name of Manuel del Mundo Jr. Sonia and I couldn't believe how much he looked like Dad. We didn't know he had now become a police officer.

Sonia approached the good-looking young officer. "Jun Jun, do you remember me?"

"Of course I do, Tita. And I still have the transformer you gave me," he smiled. A dimple appeared on his right cheek, making his face even more handsome. His hair was wavy and jet-black like Dad's. He seemed like such a boy, only a few inches above five feet, short in comparison with the other police officers. Sonia's eyes smarted. What a sweet young man Jun Jun had become. Dad would be proud.

"When did you become a police officer?" asked Sonia.

"Just this year, in fact this is my first assignment. They put me on it because, well, I'm Filipino."

"Do you speak Tagalog?" asked Sonia.

"*Konti lang,*" Jun Jun said shyly.

"A little is better than nothing," Sonia smiled at him warmly. "You probably don't know…this is Manolita…our…"

"I know. You're my Dad's favourite," he addressed me.

"And you're his spitting image," I said, a lump forming in my throat.

We looked at each other not knowing what to say.

Someone called for Constable del Mundo, and Jun Jun moved to go.

"Listen, we should get together soon, ok? " Sonia pressed.

"We need to talk. Come and have dinner," I echoed.

"I'd like that," he said, giving Sonia his calling card. "Got to go, Tita." he said and walked away. My brother, my half-brother. The same city, yet so far apart. I felt like I met the ghost of my long dead father.

Sonia still looked stunned. "My God, he's like Dad as I remember him."

"Manolita, you look like you just saw a ghost," said Tita Ching.

"You could say that. I'll tell you later," I said, realizing how many people were in the room.

The Vancouver Police officers met with Jay's friends, classmates, and known members of the Filipino gang for leads. They said they might begin to round up some suspects. Rose asked me to be the family's link on the criminal charges. I was pleased to be able to see Jun Jun more.

The Filipino community was greatly concerned. Filipino leaders offered to raise funds for the funeral, which Rose greatly appreciated. Media sought stories about the tragedy. Racism was blamed as the cause, which led to violence among ethnic groups. It was so clear in this case they said, referring to South Asian boys versus Filipino boys. "Canada prides itself in being a model of multicultural harmony, and this is what happens in Vancouver?" cried the newspaper articles. There were so many requests for interviews by media that I advised the family to hold a media conference, prepare a statement, answer questions, and give a select number of interviews afterwards. Do it all in one go. Raise the spectre of racism, make people aware of the problem, and fire up Canadians to do something about it.

That evening, Sonia and I told the whole family about meeting Jun Jun and proposed a dinner. Everybody agreed except Bobby.

"Bobby, it's not his fault," I said.

Nicole agreed.

"You can all meet with him if you like, but I'm not coming," said Bobby.

"We're inviting only him, not Carla," Sonia said.

"Suit yourself. I won't be there," said Bobby, his face reddening.

It was decided to propose a dinner close to thanksgiving, after Jay's funeral. Sonia would invite Jun Jun to dinner at the Vancouver house. Sonia would also phone mom to let her know.

The media conference was well attended. CBC TV covered it nationally, so did *Globe and Mail*, and the *Post*. Community papers of different cultures wrote articles decrying the racism in multicultural Canada. Because of the wide coverage, the funeral drew thousands of people. Ministers of the federal and provincial governments, Vancouver school board officials and the City representatives attended the funeral, with cards and flowers. Youth from Tupper School came. Leaders of the Filipino, South Asian and multicultural communities came in solidarity. Tita Rose was silent in grief. She didn't want to meet with politicians or community leaders or police or media. She only wanted justice for her boy.

The day after the funeral, I hosted a roundtable with community leaders of different cultures who came to the funeral, and political leaders who expressed interest in the issue. The Ministers of Justice, Multiculturalism, and Heritage Canada came. The Vancouver Deputy Chief of Police, the Vancouver School Board trustees, and several Vancouver Members of Parliament and Members of the Legislature came. "What can we do to prevent this from happening again?" was the question I posed. It was a sombre meeting that went for two hours. It led to the creation of a Committee Against Racism that would push for reform on many fronts: in school, in communities, in policing, in federal and provincial programs. I became its chair. ICC became the community host for the Committee, and a wide ranging anti-racism program of action was developed that would span several years involving multiple stakeholders. Criminal charges were laid against two South Asian youth.

* * *

The del Mundo dinner was held the weekend after Jay Ramos' funeral and the Anti-Racism Roundtable.

Preparations for the dinner were elaborate, a homecoming for a lost relative.

In the days preceding, we all seemed to get lost in the past, remembering Dad in our own ways.

Tito Mario relived his childhood with Dad. He wondered what kind of life Dad would have had if he did not sponsor Dad and us to Canada. He always felt a sense of guilt over Dad and Mom's separation, and Dad's tragic end.

Sonia felt guilty about neglecting to connect with Jun Jun all this time. "I've been dreaming of Dad everyday since we met Jun Jun. This time, he flashed a police badge in lieu of an injection needle. That must have been about Jun Jun. To find him among the police."

Mom was remarkably happy about it and encouraged the reconciliation, which she saw as part of divine forgiveness finally happening for her.

I felt excited about having a sibling younger than me, although I must admit to feeling somewhat jealous of him. If Dad was alive, would Jun Jun be his favourite? Did Jun Jun feel jealous of her, that she lived to be his favourite, while he never had him for a father? I liked him as a police officer. His remarks at the Roundtable were thoughtful and sensitive.

Bobby was uncommunicative about the whole matter. He left when the subject came up, as it did over and over again. "Why are you all obsessed with him anyway? His mother is why we have a broken family. He is the product of that woman and our philandering father. We grew up without a father, and Mom and I had to work doubly hard for us…because of them!" Bobby blurted out one night.

Uncle Eddie had a lot of reservations. Why is everybody keen to meet his sister's husband's son out of wedlock? He was not sure he wanted to meet this young man. It was like encouraging the whole illicit relationship that caused so much sadness to his sister.

Bekang was so excited to meet the 'secret of the family.' She brought along her Canadian husband, a businessman who was about 20 years her senior. They were happily married and now lived in a ritzy part of South Vancouver. Her mother Ate Pining lived with them, and two of her siblings were already in Canada.

Joy was thrilled to have another uncle, even if it was just a half uncle.

Sarina, Bobby's daughter, twenty years old and a ballerina, was troubled by the revelations. She knew her dad's parents had split, but didn't know that his grandfather died from a heart attack trying to shoot her dad, ostensibly because her dad dealt drugs. She was still thinking of the talk she had with her mom and her aunts about it.

"That was a long time ago, and he did only a bit of drugs to help ends meet,' I insisted.

"He doesn't do it now," confirmed Sonia.

"Why is he coming forward now, this half-uncle? And why wasn't he around before?" asked the confused Sarina.

"Just purely accidental that we stumbled upon each other. He's the police officer investigating the racial killing of this Filipino boy who is a family friend of ours," said Sonia.

"And why wasn't he around before in our lives?" Sarina repeated.

"I don't know. Better that way, perhaps, less complicated? Your dad felt bad about the whole thing. He didn't want to be reminded of our dad's betrayal, our suffering, his sacrifice to support us through those times. Then being attacked like that in the end. He's a good man, your dad, the best brother. We respected his wishes," said Sonia.

"My dad doesn't want this half-uncle. So why are we accepting him now?" Sarina cried.

"Because it's not his fault, is it?" I said. "It was never his fault, and now he's a grown man, and we're all grown from those sad times. And sometimes we have to let go of old hurts. He's a kind man, this half-uncle of yours, you'll see. He's just a year older than you I think. You'll like him."

Sarina turned to her mother. "And what about Dad?"

"I don't know sweetheart,' said Nicole. "But maybe this young man, if he's so nice, might melt your dad's hurt away."

* * *

CHAPTER 9

Canada
Jun Jun, 2011

I did not tell Mom about meeting the del Mundos. I know she no longer cared to connect with them, mostly because of the continuing toxic influence of Tita Norma. I love her, but she has such a negative presence. I was never really sure if Tita Norma and mom's relationship was more than what it appeared, and sensed that Dad also wondered. But if he did, he made no issue of it. Since Dad covered for my theft, I believed him to be a saint. Yes, he could have known and just accepted. I cherished him as my own father. I'm sure he wouldn't mind my getting along with the del Mundos. I was always curious about my deceased father's family and watched them from a distance. I was as surprised as they when we met. I was eager to meet them all at dinner. I'll decide what to tell my own family depending on how the dinner goes.

* * *

I came to dinner without my uniform. I wanted to look myself, without the veneer of authority. I wanted to be ordinary, approachable.

"What are you staring at?" I asked Manolita who greeted me at the door. "Do I look strange without my uniform? Sometimes, I feel naked without it. Oops, sorry, no offense."

"Oh no. It's just you look even more like Dad without your uniform," she said. Manolita took my arm and led me into the rom. "I'll introduce you around. Are you nervous?"

"No. Well, a little, yes." She squeezed my arm.

"This is Tito Mario, Dad's brother. He's the reason we're all here. Our sponsor." I took his hand to my forehead in the Filipino sign of respect, the *mano*. Tito Mario just stood there looking at me, his eyes moistening. Then he embraced me in a long bear hug. "*Hijo*, you look so like your father. He would be so proud."

Next was a pretty young girl and a stunningly beautiful woman who was unmistakably the young girl's mother. The young girl turned out to be Sarina and her mother was Nicole. This is Bobby's family. I feel excited about meeting my half-brother. To Sarina, I said, "Then you're my half-niece, I guess?" Manolita nodded. "Wow, I didn't know I had the most beautiful niece in the world." Sarina looked flustered.

"Sorry, I'm just...it's...I didn't mean to embarrass you. Where's your dad?" I asked.

It was Manolita who replied, "Bobby's detained by business."

Sarina kept her distance. Maybe she doesn't like me.

When I was introduced to Tita Lily, I made *mano*, and asked: "Tita, how are we related again?"

Manolita explained how Tita Lily was mom's first and best friend in Canada. "How is Tita Josie, Tita?" "She is very well *hijo*. She wanted to be here. Maybe next time she comes to visit Vancouver," offered Tita Lily. "I'd like that. She must be a remarkable woman," I said. "She is, and more," Tita Lily seemed like she wanted to say more, but Manolita moved me on to the next couple.

"Are you really a policeman? You're too young! And too good looking!" said the next woman. I liked her right away. Her name was Becky, formerly Bekang, I'm told.

"Turning twenty-one, Tita, and feeling like an old man. I have to fight with my mom to live on my own," I chuckled.

"Have a girlfriend, or several maybe?" Becky teased.

I paused, then decided on the simple way, "A boyfriend. We live together."

Becky's jaw fell. Manolita pulled me away. "Really?" She was surprised, but not alarmed.

"Yes," I said. "Are you offended?"

"Not at all," Manolita said. "You should bring him along next time." I really liked my half-sister even more. She moved me to the next person.

"This is Uncle Eddie, Mom's brother. He recently arrived in Vancouver," Manolita said.

After the *mano*, I offered, "I hope you're liking Vancouver, Uncle? If there's anything I can do to orient you around the city, just let me know. I know the neighborhoods well."

"It's ok, you're busy enough with your work. Must be dangerous," said Uncle Eddie.

"Mostly not at all," I replied. "Not where I'm currently assigned anyway — community relations. It's more like PR for the police."

"Is there not enough crime for the police? What does PR do?" asked Uncle Eddie.

"Some big cases cause a lot of community concern, like for example Jay Ramos' death, what seems like a racial killing. Or a rape murder, or major drugs. The Police assign someone to keep the lines of communication open to the community, and to report on the progress of the case, to allay fears," I explained.

"And how is Jay's case coming? Have they caught the murderers yet?" asked Becky.

"Yes, two South Asian youth have been charged," I said.

"Those *Bumbays* are such trouble makers, not to be trusted," Becky shivered.

"Actually, most South Asians are okay. Just a few bad apples tainting the whole community," I said.

"Our *Pinoy* boys should fight back, *para naman silang inaapi*. I didn't know that *Pinoys* are discriminated against in Canada," Uncle Eddie shot back.

"It's just an isolated case of gang violence, not racial discrimination against all Filipinos," I said.

"It's not as clear-cut as that," said Stephen. "One of Jay's friends said he heard one of the boys who attacked them say..."

"Dinner's just about ready," announced Sonia, breaking the conversation, which was turning serious. She gave a chastising look towards Stephen.

Tita Ching described the dishes on the buffet table.

"Do you eat Filipino food?" she asked me.

"Always," I said. "May I?" I picked up a crispy piece of pork skin from Tita Ching's *lechon kawali*, dipped it in the garlic vinegar sauce, and dropped it in my mouth. "Uhm... my favourite, Tita. Delicious!" Tita Ching smiled with her eyes which I noticed were wet.

The dinner went well. Everybody ate and chatted happily away. Until little Joy, seated way down the table, asked Sonia loudly, "How is he my Uncle again, Mom?" The conversations around the table stopped. An uneasy silence filled the room.

"I'm your mom's half-brother," I replied, in a light friendly tone.

"And what's a half-brother again?" Joy asked, as she licked her spoon.

"It's when you have the same dad, but not the same mom. It happens when two people who love each other have a baby, and then they change. And say the dad loves someone else and has a baby by that someone else, that second baby is the half-brother of the first baby. The two babies have the same dad, but different moms," I explained as though it happened every day.

"So you're the second baby, and my mom's the first baby?" confirmed Joy.

"Uhum," I said.

"My mom and Tita Manolita and Tito Bobby have the same dad as you, but have a different mom from yours. That's why you're only a half-uncle and not a full uncle!" exclaimed Joy.

"You're scary smart, did you know that?" I said.

"I know. Where's your mom? Why didn't you bring her?" asked Joy.

"She's out of town," I said, lying.

"Then she would be my half-grandmother?" asked Joy.

"Well…in a way…" I started to say.

"By the way, you're all invited to my ballet performance next weekend. Who's coming? I'll save tickets," said Sarina, diverting the attention away from the awkwardness. I caught a pleased smile on Sonia's face. I would be proud too to have a niece like that, so young and already wise.

* * *

As I drove myself home, I wondered how mom and Tita Norma could say despicable things about the del Mundos. I felt very welcome, and genuinely liked by them. I liked everyone I met. I told Nate all about the dinner that night. We discussed whether I should tell my family.

"Do they really need to know about this?" asked Nate. Nate and I became close friends since we met outside the 7-Eleven store the day I discovered that I was an illegitimate child. Slowly, and almost naturally, we became lovers. As our friendship and intimacy progressed through the years, the sexual intimacy that followed seemed so natural. When Nate kissed me one night returning from a party, I knew that more than the drinks made me return that kiss. I didn't feel it was wrong, perhaps because growing up, I thought my own mother and Tita Norma had an intimate relationship as well. My family was shocked when I announced Nate and my relationship, and that we were moving in together. Mom and Tita Norma vehemently denied they had an intimate relationship, which was a surprise to me. Things settled down. My stepdad's example of accepting Nate and me held sway in our house. Also, Nate's openness about being gay, his confidence about it, helped me carry the relationship openly as well. It helped that Nate was a famous journalist on TV. The Vancouver Police knew nothing about it, and I didn't think that would be an issue. And if they did make it an issue, I'll think up of some other work to do.

"No, but I think it will be good for mom. She will feel like she's been accepted and forgiven. It'll neutralize Tita Norma's constant griping against them. Now they are recognizing me, us. It would make both my dads happy that my other family is opening to me," I said.

"How's the brother?" asked Nate.

"Bobby. Not there. Nice wife, great kid."

"What are you going to do?"

"Nothing. I don't have to do anything."

"He caused your Dad's death."

"That's what Tita Norma says. Mom doesn't want to talk about it. Maybe I'll find out from them, later, maybe Manolita will tell me. I like her. She even told me to take you along next time."

"Really? That redneck? Wasn't she the one who turned from Liberal to Conservative? Then withdrew after being booed by her riding?" asked Nate.

"She doesn't sound like a redneck at all to me. You guys give her a bad rap," I said.

"We'll see. Elections next year, I hear she's being wooed. Let's see what party she turns up with this time."

"Lay off my sis will you?"

"Sis now, is it? You're a del Mundo now I see. Better be careful what I say," Nate chuckled, taking me in his arms.

* * *

"Now that he's a successful police officer, they recognize him," said Tita Norma bitterly.

Tita Norma managed the coffee shop Mom owned, a remnant of the karaoke bar. The one addition Tita Norma made was to bring in *barako* coffee with *ensaimada* or other pastry freshly baked by Mom when she felt in the mood to bake. Mom toyed with her coffee, absentmindedly putting in several spoonfuls of sugar. Tita Norma took away Mom's cup and made her a new one. I liked to drop in for *barako* coffee and see Mom on my breaks.

"Everyone was nice to me," I said, sipping my cup of *barako*.

"Including Bobby? I can't believe that," said Tita Norma.

"Bobby wasn't there," Mom reminded her.

"I hear the big Don is ill. Let's see how well they recognize Jun Jun in the will," challenged Norma.

"What does he need that inheritance for? Victor will look after him. He loves Jun Jun like his own," said Mom.

"Does he? Now that Jun Jun's own family is coming forward to recognize him, Victor may just wake up and give everything to his own daughter. I would if I were him," said Tita Norma.

Mom looked thoughtful.

"Josie, was she there?

When I shook my head, she continued. "You realize it was Josie who introduced Victor and me? Josie whose husband I stole? Josie supported us during the days when Manuel died and we had no one. How generous she was. I would not have done the same." She watched Norma slicing the *ensaimada*, always looking after her every need.

Mom took my hand. "How lucky I am. So many people loved me. If my first husband could only see me now. Your *lola*, our neighbors in the old village. If they could see you so handsome, and your stepdad, a famous professor. But why am I not happy? I should be happy."

"Yes, you should be. You're just missing Manuel. Eat your ensaimada," said Tita Norma with a scowl.

Momentarily, Tita Norma brightened. "Why doesn't Jun Jun go and visit the del Mundos in the Philippines? If the del Mundos here like him, they'll agree, and Jun Jun will probably charm the old man. That should remind him to recognize him in the will."

"I don't know. Maybe. Depends. What do you think Jun Jun?" Mom asked.

I didn't reply. It was too hard thinking about wills when I can't even get my head around a new set of grandparents in the Philippines, a whole new past opening up to me, the whole life of my dead father coming alive.

"What's the matter with you, Carla? You should look after your son's future better, you know," said Tita Norma. The bell by the door rang, signaling a customer. Tita Norma went to attend to business.

* * *

CHAPTER 10

Canada
Manolita, 2011–2015

In the months that followed, it wasn't clear what the bigger gossip in our del Mundo family was: that Jun Jun was a nice handsome police officer who was very much his father's likeness, a del Mundo through and through, or that he was gay, and openly at that.

Uncle Eddie thought it was very funny. He wickedly said, *"Bakla lang pala,"* meaning 'just a homosexual after all'. Sonia pinched him. 'Okay, okay," said Uncle Eddie.

Everyone agreed that Jun Jun should be included in the family, except Bobby who simply refused to talk about the matter any further. He made it clear to everyone that 'it was either him or me.'

Tito Mario cautioned the family about rushing into things. "Think of what Manuel would have wanted for Jun Jun," he confessed. "The Manuel I knew would not have wanted him too close to our father, and his wife."

"But that was so long ago. And you, do you feel the same way?" asked Tita Ching.

"The whole accident has faded, as my mom's face. Our life here has made me forget. I don't know if I have forgiven Dad, we're all getting old. He may die soon. Manuel didn't have it too good here, and carried the hate deeper. Maybe if he lived longer, became happier, he would forgive and let Jun Jun meet Dad," said Tito Mario.

"Manuel's dead. What's the point in second-guessing a dead man's intentions? If Jun Jun wants to meet his family, and if his grandfather wants to meet him, why should we deny them? Point is, do you think it'll be good for the family?" asked Tita Ching.

"I don't know. It's Bobby I worry about, losing him if we accept Jun Jun wholeheartedly like everyone seems to want. He's still hurting from Manuel's betrayal of the family, and Manuel's attacking him. He's still fighting with Manuel's ghost and Jun Jun is a perfect stand-in for Manuel. If we accept Jun Jun, then we side with Manuel and against Bobby. That's how Bobby sees it," Tito Mario explained.

"I never see him. How is he anyway?"

"I don't know. Getting rich I hear. I know how he feels, anything to escape the hurt and anger. That's how I felt when I found out about my Dad. That's why I left the Philippines. That's why Manuel left too. Bobby's trying to escape his own father. Who would have thought Manuel's son would also deny him?"

"Don't you think it's time to break the cycle of hate in this family?" asked Tita Ching.

She received no answer.

"The thing is, try as I might, I can't see my mother's face anymore," Tito Mario said.

But I could see my father's face very clearly — it was the face of Jun Jun.

* * *

Sonia followed my suggestion and took a long vacation to the Philippines. She had many missions: visit the ailing Lolo Ben, get Joy and her pampered, visit with Mom, and bring the news of Jun Jun. Lolo Ben had recovered from the heart attack and was taking it easy, relaxing at home. From the Philippines, Sonia wrote me this.

Dear Sis,

Mom advises caution. She says even if only Bobby is against it, we should not do it. She says while she'd love a reconciliation of Jun Jun with the del Mundos, Bobby has to be first. She says Bobby's not ready and we need to stand by him. Lolo and Lola want to meet Jun Jun, and Tita Marites too. Even if they know Bobby's opposed. Do you know that Bobby said he will stop doing business with Lolo if he meets with Jun Jun? Lolo said nothing. I think Lolo too needs to be forgiven now. For that affair with Lola, and causing the accidental death of Dad's mother. Mom said, don't we all need to be forgiven?

I visited Pililla and remembered Lola Iska. I sat by the stream in the backfields, remembering the feeling of Lola Iska's unconditional love. I wished it for Bobby. I felt such a sadness come over me, and pain, for the loss of Lola Iska, my childhood, and the tragedy of Dad and Bobby. Then a soft breeze blew over me. I smelled Lola Iska's black cigarette. I felt the wind brushing my hair and my back, like she used to. I felt better, thinking of my blessings: mom, you, Stephen and my now loving in-laws, the wonderful second generation del Mundos, the return of Jun Jun, Bekang and Uncle Eddie leading better lives in Canada. I felt Lola Iska's scent envelope us all like a warm blanket of love.

I miss you and am amazed at how well you turned out. Dad would be so proud.

Luv u,
Sonia

* * *

I gave up my job at BCM, and felt better for it. My colleagues gave me a rousing send off, extracting a promise that I would invite them all to my inauguration as Prime Minister. I agreed heartily on condition that each of them would raise funds for my campaign. Someone cheekily said he would raise a thousand, if he was appointed to the Senate. Another promised another thousand for the Chief Justice position, and still another promised ten dollars if he was given the post of Ambassador to TukTuyaktuk. I will miss my friends.

I threw myself into community activities. I enjoyed it so much that I felt content not running for politics if the opportunity did not present itself. I had some savings and few financial obligations. I was living in the family home and had little housing costs. I felt free as a bird to do only what I wanted. And I was in love with Armand. I was eating regularly. It was probably one of the happiest times of my life.

I helped create a political apprenticeship program for the Maple Bamboo civic engagement program, which was drawing a great deal of interest. I was close to securing a commitment for 10 new internship positions for Internationally Trained Physicians to practice medicine in Canada, valued at $10 million. The women lawyers group held an international conference of women lawyers showcasing what law companies around the world did for equal opportunity for women lawyers. I was making waves in the community about Canada's hidden secret — racism — advocating for wide-ranging changes in schools, government, neighborhoods, to encourage people to mix it up with other cultures, including the old fashioned welcome wagons for new neighbors, and ethnic street potlucks. I took the position that ethnic youth gang crimes should be met with the severest punishment possible.

It was September 2014 and candidates for federal Members of Parliament were lining up for the 2015 elections. I was approached by all three parties to run for them — 'the right-of-centre' Conservatives, the 'middle-of-the-road' Liberals and the 'left-of-centre' NDP. In fact, I felt too busy, enjoying what I was doing that I didn't want to run for office. Besides, I was done with political parties, so much kowtowing to the party line. I could not support all the positions of any single party. What reasonably fair-minded person could do that? Very few ever ran federally as an independent, and succeeded. I put it out of my mind.

The sentencing trial of Jay Ramos' assailants was more important. It was taking longer than anticipated. Filipinos were anxious about what kind of sentence would be given the two youth who murdered Jay. I was concerned for the fallout if the sentence was light. The two youth pleaded guilty to manslaughter, but they heard that the defense organized the plea just to get a lighter sentence. They said 'two years in prison, max five, if we're lucky,' based on the age of the perpetrators.

"It's not fair," cried Tita Rose. "Two years in prison for taking the life of my son? He was minding his own business. They swarmed him. For no reason other than his race. He was helpless. What kind of justice is this?" Tita Rose cried on my shoulders after a meeting with the lawyers.

"There's nothing we can do," I said. "The Youth Offenders Act limits the sentencing of youth under seventeen who commit crimes. The youth involved were sixteen when the crime occurred."

"Why can't you do anything?" asked Tita Rose with angry tears. "You can run for MP and change that law, couldn't you? Isn't that what politicians are for, to change the law for the better? Shouldn't our children be able to go to school and live in peace and safety without having to fight off racism against them? Shouldn't Canada teach these brutes a lesson that you can't do that in Canada?"

I held Rose's trembling hands. Rose snatched her hands away. "I should just go back to the Philippines, and take my boy along," she said. I couldn't really blame her for feeling that way.

In the days that followed, the Filipino community pressed upon me to run for office, "to make sure what happened to Jay does not happen again". Ethnic community leaders urged me to run as "the systemic discrimination against skilled immigrants needs to be stopped". Canada's multiculturalism was a mere tokenism, they said. "It's time to expose racism so we can wipe it out" they said. "Punish young criminals like the criminals they are." They wanted a change to the Young Offenders Act. My friends among the women lawyers and women corporate leaders said I must run "to provide a successful role model for women". Business leaders said, "A safe community, and a continuing immigrant labour force are needed for economic growth in Canada," and supported me as a "voice of reason" for these issues.

Could I run for Member of Parliament as an independent and win?

"You'd have to oppose each of the three parties in order to justify running independently, or they'd consider you a flake," said a friend with a long history in political campaigns.

"That's a lot of work and money. Why independent? Why not go for the one closest to your leanings? Nothing is perfect," he insisted.

I'm tired of the way people do politics. I don't want to play like that. People want change, and those changes cross the political lines — so why can't I just run on those issues? If it were Vancouver Kingsway, I'd only have to convince 80,000 electors, not the whole country. I began to seriously consider the option. Jay Ramos lived in this riding, and the school where he was killed is also in this riding. In this riding, immigrants comprise almost sixty percent of the population, the second highest ethnic group being Filipinos, after the Chinese. They all suggested I run in this riding, one that flip-flopped between the NDP and the Liberals in the past.

A new riding was being carved up amongst several ridings including Vancouver Kingsway, that would take its western-most portion, including the area of Jay's school, and the side that voted least NDP and more Liberal. That new riding, called Vancouver Granville, would take the southern portion of Vancouver Centre, and the eastern portion of Vancouver Quadra, and end up being perhaps the most mixed of all Vancouver ridings supporting conservative and progressive elements, with business and professional interests, youth in schools, immigrants and established communities. The new riding intrigued me. Perhaps they are the cross section of the Canada I hoped for, a diverse, but blended, not ghettoized community. I felt I was supporting issues that were of concern to enough of them, that I might have a chance of winning. I had a diverse base of support and had earned enough name recognition in the community on my own, some of it controversial, but the most recent activities gave me positive profile.

"Why are you running for office as independent, *anak*?" asked Mom, who flew in to Vancouver when I described my dilemma.

Anak. My child. She never called me that before.

"Did you really call me *anak*?" I asked, squinting my nose to my mom.

"Yes, why not? You're my child." She smiled.

"It just feels strange...you never called me that. Anyway, I'm running for office as independent because I feel I can help the community best as an independent MP, going with what the community needs, or what I feel is reasonable, and not what the party line requires," I answered.

"That's good. If you don't win, how would you feel?"

"That I did my best for the people who wanted me to help them. It means I need to find other ways to help them."

"Good. You have a genuine purpose to serve. With that, you may lose the election, but you can never truly lose. You always win with that purpose. I'm proud of you."

I liked that. I never thought of it that way.

"How about you, Mom, why did you run for Mayor, in Pililla of all places?"

"I could only ever run for office in Pililla. It's the only place I truly cared about."

"Even if we were all here in Canada?" I asked.

I could see that stung.

"Are you angry at me for leaving you?" Mom asked.

"A little, yes." Silence. "But mostly for not taking Dad back."

"I know. I was too proud. But I couldn't stomach it. He basically wanted to be with us, and her!" Mom paused to let her sudden anger subside. She looked away, and continued. "I loved him. Couldn't love anyone else after him."

Mom took my hand. "Can you forgive me for driving your father away from you?"

I didn't answer.

"Why were you so distant to me? You only ever loved Bobby and Sonia." I found what I really wanted to say.

"I was afraid you blamed me for losing your dad, and I was afraid to face you. You're so brilliant, beautiful and talented — I felt insecure with you. I felt your dad loved you more than me." Mom looked away again. "He gave me up, but you he fought for."

I never dreamed Mom felt this way.

"I'm old. I should be beyond this. But there it is. Your Mom's an ordinary human being, so imperfect."

I felt awkward.

"You are so much better than me, *anak*. I'm happy my children are better than me. Maybe it's good I went away." Mom smiled a tired smile that pulled my defenses down.

"After Dad died, I felt all alone, and pretended I could manage. I've been pretending ever since," I said. Then I broke down and cried.

Where those sobs came from, I didn't know. I never cried so much as I had that afternoon with Mom. We both cried. Then we both laughed as we cried, until Sonia came in through the door.

"What's going on? Can I join the group hug?" Sonia teased. Seeing the tears on our faces, she embraced us both. We held each other for a long time. How I loved these two women. I wanted to be a political leader ever since the beginning, but I never thought politics would do my family so much good. I didn't want that moment to end.

"We were just discussing the campaign," I said, drying my eyes with the back of my hand.

"Yes, and we were talking about how many votes we need to win, I think," Mom said, wiping her eyes with her scarf.

For me, it was a relief going back to facts. I was always better in that zone than in emotions. I estimated that with a high vote turnout, such as 60 percent, the candidates would be fighting over 48,000 votes. If the vote splits closely among four or even five candidates, including myself and the Greens, then even 9,000 votes might do it. "Yes, I think I can win that number," I answered.

"How much do you need to run a successful campaign?"

I took a guess. "Around 80,000, maybe 100,000 bucks?"

"Can you get that?"

"Bobby pledged thirty. The McIsaacs pledged five. Lolo Ben can probably come up with five. Armand said he's good for five, and can get some from his doctor colleagues. I think we can get fifty from a fundraising event. The rest we can ask friends," I said.

"Do you have enough people to help you?"

I had the numbers. More than what was required, but I needed some special skills. I gave my assessment. "Mostly, the numbers are there — for the door knocking, phoning, tweeting, putting up signs, manning the election booths. I need someone really good for polling, someone for communications and messaging, and another for policy. Someone to organize the fundraiser. And a campaign manager, a good one."

"Do you have a core team yet?" asked Mom.

"Can't say I do. A team yes, but not the core."

"Then we have work to do. We need a core team before you even start." Mom asked Sonia to write down campaign roles in one column. We brainstormed names for each role, and wrote them down in the second column. When we were stuck, we put down names of people or organizations that could refer people. Sonia and I hadn't seen our Mom this way since the early days of the catering business, directing the troops like a general. I loved it.

* * *

It turned out that I was my own best communications expert. The symbol just came to me. Maybe it was all the food in my family. All the food I rebelled against. Soup as symbol for a truly blended Canadian society. The Canadian mosaic symbol did not work — the whole was falling apart, the threads cannot hold the patches of culture together, and the country is falling into racism.

In a TV interview, the journalist asked, "Why soup?"

I explained in words that would be quoted often in the campaign. "Canada is a land of immigrants. Most of us came from somewhere else — our original home countries — and have now made our home here in Canada. It is easy to say that we should just balance these two homes, our dual identities, but there is no such thing. We have one identity or we will forever be torn schizophrenic citizens. We need to see ourselves as one whole delicious soup blended together where the onion is not crying for attention or the carrot or the chicken, but all of the ingredients harmonize to make a delicious rich soup where the combination of ingredients together is what makes the flavor of the soup distinct."

"What's wrong with a salad though? In a salad, you have greens and fruits and nuts, blended by a dressing, tasting so good as a whole, yet each ingredient is distinct in your mouth," the interviewer challenged.

"The ingredients of salads are not as deeply blended as those of soup. Soups are hearty and fill us, while salads are light and after a few hours you are hungry again. Do we want to be a country of substance or lightweights?" I said.

That started a whole debate on soups and salads and Canadian politics in the media that made me, a little known independent candidate from the west coast, a household name overnight in Canada.

Other candidates jumped into the debate with their own food analogies. In an interview the Conservative candidate remarked that 'salads are light and healthier, while soups are heavy', to which I replied 'why is it that when we are sick, we eat chicken soup, not salad?' A Liberal candidate's press release stated, 'You can't survive on soup alone; it's only a starter. An independent candidate like del Mundo hasn't got what it takes to serve a full meal.' My ads ended with the slogan: 'Soup for the Canadian Soul.' The Greens countered: "Why is del Mundo giving us soup? Canadians are not sick. She is making us sick!" "Whatever happened to our good old fashioned mosaic of many colours?" said the NDP candidate. "That's the trouble, you can't eat it," replied someone. The media loved it, and suddenly, Canadian elections were fun! I was invited for an interview on the CBC news hour. The CBC Cross Country Check-Up radio program hosted a theme: "What's your order: Canadian soup or Canadian salad?"

I built my campaign around the soup image, and henceforth, every meeting I attended always had soup served. I called myself the Soup Lady and went around giving soup to the homeless, soup to the babies in day care, to the seniors in senior care facilities, to expectant mothers, and to the sick in the hospitals. I ran a competition for soup recipes all over Canada representing their respective regions, calling for diverse recipes by geography not by ethnic origins. "As we discover Canadian Soup, so shall we discover the country that is Canada, and the values that are Canadian." People cheered to the rallying cry. I didn't know it then, but I had tapped on a hunger for nationalism among Canadians who had been programmed for decades on the idea that being Canadian was being multicultural. No, my campaign made the distinction clear: multiculturalism was salad, its ingredients distinct and apart; Canadianism was soup, its ingredients blended yet distinct.

"Isn't that the same as America's Melting Pot?" others asked.

"Far from it," I explained. "In the Melting Pot, everything melts together so that the ingredients become unrecognizable. In a soup, everything is blended together, yet the ingredients are still distinct and the whole soup is also distinct in its blend of flavors."

"But the salad ingredients are also distinct while blended together," they countered.

I gave a keynote speech at the graduation of the Vancouver Culinary Institute wherein I pointed out the real difference.

"The ingredients of salad are blended only loosely, by a dressing, the way folk dances hold 'multiculturalism' together — superficially. But the ingredients in soup are blended with the heat and time of ingredients simmered together over hours, time spent by different cultures working, recreating, and living together. That's why soup ingredients are fused and infused into a deep unity, different from the unity of salad ingredients.

In Canadianism, like in soup, people of different cultures come together everywhere. At home — parents do not reject girlfriends of their sons just because they are from another culture, as it sometimes happens now; instead, men and women of different cultures intermarry freely. In neighbourhoods — anyone can live where they want; no one is prohibited access from a neighborhood because of one's ethnicity like the campaign against 'monster homes' that discriminated against Asian extended families. In schools — young people feel welcome and safe, not afraid of being bullied or killed by an ethnic gang, as it happened tragically with Jay Ramos. At work — regardless of color and culture, everyone has equal opportunity for jobs and advancement; foreign-trained professionals can work in their field, and not have to work as cleaners, dishwashers and taxi drivers as they have to do now. In the arts — cultural institutions are permeated by all cultures; for example, there is no 'mainstream media', and 'ethnic media', but one media in which the major issues of local ethnic groups are headlined as much as those of the 'mainstream'.

In fact, in Canadianism there is no need to distinguish between mainstream and ethnic cultures as they are fused together. In Canadianism the different cultures are not just connected like in a mosaic, or combined loosely as in salad. In Canadianism, the different cultures are united by the heat of their common needs, goals and actions as one people, one broth, distinguished by the blend of ingredients which remain visible and distinct."

The speech won me a three-minute standing ovation. After it went viral, the national papers carried it. "Canadianism" became a new concept that was the cure for the racism that was growing in Canada. I built up the positives of a harmonious Canada, rather than the negatives of the racism, although I kept the Jay Ramos racial killing in the background, to remind people of what was already happening with strong individual cultures that do not blend. The speech became my platform.

I asked every group I met this question: "What does Canadianism mean to you?" I collected their answers: universal health care, jobs, economic prosperity, diverse cultures living in peace, respect for human rights, public education, enterprise, good governance, safe neighborhoods, peace and order, responsible financial housekeeping, environmental conservation, adequate pensions. I created an animation ad, representing each of these answers as ingredients going into a huge pot of "All Canadian Soup" stirred by the Soup Lady herself wearing a chef's hat. I put the video on YouTube, sending my message viral, making 'Manolita del Mundo' a household name. Politics suddenly became appetizing for the entire Canadian electorate, not just the new riding in British Columbia. Someone capitalized on the new brand and put out a line of soup called "All Canadian Soup" and put the cans in groceries.

The campaign was going extremely well.

A community campaign committee was set up with outreach into ethnic groups. I called on all my favours and friends. Sanjit Ray, my former professor and lover, referred me to South Asian community leaders. Stephen introduced me to Chinese leaders he knew. Armand hosted dinners for me with Iranian doctors and friends. Other recruits were put in charge of reaching to the business community, women's groups, youth groups, and neighborhood groups in the riding. Bobby and his in-laws the McIsaacs reached out to their connections in business and arts.

We put Mom in charge of the Filipino outreach, while Sonia scoured her contacts with all other ethnic communities. I was surprised at the response of the Filipino community, especially the caregivers. They came in droves to the campaign office, sat in the orientation sessions, manned the phones, went door knocking, and accompanied me in putting up candidate signs. Filipino seniors came to phone banks and called other Filipino friends in Tagalog. Many young Filipinos helped who did not know how to speak Tagalog. I never met so many Filipinos in my life! I did not even know most of the volunteers, yet they worked so hard for me. On the peak hours of the campaigns — the late afternoons and evenings and weekends when the campaign office was busiest — I felt moved by everyone's support. Their support inspired me to win. I found myself wanting to win for them, for the wrongs that needed to be righted, for all of them, for a better Canada. I forgot about me. I didn't realize I was doing now what Mr. Wilson my first mentor taught me about leadership: "Leadership is about caring for others."

Mom kept the campaign office stocked with *pan de sal, empanadas*, noodle dishes, samosas, dimsum, steamed buns, *baklava*, and sandwiches matching the ethnicity of the volunteers. She kept the walls plastered with photos of the events I attended, people I met with, and media guest appearances. The wall of photos became a focus of interest for everyone who came in the door. Two television screens kept running images of news and video produced for the campaign. The phone banks were constantly busy, and a hum of lively busyness filled the air. It felt like a winning campaign.

* * *

CHAPTER 11

Canada
Jun Jun, 2015

At the Vancouver Police Department office, they teased me about my half-sister the Soup Lady. They didn't mind that she stood for law and order, and promised an end to ethnic gangs. I felt proud of Manolita. A big meeting with RCMP on drugs had just finished in the conference room. We walked into the room for the weekly staff meeting. I sat at the end of the table and saw a piece of paper that must have been left from the meeting before. Classified. I read the brief memo. It said they were close to identifying the drug lords of Canada. There were only three names, and Bobby del Mundo was one of them. I looked around: everybody else was busy chatting. I placed my laptop on top of the sheet of paper, covering it. I thought about something I heard before. Could Tita Norma's story be true? I could not concentrate on the meeting. It was mercifully brief. When I left, I took the memo along.

That evening, I dropped in on Mom.

"What brings my son so unexpectedly to visit his old mom?" she said.

"*Lechon Kawali*?" I teased.

"Good thing we have some of that left over. I had a feeling you would come, so I saved some in the freezer," said Tita Norma, raising her cheek up to me to kiss.

"Bull. You always have *lechon kawali* in the freezer for me." I chuckled.

"See, it works! Our handsome police officer is here, isn't he?" Tita Norma said, opening the fridge.

Mom laughed adding, "Men are all the same. The path to their hearts always through the stomach."

"Where's Dad?"

"Fishing. Tofino."

"Save me some halibut, okay?"

"No way. Who'll cook it for you, your famous sister, the candidate?" teased Tita Norma.

"I hear she doesn't cook," I said.

"You wouldn't think that from her campaign — the soup lady, bah. I'll give you real soup here. I have *sinigang*," Tita Norma offered.

"Can't wait," I said. I let Tita Norma go to the kitchen so I could ask Mom what I came for.

"I need the truth Mom. When Dad died of a heart attack, is it true that it was because he confronted Bobby about drug use and drug dealing?"

"What's this? You prefer to believe gossip than your own mom?"

"Mom. The RCMP has fingered Bobby del Mundo as one of the biggest drug kings operating in Canada. It makes sense that it would be him if he started years ago when he was a kid. It's confidential. No one knows yet. They'll be at his house quickly, so you better let me know."

"Nothing was ever proven. It seems Bobby just dealt a little for some youth gang just to make ends meet for his family. When your Dad left them for me, they refused to take his support money. Poor kid, he was only helping his family."

"It must be him then."

Mom became agitated. "You have to help him, *anak*. It was him that discovered your dad and me. I'm not proud of it. He and his dad never talked to each other after that. Just bad blood between them. Is there anything you can do?"

From the door, Tita Norma's voice. "To help Bobby? I told you so. This time they should pay — put Jun on the will or I'll tell the papers. That should help his sister get elected." A victorious look came over Tita Norma's face.

"You'll do no such thing," I warned.

Tita Norma glared at me, and started cooking.

* * *

"No doubt it's him," I confided everything to Nate.

"What are you going to do?" asked Nate.

"I don't know."

"Are you going to warn her?"

"Why her? She may not even know. If anyone's to be warned, it should be him."

"God, you'll lose your job! You might even be charged."

"No one knows I saw it. I burned it. So? Someone misplaced the memo. The leak could come from anyone."

"Are you out of your mind? You lost your father because of him."

"No. He lost his father because of my mother, and I was the result. He did this to support his family when his dad left them. He'll have to take the consequences, but I can at least give him a head start."

I picked up my car keys.

* * *

The lights were off in Bobby's house on the mountain, except for the kitchen. Someone may be up. I parked several houses away. I walked to the front door and rang the doorbell. After a few moments, I rang it again.

"Jun Jun? Is that you?" said a voice through the intercom. Fancy security. "Yes, sorry to disturb, Tita," I said loudly.

Several locks clicked from inside the door, and a disheveled Nicole stood in a nightgown. She let me in.

"Sorry, Tita Nicole. Is Bobby in?"

"Uhh, no? Why?"

"Where is he?" Something seems to have scared Nicole.

"He's out of the country on business," she said.

"Tita, I'm here as a friend. Bobby's been identified."

"What are you talking about?" Nicole looked like she was in a panic.

"He knows what I'm talking about. If he's out of the country, tell him to stay out. And if he's here, he better get out. Now. There's no time."

A click of the bedroom on the side of the living room. Bobby appeared in his nightgown. He walked towards the hallway where Nicole and I stood.

"Why are you telling me this?" asked Bobby.

"To give you a head start."

"Why?" He demanded.

"For our father," I said quietly.

"Your father. My father is dead and wanted me dead. Why should you save me?" I sensed anger but also sadness in Bobby's voice.

"Because someone has to," I said.

Bobby sat down on the sofa and put his head in his hands. When he looked up, his eyes were red. He started crying. Nicole knelt down before him and held him close. After a long time, he looked up at me. I was still standing in the hallway.

I answered the question in Bobby's mind. "I had no father because he died. But you had no father because we took him away from you. You had to support your family. I understand. But no one else will. You have to go before it's too late."

Bobby stood up and walked towards me. He looked me in the eye.

"You're a good man. After all I'd done to keep you away, and your mother...thank you," Bobby said. He grabbed me by the shoulders and hugged me tight. "Can you forgive me, brother?" Bobby whispered.

I felt his pain. "You've done me no wrong. I've no cause to forgive. But you, brother, you need to forgive him... forgive our father."

"For you, I will," he said.

He continued. "I owe you, Jun Jun. You risked your job for me. I won't forget. You are my brother. Forever." This time, I embraced him.

I sensed a bond was born between us. I imagined the cycle of hate that had engulfed our families. I felt a glimmer of a new life, a mercy, like the hand of God that reached in to forgive me a long time ago.

"Go now. Take Nicole and Sarina. Don't come back. Leave word that you're on holidays to somewhere. When you get there, go somewhere else. Don't tell anyone where you've landed. Do not contact the family for as long as you can. There may be a leak in the papers tomorrow; you have to get out now. I'll look after telling the family. Give me a secure number, I'll call you when it's safe," I instructed them.

We hugged again. I left in the dark.

* * *

In the morning, I scanned the *Vancouver Sun*. *The Province*. The daily rags. Nothing there.

At the Vancouver Police headquarters, the superintendents were locked in the boardroom for hours. Something big was happening. It seems that media had got word of the pending arrests of the drug king suspects and RCMP and police have had to move faster than anticipated. Media gave them one day to do it.

I called Manolita. I picked her up a few blocks from her office, in my own car, not a police car, and wearing street clothes. I drove towards an old industrial area, and parked in a vacant lot.

I told her everything. The memo. Norma threatening to go to media about it. My warning Bobby. Bobby and his family's departure. The likely police hunt for Bobby. The likely media coverage. Manolita was stunned.

"This is all I can do now," I said. "I can't be seen with you. I know I'll be under suspicion as the source of the leak. They know that we're related. But nothing relates me to the drug project, no proof. No one saw me reading the memo. I destroyed it. Who would admit misplacing a classified memo? I didn't tell mom or Tita Norma about the memo, so they don't know about it. I couldn't control Tita Norma. She was likely the one who tipped them off. I don't know what she said. She denies it. But if she did, she had no proof. That's why media had to confirm it with Police. That's why the advanced arrests, for the police to get the suspects before the news warns them."

Manolita looked flattened. "That's the end of my political career. Who would vote for the sister of a drug king?" After a pause, she continued. "Where are they? Are they safe?"

"Call his office. He said he will leave word about where they went for holidays. But he will move around," I said.

"How? When…" I interrupted Manolita's confusion.

"I told him not to connect with the family for a while, it will be safer that way. You know what the office knows, that's it. He's gone on holidays in the past. He always goes on holidays, right?" I said.

Manolita's beautiful face was lined with worry. "Don't worry, we have a way of connecting if necessary," I assured her.

"So it will be all out in the papers soon?" She looked resigned, and decided on something.

She hugged me warmly. "You're a saint. Thank you so much. Dad would be so proud of you," she said. "Leave me here, I want to walk awhile and figure things out."

I held her hand. "You'll do ok, sis," I kissed her on the cheek. She hugged me again, opened the car door, and walked away.

* * *

CHAPTER 12

Canada
Manolita, 2015

Next day, the headlines hit.

"Drug King Arrested. Another Gets Away."

"Brother of Member of Parliament Candidate Soup Lady Suspected Drug King"

"Latest Ingredient in del Mundo's Soup: Drugs?"

I refused to take media calls the first day, saying I was 'shocked' and was preparing an appropriate response. I talked with the family. I consulted my campaign team. I sought Armand's advice. I prayed like I never prayed before. I asked myself what is the worst thing that could happen if I told the truth, what I understood to be the truth? That my name and my family's name would be ruined? That I'll never be a political leader? Whose family was perfect anyway? I could serve people in ways other than as a politician, wasn't that what I told Mom if I lost? I wrote down what I would say. I called a media conference next day.

The media came in full force, including national TV and press. I felt a relief, sitting in front of a room full of people in my campaign office, as though saying goodbye to old friends. I felt very relaxed, resigned to anything that would happen now, and strangely happy for a burden being lifted. Armand squeezed my hand and whispered, "Knock 'em dead." I stood up to signal that we're about to begin.

"Thank you for coming. My apologies. I didn't have time to make soup today." Laughter. I smiled at my audience. I scan the faces, and remind myself that most of the audience — campaign workers, friends, and family — are on my side. Even the journalists, while they may not be on my side, are not necessarily against me. They just want to know. The enemies, the opposition, they will be at home watching this tonight in the comfort of their homes. But I must remember that people in my riding, ordinary citizens whose votes I seek, will also be there watching. They want to know the truth. They deserve the truth. I decide that it is them I must address.

"These days have been among the toughest days of my life. My brother and his family are away, and we don't know where he is, and whether he is safe. Whatever he has done remains to be proven. If he is guilty, he must take the consequences of his actions, and I will not stand in the way. And if he is innocent, we trust you will remember that long after today.

"I want to tell you my family's story, something I have not shared widely. I was five when our family came to Vancouver from Manila. It was November and there was a freak snowfall in Vancouver. The white ice on the pole looked so much like a Popsicle, I licked it, getting my tongue stuck on the pole. Since then, my tongue has always been my problem, said my mother." I paused for the laughter that always came when I told this story.

"My father was an accomplished engineer in the Philippines, my mother a teacher at a prestigious convent school for girls. My sister Sonia was 13 then, and my brother Bobby was 15. My father couldn't find work as an engineer, and it drove him to despair. He was a proud man and did not want to work beneath his level like the others who have surrendered and worked as janitors, night watchmen and dishwashers. He tried to get recognition from the Engineers' organization that recognized credentials, but he felt insulted by the interrogation he received. His interview was cut short by a mild heart attack. He tried to get Canadian engineering education, but he was mocked by his classmates at UBC, who called him 'prof' behind his back because he seemed to be a 'know it all'. In his depression, his relationship with my mother deteriorated. It did not help that my mother was succeeding in the catering business, making him feel even less worthy. He met another woman, who had just lost her husband and child and was being abused by her employer. She was about to throw herself off a bridge, when he saved her. He helped her put back her life together, and they fell in love."

I paused. It was so quiet in the room.

"My brother Bobby caught my father and the woman in the act at our home one day when he came home from school early. He made them leave our home, and swore my father off from our lives forever." I stopped. I felt a catch in my voice. I breathed deeply.

"My father and the woman lived together as man and wife, leaving my mom and Bobby to look after us. Bobby took it upon himself to support our family, taking on several jobs and running a landscaping business with friends, while going to school. He refused any money from my father.

"One day, many years later, my father heard something about Bobby maybe being involved in drugs. He rushed to our house in the middle of the night, pointing a gun at Bobby lying in bed, and accused him of being a druggie and a drug dealer. Frightened, Bobby admitted that he dealt some drugs to make ends meet for our family, as my father had abandoned us. My father had a weak heart, and all that anger caused him a major heart attack. He fell on the floor and a few hours later, died at the hospital. Bobby promised he would stop dealing drugs."

I sighed. The silence in the room was thick as a carpet.

"Bobby has been building subdivisions and homes in Metro Vancouver for many years now. I am proud of his accomplishments. I do not know of all his activities and whether he is the drug king they talk about in the papers. He is not here to answer these charges. What I know is that my brother is a hardworking man who loves his family and whose support helped us through school, which made us what we are today. My sister, some of you know, Sonia del Mundo, Executive Director of Immigrant Communities Collective, has been helping many newcomers prosper in Canada, including helping them practise their professions, something she had promised our father. He would be so proud of her today. My mother, Josie del Mundo, active force in the community employing newcomers, mentoring caregivers on establishing their own businesses, has now answered the call of politics where she is needed most. She is now Mayor of her hometown in the Philippines — Pililla, Rizal — where she is helping transform a backwater village into a modern prosperous town.

"And me, I am the child of Canada, my home, which I love with a passion and a pride. How lucky I am to have landed in the best country in the world. A country that gives my family and me a chance to make better lives for ourselves, and better lives for others. But it is not perfect. I am doing my share, helping newcomers, women, youth, and seniors fulfill their potential. There is urgent work to be done, which is why I ran for public office.

"Our country's youth of different cultures are tearing each other apart in racial violence. Our skilled newcomers are being shamefully underutilized, when we need their skills to prop up our businesses and our economy. Our seniors are isolated because of their culture. Our women lawyers are discriminated against in their careers when they bear children, yet our country needs them to provide human resources for our future. We need our diverse peoples to come together and make Canada the paradise it can be.

"It is a privilege to help shape our country into an even better Canada, a model of humaneness for our world. It is my own call and commitment — Member of Parliament or not — to do this. I stand behind these commitments as I do beside my family, sinners or saints they may be.

"I remind us that it is I, not my brother who is running for office. It is my actions you need to judge, and not my brother's. The law will judge him.

"The day of your judgment on my worthiness to serve you as Member of Parliament is at hand. You know my track record, and the work we need to do together. I believe I have earned your trust. I am privileged to be in the company of many worthy candidates. I accept your choice, and in whatever role you give me, I pledge to continue working for a better Canada.

Thank you very much."

It took several seconds for the silence to break. I'm not sure how I did. Mom came forward and hugged me. Sonia did the same. We all three hugged as the cameras and lights clicked and flashed away. It wasn't planned that way. We stood there, holdings hands, three del Mundo women, smiling through tears, the image that made the front page of each of the papers next day.

What the cameras could not catch were the ghosts of the men hovering about us: the father who haunted our dreams, the brother who supported us through a secret life, and the half-brother who, in the shadows, saved our lives.

* * *

CHAPTER 13

Canada
Manolita, 2015

It was late in the night. The Vancouver Granville Riding was one of the last to be called, as the votes were swinging all evening.

My campaign team had now gathered in our campaign office, watching the election coverage. The feeling was that of nervous excitement, as we dared not hope for the impossible: a victory? That I was doing so well against the other candidates was a miracle in itself. I had given it up when the scandal hit. But it seems the community was willing to set aside my brother's scandal and was giving me a chance. My speech at the media conference turned things around for me, making me look human, making people feel more compassionate towards me.

"Final polls, Vancouver Granville," announced the elections officer, holding a sheet of paper in his hand.

"3,451 Greens; 7,443 Conservative; 8,256 NDP; 9,424 Liberal; 10,557 Independent"

Pandemonium broke lose.

THE END

EPILOGUE

In January 2015, the Canadian Federal Government changed its policy on how Canada would accept new immigrants.

Called Express Entry, the new system of managing immigrant applications effectively admits mainly those with job offers from Canadian employers.

ACKNOWLEDGEMENTS

This story came out fast, as though it had been simmering a long time inside me. I wrote furiously into the night, not crossing out, trusting the right-brained writing voice I'd developed with the help of my writing guru Natalie Goldberg, the first person I want to thank. Then it was time to use the left brain. After a first edit, I sought out readers for their comments. Did it make sense? Is it worth people's time? These early readers plowed through my first draft and gave me helpful comments while encouraging me to continue: Prod and Eleanor Laquian, Carlito Pablo, Patricia Graham, Melissa Briones, Irene Querubin, Baldwin Wong, Nick Noorani, Esmie Maclaren, Lara Honrado, and Mari La Rosa. I am proud to share some of their final comments with you in this book.

I was startled by a bold idea of my always creative friend Mel Tobias who suggested we do a dramatic reading of excerpts of the novel-in-progress. In an intimate gallery-turned-salon, ten actors from ACAT (Anyone Can Act Theatre) performed my characters, releasing them from paper to reality. The discussion that followed showed that the audience cared about the characters and the story's underlying themes related to immigrants and multiculturalism. For demonstrating the potential of the novel, my gratitude goes to the director, actors and production volunteers of ACAT: Mel Tobias, Mel Owen, Lee Echavez, Esmie MacLaren, Melissa Briones, Gino Echavez, Anja Echavez, Victoria Francisco, Boy Masakayan, Kenson Ho, Joey Poblador, and De Malong.

An excerpt from my novel was published in *Rice Paper*, the well-regarded Asian Canadian literary journal, boosting my publishing credential. I am ever grateful to Jim Wong Chu for inviting the submission, and Anna Kaye for helping me polish the excerpt into a stand-alone short story entitled *Angel of the Salubungan*.

When people ask, I always say writing the novel was the easiest thing. The hardest thing was the editing. Several rounds of manuscript evaluation and editing by professionals reshaped and polished the novel. Thank you, Carolyn Bateman, Sharon Miki, and Friesen Press editors. The next hardest thing was the publishing. Being a neophyte in how to get published, I sought expert coaching on current publishing practices and options, and in this, Jesse Finkelstein, Maggie Langrick, Elsie Sze, and George Verdolaga were most helpful. Part of what's so hard for me in publishing is the technology. I'm eternally grateful for my tech-wiz son Rafael Atienza who is always there for me when needed, and my brother JR Guerrero, my coach and strategist for social media.

I cannot thank enough my husband Clayton Campbell — best friend, mentor, coach, editor, legal advisor, sounding board, co-conspirator, exercise director, financier and overall supporter — who has been my constant partner in this project, critiquing characters, brainstorming plots, marking up drafts, and encouraging me onwards when I felt like giving up.

And finally, this novel would not have been possible without the many immigrants and immigrant service providers I have met, the community leaders, and various professionals and volunteers in government, business, and non-profit sector, all engaged in making Canada a welcoming home for people of diverse cultures, where paradise is not just a dream, but a real work-in-progress.

Eleanor Guerrero-Campbell

ABOUT THE AUTHOR

When Eleanor Guerrero Campbell came to Canada with a Masters Degree in Urban and Regional Planning from the Philippines and some years planning Metro Manila, she got the first job she applied for — planner for the City of Edmonton, Alberta. She continued on to plan the City of Surrey as Associate Director of Planning, and the City of Richmond as Manager of Policy Planning and Corporate Strategies.

And so she was surprised to find that in Canada, in the 80's and 90's, many highly skilled immigrants could not practise their professions. Very experienced internationally-trained engineers, doctors, and other professionals ended up driving taxis and cleaning floors. In response, she co-founded the Multicultural Helping House Society, a non-profit organization to help newcomers succeed in Canada. There she learned first hand about the problems of newcomers, and created programs to help skilled immigrants secure work in their field.

Eleanor directed the Looking Ahead Initiative, a BC wide program to improve the labour market integration of immigrants, working with multiple stakeholders. She authored *Hiring and Retaining Skilled Immigrants: A Cultural Competence Toolkit*, a guide for human resource managers of BC. She chaired the City of Vancouver Cultural Communities Advisory Committee advocating for better integration of newcomers into city life. Eleanor has been recognized with various awards as a champion for multiculturalism and immigrant integration. Eleanor is currently co-convenor of the City of Vancouver's Immigrant Partnership Program Access to Services Committee.

It became clear to Eleanor that the stories she encountered in the community deserved to be told — *needed* to be told. After retiring in 2012, she began work on *Stumbling Through Paradise*, using literary skills learned from her first degree English and Comparative Literature, courses with writing guru Natalie Goldberg, and her own experiences in the field to help shape her characters and their journey.

Eleanor writes and lives in Vancouver with her husband. When they are not travelling, they enjoy walking, cycling, and exploring the city's neighbourhoods and cultural life.

CPSIA information can be obtained
at www.ICGtesting.com
Printed in the USA
LVOW12s0038010416
481667LV00002B/76/P